THE
MERRY
MONTH
OF MAY

BY JAMES JONES

FROM HERE TO ETERNITY

SOME CAME RUNNING

THE PISTOL

THE THIN RED LINE

GO TO THE WIDOW-MAKER

THE ICE-CREAM HEADACHE AND OTHER STORIES

THE MERRY MONTH OF MAY

JAMES JONES

THE MERRY MONTH OF MAY

 DELACORTE PRESS / NEW YORK

To E. C. Braun-Munk, for absolutely no reason at all.

Hello, Eugene!

And to Addie von Herder, the Baroness, who taught me all I know about Europeans.

Oy vay, Addie!

THE
MERRY
MONTH
OF MAY

1

WELL, IT'S ALL OVER. The Odéon has fallen! And today, which is June
16th, a Sunday, the police on orders of the Government entered and
took over the Sorbonne on some unclear and garbled pretext about
some man who was wounded by a knife. There was some rioting this
afternoon, but the police handled it fairly easily. So that is it. And I sit
here at my window on the river in the crepuscular light of that
peculiar gray-blue Paris twilight which is so beautiful and like no
other light anywhere on earth, and I wonder, What now? The sky is
heavy and low tonight and this evening for the first time from the end
of the Boulevard St.-Germain and the Pont Sully the tear gas reached us
here on the almost sacrosanct Île St.-Louis. I finger my pen as I look
out from my writing desk, and wonder if it is even worth it: the trying
to put it down. M. Pompidou said, I remember, that "nothing in
France would ever be the same again." Well, he was certainly right in
regard to the Harry Gallaghers and their family.

I am a failed poet, a failed novelist; quite probably I can be, and
am, considered quite rightly to be a drop-out of a husband; why
should I try? Even the desire isn't there any more. — And yet I feel I
owe it to them. The Gallaghers. Only God knows what will happen to
them now. And probably only I, of all the world, know what happened to them then—in the merry month of May. Most of all, I guess,

I owe it to Louisa. Poor, dear, darling, straight-laced, mixed-up Louisa.

I first met the Harry Gallaghers back in fifty-eight, ten years ago. I had just decided to stay on in Paris, and was going about the founding of my Review, *The Two Islands Review*. Failed poet, failed novelist, recently divorced, but still a man of an unquenchable literary bent, I felt there was the room in Paris for a newer English-language review.

The Paris Review of then, despite its excellent "Art of Fiction" interviews, and the excellence of George's intentions, was fading away from the high standard it had declared itself dedicated to diffuse. I felt I could fill that gap. And, I did not look forward to returning to New York where although we had parted amicably enough, I would surely be forced by circumstances to see too much of my rich ex-wife at literary parties.

I went around to see Harry Gallagher and some others to see if they would consent to become among my backers. I had met Harry, and knew that he had money: an income; one a great deal larger than my own. I also knew that Harry—though professionally a screenwriter—had always stood up for the arts. I thought he might be willing to put a little money into a new review with the intellectual and artistic standards I intended to give mine. I was right.

Of course, it was the Prince Shirakhan who was the real "angel". But if it were not for Harry and several other of my richer friends who put money in it first, the Review might never have come to exist anyhow. Without them, I might never have gotten the Prince.

I had already taken a flat on the lovely old Île St.-Louis. I found Harry was practically a next-door neighbor, living at the extreme and very chic downriver tip of the Quai de Bourbon; while I like a peasant only lived—though on the sunny side, it is true—at the corner of the Quai d'Orléans and the rue le Regrattier.

Why I, Jonathan James Hartley III, should have become the number-one friend of the Gallagher family I don't know. We did not even run in the same circles in Paris. My social contacts were mostly literary. The Gallaghers ran mainly with the much wealthier and much more glamorous film crowd. That I—the reclusive, possibly austere, literary man—should become best friend of the Gallagher family has always struck me as strange enough: as if the paucity of their choice showed itself here more than anywhere.

Tall, bald, lean, Harry was a very intense man, with a long hatchet-face and tense narrow eyes, which carried a wry look about them that seemed more to be imposed on them from without than to come naturally from within. I don't think he ever had any real sense of humor, as I do, for example.

At any rate, that is what I became: the best family friend. Their son Hill was just nine at that time. I became his special counselor and his confidant. Not that Hill needed one. And when their daughter McKenna was born in 1960, I was named her Godfather, and McKenna grew up to the ripe old age of eight holding me by one hand, so to speak. Hill was 11 when she was born.

I remember that I thought of them then, all of them, that they were *the* perfect happy-American-family: the one one hears about, and sees so often in the ad photos in *New Yorker* and in all the commercial magazines, but which one so rarely meets in life. Certainly there was absolutely nothing to indicate there might be deeper darker strains to their lives they might be hiding. And I am normally sensitive about people. I really did think of them as that perfect American family.

Now Hill is 19—now, on June 16th, 1968—and I don't know where he is, and have not seen him since ten days ago, when in a numbed despondent panic he left Paris, he said, for good.

Poor Hill. When you know young people from the age of nine, much of the glamor and awesomeness of their young arrival at young adulthood, as well as its significance, are lost on you, worn away by simple proximity.

I think Hill was deeply affected by the birth of his baby sister McKenna in 1960. The experts all say that kids, especially only children, are always profoundly upset by the coming of another child to displace them as the center. But if Hill was, he never confided this to me. I remember he spent the several days of Louisa's accouchement at the American Hospital staying with me in my apartment. Louisa was old-fashioned about things like that. But Hill took it all right in stride, if somewhat morosely. He said nothing to me about it then, at 11, except once. Sitting on the arm of my one big fauteuil at the window, he turned from watching the river and the barges moving on it, found me with his eyes, and, looking straight into my own, said enigmatically, "I know where babies come from. And how they got there. Don't think I don't." I was sure he did. Confused and embarrassed, I chose not to pick up this 11-year-old gauntlet at the time.

I used to take him fishing. At that time, at age 11, it was down under the bridge on the Island. We would sit under the big trees on the big uneven cobbles of the lower-level walk that runs beneath the Pont Louis-Philippe and Pont Marie almost around the Island, where the picturesque old Parisian duffers spend the years of their retirement with long bamboo poles and nylon leaders, snatching panfish even in the worst rainy winter weather. Later on, when he was older, I took him out of town up the Marne, where we fished for perch and trout from a rowboat along the banks and between the grassy tree-studded little islands, in scenery that made you think of nothing so much as the nineteenth-century Impressionist landscapes of a Monet or a Sisley—a nineteenth-century landscape unchanged and, in France, rural France, hopefully perhaps unchanging forever.

I remember it was just such a warm sunny cloud-dappled spring day, in just such a nineteenth-century Monet setting on the Marne, that he brought up to me for the second time his sister and her birth and her life. He was 15 at this time and McKenna four. There was no question how much he loved her. There was no question how much we all loved her, the bright little thing, so perspicacious, with her dancing eyes and ready smile and her ardent curiosity about everything, like an unsedate kitten's. She had wanted to come with us, and had cried when Hill refused her on the grounds that she was too little and would be a liability and get in the way. She would not be a lia-blility, she said. I'm sure she didn't know what it meant. On the river he had just back-rowed us in toward a grassy overhang held together amongst the parklike fields by the root systems of three giant oaks. "What do you think of the kid?"

"McKenna?"

"She's a dollbaby isn't she? Smart as a whip." He did not look at me, and got his line out. "But they're spoiling her already. She's got to learn there're going to be some hard knocks out there for her in the big selfish world when she gets there, and how to survive them. She can't

have her way all the time forever. I hated to do what I did, but I had
to do it. She's got to learn."

I interpreted. He was apologizing, in case I had indicted him
privately for cruelty, for what he had done.

"She's got to learn," he said again.

"I suppose so."

Hill reeled in his hook and made a big thing about inspecting his
bait, which did not need it at all. He tossed it back out. "I don't like
the way they're handling her. They're spoiling her rotten."

"Well, I guess it's pretty hard not to spoil McKenna," I said.

"Oh, sure. But with them it's something else. They give her everything she asks for, and half the time they anticipate, and give it to her
before she even asks. They never should have had her."

"What do you mean!" He had made me angry. I was shocked at
him. I guess I loved my Goddaughter right then more than I had ever
loved anything, as only a man can who has never had a child of his
own and regrets it. And I suppose, now, that there was more guilt in
my anger than I was willing to admit then, because I knew that Hill
in one way was right.

"They should never have had a child at their age," he went right
on, not noticing my reaction. "They haven't got the resiliency, the
spiritual and psychological flexibility. They're much too old to have a
child her age."

"Now, wait a minute!" I said.

"Then, there is a second thing. Why, they were about to break up,
when she came along. And she sort of brought them back together. At
least on the surface. Didn't you know that?"

"No. I certainly did not," I said, hollowly. I hoped he wouldn't
notice the tone.

With that adolescent insouciance? I could have saved my worry.
"Oh, sure," he said. "If they hadn't had McKenna, they'd be divorced
by now. I thought everybody knew that. And so now they treat her
like she was some kind of a special, God-given event—a *blessèd*
event!—that came to them from heaven. And go on pretending they're
happy together. And meantime they're ruining the kid."

"Well, I think they *are* happy together. In fact, I know they are," I
said. "And I'm glad for *you,* glad for them, and glad even for myself,

that McKenna did come along and bring them back together. We're all certainly a lot better off."

"Oh, I don't know," he said. "I think we'd all be better off if they'd divorced. Certainly it would be a lot more honest. I think she should have left him. If she'd had the guts.

"I love the folks, you know? Really love them, the poor sods. But they're awful hypocrites, you know. Acting so lovey-dovey all the time. When I know better. I wonder what they say when they're alone?

"And they're teaching poor McKenna all that monogamistic-love crud. Teaching her she must keep her legs together. She mustn't run around without pants on. Teaching her she mustn't spread her legs on the couch and show her butterfly without pants on."

"Good heavens! You wouldn't want them not to teach her that, would you?" "Butterfly" was a direct translation from the Italian *farfalla*, a euphemism for the female organ Harry had picked up working down in Rome, and which had become a family word since McKenna.

He didn't answer me. "Teach her all that crud about saving it, keeping it like gold. Romantic love. Saving herself all for one man who will love her always and only her forever and ever. Keeping herself for one great love that will last all her life. Monogamistic crap."

"Hill, I doubt very much if your parents are yet teaching little McKenna to save herself for monogamistic love," I said.

"But that'll be the next step on the agenda," he said. "Believe me it will. And all of it hypocritical lies."

We fished for a while.

"Maybe they don't want her to get hurt," I said finally, fiddling with my reel. I felt inadequate.

"Hurt! How's she going to get hurt if she doesn't fall in love with them? And all that crud?"

"Hill, have you ever slept with a girl?"

He looked up and grinned. "No. No, but I'm working on it." Fifteen-year-old confidence! I guess I never had it, even at 15. Then his face sobered. "But we talk a lot more about it openly, boys and girls, than you people did. At school and at parties. Don't think I haven't had chances. I'm saving my first one for a girl who'll appreciate it and enjoy it like I will, without all that falling in love crap and monogamy crud. A girl with my sensitivity and sensibilities. Certainly I won't rush off and marry the first girl I get a good piece of ass off of. Like all you folks did. And I won't take on a girl who expects that. And I hope McKenna won't—with a boy—either. But then we don't have as many monogamy-oriented kids like that in our generation the way you did."

I had no answer. But Hill did not press it. In fact, we did not talk about it again. Not then or later. Or about his parents. Or about his parents' treatment of McKenna. Naturally, I did not tell his parents of our discussion. I felt it would be a violation Hill would detest me for, one which would make him stop confiding in me. But he didn't confide in me anyway. I assume he got his piece of ass, the next year, or the year after. Several of them, a whole string of them. But if he did, he didn't tell me about it.

But he was always a close-mouthed, quite self-contained boy, Hill, even back then; and I never knew much about what went on, was going on, in that ballooning, swiftly growing mind of his. Not, at least, until the *Mouvement du 22 mars* at Nanterre and the *Révolution de mai* unlocked his voice, and he began to confide in me things he had never spoken about before.

I'm sure Harry had no idea of the way he was thinking, either. Any more than I myself had. Not, anyway, until that night of April 27th of this year, when Harry called me.

He called me around two-thirty. He knew well I worked late editing and reading and never got to bed before three-thirty or four.

"The kid's not home."

Kid? I thought in panic. McKenna? My Godchild? Eight years old? Not home?

"No, no!" Harry said impatiently into my silence. "Hill! Hill hasn't come home."

"Is that bad?" I asked cautiously.

"Well, he's never done it before. Not without letting me know. I'm worried. We're sitting here waiting up for him. Come on over. I'll break out a bottle."

"All right," I said. "I'll come. Do you think there's anything wrong?"

"How the hell do I know? Come on over."

It was certainly pleasant strolling down the quai in the soft spring night. Everything seemed so calm. Certainly I had no inkling that young Hill was wrapped up in the student troubles. Hill had been studying both Sociology and Cinema at the Sorbonne for three years, without saying much of anything about it to anyone.

The Gallaghers' apartment was lovely. That was the only word for it. Back in fifty-five, before I knew them, when Harry had come into his inheritance, the Gallaghers had taken a long-term lease on an entire floor high up across that terminal building at the end of the Island, the one owned by the Princess Bibesco. Four tall double-doored windows looked out across the downriver tip of the Île St.-Louis toward the Pont d'Arcole and the river, for all the world like some luxury-liner captain's bridge looking out across the prow of his ship. Harry had done it all in superior Louis Treize. I'm a Second Empire man myself. But I had to admit the dark, heavy, massive Louis Treize with its somber deep reds and greens looked very fine in the long sunlit expanse of Harry's living room when I saw it that first time. And it looked just as nice now, with the lamps lit in their velvet and parchment shades. And over all of this Louisa presided like the casual but considerate hostess that she was.

Dear Louisa. Well, we sat around waiting and talking—about writing, about films, as we always did; and we went through one bottle and then through another. Even Louisa was a little high. "He knows he's always supposed to be home by one-thirty or two," Harry said. "He always has before." It was nearly six o'clock when Hill finally came in.

"Where the hell have you been?" Harry demanded.

"Just to a meeting." The boy made as if to go on to his room.

"No, sir! Come back here, sir!" Harry called after him. Hill did, and stood by the archway with his shoulders slumped.

"I want to know more than that," Harry said. "I want to know where you've been. You know you're supposed to be home by one-thirty. Or at least call me," he added—somewhat inconclusively, I thought.

"I've been to a meeting!" Hill cried. He looked up then, and his eyes actually blazed. "A meeting! A students' meeting!" We followed the papers, but we wouldn't get tonight's news until tomorrow morning. "The police arrested Dany Cohn-Bendit today," Hill said. "They let him go tonight. Because they're afraid of repercussions. But if they think that'll stop us, they're dead wrong. We're organizing. We're organizing, and we're going to make them stop and think. Maybe we'll do more than that," he added darkly, and glared at all of us as if we were personally responsible for the arrest of the student leader Cohn-Bendit. I found this suddenly funny, but decided not to say so. I, for one, rather liked young *Dany le Rouge,* and wished him well on his crusade.

"Well, I'll be damned," Harry said, and then he grinned with that hatchet-face of his. "So you're in on all of that. How long?"

"Oh, we've been talking," Hill said sullenly. "You don't think it's only Nanterre, do you? The Sorbonne's involved, too. Every university in France's involved. We've had a bellyful of it. And we're not going to take it lying down."

My ear loved his use and command of his father's type of American English. But Hill's French was equally as good, was perfect. I had a tendency to forget that sometimes. But in fact he was at least as much French as he was American. He had lived in Paris almost all of his life.

"Well, I'm proud of you," Harry said, still grinning his hatchet grin.

"You're proud of *me!"* the boy cried. "What do I care whether *you're* proud of *me!* You, with your money, rich, and writing those crappy films you write! Look at you, all of you: sitting there boozing it up! Boozers! Lushheads! Getting fat in the belly and fat in the mind! With your old Louis Treize and your ritzy apartment! *You're* proud of *me!* After what your generation did to the world?"

"Wait a minute!" Harry said. "Wait just a minute, kid! My generation inher—"

"You wait a minute!" Hill said. The tirade seemed out of all proportion to the offense, if there was one; out of proportion even to his own perhaps over-excited emotions left over from the student meeting; but he went on.

Harry had stopped grinning.

"Hypocrites! Absolute hypocrites, all of you! Well, we're going to pull you down. Pull the whole damn society down. Down around your ears. We haven't got anything to put in its place yet, but something good—something better than what exists—has got to happen." He caught a breath. "Oh, what's the use of trying to explain anything to *you?* Old phonies like you?" He turned and fled.

Harry had gotten half up out of his chair, and looked as if he were undecided whether to chase his son and hit him, or let it go. Slowly, he dropped back into the chair.

"Well, I'll be God damned," he said. Then after a moment, "How do you like them apples?"

"Harry," Louisa said softly from the lovely Louis Treize couch they had hunted over a year for. "Take it easy, Harry. Take it easy." She got up to pour us all another drink.

Darling, solid, level-headed Louisa. I still think it was a good thing that she spoke. Harry's face was a sight to behold. There was a kind of numb snarl on it, and underneath that a bitter hurt the like of which I have rarely seen. And though he had sunk back, he was gripping his highball glass with whitened knuckles as if he might hurl it into the fireplace. And if he had, I don't know what might have followed. I think he would have gone for Hill. But Louisa kept his thought distracted. She refilled my glass, his, and her own, talking inanities about younger generations. She sat back down, finally, and nobody spoke for an uncomfortably long time.

It may seem that Harry's reaction was out of proportion to his son's offense. The key lay in the fact that Harry was a man who all his life had been proud of himself as a fighting Liberal. Now here was this man being upbraided by his own teen-age son for being old, a phony, an arch-Conservative, a member of the "Establishment". It was apparently the first time it had happened.

In the uncomfortable silence, in which I could hear far too loudly the swallowing mechanism of my own damned throat, I finally got up and took my leave, saying I ought to be getting home, since Hill was obviously all right.

"All right?" Harry said in a dazed way. "All right?"

I suppose it wasn't the best thing I could have said.

Anyway, I left. I had no concept, no premonition, no idea, nor even any concern, that this might be anything more than a normal father-son squabble, that an element might exist in it which would demolish, would flatten the whole Gallagher family as Hiroshima was flattened.

2

. . . . . MY DOORBELL IS RINGING. I know who it will be. It will be
Weintraub. Weintraub, coming by with gossip tidbits about the
taking of the Sorbonne today, or perhaps some news about whether the
students will be out protesting tonight. Weintraub. David Weintraub,
who brought The Catalyst into all our lives. I suppose I must go and
let him in. But the thought of seeing him now, depresses me.

But first I am putting these papers away, and locking the desk.
Weintraub avidly and openly examines everything that is lying
around loose in any apartment that he visits. . . . . .

Weintraub. Weintraub the clown. Weintraub the clown has gone.
And he did not see any of these papers of mine. And yet somehow I
have a hunch that he suspects that they exist—even though I only
began actually working on them today! He has that kind of a ferret's
mind, a kind of immensely aware animal cunning that is not inhibited
by any short-circuit of shamelessness on his part, or by any deep-riding
sense of the right of privacy of others. Totally open about himself and
his private (or what ought to be private) experiences, to the point of
embarrassing his listeners, he accords others the same right by prying
shamelessly and incessantly into their private experiences as far as they
will let him. He made at least two allusive remarks about the fact that
I might be working on something, writing something, about the

Gallaghers and the events of the past six weeks—remarks which I parried deftly without giving him any information one way or the other.

It is next to impossible to give any kind of accurate description of Weintraub to someone. "Hello, Jack Hartley!" came that deep, booming, falsely hearty voice from the stairwell, as I pressed the button that opened the outside street door a flight below. "I have great news for you tonight! Weintraub has finally been beaten up by the flics! After all these weeks and days of being in the forefront rank of the *Révolution,* Weintraub has finally made it! I got the bruises to prove it! I'll show you!"

"Come on up, Dave," I said, deliberately making my voice superquiet, to contrast with his effusiveness. He always has affected me that way.

One word here about my apartment. It is in one of those old buildings built around 1720 by some long-vanished entrepreneur who was a big wheel in the King's Finance Ministry or someplace like that, and whose now-forgotten name adorns the wall outside on the quai on a seldom-polished brass plate. These houses were all built as town houses for some rich family or other. Now of course they are all broken up into apartments. And at some time in the last century somebody, for reasons unknown to me, decided to split the high-ceilinged rooms of the ground-floor apartments into two by putting a new floor squarely across the center of them, thus creating two apartments. I have the upper of these. It is, necessarily, low-ceilinged; but I like that. I like being able to reach up my hand and lean on it against the natural-wood beams. Of course Harry, who is tall, and vulnerably bald, always had to duck a little when he came into it, but hardly anyone else did. And it was perfect for me. I had a spacious living room, a small dining place beyond a high arch which did not cut down on the passage of sun and air, two tiny bedroom-cubicles, bath, an adequate—if small—kitchen where I often cooked, good-drawing fireplaces in every room, and a Portuguese maid who lived on the Island and came in every day. What more could a single man ask? I seldom entertained at home, but I could when I wanted to. And beyond my three French-doored windows on the quai, which could be flung open to the sun in summer, was one of the best views in Paris: the back of Notre-Dame

with its soaring buttresses almost close enough to touch; the high
wedding cake of the Panthéon on its hilltop floating above the old
Left Bank houses; and always the river, and the barges, a never-ceasing
source of interest to the eyeball. I had had my writing desk placed
right in front of one of these windows. And down below were the old
trees, and the ancient cobbled ramp, framed in ancient white stone,
where the poor people from the tenements in the center of the Island
used on Sundays to run their cars and motorbikes down to the water to
wash them. It was a great place to live back in fifty-eight, when I first
got it.

Of course, all that has changed now. The Island has become terribly
chic, a dozen new restaurants have opened up, and the honest poor
people's tenements have been bought up by entrepreneurs and cleaned
up and turned into studio apartments, where young white-collar
executive couples, working so hard to build the new Technological
Consumers' Society of France, now live with their narrow black
briefcases like a New Yorker's.

It was into this place that I ushered Weintraub, and offered to make
him a drink. Not that he had not been there before and didn't know
his way to the bar perfectly. He made straight for my writing table
before its end one of my three windows, and began rummaging through
old material for my Review that I had lying there.

"Yeah, God, Hartley," he said in passing across the room, puffing
out his chest and again deepening his already deep, resonant voice; to
show sincerity, I suppose. "I could do with a good stiff Scotch. *Les flics*
really racked me up tonight." He put down my papers with a gesture
that said they were not of interest to him and that he had already seen
them before. "Yes, sir, they really racked old Weintraub up. You want
to see my scars?" He began unbuttoning his short Eisenhower-type
jacket.

I handed him his drink, and then made a stiff one for myself.
"Scars?" I said.

"Well, bruises," the deep, immensely self-important voice said. "But
deep bruises. Those rubber *matraques* with that iron rod in them
really sting. And they bite deep. They hurt deep." He already had his
jacket off, and was starting on his turtleneck.

The jacket of Weintraub requires description. I had never seen it on him before the May Revolution came along. It was made of near-white cotton chino, instead of olive-drab wool like the jacket Eisenhower copied from the British, and since the Revolution started I had not seen Weintraub wear anything else. I am convinced he bought it solely to be his Revolutionary uniform, to wear along with the white Levi's he now affected, in contrast to the dark suits and narrow New York ties he used to wear before. Because the May Revolution, the Students' Revolution, had become a personal symbol, a deeply personal cause to Weintraub.

He always claimed it was because his *hôtel pension* in the rue de Condé was so close to the Odéon, and the center of it all, that he could not avoid becoming involved. The students had, he said, during one of the scares that the police would attack the Odéon, removed all of the files of the Cinema Committee and hidden them in Weintraub's room to protect them; and that from that time on he was forcibly committed. I always doubted this. Not that the Committee had hidden their files and shot film in his room; but that they would do so without first knowing him well, and knowing that he *was* committed. I suspect what really happened was that he took to hanging around the Odéon after the students captured and took it over, found the Cinema Committee's room up in the gloomy recesses upstairs in that old theater, attached himself to them, and later offered his room as a sanctuary for their files and film. Weintraub always denied this though; I don't know why—out of embarrassment perhaps.

Why this American male of 45-plus years (Weintraub would never admit to more than 45) would attach himself to a group of 19- and 20-year-old French students involved in a visibly hopeless revolt, was something else. To understand that you had to know Weintraub.

Weintraub by profession was a harpist. And a fairly accomplished one. But he didn't like it much. He played harp in the Paris Opera orchestra regularly, and also played in any theater orchestras and concerts around town that required or wanted a harp. This was how he survived and made enough money to eat and live. But what he wanted to be was an actor. A movie actor. There was not anything about the movies he did not love. Indiscriminately, he loved movie stars, movie producers, movie directors and movie writers; and the more famous and successful they were the more he was inclined to love them. When not playing the harp for bread, he hung around in the expensive joints where all these people hung out, together, places like Castel's, New Jimmy's, the Calavados. The only way he could get himself accepted by them, since he could hardly afford to pay his own way in these expensive places, was to play the role of the buffoon, the group clown, which he had figured out for himself. He deliberately made himself into a punching bag and straight man for celebrities. It was in this way that he had attached himself to the Gallaghers, and through them to me, though he had little real interest in my literary pursuits. He was not entirely unknown, having played a number of bit roles in films, several of which Harry Gallagher helped him get. He also wrote bad poetry and painted bad pictures.

His buffoonery and role as the fool, of course, could not keep him going long with any one particular group. They soon got bored with him, and he further alienated himself by his increasingly exotic demands such as ordering on the star's tab caviar or Scottish salmon when the rest were ordering steaks or hamburgers, by borrowing without repaying, by asking movie stars to get him roles in their productions or invest in his bad paintings, so that he was reduced to moving from group to group to group till he became known to all of regular Paris. Finally he had to attach himself to visiting stars or directors who were in town for a single production. He had about reached this point of no return with the Gallaghers, than whom there were no softer touches in the world, when the May Revolution came along.

I am convinced the reason he involved himself so completely with the young members of the Odéon Cinema Committee, outside of the fact that they had to do with cinema, was partly because he was such a lonely man. The other part I think was the fact that this was the first time in a long time in his life that he was being taken seriously by anyone, at his own face value of himself. These kids believed him when he namedropped the stars he said he knew, and almost certainly saw him as perhaps their major, if not their only contact with that outside cinema world they hoped to get to help them. Later on in the Revolution I went with him many times up into those dark grimy cubbyholes and upper balconies at the Odéon to see—and work with—"his" Committee, and I do not think those children ever did see through him as he really was. And I believe Weintraub needed that, as other men need liquor or dope.

And this was the man who now stood before me in my apartment, his precious Revolutionary's jacket flung down on my Second Empire couch, while he struggled with his black turtleneck, peeling it up over his bare back to his neck and to the knotted bandanna around it which he had affected since the Revolution started, even during the daytime when there were few or no tear-gas bombs being thrown. This was the man who had brought into our more or less stable, more or less secure midst the woman (woman? woman, hell! Baby girl!) whom I call, called, the Catalyst: all unwittingly on his part, it is true, and, in the end, quite painfully for himself.

"You don't need to show me, Dave," I said, with a faint edge of irony in my voice. "I'll take your word."

But he had already shucked the shirt up, arms crossed above his bowed neck and bent back, and I saw eight or ten blue-black stripes about the width of a thumb and a foot long, crisscrossing his shoulders and lower back. "I got to admit I'm kinda proud of that," he said in the resonant basso. He pulled the shirt back down. "Of course, it doesn't mean anything really. I just happened to get caught between two lines of them. I didn't see the second line coming down the side street."

"But you're glad just the same." I smiled faintly.

"In a way," he said, and walked to the nearest of my open windows. He stepped up onto its parapet and leaned his arms on the *fer forgé* protective railing and looked out at the river. "We're not going to give up, Hartley. We're not going to quit. The Revolution will continue."

"What's happened to the Cinema Committee now that the Sorbonne has fallen?"

"They've moved to the Censier." The Censier was an annex to the overcrowded university in the rue Censier almost a kilometer from the Sorbonne, and still in student hands. "They'll stay there for now."

"Not unless the Government wants to let them, they won't," I said.

"We'll never give up," Weintraub said, still looking out over my river. "We've done too much, and come too far, to ever give up now."

"I'm afraid there isn't any choice. And never was," I said.

"You've never really been with us, have you, Hartley?" Weintraub said, deepening his voice again, but grinning as he did so, thus making of it a parody of an accusation instead of a real one. It was a trick of his.

"I've been with you. And you know it. But I'm also a realist. And I've known all along—as you've known all along—that it could never be much more than what's been, never achieve much more than what it's already achieved."

"No," he said solemnly. "It isn't over. We'll go on. Somehow. We'll do something."

"What? Go underground? And form a new *Résistance?*"

"Maybe," Weintraub said though my remark was patently ridiculous. It was plain he could hardly stand to lose his precious Revolution. But I on the other hand did not want another over-precious lecture on his precious Revolution. And I did want to know more about the woman—girl—(God, I hardly know what to call her, really) —whom I have called our Catalyst. "Have you had any news from Sam?" I asked.

"Samantha?" He turned back from the window's railing.

"Samantha-Marie," I countered.

He smiled. But under the grease of the protective coating of the smile there was a look of bone-deep sadness, an exhausted anguish, in his eyes. "I had a letter from her from Tel Aviv three days ago. She's back with her Sabra girlfriend. They're making it great together. And she wants me to join them as soon as I can get down there."

"And you're going?"

"Where would I get the money?"

"Umm," I said. I changed the subject. "She taught you a lotta things, you told me once."

"Yeah, she did," Weintraub said, still smiling an only-skin-deep smile. "She gave me a taste for some pretty exotic stuff. . . . Aw, fuck it. She don't want me. We both know it. Have you heard anything more from Harry?" He paused. "Or any of them? I walked past the house down there tonight. Their apartment's closed up tighter than a drum. Not a light anywhere."

"Hill has left Paris," I said. "Ten days ago. You knew that. I've not heard from him. Louisa, you know about. The baby, McKenna, is staying with Edith de Chambrolet—you know, Louisa's Countess friend."

"Have I met her?"

"I think you have, at their place."

"I don't remember. And Harry?"

"You saw the telegram I had from him yesterday. He's arrived in Tel Aviv."

"You think he'll ever catch up with her?" Weintraub asked. "With Samantha? Make it back?"

"I haven't the least idea," I said. "You would know the answer to that better than I would."

"No," he said, and hollows showed under his eyes. "No, I wouldn't really. Really."

"Well, I certainly wouldn't have an inkling," I said. "Dave, would you like another drink? I'm pouring. But would you mind making it a quick one? I've got some things I've really got to do tonight."

"Sure. I would like one. And I will make it quick. What are you doing? Writing something about our past six weeks, our *Révolution?*"

"No," I said. "But I suppose I will have to have something done about it for the Review."

He actually leered. "But you're doing something on it yourself?"

"No. I think I'd much prefer to have a French political expert— Left, of course—do it for me. I might translate it myself, though."

He pulled himself up to his full five-foot-four, and grinned—again; this time a genuine one. "Don't forget to have him tell what part Weintraub played in the transpiration of this Revolution! Including the one at Harry Gallagher's!"

After he left, I wondered if his very last remark was not still a further allusion to these papers, to his awareness of their existence, and that he was giving me permission—no, was *asking* me, please to include him in anything I wrote about the Gallaghers. History he wanted. Well, I would certainly have to include him. He certainly did play a role. A key role. But somehow it depressed me. It depressed me even more than I had known that seeing him would do, and I went myself to my window. I leaned on the protective wrought-iron railing looking out at the sadness of the flowing river. As Weintraub had done. It was always there, that sadness of the river, of the flowing of the river. But I've never been able to isolate why. But it was always sad. That was one thing I could count on.

Night had fallen since he had arrived. And the Paris streetlights had come on along the quai. Across the river, lights were coming on in the Left Bank apartments. And in the *Quartier* itself there were no more thuds of gas grenades igniting, no more fires flickering from barricades to light up the rising clouds of smoke and tear gas, no more flashes and the cracking reports of the percussion grenades. Something indeed had truly ended.

By leaning out I could look up the quai to the Pont de la Tournelle and see that the two squad cars of police were changing shifts. Twenty-four hours a day they guarded that bridge's access to the home of M. Pompidou on the Île's Quai de Bethune.

I made myself another, very stiff drink, and downed it. Then I made another, and downed that. Damn it, I thought, I'm going to bed. And if I can't sleep, I'll take a Mogadon.

I didn't take the Mogadon.

I feel I have not given an adequate picture of Harry Gallagher. To understand him you have to understand something of his background. Harry at 49 comes of an old Boston Irish family, who left him an income of some 20-odd thousand a year. In spite of that he has made a considerable name for himself as a screenwriter, and makes an excellent living on his own. He is famous enough and competent enough—what they call a "star" writer in the industry—to be in demand by big-money American producers. He has published two novels in the past six years. He has written screenplays for France's most successful young avant-garde movie makers. In short, Harry was a winner, a man who, entering the bottom edge of middle age as he was, could relax a little and look back without anger.

When he was 19, Harry left Harvard in his junior year as a social protest, to become an actor in New York with the idea of writing plays of social protest somewhat in the manner of Odets. When his first accepted play was in production, but long before it actually reached the boards to flop, he was on his way to Hollywood—at what then seemed a fabulous salary—to do his first screenplay, and on a big production. An old Communist-buddy director pal of his from the New York stage, who had gone out there before him, had asked for him and got him.

I will not go into any moral issues here about their going to Hollywood. Suffice it to say that they two (as well as a whole generation of them, I guess, who went out there then) felt that they could reach more people with their message through films than through the theater. That was in 1939. By the time the war came at the end of 1941, at the age of 23, Harry had written two hit screenplays and was a boy-genius in the industry, with a big name.

After Pearl Harbor, Harry threw all this up. Unlike his dedicated Communist confreres, who mostly received commissions as Lieutenant Commanders and went right on, making propaganda films for the Government now, Harry enlisted in the Marines where he fought the war in the Pacific as a Sergeant.

After the war, of course, he had to start all over. A lot of new blood—that voracious, clamorous, greedy-ambitious new blood—had come in and taken over every place that was not occupied, and a lot that were. But he re-established himself in Hollywood as a top writer; and though his friends who had fought the war on the Silver Screen had trouble looking him in the eye, he became again a wheel and involved himself in the intellectual and humanistic Communism-Marxism side of the film-industry community which he had always been drawn to. There is no use here of my going into the relative goods and evils of Communist-Marxism as they were seen in the 1930s and '40s. A lot of things that have happened in the world since then have changed an awful lot of things. But back then everybody was a pearly idealist. And Harry Gallagher was one of them. And, in 1947, on a visit home to Boston to his conservative Irish family, he met and married young Louisa Dunn Hill, another dedicated Marxist-Liberal idealist from an old Boston Brahmin family whose line and whose Liberalism dated even from before the days of Thoreau and Emerson and the Transcendentalists. Together they carried on their political activities in Hollywood, although neither ever actually became a card-carrying member of the American Communist Party. She immediately bore him their first child, Hill, in 1948.

In 1950, when the House Un-American Activities Committee anti-Communist hunt got going full blast in all its glory, and the Hollywood Ten had finally been jailed, Harry (often jokingly called Number Eleven of the Hollywood Ten—although a number of others claimed that title, too, I gather) was investigated. Somebody had given

in his name, obviously. Rather than talk to the Committee and give
the names of friends as most of his friends did, Harry chose to skip out
to Canada and make his way to France, later sending for Louisa and
Hill when he got settled. I do not choose to comment on what will be
history's verdict on these ignorant, primitive, self-seeking American
politicians who could tolerate and even defend a Rankin and a Joe
McCarthy, though they will probably be slightly less badly thought
of than the Catholic Inquisition.

Even had he stayed and not gone to jail, he could not have gotten a
job anywhere in the American film industry without talking for the
Committee because of the secret blacklist—the blacklist which the
industry denied existed but which in fact did exist. We tend to prefer
not to remember all this today whenever we righteously criticize the
Russians for putting their outspoken writers to jail.

Harry's first two years in France were very hard indeed, because of
the language problem. But without help from his family (his parents
disapproved of him and had not quite died yet to leave him his inheritance), Harry started over. He played bit parts as Americans in
French films, became adept at the new industry of dubbing American
films into French for the French market, and finally was writing
screenplays in French—now for the young French *Nouvelle Vague* film
makers. And as the years passed and the McCarthy Era blew finally
away back home, more and more American producers were coming to
him for screenplays of productions to be done in Europe, and finally
for screenplays to be done at home. It had been discovered Harry had
a natural talent for American love stories, and for America's morality
play, the Western. Success followed success.

So it is true that on that night of April 27th, when young Hill threw
his first young monkey wrench into the machinery, Harry Gallagher
was an unqualified, even a disgusting success.

But Harry had paid pretty dearly for never compromising his
principles. It was, Harry felt, something to be proud of. And it was
that that stunned him so about Hill's accusation. It was as if everything he had done and stood for had gone by the board, been thrown
out, negated, denied existence by his son in a wild youthful jettison, as
if in his housecleaning young Hill was throwing out the furniture and
rugs and even the wall fixtures, along with the dirt.

And yet they were not all that far apart. Hill with his anti-Capitalist, anti-Communist *Nouvel Anarchisme* and the black flag of Dany Cohn-Bendit was not all that far from Harry's viewpoint. Because Harry had given up on Communism. After watching the developments in Russia, China and elsewhere during the '40s and '50s and the '60s, Harry had become convinced that while these societies might be— probably were—helping the lowest common denominator of humanity, their demand, their drive to compel rigid inflexibility of belief from every citizen (as the Church had also done in its day of power) was diminishing, impeding the movement upward of the highest common denominator of the race: its growth, which was where the true creativity, the talent for innovation, and genius for change and spiritual growth were situated. And for him, however reluctantly, that meant a return to enlightened Capitalism as the lesser evil of the two. But he didn't like that Capitalism, either. Or what it stood for. Spiritually, that made him an Anarchist too.

But try and tell that to Hill. Certainly I couldn't. And Harry was not about to.

I suppose really the only difference between them was that Hill was activist. He, like the rest of Dany Cohn-Bendit's group with their black flag, wanted to *act* on his Anarchism. Believed you *must* act on your Anarchism. He believed in organization of the Anarchists, already an anomaly, of course. Hill believed Harry had become cynical, I suppose you could say—an old man's right. Wisdom is the right of the aged not to declare themselves. But where, in our day and age, were the old men going to be left to rest peacefully and with dignity upon their laurels? As far as Hill was concerned, all that belonged to the disenfranchised past. To Hill it was the most profane sacrilege.

Perhaps, after all, it was only a problem of the generations. Hill— very jealously—was not about to let his old man get into the act and usurp his youthful rebellion.

Now, I really must sleep.

3

MY OWN MARRIAGE HAD ENDED in the spring of 1958. And it was while my wife was doing her Reno residence time that I departed for a European trip, never dreaming I would end up staying there, in Paris on the Île St.-Louis. Our marriage was always a New York marriage, and a literary one. We lived the whole nine years of it in Manhattan, in a rather grand apartment on Central Park West, and entertained lavishly everybody during that time who had made it on the New York literary or theatrical scene. We were both would-be writers, I in poetry, she in the novel and as an essayist, and Eleanor was wealthy: rich: the heiress of an ancient publishing and writing family that had made millions back when a million counted. Fortunately, we were without issue.

It is difficult to go back to teaching Lit. at some school, even a ritzy one, when you have lived nine years married to an heiress. And we had practically lived together the two years before that, before we married and I gave up my teaching job. My book on *The Rhythms of Early English Prose* came out to very good reviews, and sank. As expected. My two slim poetry volumes got very bad reviews. Eleanor's first long, long novel, very Joycean in style and very Virginia Woolf in outlook, appeared, died, and joined my three books. And that was probably what did it. We continued to entertain, even stepped up our entertaining. Eleanor drank more and more at night, and so did I. Our parties got oftener and oftener, and longer and longer, often lasting deep into the morning. We got so we each hated to see people leave and go home, begged them to stay for one more drink when they tried to leave. In desperation I tried a tough realistic novel which I never did believe would work. It didn't. And that was just about it.

I never did believe, as Eleanor accused, that it was all my fault, that I caused the withering and downfall of her talent by my own lack of one, by my budding "alcoholism". She has never published anything since then, and has married twice and divorced twice. I am sure she had a string of literary and theatrical lovers during our last years, and maybe she had them sooner. But she did love the arts and artists. And I feel that I did fail her there. It left me with a strong guilt. Fortunately for me I still had my own small income which my family of successful New York lawyers had left me:—my family of New York lawyers who had always disapproved of me as Harry Gallagher's family of Boston bankers and doctors had always disapproved of him.

In late September of 1959 Louisa Gallagher came to my apartment alone for the first time. She called ahead of time and asked to see me and made an appointment. At that time I had known her pretty well for almost two years, and she and Harry had been to my place often. But this was the first time she had ever come there alone. In fact, it was the first time Louisa and I had ever been really alone together anywhere. She certainly had never been to my apartment alone.

If I seem to dwell on this point unduly, it is because Louisa herself made me so aware of it. Not that she ever mentioned it openly in words. She didn't. But there was about Louisa a kind of quasi-Puritanical quality which seemed to make her always aware of herself as a sexual object, in a sort of guilty and uncomfortable way. Dear Louisa. For instance, she was always very meticulous, even prissy, about her person—always carefully adjusting her skirt when she pulled her lovely long legs up under her; always feeling almost guiltily at her skirt to make sure it was properly adjusted whenever some man looked admiringly at her legs; always sitting primly with her knees pressed tight together when she was in a chair. Even with me, whom I believe she liked more than any other friend they had, there was often this look of guilty start on her face, as if it had again occurred to her that I might find her attractive, and that this was her fault.

I always supposed this was part of her New England heritage. Her New England heritage was evident also in her lanky, almost rawboned build, and in her long, sharply sculptured horse-face. When she grinned, two deep lines would appear beneath her high cheekbones. And yet she was extremely beautiful as a woman, with her lovely long legs and vague, eager eyes. An extremely reserved person about herself, she was by fits and starts almost hysterically talkative about just about everything else, especially politics. Even back then Louisa was already violently and volubly anti-de Gaulle, saying he had only saved France from the militant Rightists of the OAS to impose upon it a gentler Rightism of his own, which would make it that much harder to fight for any truly modern economic reforms. But it was not about de Gaulle that she was coming to my apartment alone to see me that September.

Naturally, I was curious and puzzled. To call me for a rendezvous alone in my apartment was certainly not the usual Louisa. When she came in, I offered her a seat and suggested a drink.

Well, for a moment that startled, wild-deer look came into her eye and I seriously thought she was going to bolt out the door.

"Oh, no! No, no! No drink!" she stammered—as if to accept a drink was the first step along a path that must end in her seduction there in my own apartment. For a few moments I thought she was actually going to refuse to sit down on my Second Empire couch.

There was always about Louisa the feeling of tension as of a tightly drawn wire, but now the drawing was so tautened you actually felt you might hear the wire snap singing in the air.

It was about Harry that she had come to see me. "I'm leaving him, Jack," she said without preamble. "I'm taking Hill and I'm going back home to America to my family."

"You're *what!*" I exclaimed.

"That's it. That's what I'm going to do."

"You must be out of your mind!" I said. "Harry loves you! He adores you!" The thought of their marriage foundering, too, made me actually physically sick at my stomach.

"If he does, he does not show it in any way which I can any longer tolerate," she said firmly.

I had heard some pretty explicit gossip about Harry Gallagher's sexual flings with young actresses and such. When people find out you know someone, they hasten to tell you everything scandalous they have heard about them. After his first successes in France in the mid-'50s, Harry apparently had gone through quite a list of young actresses and would-be actresses, of just about every nationality—a number of whom both European and American are today world-worshipped sex symbols.

At first I was shocked by this talk. I still thought of Harry and Louisa as my perfect happy-American-family—something I had perhaps failed to achieve, but was glad nevertheless to know did exist. But then I decided if Louisa did not care, why should I? And obviously Louisa didn't. And after all what could be more truly American, than that the man of the family should have his peccadilloes and that the wife should forgive him and not care as long as she had him himself and his love. That was *truly* the perfect happy-American-family.

And of course, Harry was working on scripts for most of these girls; and in his favor it had to be admitted that they all certainly made themselves exceedingly available. Whether it was simply their supreme availability, or whether something deeply important inside Harry had been torn apart by the ignominy of his forced flight from Hollywood, I would not presume to judge.

But now suddenly in my apartment it all came out. Louisa did care. She had only been putting up a front. The story I had heard was substantially the story Louisa unfolded to me that day in September of '59 in my apartment. And not only that, the same thing had been going on a long time before, even out on the Coast, long before Harry fled Hollywood and the Un-American Activities Committee for France. And now the crowning indignity had come.

Harry had been writing a screenplay for a French producer which was designed to hit the American market with a new young French male star, and for it two beautiful American actresses had been imported. One of these was *very* young and beautiful, and in fact would soon marry the French producer and go on to become a big international sex-star. And the other, while older, was still not anything to be sneezed at. Well, each girl had (individually and privately, of course) invited Harry down to Cannes to visit her, where each hoped he would be able to enhance and expand her role in the film. Each girl felt that her role was not quite up to snuff and needed expanded characterization, particularly when confronted with the role of the other girl. Each had written a warm letter to Harry, after her private dinner conference with Harry and the producer. And Harry had gone, Louisa said. Of course, he had had to go anyway, to work on the script with the producer. But both ladies had written him very warm thank-you letters to his Paris address after his return from Cannes, each saying how much she had enjoyed working with a writer of his understanding, of his sensibilities and discernment about roles and characterization.

"And he didn't even bother to hide the damned letters!" Louisa said, red-faced, and blew her damp hair back off her forehead. She was 31 then in 1959, and exceedingly attractive. "Neither the first ones, nor the *thank-you* letters that came after!"

Insensitive as it was, I had to fight down a grin, and swallow to keep from laughing: thinking of Harry down there in Cannes, slyly doing both of these girls, these ladies, turn and turn about every other night apparently, and paying them for their favors by working secretly on each's role against the other's in their greedy competition.

But there was nothing funny at all about it to Louisa. "Maybe he didn't think you would stoop to going through his mail?" I suggested gently.

"Well, I did," Louisa said, totally without guilt here. Her guilts all seemed reserved to pulling down her skirt, which she suddenly and primly did. "And my family is perfectly willing and capable of taking care of us, of Hill and me."

That, they certainly were. Unlike Harry, whose wealthy, conservative Boston-Irish background did not go back much beyond 1880, when the first of his Irish forebears broke out upward from the Irish working class via banking, Louisa's intellectual heritage, unhampered by the need to earn a living, went in unbroken line back to Emerson and far beyond. She was even a distant cousin of the Jameses. They certainly could take care of her. Particularly they could, mélanged as they were of equal parts iron self-restraint and strict New England Puritanism.

"Well, what are you coming here telling me all this for?" I asked. For a moment I thought she would cry. But of course New England would not let her.

"I just had to talk to somebody about it, Jack," she said. "I had to."

"You're not even going to tell him you're leaving?" I said. It had somehow sounded like that.

"No, I'm not," she said. "I'll leave a letter."

"And how old is Hill," I pressed her grimly.

"Almost eleven."

"Almost eleven! Louisa, Louisa! Good heavens!"

She looked back at me with a powerful New England stubbornness. "I know. That's the worst part. But it can't be helped."

I drew a deep breath. I was sitting there beside her on my Second Empire couch. For a moment I thought of reaching for her hand. But I knew better. She would have run. But good God! Even divorced, particularly because divorced, how could I countenance and be party to breaking up a marriage—especially this marriage? "Well, you know that I'm Harry's friend," I said tentatively. "Maybe one of his best ones."

"The best one," she said.

"Well, I'll tell you what I'm going to do," I said, making my voice cold and quite literary, as I've often had to do when rejecting manuscripts—though it always pains me. "I'm going to call Harry up on the phone, right now, and tell him what you've told me. Unless you promise me right here and now on your honor that you won't leave Paris till you've talked this thing thoroughly through with Harry. And you must come and tell me that you have, afterwards!"

"But that's *unfair!*" she cried, "I *came* to you! That's not fair at all. I came to you as a friend."

"Unfair or not unfair," I said in my best tough-editor's voice. "There's no choice."

Louisa looked helpless, a little stunned. "You'd really tell him!" she said. "Then I guess I don't have any choice then, do I?"

"You do not," I said. I reached out for the phone.

"All right! All right! Don't do that! I'll promise!"

"That's on your New England honor," I said.

"It's on *my* honor," she said. "That's enough."

"It is," I said. "Now, you go on home and see Harry."

She sent young Hill over to stay with me that night. I assume that they had it out then. Young Hill, aged ten and a half was a little disgruntled.

"What's goin' on at home?" he asked me with angry suspicion.

"Why, nothing that I know of. Why?" I said.

"Well, what're they sendin' me over here to stay with you for then? This is only the second time I've ever stayed at your house. And the other was when I was only a little kid." He meant a year ago.

"I just thought you might like to see your old Uncle Jack," I said, "and have dinner with him for a change. So I asked your mother."

"Well, *I* think there's somethin goin' on," Hill persisted.

"Well, if there is, I don't know about it. Look, I've got some great steaks. Or would you rather have a big hamburger steak?"

"I like escargots. Have you got any escargots?"

"You know damn well I haven't got any escargots. All right. We'll go out then. Down the block. Quasimodo has excellent escargots."

"Great!" Hill cried. "Fine! Oh, boy, do I love my Uncle Jack!" But afterwards, walking along the quaiside to the restaurant, he still looked at me narrowly, even sullenly, as if he suspected I knew something he had not been let in on. "I suppose you know about Dad's girlfriends, don't you?" he said finally. We were just crossing the rue Boutarel. It was one of those lovely, winey September Paris days. The restaurants were full or filling, but it was not yet dark. In the west behind the loom of Notre-Dame the sun had not yet lost its influence, and was shooting last rays up into that special île de France fair-weather cloud structure.

"Girlfriends?" I said. "Girlfriends? Do you mean lovers?"

"I guess I mean lovers. Lots of them. He's got loads of them. It's pretty important. Not many fellows got so many."

"Where did you pick up all this nonsense?" We had almost reached the restaurant, I noted gratefully. I looked into its picture windows with their potted plants, but Hill was too short to see in. It was crowded with smiling diners.

"Just keep your eyes and ears open. That's all. Like I do. And you'll learn," Hill said. "It upsets Mom a lot, I don't know why exactly. But she hides it. Dad doesn't know. But I can tell."

"I think you're just making up a story," I said. "If your Dad had girlfriends, I would know. He would tell me." I stopped at the door to take a last look at the evening, and the evening's sky. Why couldn't we all be as serene as that was?

Hill didn't answer. And we went on in. The portly old maître d', who has owned and run that place since before the Third Republic I guess, knew Hill and knew me, and made a big fuss over us as residents of the Island, who are always treated special in his restaurant. He made a big thing of Hill the jeune monsieur out for an evening with a friend, without his parents. Hill ordered and ate a dozen escargots, sopping up the butter sauce from the little cups in the tin plate with his bread, then tried to bring the subject up again. But I avoided it, and tried to give the impression that I considered the matter closed, as we ate our coq-au-vin. I don't know what else I could have done. But I was to suddenly remember that evening four years later that day up on the Marne—particularly, strangely enough, I remembered the way the sky was. However, he slept very well that night at my place, and nine months later in late June, nine months almost to the day, my Godchild McKenna Hartley Gallagher was born, a small level-eyed girlchild whose New England background could never be mistaken.

I value it highly in some way that Louisa never thanked me. Not only did she never thank me. She never even mentioned it again. In fact, it was as if it had not ever happened.

I think that after this near break-up, which I averted, the Harry Gallaghers became that perfect happy-American-family I once imagined them being. I know Harry stopped going out with his young actresses. Certainly there was no more gossip. And Louisa seemed completely happy.

I know Harry stopped going out with the actresses because he told me. There was no reason he should tell me, but he did. I believed him simply because there was no reason for him to tell me.

This was a long time after the birth of McKenna. Six years after.

And Harry had no idea of the part I'd played in that.

It was, also, quite a while and almost two years before Samantha Everton and the May Revolution, the Events of May as the French still like to call it, came down upon our heads. No, there was no reason Harry should tell me except that it happened.

I know it was after McKenna's sixth birthday because I gave a special Halloween party for her at my apartment that year, which was her first year in serious school. I invited all her little school playmates. Hill was thus at least 17, and already a student at the Sorbonne. God, you never saw a happier, more delighted kid than McKenna was at that party.

My confessional session with Harry that same winter came about because Harry was trying to decide whether to take a job or not, and he wanted my advice. Why he should ask my advice about a film job has never been explained. But that was the reason, the excuse, that I was asked for dinner that night. The job he had to decide about was whether or not he should contract to write an Italian Western in Spain.

He had invited the two producers, one French and the other an American, to dinner at his place that night. That was the real reason I was there. I was to be his ploy, his foil, in his Hollywood one-upmanship battle with the two producers. Around film people, I was always sort of Harry's literary weapon, his artistic broadsword. The *Two Islands Review* was known by this time, and I as its editor was known with it. Harry liked to defer to me as his expert on artistic and esthetic points. He also liked to bring up as a throwaway that he had put money in the *Two Islands Review,* which indeed he had.

The Frenchman fought him back valiantly that night, with that over-loquacious, over-adrenalized valor which the French are addicted to, and could not avoid even if they wanted. The American, who was a former distributions executive for Warner's or Fox or M-G-M and looked like one of those hairless pink cupie-dolls you win at a village fair, listened and watched everything keenly in pregnant silence and did not say more than one or two words all evening. I found out later that he was not smart at all. That was just his gimmick. As I was Harry's. And loquacious valor was the Frenchman's.

This thing of a film-job thing is a complicated matter. Nobody tells anybody anything. It is like pulling teeth to get anything out of somebody.

The mechanics themselves are complex enough. Harry's writing job was only a part of it. The whole thing entailed a lot of film world high-finance shenanigans, a lot of reputational jockeying back and forth, demanded much talk about markets and distribution deals. I tried to understand it as they tossed it all back and forth between them after dinner, but I'm afraid I did not understand it at all well.

The trouble seems to be that nobody knows or can figure out ahead of time what will sell. So most film makers (and I don't mean just the small fry) are copiers. That is, if a Broadway musical is a hit, they will rush to make a Broadway musical; if a Western is a hit, they will make a Western; if a Pinter play is a hit as a film, they make a Pinter-like film.

Harry's Frenchman and American were after making an Italian Western in Spain. Mainly this was because Italian Westerns had become a big hit in America and therefore now were big business. Italian Westerns (I found out) were distinguished by the fact that they were made in Europe at a cost the Americans with their high union wage could not compete with; they were also different in that the Italians had thrown out the classical American morality-play angle, done away with the concept of hero and villain, and were making their Westerns into an entirely new thing: tough, extremely violent, and totally amoral. And American audiences were loving it. Our two producers thought they could compete with the Italians on their own ground, and even beat them at it, by making the films in Spain where it was even cheaper than Italy. The American had a deal to use the Dupont-Bronston studios and facilities. They had a great deal of money behind them to do it. They wanted Harry to write the first one for them. And if the first one was a hit, there was no reason there couldn't be a series of them.

All this was not only just for the money and profit, mind you. Even moreso the film maker wants the notoriety a big hit brings, the fame of being famous, a globetrotting celebrity, the right of success which is the right to give lots of people lots of orders and spread much largess, and be like Mr. Darryl Zanuck or one of those. You could almost smell it oozing, exuding from our two.

But there were further complications. For example, almost all films today are what they call "packaged". This presents another problem. "Packaging" means that the "independent" producer (who isn't really independent at all) must first set up all of his whole film production ahead of time, before going to his major studio or big-money people who are advancing the million or millions required to actually make the film.

Thus a producer must first get a "property", which means a story, then find a writer who will write it as a script, and then a director, and if possible a star actor who will agree to act it,—all the while laying out out of his own pocket, the producer, the 20 or 30 or even 50 thousand dollars to bring all these people together, while hoping against hope as he does so that they all can get along together and work together congenially, something which according to Harry apparently happens very rarely.

I felt rather sorry for the poor producers. But Harry didn't, although he pretended to at the appropriate times.

I knew from the moment we sat down that Harry was going to take the job. I don't know if anyone else could have seen it. Certainly the two producers didn't. And Louisa had left us immediately after a coffee. Dear Louisa. But over the second coffee and the brandy, Harry began to bring out a formidable and almost interminable battery of objections. These lasted through the brandy and well into the Scotch. And they were pretty devastating, and pertinent, objections. Or seemed so to me. The whole thing must have lasted until well after three o'clock.

In between belts at their Scotch, and sunk down in the cloudlike wreathes of expensive cigar smoke which gave me a fearful headache, they continued to throw it back and forth, as they called it, and Harry went on elaborating his list of objections. He demolished those poor producers (and they were not small fry) so thoroughly and with such relish that I was embarrassed for them.

I was his esthetic objection. I had read it (I hadn't; but here I nodded and frowned) and I agreed with him that their property, the novel they had bought, was worthless. Harry would have to do it all. Only one or two scenes could be used at all, and these only when highly modified by Harry. He looked at me, and I hastened to smile and nod my agreement.

Then there was the objection of Harry's reputation. As they well knew, it was based on, and he was noted for, writing good old-fashioned American morality-play Westerns, complete with dovetailing love stories he was famous for and that touched and moved his audiences. Harry was not sure he wanted to leave that role, step out of that well-fit suit of clothes, to take on some new gimmick like this Italian-Western, so-called "modern" stuff. It might easily ruin his other reputation.

And what about the director? He could not write for just any director. Harry elaborated on this for a while.

And the star? They had no real contact with a star for it, yet. And Harry could not write the star role properly unless he had some idea what star he'd be writing for. As they well knew, a Burton role was not a Steve McQueen role. They discussed this a while.

No, he just did not think he was the man for their job, Harry said finally.

They came back with all the right answers. They knew the original story was not much good, they said, but they were depending on Harry to fix that. As for his reputation, they thought such a film would enhance his reputation, not damage it. And the director and the star of course depended a great deal on whether they had a Harry Gallagher script or not. They were really ladling it on. They both looked a little puzzled somehow, as though somehow they could not quite figure out how they had got put into this position, this role. Matter of fact, they went on, they could even use a phony name, something like Enrico Galignani, say, if Harry liked that idea. Of course, the director and star would know Harry Gallagher really wrote it. After all, Harry Gallagher was a "star" writer, the kind whose work directors and stars delighted to do. Who did he have in mind, who did he think he would like, as the star and director?

There then followed a long discussion, over more Scotch and cigars, as to what director and what star would be good for it and could work together well. It was flattery of the worst order really, and I could see that Harry was quite aware of that. Finally they left with the tentative agreement that Harry would think about it a few days and let them know whether he would accept or refuse, or whether he wanted to discuss it further.

"Who the hell do they think they're bullshitting?" Harry said the instant the door closed. He was grinning. We went back into the smoke-fouled living room.

For a moment Harry stood and looked at it. "Jesus!" he said suddenly. He slapped himself on both thighs. Then he went up on his toes, stretching himself to his full height in the dark narrow-cut suit, and spread his arms above his head. Momentarily he looked like some kind of witch's demon. There was in it such force, such a power of long-sat-upon, painfully contained energy and exuberance, that I half expected to see sparks crackle in streams from his spatulate fingers.

"Jesus!" he said again, and threw himself down in an overstuffed armchair like a sack of old arms and legs. "I've been waiting for a shot like that for over a year. Ever since those Italians hit the market with their product."

He wriggled in the chair. "I've been waiting longer! Five years at least. To make that kind of a Western. But nobody in America had the guts to go against the taboos and try it." He gathered himself and got to his feet.

"Come on. Let's go upstairs. Up to my office. We need to cool out, you and me. Over a bottle of Scotch. I feel like I've just gone fifteen rounds."

He led us out. On the dimly lit exterior stairs of the building he turned back, grinning with his hatchet-face in the faint light, and said, "You have to play poker with them. It's almost a ritual. That's just the way it is in this business."

He climbed on, and his voice continued, coming back over his shoulder in the pale, just barely sufficient light of the *minuterie*. "If you ever let them know that you want it, they'll kill you. If they even get any idea at all that you're in fact aching to do it, they'll shit all over you all down the line. They'll stick a knife as big as Jim Bowie's up your ass and make you dance the hoe-down."

The keys jingled in his jacket pocket as he withdrew them. He reached inside and snapped on the overhead light and led us in. By the time I was inside and had shut the door, he was already sitting tilted back in the big black leather swivel chair behind his antique wooden desk. "You just can't level with them," he said. "Anyway, I'm not sure I want to go down to Spain to work that long really. I'm not sure I want to be away from Louisa that long."

The desk and the Louis Treize table set at right angles to it were covered with manuscript and stacks of research materials. Beside the chair stood his IBM electric on a rollered typing table. Beside that stood a tiered paper, carbon and notebook holder on rollers. I sat down on one of the two middle-height Louis Treize armchairs across from the desk.

"I'm not at all sure I want to be away from Louisa that long," Harry said. He got up and moved toward the bar for whisky, Perrier, glasses and ice. I looked around. Again.

"Anyway, it's already been done now, in Italy," he said from behind the bar. "It's not the same as if I would be doing it for the first time." I didn't answer.

Harry's studio was such a massive projection of Harry's personality that it was almost a caricature, or something made up by a screen-writer of one of Harry's own American he-man love-story films. On one wall hung a Watney-Mann "Red Barrel" dartboard in its Watney-Mann cabinet identical to the one in any London pub; and on the floor under it stretched the authentic Watney-Mann rubber mat with its eight-foot and nine-foot marks. On another hung Harry's collection of Western arms and cartridges, Bowie knives, Indian lances, bows and tomahawks. In a corner leaned six or seven modern shotguns, and three modern fiberglass bows, unstrung.

Harry had taken over three maids' rooms on the top floor of the building up under the roof, back when he leased the apartment, and by knocking out portions of the walls between had made them into one studio. So he had more than four walls under his slanting ceiling; he had about seven. It had its own complete kitchenette, and its own ample bathroom. Half of one of the small rooms had been covered with a sort of raised dais a foot-and-a-half high covered in some kind of a heavy blue felt material, and on this for a bed was a made-up double mattress with a reading lamp over it, leaving plenty of space on the dais for books, ashtrays, a tray of drinks, and a chess board. A small fireplace had been built to serve both the dais area and Harry's black chair behind the desk. It had an extremely cozy air, with its slanting ceilings and small windows, and made me think of nothing so much as a secret *pied-à-terre* place of assignation to bring a girl. Harry had the only set of keys in the household, which once in a while he would give to the one maid he allowed in to clean it. Nobody else was allowed in it. And in all the years I had known him, I had only been invited up there three or four times.

One entire long wall had been completely covered in bookshelves, about a quarter of which had locked glass windows in front of them and housed Harry's famous pornography collection. Another shorter one had cabinets built against it, which stored all Harry's charts and carried on its top under its special lamp all his navigational tools and his *Mixter* and *Bowditch.* Though Harry had never owned a yacht that I know of. A third wall was hung with the plaques and framed certificates and citations of his life, and other memorabilia. Harry called this his *Shit Wall.* There were things like his Life Memberships in the National Rifle Association and National Skeet Association, his citations from the Screen Writers Guild for Academy Award Nominations. There were his framed Silver Star and Bronze Star citations from the war, a certificate making him an admiral in the Great Navy of the State of Nebraska some fan had sent him, some newspaper clippings, a menu signed by himself, Irwin Shaw and William Styron from the South of France, several poker hands, a framed tie from a club he had become a member of, a framed key from the Chief Purser of the old *Liberté* which would let him into First Class, framed covers of *Newsweek* or *Time* with the portraits of friends who had made it, and a framed photo of some anonymous girl's bare behind all bent over cunningly so that nothing shocking really showed except her pubic hair peeking through under. Harry would never say who she was except that she was a famous movie star he had known.

In the other corners around not counting the shotgun corner were scattered a couple of scope-mounted hunting rifles; his skis, his poles, and his boots in their carrying rack; his Aqualung tanks and regulators; several pairs of different types of crutches and some canes; and near the bar was a folding table-like thing called an Adams Trainer Exerciser. About the only thing missing was a Ping-Pong table. But there wasn't room for one.

"No, I'm not at all sure I want to be away from Louisa that long," he said, coming back from the bar with a tray, and sat back down in the tall-backed black leather swivel chair.

"You could take her with you," I said.

He looked at me with surprise. "I could, couldn't I?"

"Install her in Madrid."

"Except there's nothing to do in Madrid. She'd be bored. I'd be out at the studio all the time, or out on location."

"Shopping."

"There's nothing to shop for in Madrid. Maybe some of those knitted Spanish rugs is about all."

"Museums. She's never seen the Prado. Has she?"

"That's true," he said thoughtfully. He rocked himself in the black chair several times. "That's true."

"She'd love it," I said.

"Maybe," Harry mused, "maybe. Well, I sure don't feel like going without her," he said. Then he grinned, to make sure I knew what he meant. I think he was still feeling particularly high after his session with the two producers.

I took a drink, then left my nose in my glass and studied the ice in there. Harry and I had never really talked openly about sex—except for what was implied when he nudged me and smiled or nodded imperceptibly over some especially well-endowed girl at a party, or who would pass by us in the street. I did not particularly want it to begin now. And I certainly did not want it to start with something about Louisa.

At the desk Harry swung himself around toward the Watney-Mann dartboard and looked at it a moment. Then he swung back, and placed the soles of his black short-boots on the desk's edge, jackknifing his long body. His eyes had become brilliant, and curiously shallow, like jewels. The leathery soles of his shoes stared me in the face, framing his head. This was grinning at me in a super-diffident way, which at the same time was oddly conceited and quite proud. I realized I was on the brink of some revelation.

Harry said from between his feet, "You see, I haven't slept with another woman except Louisa for six years. Not since McKenna was born. Not since she was *conceived,* in fact." He peered at me between his boots as if I were expected to react to this in some way.

I on the other hand did not know what to say to this statement, so I said nothing.

Harry shifted his position to stretch out his long legs, and crossed his ankles on a corner of the desk while he lit a cigar. He poured more straight whisky into his glass. "You may not know it, but I used to be quite a rounder. I was quite a womanizer at one time. Before Mc-Kenna. For quite a long time. All my life, in fact. You probably never guessed that." He paused.

I still did not know what to say, so I coughed—but politely—to show my continuing interest. I had a hunch he would continue anyhow, whatever I did. I somehow knew somewhere inside myself that at this point nothing was going to stop him. I also knew, to give Harry his due, that in fact in that six years since McKenna Harry had spent several quite long periods away from home, working in Rome or in London.

With his jewelly eyes, Harry said, "I don't think I'm inordinately attractive to women. I mean, no more than some other. So I don't take credit. But I've had more cunt in my time than most fellas ever get. Twice more, probably. I've just about done them all. I've fucked the great and the near-great." He paused and grinned diffidently at me. "You never even imagined that about me, I suppose."

It was not quite a question, but it almost was. And I felt I was expected to answer. Since I couldn't, I leaned forward suddenly and held out my glass, to dissipate his attention; and he poured for me, straight whisky, from the bottle on the tray among the manuscripts. I put in the Perrier myself.

Harry said, "I've found, in general, that most girls will put it out, and think nothing very much about giving a little bit of it away, if it's to their interest. After all, there's always more of it left. And girls learn that, fast. And they do like writers, especially script-writers. So I don't take credit."

I cleared my throat, cautiously. I felt we were fast reaching the point where I must answer with something. "I think that's pretty damned magnanimous of you to say so, Harry," I said; and peered again down at my ice, which was shrinking.

He waved his hand, as if shooing an irksome fly. "Anyway, Louisa came to me about it. About my other women. Well, I was flabbergasted. I had no idea that that meant anything to Louisa. Hell, I didn't even know she was upset about it. But she was. Upset, and mad. Shi-*it*, was she mad! She wanted to divorce me. She was going to leave me. She wanted to take Hill and go back to America. To her family.

"Some sense of her own inadequacy, you see. She felt she had failed as a wife. She felt she alone wasn't enough for me. She couldn't satisfy me enough to keep me at home. She felt I didn't love her. Or no longer loved her. Or, had never loved her. All that stuff, you know.

"—All of which, of course, was absolutely untrue.

"I don't mind at all telling somebody close like you, Jack, that Louisa has always been more than adequate in the bed with me. She's basically a real woman, which means she's basically a masochist-type. She likes to have things done to her, instead of taking the initiative herself. Which is what a woman ought to be. Sexually, she's always been adequate, more than adequate, for me. We're well-matched like that."

"That's nice," I murmured, then felt it wasn't adequate. "Nice to hear, I mean." It's strange how things which have terrified you so in your imagination, when they actually come to pass, are digested so easily, and with such dispatch.

He only made a kind of gesture with his cigar. "How do you explain to a woman that you can love her and adore her and still want to fuck around a little on the side?—especially when it's all right there waiting for you, practically, so to speak? All ready to fall back down on its back and open it up wide for you?

"Well, I didn't try to tell her that it just was different with men. That it's a kind of adventure. What was the point? You couldn't talk to her. So I made her a solemn promise instead. That night. And, that night, as you may have guessed by now, was the night McKenna was conceived. She wasn't anticipated or planned for. But I know that happens with lots of people. It's happened with lots of my friends. I call them Reconciliation Babies. Some deep emotional spark down deep inside them somewhere makes contact and catches hold and sticks.

"And I haven't laid a glove on another broad since." He moved in the chair.

"But wasn't that miraculous? That she should come to me like that? I mean, she didn't have to. She could just have taken Hill and left, and left me a letter. Or not even left me any note at all! And where would I have been then? No, I think that part was marvelous."

"Yes," I said from deep within the open mouth of my glass. "That part was certainly marvelous. But then, she's a marvelous woman, Louisa."

"She sure is, and I don't mind telling you that I've had several pretty long hard dry spells because of that solemn promise, since then," Harry said. "That's why I'm not so very hot on going down to Madrid for this job without her."

Such self-centeredness as that demands a certain respect. He reached for the bottle. I quickly held out my glass. It had been a brand-new bottle when he got it from the bar. But I felt I needed a drink. I felt dishonest. But I did not quite see how I could tell him now, six years after, about my share in his reconciliation with his wife—and by extension, in the conception of his daughter. It was too personal. It was too—intimate. The very idea embarrassed me. And yet some devilish part of me was enjoying having my secret with Louisa, even if she wouldn't acknowledge it. At that moment, I hated the whole evening.

Harry poured himself more than half a tumblerful of straight Scotch, and poured almost as much for me, before I stopped him. He took very little Perrier. I took more. I never was able to drink and keep up with Harry drink-for-drink, though I'm a serious drinker. The studio kitchen had its own refrigerator and ice, and Harry knocked some loose. Then when he sat back down in the big black leather chair and put his feet back up on the desk corner, I realized he wasn't finished.

I was pretty well worn-out emotionally, and I didn't want to hear any more. The thing I was most terrified of hearing—his revelations about his sexual life with Louisa—had come and gone rather placidly, without causing any earthquakes or seismographic oscillations, and I thought that was enough. Of course, he had not been very graphic. But I still thought it was enough. But I apparently did not have any way of communicating this to Harry; or if I did, it was not getting through to him. For whatever reasons of his own, Harry had gone beyond receiving any signals from me.

I'm convinced that the emotional tensions of the evening with the two producers were the initial cause of it. Add to that all the brandy and then all that Scotch, and those ungodly strong cigars. Top it off with the morbid speculations about having to go to Madrid for a long period without Louisa which the conversation had called forth, and you had a Harry Gallagher in a nervous fit of irresponsible soul-searching, with me as the captive audience.

Other people's intimate sexual disclosures have always made me nervous. Several times in my life I have been trapped and made the victim for such soul-searching declarations by men I knew, and every time it has resulted in the loss of a friendship. The next time they see you the eyebrows go up and the eyes get flat and funny, and an impenetrable wall of plastic descends. Harry remains the sole exception to this rule, but I didn't know that then. And I was made more unhappy by having been forced to be dishonest with him.

"Of course, there's more to the whole story than that, naturally," was the way he began. O, foreboding sentence of a miserable night in store! How many times have I heard you? And how many times have you portended spiritual bad digestion to come?

He always was a very highly sexed individual, Harry proceeded to tell me. Even back in his earliest young youth, and as far back as he could remember. He didn't know why exactly. It was just there. He had an abiding love for the female body, both in toto and altogether in its form (he said) and in all its details, down to its tiniest parts. And it didn't matter much who inhabited it. He liked female bodies. He liked to look at them and touch them and smell them, and study them inside and out, in the same way that other people like to find out what is between the covers of a book. He collected women—in the same way other people collect books. And he had to admit to me he saw absolutely nothing wrong with this in any way. That was why he honestly, truly could not see what had upset Louisa so.

Of course, now he understood that it was some tremendous, baby-girllike insecurity of her own (she had, incidentally, always been a great adorer of her father: for example) . And, of course, now all that was over for him now.

But it was a phenomenon he had noted (over the years; talking) in a great many American men. They were all of them—or a great, great many; a very high percentage—absolutely cunt-struck. They were almost all, like himself, completely cunt-oriented.

I sat nursing my drink and nodding, without looking up too often, and watched the level of my glass descend too fast, despite the Perrier I kept adding to it. I was sure that my ears were burning fiery red.

Harry was always quite a swearer, using all the four-letter words with great freedom, even in mixed company, and right now he was not worrying about niceties. And, I was well aware that in the past few years it had become chic to use them liberally in conversation, particularly in front of women. I was publishing them in great quantities in my Review. But my primitive upbringing never allowed me to feel comfortable around them, even when females were not present. I never used them myself. I was aware this was a fault, but there was nothing I could do about it. Besides, there was no more point in interrupting Harry than there would have been in trying to interrupt that bursting dam in Fréjus several years ago.

I have always been a low-keyed man sexually; female bodies interest me less than female minds, so to speak. Sex, while undeniably pleasant, and not something to be avoided, always seemed to me something that the pursuit of cost one a great deal more energy than the final results achieved were worth. So I don't think I ever did really understand that part of Harry well. It was almost as if there were some actual basic biologic difference between us.

Cunt-struck, Harry was continuing, incognizant of my red ears, cunt-oriented: those were the key words to remember. When the true history of his generation came to be written, it might well go down to posterity as the Cunt-struck Generation. By extension they could then be called Cuntniks, as Kerouac, Ginsberg and company, a few years younger, were Beatniks. Harry laughed suddenly, ha-ha-ha, in a kind of crazy way. But the very first memory of his life was of sex. It was of lying in bed on a sunny summer morning jacking off. He couldn't have been more than five: too young even to know what coming was, in any normal way; but lying there jacking his cock just the same. And what was in his mind? What were his thoughts, his fantasy, at the time? Cunt! The little girl next door! The little girl next door, when he was too young even to know what a cunt was, or looked like.

He had been a dedicated pussy-eater since the very first time he had indulged the pastime. Had been one before, even; since first learning such a technique existed via the pornography shown him by older boys. His own young porno collection had swung more and more toward pictures, stories, drawings, any material having to do with cunt-lapping. But the girls of his generation, at least while young, were backward in this respect. His first real opportunity did not come till he

was 17, when he took out in his father's big Studebaker a younger girl
noted for going out with all the boys, and had gone down on her
before he fucked her. She had not been at all surprised. All the boys
liked to eat her pussy that way she said, and she herself loved it. She
was his first blow job, and his first real fuck. He would never forget
her. Wherever she was, he wished her well. But she was quite a contrast to the rest of them, who all seemed to feel that licking their cunts
was dirty and immoral, a perversion; which of course only excited him
all the more. Perhaps it frightened them because its intensity was so
great, and made them find they were sexual creatures after all. Whatever, it gave him some anxious moments about his "perversion". And
as it was with sucking, so it was with fucking. *There are other things
in life besides sex, Harry,* spoken in a high, protesting highschool—or
college—soprano, was a sentence that would remain in his head the rest
of his life. Later, of course, as he moved on from Boston to New York,
and then to Hollywood, and then into the Service, and back to Hollywood, he realized that what he had found and taken unto himself;
what he could, indeed, almost be said to have totally and alone
created for himself, i.e., this preoccupation with and adoration of
female cunt—was after all not really all that much of a singular experience at all.

His entire generation, or at least (here he nodded at me, allowing
me existence, too, alongside himself), at least one element of his
generation, had it, and suffered from it and enjoyed it.

He had analyzed it and analyzed it and, if you took away all the
commercialization of it (cunt; and the adoration of cunt) in the
advertising world; all the promulgation of it in films and magazines
and radio and TV; if you took all that away—*it* was still there; still
there, and existing in and of itself, by itself, antedating all the rest of
it, all the media saturation. He thought maybe it had to do with some
brand-new element of male masochism, introduced by whatever matri-
archal environmental factor he had never been able to isolate. Masochism in the distorted male pleasure principle: the pleasure of giving
pleasure to the woman. That, of course, was unnatural. Imagine a
male dog or cat or lion concerning himself with giving pleasure to the
female! Ridiculous! But men did it. And it had to be masochistic.
There was something perversely pleasurable in *making* a woman enjoy

sex. For example: You take a woman and, by whatever means, bring her on toward coming—toward her orgasm—and before long, you reached a point where you ceased to exist as you for her. You ceased to be Harry Gallagher for her and became just a man, any man, who is giving her excitation and stimulation. Carry it a while further and you ceased to be even a man, and became just some object, some thing which is causing her to have pleasure. Carry it on all the way to where she comes and you ceased even to be an object. Because in the midst of her come nothing exists except herself and what she's feeling. So that, through her, what you've done is "stimulate" yourself right out of existence. What you've really been doing is to be present at and assist in your own cuckolding. In reality— . . . you have been cuckolding yourself! . . . Man, we're masochists, man! he cried at me, his eyes jewelly in the light. All us cunt-lovers!

I think he was a little drunk by then. Anyway, it was certainly a new idea to me, and the logic seemed impeccable. I mainly kept my eyes down and nodded, pretending to peer reflectively into my by-now empty glass, in order to avoid being further embarrassed by exposing the embarrassment I already felt. At one point once, I thought fleetingly of asking to have my glass refilled. But before I could even do it, Harry had leaned forward with the bottle in his hand and poured whisky in the glass, his jaw continuing to wag and rotate at me, without even slowing.

I got very drunk. Things began to come and go in what film people call fast dissolves, and then would suddenly arrest themselves in those sudden stop-shots in which everything freezes and the man with the pointing finger remains fixed, frozen, in front of you for what seems an inordinate length of time. I began to see things in splintered images as if the mirror glass had broken; and I would find myself present at the beginning of something only to disappear and find myself, next, far into the middle part of something else without having been present at the ending of the first or the beginning of the second. So I am somewhat vague about the rest of what transpired.

I remember Harry talking about his pornography collection, which is famous in the American colony in Paris, and saying he would get some of it out to prove some point. Next I was sitting forward in my chair with my knees together, poring through a whole flock of precisely focused, glossy finish photographs in series of fives in my lap, all of which Harry apparently had said he'd bought in London, I remembered vaguely. Beside me on the low Louis Treize table was an even greater flock of them which I apparently had already been through; and beside these was a stack of Olympia Press and Ophelia Press books I must have looked at too. All of this is crystal clear. The photos were of varied subjects, but most of them were of two women making love in various ways. Some of them were of white girls committing fellatio upon young Negro males. The girls changed from series to series.

"That's the trend it's taking," Harry was saying beside me from over my shoulder. "More and more. Lesbianism. Or not even true lesbianism. Just two women, two normal women, making love together. I don't know why it turns me on so, but it does."

Then I disappeared again. When I returned, Harry was locking up the pornography collection in its glass-doored shelves. I was aware dimly that he had been talking about "his Fantasy". He himself had capitalized the word with his voice, and it had something to do with making love with two women at the same time, instead of the normal, usual one.

"You wouldn't believe it," he growled over his shoulder, as he turned the key on the last great batch of the pornography. "But it's the God's truth." Apparently he had just been talking about something else, too. "If I didn't lock them up, they'd disappear in a minute. That's why I had the doors put on. Why, I've had producers and directors staying up here working on a script with me, big important men I mean, and making plenty of their own money. Well, by God, after they'd leave, I'd find one or two of my choicest items missing. Stolen." He put the keys in his jacket pocket protectively. They were on a different ring from his other keys. All of this was crystal clear, too. "I don't know why it is. But pornography just is considered fair game. By everybody. An honest man that you could leave all sorts of money lying around in front of, and just let him loose around your pornography!" Harry said.

Then he was suddenly sitting in the black chair talking again, without having walked there or sat down in it—just as if some film cutter in a studio working in front of a Moviola had expertly clipped that unnecessary footage out of the scene. Harry was talking about his Fantasy again.

"And that's it. That's what it is: Me and two women in the same bed together, as you may have surmised by now."

Surmised? I peered at him owlishly. I was incapable of surmising anything. Harry was leaning forward pouring again, first his glass, then mine. This was clearly not the same bottle. Feebly I tried to stop him at my glass, and failed.

"Me and two women, doing everything to each other, to the other two, and all of us watching it all with great relish and the greatest of pleasure.

"Are you listening to me?

"I remember the first time—First?—the *only* time I ever had it. One spring day I drove through the pass and over into the Burbank area. It was flat, for miles before you got to the actual city. There used to be lots of massage parlors over there, back then, where you could get laid for anything from ten dollars up to fifty dollars, depending upon what exactly you wanted. I was a pretty big shot then, and not married. I picked out this slender young girl with nice boobs, one of the three who worked there. Slim young thing. She had sneaky eyes and she looked me over closely, a real scrutiny, and then asked me privately if I'd like for her to bring her friend with us too. I was hot instantaneously. Well, we did just about everything three people can do together, I guess. I've never had another scene like it.

"I went back there later, and saw my girl again, but her friend had left. I asked her about our scene, and she said sure, and she got another girl. But it wasn't the same. The two of them were just putting on an act for me, the second time. I suppose my girl didn't want this other strange girl to find out she really liked it. I learned one thing. The women have to like it, or it's no good.

"I've known women since then that I thought might like that kind of action. Some of them, when I was making it with them, I was sure had been making it with other girls. But I could never quite get my nerve up enough to ask them. And none of them ever asked me.

"So that's the one time I ever really had it. Maybe that's why it haunts me.

"I tell you, Jack, there's nothing like lying there watching two women go down on each other while one of them is gently jacking your cock. Or one of them sucking the other, while you're fucking the one.

"But I think it takes a special kind of woman. She has to like men too.

"Oh, I know it's just a fantasy. For a man in my position now, married, and with a wife and all, and a family. It's like one of those fantasies you have about taking your wife to one of those undressing orgy places, like Olga's, where you take off all your clothes before you even go into the bar. You imagine it, but you would never do it. It would hurt too much. If it was your wife. You can't do those things with a woman you really love.

"Oh, I know all about fantasy. Enough to know that when you try to put them into reality, you're liable to cause mayhem. Or murder . . . —or else they'll just be ridiculous."

He moved then, and stretched his muscles stiffened by sitting immobile too tensely too long, and I realized in my befogged, dimly apprehending way, suddenly, that he had not moved at all in a long time.

"I don't know what got me onto all of this. —? Oh, yes. See, I know it's only a Fantasy. But it haunts me. Haunts me like some haunting melody. Maybe because I only had it that one time. But why should it affect me so? Well, see, I think it has something to do with that male masochism I was talking about earlier when we—."

. . . It was exactly as if a black curtain had descended between us, cutting off the play in the middle of the second scene of the third act. I had departed again. Later I found myself out in the street, weaving along trying to find my way home.

I tried to stand up erect and straight, in case any police or youthful muggers after my gold wristwatch passed by. But when I stood straight, I found I had a tendency to lean too far over backwards. When I corrected for this and leaned forward again, I would almost fall on my face. The chill A.M. air tasted good, but did not aid me. I had only to make it from the end of the Island up past the darkened deserted Brasserie and the rue Jean-du-Bellay, past the rue Boutarel to the rue le Regrattier. That wasn't far. I could remember dimly something about Harry offering me the big couch in his living room, but I had refused. I did not want McKenna, or even Hill, to see me there in the morning, when they got up to go to school. I kept one hand pressed firmly to the top of the stone parapet that lined the quai's sidewalk to keep people like myself from falling to the lower level and cracking their skulls. I had my umbrella in my left hand and my winter overcoat, I'm sure, hunched up messily across the back of my neck. In the morning I found I had pressed the parapet so firmly that the skin of the fingertips of my one hand looked successfully sand-papered.

But mainly I was worried about Harry. I was terribly afraid he would never want to see me again, after all he'd said. I knew I wouldn't, were I he. And after all, I *was* McKenna's Godfather.

But I needn't have steamed up. Not with Harry. Not only did he call me at one the next afternoon, but he invited me to a late lunch at Lipp's that same day. There we ran into both Mary McCarthy and Romain Gary, both looking too terribly bright and chipper, though at separate tables, of course. Harry said hello to them both.

4

I AM CONVINCED THAT had the weather not held good through most of May, there would have been no Revolution. There might have been a few flurries. But rain and cold cool the hot philosophy of the demonstrating Revolutionary more than just about any other thing. I know that sounds cynical. But I believe it's true, and so did the Paris police believe it. I understand the officials at the Préfecture gathered every day at noon to study the daily weather projections.

But the weather did hold. Day after day the sweeter, less violent European sun rose to a nearly cloudless sky, pouring its unexpected bonus of warmth down upon cobblestone and leafing tree, demonstrator and cop alike, calling us all to come outdoors: warming even the gray Paris stone, which even in 1968 was still permeated with medieval damp and chill. Such weather was an almost phenomenal thing in Paris in May. And day after day officials scanned the reports, and the sky itself, for the rainclouds that ought to be coming along, but didn't.

Hill Gallagher came by to see me on the Saturday of May 4th, the day after the closing of the Sorbonne by the Rector, one M. Roche. Beams of sun were streaming in my opened windows, and people strolling along the quai sent up a constant murmur of pleased voices. Hill had four of his student friends with him: three boys, and one girl.

The first thing I noticed about Hill was that he had a beauty of a black eye. The second thing I noticed was that he was—they all were—dressed in what was soon to become the uniform of the Revolution: blue jeans, flannel shirt, running shoes (i.e., tennis shoes), and a large bandanna knotted loosely around the throat.

There had been rioting into the night by the students the night before. And I had sat at my desk pretending to work, and watched the clouds of gas and smoke rising in the glare of light from the Latin Quarter across the river, and had listened to the two-toned French sirens hooting across the night: and the dim shouts and chants of the students and the soft plops of the tear-gas grenades exploding. The morning papers had stated that 496 arrests had been made by the police, most of them students.

And now here they were, five of them, in my living room—one of them a girl. And I soon learned that that girl was not to be discounted. She would have made a saint angry.

Hill had come up first alone. In all my dealings with the students and their Revolution I have never known one of them not to be absolutely polite, thoughtful and respectful to me when I was with him. "Listen, I've got a couple of buddies with me," he said when we had said hello and I had commented on his eye. "They're waiting downstairs. Would you mind if I invited them up? And offered them a drink?"

"Absolutely not," I said. "I'd like to meet them."

"It's perfectly all right if you do mind," he smiled.

"No, no! Ask them up."

We walked to a window and he leaned out and whistled down to what appeared to be four long-haired boys, dressed substantially like himself, lounging against the white stone of the quai above the river. He waved down to them on the crowded sidewalk and motioned them up. It was not until they were inside my living room that I realized one was a girl. It was hard to tell at a distance, with them all dressed alike, because of the long hair. And she had almost no boobs at all. What little she had, along with the not-negligible swell of female hip in the tight jeans, was hidden by an imitation American Indian's buckskin jacket complete with fringe, but made of suede.

They were absolutely handsome kids. Anyone should have been proud to be their parents. Since they were all French and had little

English, we spoke mostly in French. Hill had let his own sideburns and hair grow out some, although he hadn't grown a beard. But these boys' hair hung literally to their shoulders. One of them was bearded. If anything, the girl's bobbed hair was a little shorter than theirs. And one of the unbearded ones, the taller one, had the most beautiful head of hair I've ever seen on anyone. Any woman would have given her eyeteeth to have his hair. Parted in the center, it fell in tight natural waves all the way to his shirt shoulders. And below it was the most innocent, sweet, open, trusting face imaginable. I gathered his name was Terri. The bearded one, though perhaps less striking, was no less handsome: with his full, pointed black beard and the intelligent, sensitive eyes peering out at you from above it.

What the hell? I found myself wondering to myself. What was so unmanly about long hair? Hell, in the eighteenth century you would have called a dandy's long hair unmanly at your direst peril.

I hustled around to make them drinks, trying to show them my feeling for Hill included them. It was easy to see that a Scotch *"un ze rucks"*, which was what they all asked for, was quite a treat for them at this stage of the game.

It is hard to explain how much and why the Sorbonne means what it does to the students of France. It is only one of five autonomous colleges of the University of Paris. Yet it is the spiritual and symbolic head of all the universities of France. Probably just its history alone accounts for a lot of this. It was founded in the thirteenth century, and dedicated to those elite problems of the age: religion and politics. Throughout the Middle Ages it attracted the greatest scholars of Europe. St. Thomas Aquinas was one of its great masters. Latin was its language then, and its men played very important roles in nearly every big intellectual question of the age—such as how many angels can stand on the head of a pin. As the big religious problems of that period faded under the pressures of time and living, philosophy naturally moved in to replace these and became the Sorbonne's almost exclusive province. Always its students, and usually its teachers, stood for freedom of expression, freedom of the right to think new ideas and say them. Closed down during the worst part of the French Revolution, it had been re-opened by Napoleon in 1808 with a series of sweeping educational reforms—and it had changed almost not at all since then. But to French students it remained the holy of holies of the true French education, and in all that time it had remained the students' private preserve and sanctuary against their hereditary enemies of the status quo: the police. An old law dating almost from the school's inception 700 years before stated expressly that on-duty policemen could not enter the students' revered Sorbonne without the particular invitation of the Rector.

However antiquated and quaintly medieval all this might sound to an American system in the first miseries of a World Technological Revolution, it meant a lot to the French kids. And that M. Roche their Rector could utilize this old rule as a Government ploy to call in the cops—and without even letting them know he had done so—that was the greatest betrayal and insult he could have handed his Sorbonne students. They knew where he stood, now.

The morning papers had presented a somewhat garbled, Government-censored communiqué stating there had been a fight, or near-fight, in the building's courtyard: between the Leftist students holding a meeting and a Rightist student group calling itself the *Occident*. This fight, the Government said, had forced the Rector to ask the police to intervene. But young Hill with his bruised face told me quite a different story.

Hill's ran this way: Young Dany Cohn-Bendit (There was that kid again.) had been making his first speech at the Sorbonne, hoping to get converts for his 22nd of March Movement. His Nanterre group wanted to boycott year's-end exams until the Government agreed to their proposed reforms. Rumors that could never be traced ran around the meeting saying the *Occident* boys planned to attack the courtyard and break up the meeting. So a student group posted itself at the entrances to the yard armed with sticks and old table legs. What appeared however was not the *Occident* but a line of police who filed in and lined up along the four walls of the court wearing helmets, gas goggles, their heavy protective fighting raincoats and carrying the long light hardwood riot sticks. Then, and only then, the students were informed the Rector had called for the police. They were ordered to leave quietly. The implication was that if they did, they would not be bothered. So their leaders urged them to go peacefully. But when they did, they found all the entrances to the Sorbonne tightly cordoned off by riot police out in the street, backed up by their "Black Marias". The students had walked out into a trap where they could be arrested singly or in twos and threes.

This was the first establishment of a pattern which the police, and the Government itself, would use on the students during the rest of the troubles:—a pattern of dissimulation, false promises, and down-right lies to gain their ends. In this case the end was the arrest of the Leftist students. The riot police began carting them off by the van-loads.

"And that was when the fun started," Hill said cheerfully with a big grin. "There were plenty of us in the area still, and we began to drift back and jeer the police, when we found out what was really happening. They charged us and started throwing their gas grenades. We retreated to the Boul' Mich' and started throwing up barricades. But they had every side street occupied in advance, and closed in from all sides. That's how they caught so many of us. We'll know better next time. We'll have our lines of withdrawal planned. That was our baptism of fire."

I couldn't help noticing the military usage. I sympathized with their anger at the dishonesty of the Government and its police. But the military usages irritated me. I was an old soldier myself, though maybe not on Harry's level. I didn't like military usages.

Hill had been at the meeting, it turned out as he went on, but had left early because Red-Headed Dany had reached that part of his speech where he began to use rhetoric and oratory and was essentially repeating himself. So had some of the others in the know, and that was why they had not been caught in the first net.

That comment irritated me further. I had heard too many ambi-tious politicians talk about the values of oratory on the ignorant populace. But I didn't want to make an argument with Hill. I seized on Red Dany. Did Hill know *Dany le Rouge?* No, he didn't really know him, he had only met him a few times briefly, and had talked to him: and he agreed with everything he stood for and believed. Well, how come he had left, then, during his speech?

Well, you had to understand, he explained, that not all students, just because they were students, were equally smart, or sensitive. Percentage-wise, statistically, intelligent students (on their somewhat higher levels) were just as rare, just as small in number as intelligent workers or intelligent bourgeois were on theirs. And the latter part of Dany's speech was planned to appeal to that greater mass of the less-aware students, which was where the needed power lay. So there was no reason for the ones in the know to hang around. Dany and his boys all understood that.

I found it hard to believe he was telling me this in all innocence, as it appeared. But wasn't that sort of—cynical? I asked.

But yes! he said in French; certainly yes. Shit, yes! How would you think that my General makes it so well?

Okay, I thought: I stopped right there. But Hill must have caught some look he didn't like that flashed across my face, because he looked disturbed and went back to it: on the other hand it was not cynical at all because they were only saying what they truly believed, and what the other students when they understood it and felt it, would also realize was the truth.

I did not pursue this sophism. I easily could have, but I didn't want to or feel like it. I wanted to be with them. But as a matter of fact I would not have been allowed to pursue it, anyway. Because this was where the little girl Hill had brought stepped in.

"Would you not, then, allow us the same rights to orate, to rhetoricize, to propagandate the populace that you allow of the Government?" she demanded in a cold voice. "Is that of fairness to you?"

"I would allow you anything," I said, and made her a little bow. Something about her way of speech forced me to. That girl instantly inflamed me. "Or rather, anything you can TAKE and KEEP. But that has nothing to do with moral right. Dialectically, you have no moral right at all. So I find it droll that you resort to the same bad methods which you hate and attack the Government for using."

"Because to us they do not permit some choice!" she said flatly. "They make us to make it!"

"You would make war to stop war," I smiled. That was one of their big bitches, already. "Will you not become as rotten as they, then, in the end? If you use their methods?"

"Not we!" the little girl declared with a cold contempt. "Because we are *right!* And *you* know it! We love. And we have only the good in our heart."

She infuriated me. "You say so. It has not been proved to me," I smiled. "And if it were proved for this week and this group, it would not be proved for next week and some other group."

"But that is sophistry. Is it not bad that—" she began. Then she stopped. It was as if some invisible signal had gone round the room: I was one of *them:* one of the old ones: I would never understand. None of the old ones would. Why bother? In the new silence not one of the five, including Hill, offered to fill the gap or say something; and they all five simply stood, smiling pleasantly at me.

"Excuse me," I said. "I'm sorry." And I guess I was. But that little girl just automatically ignited me. It had nothing to do with being an old one. It had to do with her absolute righteousness. She had a built-in inability, that girl, even to conceive—let alone admit—that she might ever, once, one time, be even four per cent wrong. She looked at me the way some Communists did. She was the teacher and I was the pupil. She had awarded herself total moral superiority. Not only must I come to class, but I must learn my lesson, or she would smack my hands with her ruler.

Physically, she was a tiny little thing really. A blonde French, with arms like sticks, and nearly stick-like legs, a neck I could put one hand around almost; and out of that pale, ivory complexion beneath the bobbed pale-yellow hair, a pair of pale-blue eyes peered at me with a total, contemptuous, fierce belief.

I wasn't being political. I had seen Americans look at me that same way: some Liberals, some redneck reactionaries. In fact, I had seen her type often. She was one of those who even if they made a public declaration that they were three-and-three-quarters per cent wrong about some thing, it would only be to prove to themselves and to the world how absolutely good and right they 100 per cent were.

"Let me get all of you another drink," I smiled at her—though it hurt my face. "The same? Scotch on the rocks?"

"With intense pleasure," she smiled back. The others, the boys, all nodded, still smiling, that they would like the same again.

It was a thing, an attitude, I would come up against again amongst the students, all during the rest of the Revolution. But I didn't know that then. They *had* to be morally right. I was willing to admit they *might* be right; but that was not enough.

In any case Hill had been sitting in one of those student-haunt cafés on the Place Sorbonne when the arrests began, he went on, and had helped lead in the jeering, and in the retreat to the Boulevard St.-Michel. He laughed happily, suddenly. "I got hit later on in the evening, with one of those long hardwood clubs. But I managed to get away. A lot of us did. But I know by God we dented a few of their damned heads."

My thing with the girl appeared completely forgotten. For our own reasons, we all saw fit to drop it completely. I went around with the ice and the bottle. Hill went on with his story of the night.

"Excuse us, please. We have a thing to talk," Hill said in French after they all had their second drink, and motioned to me toward the kitchen. From their faces as I followed him I could tell they all knew at least something about why he was there: none was surprised.

Out there, I looked again at the ugly mark on his face. Seen more closely, it was not a black eye at all. He had taken a horizontal smash along the ridge of the cheekbone. A blue and yellow tear-shaped splotch tailed back toward his ear, and dark venous blood from it had seeped over into the hollow under the eye.

"I've got a nice big chunk of beefsteak you can put on that if you want," I said. "They say that helps." I tried a joke. "I can always cook it later just the same anyway."

Hill brushed all this aside. "No, no. That's not important. I'll get worse than that before I'm through with this. That's not what I came for."

It turned out none of the previous discussion was what he had come for. He had come to speak to me about his father.

"What about your father?"

"Well, you see, this thing's a long way from over. We're just not going to let it drop. A lot depends on what the judges do with our innocent comrades that've been arrested. We're almost certain they won't release all of them. But even if they do, we're not letting it drop. We're calling a big protest demonstration for Monday the 6th. They've made a terrible tactical blunder. They've called police into the Sorbonne; M. Roche has closed the entire college until further notice; they've beaten up and arrested hundreds of innocent students.

They've made an awful blunder, and we are going to exploit it. We'll have every damned student all over France out in the streets on strike!" He was very excited, and his eyes were snapping above his happy grin. I on the other hand could not help but remark his blatantly propaganda usage of the word "innocent". He went on. "There'll almost certainly be a lot more fighting in the streets after Monday and the big demonstration." He actually said "Manif", instead of "Demonstration", which is the argot short form for the proper French word *"Manifestation"*. In France, in order to have a public *Manifestation,* any group must first ask for and get express permission from the police. Hill was sure this permission would be refused. "Which will only make it that much better. Because we'll have so many people out there they won't be able to stop us."

"But what has your father got to do with all of this?" I asked.

"Oh. Well.

"Well, I didn't get home last night. What with all the meetings and all. And I don't expect to get home tonight, either. In fact, I don't really anticipate getting home again for quite some time, now that this has happened." He looked at me anxiously.

"Yes?" I said. I realized, quite suddenly, that Hill had gotten at least as tall physically as his father was. He seemed to be leaning down over me.

"I want you to tell dad that for me," he said. "So he won't worry. Just go and see him and tell him you saw me, that I'm okay, but that I'll not be coming home for a while. So he shouldn't expect me. Don't tell him about the eye."

I nodded. But I felt I ought to say something. "Well, where will you be staying, Hill?"

"Oh, we've got access to a couple of lofts where we're holding our meetings, and sleeping, when we have to sleep."

"What about your clothes? And all that."

"We'll wash them. None of that matters. I'll tell you a little secret. We expect to be holding our meetings and doing our washing in the Sorbonne itself. Before very long.—

"And we'll throw it open to the whole world! Students, teachers, workers, Government officials, everybody. Everybody will be welcome!" He coughed, to contain—and to hide—his emotion. "But don't tell my dad that. Just tell him what I told you to tell him."

"But I think you should go and tell him all this yourself," I said.

Suddenly his shoulders came up towards his ears, and he looked at the floor. It was not so much a shrug, as it was that same look of dejection I had seen on him that night at their house: head down, shoulders up, his over-big, pup-like paws dangling at the ends of his long arms. "Aw, you know I can't talk to him. He won't listen to me. I could talk till I'm blue. He filters everything through those hypocritical self-indulgent ideas of his; and comes out believing exactly what he wanted to believe anyway. If I go try to talk to him, it will only end up in a fight. And then he'll pull rank, and *forbid* me to go out with the comrades. And then I'll have to tell him to go screw, and go anyway. He doesn't know I'm grown up enough to decide—and have been for quite some time now. He won't admit it." He looked up at me then. "I don't want to see him." It had a stubborn, unmovable finality.

"What's your mother going to feel about all this?" I said as gently as I could. I was beginning to get irritated again.

Hill swung his gaze back onto me, and his eyes flashed dangerously. "What do I care what *she* thinks! *Or* feels! Es*pe*cially her! *Both* of them! With their phony parenthood, and all that family Togetherness crap they try to sell so hard but don't live up to!"

"All right, all right," I said soothingly. I could see I wasn't going to change his mind. "I'll talk to him. And I'll tell him exactly what you want me to. But I want you to know that *I* think you're absolutely wrong about your father. *And* about your mother."

"Okay okay okay," he said. "I know you love them. And I love them too. That doesn't mean I should forgive them for what their hypocrisy and all the others like them have done to the world. The world doesn't have to be like this. Like it is. We all know that, Jack.

"Besides, you don't know everything that goes on all the time everywhere," he added with a dark look. "You're pretty innocent, at least about your friends."

I did not know what he meant by this last. Also, it was the first time he had ever called me "Jack"—at least it was the first time that I could remember—instead of "Uncle Jack", or "Mr. Hartley". I had sense enough to know it was a sort of trial balloon. I slapped him on the back.

"All right, I'll talk to him," I said. "I'll go down there this evening. And I'll lay your case out to him exactly as you've told it to me. Whether you believe it or not, *I'm* sure he'll understand."

Hill grinned at me. "Thanks."

"Now you tell me something," I said. "Tell me, is that little girl?— What's her name?"

"Anne-Marie?"

"Anne-Marie. Is she your girlfriend?"

Whether it was my accepting him on a first-name basis, or simply what I said about talking to his father, he had changed suddenly from the unhappy, misunderstood son back into the excited grinning student Revolutionary. And now he changed again, just as suddenly. His eyes got funny, and faraway-looking. "Girlfriend?" he said. "You mean *lover*."

"Well," I said. "Yes, I guess."

Hill's shoulders came up to his ears again, and he sort of spread his hands. "Well, she's . . . she . . ." Abruptly, for all the world like some adult switching to protect the supposed innocence of some child, he switched to French. *"Elle nous fait des pipes à tous les quatre. Elle nous fait des pompiers."*

I almost shouted. "What!" I was half badly shocked, and half laughing.

"She goes down on the four of us. She blows us all," Hill said in English.

"You mean she . . ." I began. "All at the same . . . I mean, all in the same . . ."

Hill's brows came together in a mildly irritated frown. "No, no. No, no. We're not orgiasts. I mean, we have some orgiasts. Quite a lot. But we five just don't happen to . . ."

"I was *afraid* you wouldn't under—" he started. "Look. We're all on the same Committee: see? We're all Cinema students, and we're all on the Cinema Committee. We all happen to be Sociology students, too. But that's just an accident."

I was nearly openly laughing, now. "And are there other girls on your Committee?"

His brows knit further. "Oh, sure."

"But you don't, uh . . ."

"Fuck them? I mean, have sex with them? Oh, sure. Every once in a while. I mean, sometimes. Maybe. But . . . look: see: We're all sort of a *sub*-committee, us five, with*in* the Cinema Committee. We have been assigned a—a certain area of exploration, shall we say."

"And she, Anne-Marie, is a member of the . . ." I said. "But she doesn't like to . . ."

"She prefers it the way I told you," Hill said, frowning.

"She knows about the pill?"

"Oh, sure: she knows about the pill. Look. See, she doesn't *have* to do anything at all. Anywhere. I mean, she's not required to . . . I don't think you understand."

"Oh, I understand," I said. "Of course, I understand, that." I tried to smother my silly grin. "But, did you really feel you had to go into French to tell me that?"

"Well. I don't think you really understand how things are with us: our generation," Hill said. He grinned a little bit himself, now. "I mean . . ."

"Of course," I said. "And perhaps not. I am older. But, my God, Hill, I'm not that much older! To lapse into French with me, as if you were speaking in front of McKenna!"

"I think it's a pretty phrase in French," he said, defensively. "It's a cute phrase."

"Descriptive," I nodded. "It is pretty. It's a pretty, and descriptive, phrase in English, too." I was suddenly reminded of the current American-English joke about the young man explaining to his fiancée that "blow" was just a figure of speech, and almost collapsed. I wanted to let out a roar and laugh out loud, but restrained myself.

"I don't *really* think you really understand how it is with us, Uncle Jack," Hill said, peering at me with a frown again. "We're a sort of a— of a family, really.

"I don't think you understand."

I caught that return to *Uncle Jack.* "Sure I do," I said. "Of course I do. You're all on the same committee—*sub*-committee. And Anne-Marie is the only girl on the *sub*-committee. And she feels . . . She wants to . . ."

"No, no!" Hill said. "She *likes* us all. It just *happens* that we're all on the same *sub*-committee."

"Of course," I said. "I understand that. I'm really not as old as you think, Hill. I mean, it's not like as if I were your grandfather. I think we ought to get back out to your guests, in any case."

"—" Hill reacted, but didn't answer.

"My God, didn't you ever read a copy of my Review!" I couldn't resist crying.

"Yeah; it's pretty hip," he said from the door.

They were all still standing, or sitting, just exactly as we had left them, in exactly the same positions exactly, as if, when I disappeared from view, they had immediately and at once frozen themselves in the postures they had had, so that, when I eventually and inevitably returned, I would be able to see at a glance that they had not been nosing around or poking into any of my things, or peering at anything. I could not help thinking that, even for French politeness—and the French set a great store by politeness, more than Americans do—this was going a bit too far.

"Well, kids," I said, "what about one more drink!"

I went around with the bottle. I could not get rid, whenever I glanced at her, of a sort of imaginative picture like a film clip double-image of Anne-Marie standing like a sergeant before her four ranked boys, all standing at attention with large erections projecting from their Revolutionary uniforms, and her going down the line like a good Commissar, or dutiful Den Mother, doing each in turn so that he could keep his mind where it ought to be on the Revolutionary business at hand and stop thinking about his crotch. Therapeutic service. I kept having to blink. And around me, they all sat and talked together easily, about the Revolution. Everybody had accepted the drink, after a confirmatory glance at Hill.

They were clearly all working together, it came out as they all talked, on the formation of this Committee having something or other to do with Cinema. But mostly they talked about what would be the fate of their comrades who had been arrested the day before. No word had been heard about them yet, and they were still locked up. The big question of the moment was whether they would all be freed or not. None of Hill's gang thought that they would *all* be freed; and *all* was what the students were demanding.

As they left, Hill said to me in English in a low voice, "Don't forget what we talked about, about home?"

I nodded and winked and, after they had gone, went to the window to watch them walking together arm in arm, two in front and three behind, down the quai toward the old Bailey bridge footbridge that crosses over to the rear of Notre-Dame. I watched them swing along through the crowd, and discovered I had a definite lump in my throat. In spite of Anne-Marie. As they passed from sight around an angle of the quai, I found myself thinking that nothing could ever really hurt them. Not, at least, the them of this moment, now. That particular them was eternal.

Then I got ready to go down and see Harry at his apartment. I called him first.

Hill came by again the next evening, Sunday the 5th, just at dusk. This time he came alone, all by himself.

There had been very little happening, as far as I could tell, during the day. The French, even young French Revolutionaries, take their Sundays pretty seriously. M. Alain Peyrefitte, the young Minister of Education, had put out some rather threatening communiqués saying substantially that the small groups of dissidents causing the trouble would be dealt with summarily by the college authorities if they did not desist. But if these were meant to quell the student troubles, they were apparently having just the opposite effect.

But Hill, and his friends too he said, were more concerned with what had happened Saturday night and Sunday morning at the Palais de Justice, that huge and frightening grinding mill of bureaucracy situated like some great pile at the other end of the Île de la Cité. The judge on duty for the weekend, one M. Isambert, had been lenient on Saturday. In the end only a few, six to be exact, of those arrested actually came before the judge, and he let them all off with small suspended sentences and light fines. But today on Sunday at eleven A.M., Hill told me, Judge Isambert had sentenced four students to two months in jail. Maybe his breakfast was burned. More likely it was on Government orders. This was going to play a big part in the coming demonstration tomorrow, Hill said. Before anything else, their comrades must be freed.

In spite of my little fight with Anne-Marie, they apparently had taken me in and accepted me as one of them, Hill told me, or at least as one sympathetic to their cause, in front of whom they could talk freely. Of course, Hill had introduced me to them all as an editor of an American review who very likely would write something in my Review to aid their cause.

But all of this was not really why he had come. After he helped himself to a Scotch and soda at my little bar, he brought up Harry. "Did you talk to dad?"

I nodded.

"Well, what happened?"

"Well, as you probably suspected—or at least as I suspected—he was hurt that you didn't come to him."

"Well, what did he *say?*"

"He said in effect that if you should need anything, like money or help or legal help or whatever, all you had to do was let him know or come and ask him for it."

Hill frowned and made an irritable gesture.

I waved him down and continued. "Or that, if you didn't want to do that, you could use me as go-between and convey any messages or requests to him through me. If you didn't feel like coming home and asking him for it yourself."

Hill was suddenly and absolutely outraged. "God damn him! God *damn* him! *Both* of them! Wouldn't you know he'd pull some cheap trick like that? I *knew* he'd pull something like that! Doesn't he know, don't they both know, that I don't *need* anything they've got to give me? Don't *want* anything they've got to give me? They just can't keep from trying to get into the act, can they? Cheap hypocritical liberal bastards!"

I was completely taken off balance. I just gaped at him. I didn't see anything at all wrong with what Harry had said.

And as if aware of me suddenly, Hill got a hold on himself. He drew a deep breath in through his clenched teeth, clenched his fists tightly against his flanks at the ends of his long arms, and shut his eyes. He exhaled through his nose.

At the time I thought it was a bit theatrical, but later I wondered. Because Hill had a hard time reestablishing himself in the high mood he had come in with. He flung himself down, with a gesture curiously like his father, in one of my armchairs; and there he brooded. Talking to him was about as worthwhile as talking to a stone post. When he finally left he was himself again but it seemed to me it had cost him a considerable effort. As he started to get up out of the chair, he looked at my windows and said wistfully, "It sure is nice here!" He turned back to me at the door.

"I'll try and keep you informed of what takes place. But if what I suspect is going to happen happens, after tomorrow, I may not be around to see you for some days. In any case, don't worry about me. I doubt very much if I'll see much more action on the barricades.

"You see, what this group I'm with—the whole group, not just our sub-committee—is trying to do is arrange in some way to have a true film record of what's going to happen between us and the *forces of order.*" He italicized that last phrase, in a deadly way. "We're in the process of forming a Cinema Committee of the May Revolution. All of us are Cinema majors, you see: the future directors, producers, screenwriters of the New France. If it works out, as it appears it will, I'll probably be spending most of my time behind a desk organizing the shooting of what transpires in the next few weeks—so *our* side can present *its* picture to the world, to contrast with the Government's propaganda films. You can tell my father that."

Then he added, "If you want to."

I nodded and we shook hands, hard and tightly: for all the world like two combat men being sent off on different missions from which we didn't really expect to return. It was silly. And yet I couldn't help it.

After he had gone, I went again to my window, and watched him swinging off down the quai toward Cité, in his young Revolutionary's "uniform". It was then I noticed, after leaning out a little and looking up the other way, that for the first time the two dark-blue camions of police had been stationed on the Island side of the Pont de la Tournelle beneath the Tour d'Argent, in position to block off the Quai de Bethune where, as every inhabitant of Paris knew, M. Pompidou the Prime Minister lived.

It was the first time the dark, sinister-looking little vans had appeared there, but they were to become familiar.

5

It was some time during that week of May 6th to May the 12th that some of us Americans established a pattern of meeting at the Gallaghers'.

Every evening around seven, a group of Parisian Americans would congregate at Harry's apartment. It was like a sort of late cocktail hour. We would discuss the day's events, stay to watch the eight o'clock news on TV, drink a good deal, and speculate on what might happen tomorrow. Then we would move on to our dinner dates, or whatever we had lined up for the evening.

As the rioting got worse night after night, the Government-controlled French TV showed less and less about it. Finally it was hardly worth turning the TV on. The Government had decided it was going to play the whole thing down to the French people. Apparently, it hoped the problem would just up and disappear. We got news about the forthcoming Vietnam Peace Talks and Ambassador Harriman, and about how many the Americans were killing out in Vietnam.

Hill Gallagher, of course, had not been seen by any of us since the Sunday night when he had stopped by my place alone.

There were student riots every night now. In the French press they were already calling the students, more or less as a compliment, *les enragés:* the enraged ones. Hill's *manif* (I always thought of it as that, somehow: as if he had personally arranged it all), Hill's *manif* on the May 6th Monday, although not allowed by the police, was a howling success as a call to arms. On the Tuesday of the 7th some 15,000 students paraded all around Paris in a 12-mile march, and the police let them. On the Wednesday the Government offered to reopen the Sorbonne: the students immediately threatened to "occupy" it. So the Sorbonne stayed closed.

Nobody thought that soon France would be literally paralyzed, in the throes of one of its worst social upheavals in this century. Yet somehow our pattern of clustering together established itself anyhow. Everyone was excited and there was a vacation feeling in the air. More than anything, it reminded me of the first weeks of World War II back home. It was almost the same. Everybody knew it was holocaust: that catastrophe, that too much useless killing, was coming. But we enjoyed the beginning anyway: it was a welcome break from the hackwork of daily living and of screwing only your own wife. It was like that in Paris. I know it was during that week I started showing up every night at the Gallaghers'. And it was during the tail-end of that week that Dave Weintraub first brought Samantha-Marie Everton there.

We were a pretty catholic group even for Paris-Americans. And almost all of us had some other reason for needing to be near there. I lived only just down the street, and I had no TV. Then there were two separate painters whom the Gallaghers had been buying, who both had apartments just across the river in the Latin Quarter near the Place Maubert. They were finding it hard to get home at night sometimes, if the students happened to be rioting at Maubert.

Then there was an American TV commentator who was quite a famous face back home and was an old poker buddy of Harry's. He had to be out shooting and commentating the nightly riot every night. So he would stop by for a few drinks and some "Revolution" gossip, before he crossed the bridge and with his press armband on his arm plunged into the tear-gas clouds of the Quarter like Tarzan plunging into the jungle.

There was a very young twenty-two-year-old UPI man who was doing the same thing for UPI, without a cameraman. He was a friend of Harry and Louisa because he wanted to be a screenwriter, and also a novelist, if he had the time.

There was a wealthy, good-looking American businessman who was unmarried and lived on the Island. He would show up with any one of an apparently endless string of lush young—well, "humpers", I believe they are called—that he had access to: humpers, that is, who do it with rich men for kicks and presents, as distinguished from call girls who do it for set prices of hard cash; and all of whom always lived in the heart of the Latin Quarter, naturally.

There was a portly young redheaded Jewish-Hungarian-American publisher's assistant to a French publishing house whom Harry had met somewhere, who at 32 was so Continental he could hardly be classified as American any more, and who delighted in entertaining the gang of us with snobbish employments of the monocle he affected. He would stop by every night after walking out from his office in the depths of the Quarter, to have a few drinks to clear the tear gas out of his throat, he said, before calling a cab and going off to Auteuil where he lived.

There was Weintraub.

There were some others; and there were still others whose faces changed night to night.

And it was into this homogenized milk of Americans that Weintraub finally introduced the lactic acid of the young nineteen-year-old American Negro girl, Samantha-Marie.

Looking back on it from after the end of the ballgame, that week seems like a pretty dull inning now. Sure, it was a week of student demonstrations, and students rioting all night almost every night. But none of us felt that this student revolt could actually penetrate to the very heart of French life, and jerk it to a standstill. Normal life seemed to go right normally on. Housewives out shopping pushed with unconcern their baby carriages along the sidewalks of streets down whose centers students and police charged shouting or retreated, heaving paving stones and gas grenades at each other. (Sometimes it was very funny: to see the carriage-pushing mothers weeping as if their hearts would break as they pushed along; and then look down and see the babies sitting quietly in their prams blinking and weeping, too.) And—at least, that week—the Metro subways ran, autobuses and taxis continued functioning, you could still call New York (or in Harry's

case, the South of France, where his current producer was shooting).
Food was plentiful, and there was not yet any talk of hoarding sugar
or flour.

Sometimes the traffic got blocked up on the Boulevard St.-Michel
and the Boulevard St.-Germain when the students were out, and there
would be a great deal of illegal horn-honking, and a long wait. But by
detouring around the Latin Quarter entirely, you could get to where
you were going in Paris in the normal amount of time.

The students had three basic demands back then, during that first
week: they wanted their seven convicted comrades released; they
wanted the special riot police (the CRS: *Compagnies Républicaines
de Sécurité*) withdrawn from the Latin Quarter; and they wanted the
Sorbonne reopened and classes resumed. At the same time, they
maintained they would continue to boycott the year's-end exams. But
they would consent to sit down with the Government and discuss their
program for the reforms they wanted.

You have to understand that it was all really a question of *timing*.
For example: To the eternal credit of their profound perspicacity and
insight, the Government started off the week by refusing all three
student demands. The arrested comrades were not released, the police
were not withdrawn, and the Sorbonne remained closed. Only a few
agitators were causing this, they stated in their news leaks, not the
great mass of the student body. So on the Monday of May 6th, their
big demonstration banned officially, the students took to street-fighting
again and to building in the Quarter their barricades of paving stones,
tree guards and traffic signs; and they kept it up for 14 hours all
through the night. On the next day the big, nonviolent, unauthorized
but uncontested, six-hour, 12-mile march was made all around Paris by
more than 20,000 students some said (anyway, a number which
obviously startled the authorities), only to end in more barricades and
street-fighting when the police tried to break it up after the march was
finished. And it was happening now in other cities, too: Toulouse,
Strasbourg, Lyons, Bordeaux.

Two other young leaders had emerged alongside *Dany le Rouge*:
Jacques Sauvageot of UNEF, the biggest students' union; and Alain
Geismar of SNE Sup., the young teachers' union. On Wednesday the
8th, after four days of refusal, the Government finally offered to

reopen the University—if the students would stop demonstrating; the response, instead of the agreement the students would have given three days before, was now a wild student sit-in in the middle of the Boulevard St.-Michel, tying up traffic for three hours, and a stated threat by young M. Sauvageot that if the Sorbonne was opened, the students would take it over and occupy it. So on Thursday the Government announced the Sorbonne would stay closed, and the demonstrations and street-fighting began again, this time early in the afternoon.

It was all one long history of changing their minds, inefficiency, bungling, blundering, and execrable, inexcusably bad timing. Our group of Americans, in our almost ritualistic pattern of meeting at the Gallaghers' every evening, watched and read and discussed it all. Almost everybody had been out at some time or other to watch.

I had not been out to the riots myself. I had been working hard, I had a considerable number of dinner dates that week, and the whole thing bored me. But Harry had been out. He had been out quite a number of times. But there seemed to be strangely little he could tell about it. He said there was a strangely nonserious air of gaiety about it all. It was too vivacious. He didn't think it would accomplish much. To me he seemed irritated, even angry, at the students. You might almost have said he was jealous in some odd way.

They had not heard from Hill since the previous Sunday when I delivered them Hill's second message. But Hill had had some young woman (*Anne-Marie the pipiste, I wondered?*), who seemed to be "working" as his "assistant" they said, telephone them a couple of times. And he had been home once, they found out from their maids, to pick up his big Bolex 16-mm zoom-lens movie camera. But he had sneaked in and out without seeing them.

I found them both strangely unworried about it all. I knew I was worried about him. But they just seemed to go right on. Harry had made a deal two months before, and was deep into the writing of a new, *American*-Western. Louisa went out to her lunches at Lipp's or Alexandre's with her friends, shopped afternoons, entertained at home nights or went out with Harry. They both seemed to have at least their usual amount of fun. It was more as if Hill were away at school at some American university back home, instead of maybe running for his safety from the tough Paris cops.

"Naturally, we're worried," Harry said when I finally asked them. But then he stopped. And he went on with whatever it was he was doing: fixing himself or me a drink, I guess.

I had been very careful with them, when I told them about Hill's second visit. I had underplayed Hill's reaction to Harry's offer of help. I hadn't lied. I had told them the offer angered Hill. But I had not told them how angered. Neither of them had reacted. Not in any way I could see, anyhow. And I went away with a distinct feeling that if I *had* told them: told them how first strangely furious and then melancholiac Hill had acted, that they would not have reacted to that, either.

Finally I stayed late one night. I waited till all the congregated eight-o'clock news watchers had gone. I wanted to bring it up again. This all was a long way from the powerful parental reaction I had seen that night back in April, when Harry telephoned me to come over because Hill wasn't home. And I wanted to know what was going on with them. This time it was Louisa who answered me.

"Of course we're worried," she said, just like Harry. But then she smiled one of her superior New England smiles at me, the kind that always irritated me, though I'm sure she never knew this, or was even aware of the superiority.

We three were all alone. The Portuguese maids had cleaned away the TV-and-cocktail debris of glasses and hors d'oeuvre plates, and had retired to the kitchen. McKenna was in bed asleep. But then when I brought up Hill, Harry seemed to just sort of fade away and disappear, too: fade right into the wall; or bend and secrete himself behind the bar or a chair somewhere.

So that Louisa and I seemed alone.

I was dimly aware of him somewhere there behind me; but I could not turn to look for him without taking my eyes and attention away from Louisa. And this quickly became increasingly impossible to do. I recognized dimly in some other part of my mind, with a small inner start, that to do so would be to insult her seriously, perhaps irreparably. I had seen her get the bit in her teeth this way several times before, some about politics, and once about summer camps. You simply dared not disagree with her.

"On the other hand, we know he's doing exactly what he wants to do," she said. "And what he wants to do is what we want for him: what we want him to do, too." Her faint New England drawl seemed to get visibly longer and more prominent as she spoke.

Sitting on the couch, she tilted back her head and let her long New England jaw drop at me. And her veiled green eyes, always a prominent thing with her, seemed to come out, pop forward, in her face: now, they looked like two spot-lighted marbles. The smile seemed to tell me she was thinking very critically of me, her old friend Jack.

"After all, it was Hill's decision to make. And *we* would certainly not attempt to interfere in that. So that, in quite another way, I can say that we're not worried about him at all. We're glad: that he's there. We're proud: that he is out there where he is."

"Well," I said. "Yes, of course. I mean, there's very little chance of his—"

"Getting killed? None at all, or almost none," Louisa said. "But even if there were. Even if there were, we should still want him to be where he is. We, Harry and I, are totally and without reservation on the side of the students in this thing. We'd be rather ashamed of Hill, if he were anywhere else.

"We wouldn't want him to have to be coming home every day to reassure us, when there are important things he ought to be doing instead. We do not even expect him to telephone us. I told that little girl that. We will go right on carrying on here, I told her: that is the best way we can help Hill. Help them all."

I could imagine what Hill would say to Anne-Marie about that.

"Well," I said—somewhat inconclusively, I suppose.

But I found myself, without knowing why, on the defensive. Something had got her up on her high horse and from up there there she was looking down with those marbles for eyes and haranguing me, while I down below stood feeling I had put my foot dumbly into some bear trap, steel-sprung and saw-toothed.

"I expect we have all the normal parental anxieties, Jack," she said. She shook her head. "But those count for little. And since Hill was not raised in any hypocritical background, I don't see how we could expect him to do anything else than what he's doing."

"Well, yes," I said. "Yes, of course not. But I just thought that, if you both wanted to, if there was any way to—"

She said it for me. "Contact him?" The superior smile seemed to writhe around on her face for a bit. "And how would that get done?"

"Well," I said. Of course she was right. "You're right, of course," I said. "He did say something to me about some lofts. But he didn't give me any addresses."

"There you are!" Louisa cried, triumphantly, as if she had won a whole war from me.

I was beginning to wish Harry would turn up, from wherever it was behind me he had hidden himself, and get back into this.

"I just think that it's horrible for them to set their police brutes on those children," Louisa said. "Those kids are young, and idealistic, and they have a perfect right to protest against this hypocritical society that they're forced to inherit and live in without any choice in the matter. If the young are not going to protest, who on earth is going to? Harry and I have been fighting the same two-faced, hypocritical human society all our lives. We are backing these kids all the way, Harry and I, and we are going to do everything we can to aid them." The green marbles of her eyes seemed to have gone unfocused. "We are whole-heartedly behind everything these youngsters are doing. Isn't that so, Harry? Isn't it?"

"Absolutely," Harry said from behind me. "Yes, absolutely." He came up. He was carrying three new drinks. He gave one of them to Louisa, and then another to me, kept one. But I had a distinct impression he had used the making of them to keep out of the way, and out of the conversation. "To see those kids out there, taking those beatings from the damned CRS, is just beautiful. It's just something beautiful to see."

From the corner of my eye I saw Louisa bob her head emphatically from the couch. She smiled on us a kind of breathless, aggressive smile. And the eerily brilliant green eyes in her long face seemed to be looking far away. I am sure she was unaware she had a drink in her hand.

It is a hard thing to explain. I am sure Harry went away deliberately. And when he came back, there seemed to be just the slightest hint of a less than full enthusiasm in Harry. Let me put it this way: His passion for the student movement, while every bit as heartily stated, was a hair less fervent than hers. Still, this was a long distance from the way he had been talking the past days. I had an uncanny but powerful feeling that something here did not have to do with Hill at all. Did not have to do with the student movement, either. Did not even have to do with that "hypocritical" human society they all, and me too I guess, disliked so much and were against. And Louisa seemed to have hypnotized herself into a kind of breathless, quiet female hysteria, with her talking.

I am convinced that when people are crazy is when they over-symbolize. I mean when every act, gesture, word symbolizes more than it itself is in its own nature is when people are crazy; certifiably nuts.

"If they had come to *my* apartment, Jack," Louisa smiled, "*I* would have moved heaven and hell. *I* would have left no *stone* unturned until I went back out in the streets with them, back to their lofts and their unwashed washing."

I was upset. It all made me nervous. And not only that. I found myself placed suddenly in the position of the villain. Without any preparation. I was held responsible with regard to Hill and the student movement, by the both of them. Me, who had been publishing pieces in my Review on Berkeley and the student troubles in America for over a year. Both of them began to talk at me about how little I was doing, and how thoughtlessly selfish I was being, and what *was* I doing? and why *wasn't* I doing?

Finally, when I could finish my new drink politely without seeming to have tossed it off in too much of a hurry, I took my hat and crept quietly away, feeling somehow guilty. As if, in coming to them about Hill, in having seen him and brought them news of him, in fact by having allowed Hill to visit me in my apartment at all, I had become responsible for everything bad that might happen to Hill, *and* to the student movement, *and* to the Gallagher family itself.

Louisa saw me to the door. But her glassy eyes and her voice were both far away.

Outside on the quai it was dark. I set my hat properly, and grasped my umbrella, and tried to shake off my awful feeling. Over in the

Quartier sirens wailed, and tear-gas grenades thudded above the chants. Up in the air between some buildings over there, there was a bright flash, and then a deafening report. It was one of the new percussion grenades the police had begun to use now.

And up on the corner of the Pont de la Tournelle squatted the dark little vans of special police, like two awful bugs in the dark night.

6

I REMEMBER IT WAS the next day, Thursday, Thursday the 9th May, that I first went out to look at the riots for myself.

I do know what special thing made me decide to go out that particular day. But I do not know if I can describe it. As I've said, at that time the whole thing bored me. I had other interests going. And I had no desire to get myself mousetrapped against some apartment building as innocent bystander, and get beaten up by half a dozen CRS riot police. Perhaps if I were a lot younger, and still venturesome. But I was not that naïve any more. Not the cynical Jack Hartley of today: divorcé; small time editor; failed writer at a variety of forms, and 47 years old with two arthritic knees. I preferred to ignore it.

But that Thursday something happened, something in the air, that made it impossible to ignore it any longer.

I must try to get this down exactly. I had risen as usual around eleven, had my coffee and orange juice served me as usual in bed together with the mail by my Portuguese. Then I made my usual morning toilet. Now, my morning toilet is always one of the best parts of any day for me. Showering: then shaving slowly and leisurely with one of my set of straight razors given me by my grandfather: selecting one of my several Caswell-Massey cologne waters, a luxury indulgence on my part I admit, since they could not be bought in France, and had to be sent from New York: attending to my ageing teeth with a Water-Pic treatment after a firm brushing. As my grandfather used to say: If you don't look after your teeth, you can't eat; and I love to eat, as did he. It was one of those times of the day when being a bachelor really paid off. No women running around scattering powder everywhere and leaving the water taps not quite turned off. No female hammering to get in and use the john or the mirror or the toothbrush—just when you were about to apply bared blade to lather for the first sensuous stroke. There is no instrument invented that will give you the absolutely close, clean, satisfying, esthetic shave that an old-fashioned straight razor will, if you keep it cleaned and take care of it. Then, feeling marvelous, I had dressed and gone to work at my desk editing a revolt piece which had just come in from a professor-friend contributor at Berkeley.

I think now that I must have become aware of excitement in the air while I was making my toilet, but that I failed to notice it because I was enjoying myself so much.

Anyhow as I sat down with the revolt piece I realized immediately that I had been sensing excitement for some time. Almost at once I found I couldn't concentrate on anything, certainly not on editing an intellectual revolt piece.

It was another sunny day. There was a breeze on the river. A lot of people were out, on both sides of the water, walking along and enjoying the exceptional weather. None of this was unusual. But something else was. It is my habit to keep my quai windows tight shut when I am seriously working, but now the closed windows could not keep out the electric quality that was in the air.

More than anything it was like a bullfight day in Spain. I thought immediately of the San Fermin Festival in Pamplona: in the morning when one first gets up, late, after staying up all night drinking and waiting for the running of the bulls. Nothing was happening, but people were preparing themselves, just the same. There is an indefinite buzz over the town, its source cannot be isolated, soon people will begin to leave the hotels and houses and move toward the bars and cafés for talk and the first drinks, then there will be a long leisurely lunch with a lot of sangría while the excitement mounts higher, and finally the general exodus toward the bullring in the thickening buzz:

Something is going to happen today: There will be danger: Maybe someone will even be hurt: Oh, boy: And we are there: We are the excited audience.

That was it. That was what it was. The audience. There was an audience in Paris. And the audience was preparing itself to go to the arena. A low, constant murmurous sound as of great crowds of people, an oceanlike sound, it seemed to seep in through the very walls themselves and through the glass panes of the windows. It was monotonous, did not rise or fall in intensity or pitch, and it carried on its low soundwave this air of intense holiday.

I tried to go on working. It was useless. Finally I walked over to the windows and looked out. Nothing was especially different. It was still the sunny day. It was still the same quite-a-few-people abroad, walking and enjoying the sun.

Then I opened the window. It was like opening a dam. I was engulfed in a torrent of sunny, happy, gabbling excitement like an electrical charge, that churned in and swept through the apartment and washed against its walls in a golden flood. The soft air puffed at my face and the sun touched it, as if it too was sucked in with the torrent's gush inward. I leaned out.

Down below people strolled along the quai in twos and threes. On the wide cobbled landing at the top of the ramp under the trees below my windows, a kind of loafing place alongside the moving foot traffic, a group of at least ten was staring off intently toward the Left Bank across the river. Children, and older people too, ate *Esquimaux* or munched on the large waffle-like *crêpes sucrées*. I felt I might truly be in Pamplona, preparing to leave the hotel for the first drink and bullfight talk of the day.

And with the window open now, I could hear faintly the isolated shout, the chant, a thin piping command, the thud of a gas grenade, the great rending crack, though muffled by distance, of a percussion grenade. The cops and the students, they're putting on a show! Putting on a show! Let's go! Let's go! It was noon. The Festival was starting.

How could anyone work? I put my foot up on the windowsill.

There was a larger number of students than normal among the strollers. Most of them were dressed in the by now recognizable "running shoes and bandanna" uniform. All of them were laughing inordinately. Happily they strolled along in twos and threes, sometimes arm in arm.

They were coming from the Left Bank, across the Pont de la Tournelle at the rue Cardinal Lemoine, passing indifferently by our two camions of CRS police, whose men studiously ignored them. They walked downriver toward Notre-Dame, presumably to recross the river there via the footbridge, and the Pont d l'Archevêché which butted on the rue des Bernardins, which led to the Place Maubert where they were apparently fighting for the moment. There was an awful lot of them, and they did not stop coming.

So, their damned Revolution had finally come to the Seine islands, had it, damn them, I thought grimly; and found myself grinning. You couldn't help it.

But the air of electric gaiety and holiday did not come solely from them. It was in the faces of the older people, too—the rotund little Frenchmen with their gray moustaches and dark caps and baggy suits; the older women dressed in dresses designed not to hide but simply to cover their good French fat; the younger ones in their New York-cut suits and ties and miniskirts. They were all in it together, whatever it was; and whatever it was, it was fun.

Behind me my Portuguese came in and interrupted me. This was something she almost never presumed to do. She told me she had just heard on her kitchen transistor radio that there was a big bagarre, a truly big fight, going on over at the Place Maubert.

I gave up entirely on my Berkeley piece and stayed in my window to watch. I could almost see Maubert from where I stood, but not quite. The tall houses along the Left Bank cut it off from my view. But I could see the cloud of smoke and tear gas above it. Maubert was a marché, a street market, on the Boulevard St.-Germain almost on a level with Notre-Dame, where St.-Germain junctions with the rue Monge, which can be considered just about the eastern boundary of the Latin Quarter. It made a nice large junction for erecting barricades, when all the market stalls were taken down.

The sun was pleasant and warm on my face and shoulders. I saw, picked out, the high bald dome of Harry Gallagher glistening in the sun as he crossed the Pont de la Tournelle. Harry was striding in his tweed jacket among the students like a senior professor. When he was below me, I leaned out and called down to him.

"Wait up. I'm coming down."

We stood against the sidewalk's belly-high stone parapet. Students who passed us on the sidewalk grinned merrily at us. I grinned back at them.

"You've got to admit it's exciting," I said.

"Oh, it's exciting." Harry had been up to the Brasserie Lipp in St.-Germain for lunch and had walked home through the students' quarter.

"I couldn't work," I said. "I had to give it up. There's too much excitement all around."

Harry gave me a professional smile, but he looked as if he had not heard me. All through the Quartier the students were out in roving bands, he said, and the place was alive with platoons and companies of riot police, not only the CRS now but also the *Gendarmes Mobiles,* really a military force, armed with unloaded carbines and under the authority of the Army, but capable of being requisitioned by the Prefect. Barricades were up all over the place, and either being defended, or abandoned, or breached by the police, and then torn down by the truckloads of public-service workers who followed them.

"But they have been doing that for days," I said. "What is so different about today?"

"Something is," Harry said. "I don't know. But it's gotten bigger. Whatever it is."

"They've been fighting at Maubert before today," I said. "But it never bothered me from working. What has changed?"

"Something has," Harry said. The students were apparently trying out a new tactic, he went on, which consisted of raising a barricade at some undisputed point, which of course would bring the police in their camions, then after a small fight retreating and fading away, while by radio or motorbike informing another group to begin doing the same thing somewhere else. They were keeping at least a dozen big task forces of police busy in this way. They seemed very well organized. In addition, large contingents of police were blocking off all the bridges on the Left Bank side, from the Pont Alexandre III at the Invalides to the Pont au Double at the front of Notre-Dame.

"They're not going to have any police left," Harry said, "if they don't watch out."

Place Maubert had been one of the big fights today, he said. Barricade after barricade had been put up, lost, sometimes retaken there.

Both of us looked across the river. We could still hear the occasional chant or shout or muffled thud of a grenade, coming across. And the tear gas made a high, rising cloud of white above the tops of the houses over there. Right then, I made up my mind to go over there, and have a look at it.

"Well, I certainly can't work around here," I said.

"It's amazing to see them put one of those things up," Harry said. "All they need is one crowbar to start it, and then a couple of shovels to keep it going. They form human chains to pass the paving stones along. There's something truly ritualistic about it."

"Well, they've certainly had enough centuries of practice at it for it to become a ritual," I said. I coughed. "I can't get over the feeling that I'm at Pamplona for San Fermin."

Harry grinned. "It is like that. Everybody's having a ball, all at once. The whole town."

"I'm going over there and have a close look at it. Do you want to come along?"

"No. I've already been. I'm going home. You're not going to work any more? Come on walk down with me toward my place."

Just then, suddenly, across the river, a mass of running bodies, students' bodies, squirted around the corner of the narrow rue Cardinal Lemoine. It debouched onto the Left Bank quai, moving toward the Pont de l'Archevêché at Notre-Dame. No police came after them.

"We'll have a beer at the Brasserie," Harry said after the flurry had passed away.

We moved out into the stream of walkers, and I walked along with him. I could not get over a feeling that Harry was wanting to talk to me about something.

"What was it you were going to say, Harry?"

He didn't answer for a moment. "I wasn't going to say much of anything," he said.

We walked some more.

"I just can't help but think that they're not doing any good," he said in a different voice. This clearly was not what he had been meaning to talk about. "The kids, I mean. They're getting themselves all beat up for nothing. And I don't think they're going to do any good. It's all just too—too frivolous."

"It does appear like everybody's having a good time," I said.

"Hell, when we were kids demonstrating back in the Thirties, we didn't have any of these kinds of attitudes, or act like this. We didn't do this."

"What did you do, Harry?"

"Well, we . . ." It trailed off, as if he were taking a moment to formulate something. But then his silence continued. We were just strolling again.

"I suppose it's that I don't like being relegated to the sidelines," Harry said, and made a rueful smile. "I don't like being classified as an old fogy and tucked away on a shelf. I don't like being told I'm an old-man member of a conservative Establishment who doesn't understand, and never knew what it was to revolt." He paused. "But it's more than that. I don't like being told it's my generation that's solely responsible for everything that's wrong with the fucking world. Christ, didn't any of them ever read their history? Didn't they hear about the war we fought with Hitler and Tojo? Didn't they ever hear about the Depression and the New Deal? The House Un-American Activities Committee in 1950? Who the hell do they think they are?"

I did not try to answer this. It was rhetorical, anyway.

"They don't want us," Harry said. "They don't even want to utilize our knowledge and experience to help them."

—Another trio of laughing students passed us and grinned happily at us.—

"They don't want anything to do with us or our past, and I don't like that. I also don't think it's very sane."

I had been thinking and feeling a lot the same way, since seeing Hill—and his Anne-Marie.

"Maybe you just don't like not being young, Harry."

"Maybe. And I've thought of that. But I've never thought of myself as young, or not young. It's never been a criterion I've ever applied to myself."

"But now they are applying it to you. Through their eyes we must look pretty 'old', Harry."

"Well, I don't mind being old. I even like it. Let somebody else pick up the old torch. But I refuse to be 'old' just because these kids think I think 'old'. Hell, I can still get it up three or four times a day. Anyway, at least you would think Hill would know differently."

"Why? I think Hill least of all would. Hill is the young bull pawing and snorting to take on and pull down the old bull."

"And take over the herd. Sure. Chart-class Freud. The young buck wants to screw the doe I'm screwing, even if it is his mother. Especially if it is his mother. Chart-class Freud. Christ, Jack!"

"Okay. I know it's so general it hasn't got any applicable meaning. Still, I think you probably did exactly the same thing when you were young."

"Yee-ah." He said it, half-breathed it, in the old tough Hollywood way that Julie Garfield used to say it in his films. "You and your analysis. A great lotta help. And I wish you'd stop saying 'when you were young' like that to me, for God sake.

"I hope he's all right," he added.

"He's all right. Nobody's been killed yet."

"As far as we know," Harry added. "Yee-ah!" he said again.

We had reached the Brasserie. That was all we ever called it. Its full name was the Brasserie of the Red Bridge of the Island of St. Louis: *Brasserie du Pont Rouge de l'Île St.-Louis.* There wasn't any red bridge, but apparently there had once been one, way back. It was our local pub on the Island. It squatted in the ground floor of a building at the foot of the rusting green Bailey bridge footbridge called Pont St.-Louis which had been put up temporarily in 1940 when a *péniche* barge had crashed into and weakened its old stone predecessor, in a tiny *Place* where a few late beer-drinkers stationed their deux chevauxs late at night, and it served the best beer in Paris in stone mugs. It was generally closed Thursdays but it was open now, and it was crowded with people, and the bridge was crowded with people. A group of its patrons and habitués stood outside its painted windows on the sidewalk with the gray stone mugs in their hands, and stared over at the Left Bank. Harry stopped.

"I think I'll beg off on that beer, Jack, and go straight on home." He put his hands in the pockets of his khaki drill pants. He jiggled some keys. "No, about what I was going to say before, back up the way."

For a moment I couldn't read his reference. Then I remembered.

He peered at me quizzically. "I was just going to say that I hoped you weren't upset or angry about the way Louisa and I jumped on you last night. We lit on you pretty hard."

"—" I didn't want to complain about it; but neither did I think I ought to pretend it had not happened.

"There certainly wasn't anything personal in it," Harry said. "We weren't attacking you. Hell, you're the best friend we've got. Louisa, I think, feels that even stronger than I do. And you know how I feel."

"You don't have to tell me that," I said.

"It didn't really have anything to do with you at all. We're in a strange position, with Hill out there. I guess a lot of parents are." He lowered his head, and looked down at his shoes. "Politics and college kids are two things that really turn Louisa on. Put them both together in something and . . ."

"It made me feel guilty," I said. "In an oddly strange way. And I don't think I deserve to."

"Fuck, you certainly don't," Harry said. "But you know how Louisa is about politics. She wants so badly to *help*. We're really behind these kids, Jack. *Really* behind them, all the way."

"I thought somehow that maybe there was something more behind it than that," I said. "I mean, I felt that."

"Well, there wasn't," Harry said, looking me squarely in the eye. It seemed to me he was looking me too straight in the eye, or doing it too carefully.

"Well, I'm glad," I said, simply. It wasn't my business, anyway.

"Louisa wasn't—We weren't after you. Louisa's always gotten these moody spells. Especially about politics. Louisa hasn't ever been able to do all she'd like to do. It's pretty hard being a parent, in this. Quite a lot of them feel that, I expect. It's worrisome. I know Hill's younger than I am."

—To me that seemed a strange thing to say.—

"And I wouldn't have it any other way. I mean, it stands to reason any father's got to be older than his son. But I sometimes don't think Hill sees it that way. And sometimes I don't think Louisa does."

"I think Hill sees it," I said noncommittally. "I don't know about Louisa."

"Well, I just wanted to explain. Louisa wasn't—We weren't after you, last night."

"Oh, forget it, Harry. I don't really care. Tell Louisa that."

"Be careful over there," he said as he left. "I mean, you don't run so good any more. Just don't get caught between the lines. Especially when a charge is working up. I've found that if you want to change sides, to observe, it's best to circle back around on another street that isn't in dispute." He waved, in a kind of awkward way that made me feel sad for him and warm.

I still had the feeling that he was trying to tell me something about Louisa that he had not been able to say. Or that I had not been able to get.

In the fact, I had seen her in those strange moods before, a lot of times. But her attacks had never been directed at me before. You had the feeling when she was in those moods that if you disagreed with her even in the slightest way, you would destroy her whole psyche, crumble her all up like a handful of soda crackers. She seemed to expect that you would, and how dare you? You felt she might brood for weeks, for months over it. Yet I had never thought of her as being goofy, or even very neurotic. I was sure she wasn't goofy.

I still had my feeling that there was something more there, something still, that had nothing to do with what we all had said.

I went in the Brasserie.

It was cool and dim in there. They kept a thin film of sawdust on the tile floor around the bar in the front. I ordered my beer. It was served in my own special stein, with a pewter top. All of us habitués had our special steins, which were all kept apart, on a separate shelf.

The long dining room in the back had hardwood floor and no sawdust, and it was crowded with luncheon eaters. I had been coming there for years, and knew all the waiters by their first names. But I suddenly felt constrained about asking them about the riots.

Anyway they were all very busy. The bar was crowded too. The waiters all wore white shirts, black four-in-hand ties, and in winter little red sleeveless sweaters, above long blue-denim aprons that wrapped around the back and tied in the front. The place was owned by Monsieur and Madame Dupont who ran it themselves aided by a series of brothers-in-law, Madame Dupont's brothers, and one thin little old grandmother with an old white dog. Today Madame Dupont was on duty and sat up on a stool behind the cash desk which was placed against the wall, between the bar and the dining room. The waiters from the dining room had to pass this cash desk and run behind the bar, shouting their orders, to the kitchen which was on the other side. Sometimes the grandmother sat up there, sometimes Monsieur Dupont, and other times one of the brothers-in-law. Beside the cash desk was a table usually considered the family table. The waiters had a table on the other side near the kitchen.

The Duponts had bought the place the first year I lived on the Island, and had been doing a huge business ever since, huge enough that Madame Dupont now sported a leopard coat and purse and wore Chanel suits which, whether they were high-class copies or not, looked like real Chanel. They had a 14-year-old daughter, whom I had watched grow up from a tiny girl.

She was sitting at the family table, and came over to me to say hello, her young breasts covered only by a slip under her sweater. She had nice legs. It was astonishing to think I had watched her grow from almost a baby.

"Well, what do you think of it?" I asked in French.

"It is certainly something, isn't it?" she smiled.

She always smiled shyly at me, and always blushed. I was sort of the place's "very own American", more than Harry, and maybe that accounted for it. She had the short pert Bretonese nose of her father, who was a tough hombre, and she was sweet when she blushed.

"You are on the side of the students?" I said.

She blushed again, and smiled more. She was really very tiny, dark and olive, with black hair. "M'sieu, the police have entered the University. That has not happened in a very long time. There is an old and valuable tradition against that, and the police have flaunted it. Also, the reforms of the students are good reforms, and are necessary in the modern world."

"You're not at school today?"

"My school is closed," she said shyly. "The students there are on strike, also. Many of them are out marching." She went to a *lycée,* the equivalent of our high school.

"The *lycée* young are out, too?" I asked.

"Oui, M'sieu," she smiled. "Certainly. Many of them are. My school is."

I grinned at her, because I thought I already knew the answer. "But you are not marching with them?"

She blushed again. "Maman would not let me. She doesn't understand." Still smiling, she cast a loving look over at her mother.

From the cash desk Madame Dupont, who had been listening to us with attention, and who had the long aquiline nose of the Central Plateau, smiled at me and rocked her head on one side and put her hand up by her ear. "The young. Mind you, I am with the students, I think they are right. But they are very young. And a young slip of a young girl like that, out marching against the police. It isn't even sane." It was from her that Marcelline got her olive coloring. She was a good-looking woman, with a fine figure, though perhaps her bottom had spread a little with the ten years of success.

"I wanted to go," Marcelline said simply, blushing.

"Maybe you ought to let her go," I said to Madame.

"You see!" Marcelline cried, clapping her hands. From the background the oldest of the brothers-in-law, Marcel, smiled at them fondly.

"M'sieu Jack!" Madame said. "You do not really mean to say that."

"I am perhaps only thinking of the possible dental bills, that is all," I said.

Madame Dupont nodded wisely, smiling her fine smile at me. "As well as possibly other bills." She was a very attractive woman. She couldn't have been much more than five or six years younger than me. She would be just about my wife Eleanor's age. I looked at Marcelline, 14-year-old Marcelline.

The two of them, mother and daughter, exchanged a look of open love.

"In any case, M'sieu," Marcelline said, blushing, "I thank you for your aid! I shall not forget that!" I shook hands with her formally, gravely.

It was all a joke, all a warm family joke, with Marcel the brother-in-law participating, and on the periphery of which I participated a little. But it was good to see open, honest family love, that was not dominated by either open or hidden resentment of same.

"Plenty of time for her to go out marching against grown-up police later, if she has to," Madame smiled, as I finished my beer and paid at the cash desk. "She's not even University yet."

"But I will be!" Marcelline said.

"Plenty of time, plenty of time," Madame said. "You be careful over there," she said to me, as Marcel the brother-in-law shook hands with me formally for having stoppped by.

I nodded and winked at them.

Harry had said the same thing about being careful over there. Well, I certainly intended to be careful. The footbridge seemed equally crowded with people going to the Left Bank and people coming from the Left Bank.

There was a steady two-way stream across the Cité behind Notre-Dame, and on the Pont de l'Archevêché. The Left Bank quai was jammed up, with a veritable mob of people moving under the leafy shade trees. But the old cathedral looked the same. That old stone barn, raised to tribal blood gods, had been sitting there on its haunches brooding over the bloodletting rituals of mankind for centuries. Beautiful and useless, it squatted over us all. With its high-flung buttresses and stained windows it was certainly a monument, to something or other. In the street lots of the children carried balloons.

I did not feel scared. It was impossible to feel afraid in the gay excitement. This was completely different from the war, and the dense excitement that comes on you like an additional weight of gravity, before going into an attack.

I crossed the Quai de Montebello, after waiting on the traffic light. I entered the narrow mouth of the rue des Bernardins. At once, the crowd stopped moving so much, became almost stationary.

In front of me mainly what I could see were the backs of many heads. Mostly they were the backs of heads of Arab Algerians, who largely lived in this quarter. It is as easy to tell an Algerian by the back of his head as it is a Chinese. They shuffled and craned, but forward movement had stopped. They were not densely massed, and it was easy to slip in and out among them.

Up ahead a big roar went up from the Place Maubert, fading swiftly as it was passed backward through the crowd by all the heads in front of me. The crowd stirred a little on its feet. I went on, slipping in and out, slipping in and out.

At the moment I did not give a damn, and I wanted to see what all this crap was about, that Harry had been talking about in the past few days so proprietarily.

You have to understand the topography of the Left Bank and the place of the Place Maubert in it, to understand its importance during the weeks of rioting. The Seine flows through Paris in one long curve from the East to the Southwest, cutting off as it does so about one-third of the city from the other two-thirds. This one-third is called the Left Bank, and of it about one-fifth, roughly bounded by the Boulevard Raspail on the West and the rue Monge on the East, is called the Latin Quarter. The area is largely dominated by the great pile of the Panthéon, which was built on just about the top of the area's one hill. It was built as a church, but later was taken over and made into a lay memorial to the French Revolution and to France. The bloodletting rituals played an important part in its history too, and were conspicuously present in its murals and sculpture. A couple of blocks below it, west and toward the river, lies the Sorbonne. And a couple of blocks below that is the junction of the boulevards St.-Michel and St.-Germain.

These two main arteries cross the area of the Latin Quarter in roughly the shape of a crucifix, if you placed Christ's head at the river. And their junction, called the Carrefour St.-Michel, is the spiritual and emotional heart of the *Quartier Latin*. From it Boul' St.-Germain curves gently northeast to meet the river at the Pont Sully, and about halfway between these points on the Boulevard lies the Place Maubert.

Maubert is a sort of arrowhead-shaped square and market into which run about six streets, two of which run steeply uphill crossing the rue des Écoles (Street of Schools to you, in English), and dead-end themselves in the big square that surrounds the huge mass of the Panthéon.

Thus, this area is almost in the heart of University ground. The students could descend easily in swarms to fight there from their home-base around the Sorbonne and the Panthéon. They could, as well, fade away and retreat back up the hill when over-matched or out-powered.

And the Place Maubert, in addition to having the largest local food market in the area, also had the advantage of being supremely disruptive of traffic, always a student objective, since it junctioned with a main artery from the south side of Paris, which was the rue Monge.

It was almost as good a place to fight as the symbolic Carrefour St.-Michel, and some ways was even better since it had more choice of escape routes and its arrowhead square gave more room to maneuver. It was the perfect place for the students to make a diversionary fight when they wanted to take pressure off the Carrefour.

I came out of the rue des Bernardins into Maubert in exactly the kind of situation Harry had told me to avoid. The police were preparing themselves to charge the students' barricade. I came out right in among the extreme left of their line. I could have laughed out loud, thinking of Harry, except I realized instantly that any laughter would be exceedingly out of place right here and now.

Across the square a kind of not quite visible fog hung everywhere. The sweetish, acrid smell of tear gas was strong. Already, my eyes felt scratchy. Four automobiles and a couple of grocery bikecarts lay on their sides across the Boulevard St.-Germain right in front of me, but the students had abandoned this barricade. They had slipped their line left over to the mouth of rue Monge across the square, where they had pushed a couple of cars out but hadn't had time to overturn them. Behind these they pranced, and jumped up and down, and chanted, and whistled and yelled at the police. A couple of them threw one each of the square granite paving stones with which so much of Paris is paved, which fell far short of the police line.

A policeman darted out, threw a gas grenade, which fell just in front of the cars, exploded with a puff, and then lay there smoking.

These were the CRS, armed with the long hickory riot sticks, and carrying shields. They had a different kind of helmet, with a silver strip of ornament running back along the crown. A couple of them right beside me who could not have been more than 19 down there inside their uniforms, goggles, helmets and gloves, glared at me with all the bloodthirst of dedicated head-hunters.

I stopped dead still. There were other people standing around, too. But they had been there. And I was new. In fact, all around the square things were going on normally, only inches it seemed away from the combat. People went into the *tabac* and bought cigarettes and came back out to watch. I stood absolutely still, my hands quiet at my sides. The two boys muttered something, growled almost, tapped their sticks suggestively in their palms, and glared absolutely wall-eyed at me, like horses, with wild-eyed absolutely contemptuous insult.

I knew explosive hatred when I saw it. Every animal does. So much adrenalin pumped into a system has to have release, and the animal part recognizes that. I could probably have backed off, with an obsequious movement. But some other part of me calmly did not think that was the right thing to do, and said quietly inside my head: stand your ground; just, don't move. But then, any movement of mine at all might have triggered them, and both of them would have me on the ground that quick and be on me beating me. So we stood. Then the officer down the line shouted a command, and my two boys turned and began with the rest of the line to run across the *Place*. One's coattails brushed me. The moment was over, I was no longer the subject of attention.

Across the square the students, there were about 30 of them, faded away: into the side streets, or running back uphill up rue Monge. They stopped after they had gone one block. The police stopped after they had passed the improvised two-car barricade.

Of course, everywhere traffic had ceased on the two thoroughfares. I got out a cigarette, and noticed somewhat abstractedly that my hands were shaking a little. I still was not scared, and had not been.

The students had certainly made a mess of the square. Broken glass, wet black ashes of cardboard and wooden crates, piles of the paving stones, and the overturned cars with their windshields and headlights all broken out now littered the area. Large light patches of yellow sand showed where the paving stones had been taken up by the hundreds, the thousands. Fire trucks had sprayed the burning crates and boxes, and the water had carried the greasy black filth of the ashes everywhere. Every shop in the market around the square was closed and shuttered. It was for just this the French all had and firmly maintained iron shutters on their shops. Two ambulances stood silent in the middle of the street, their top lights winking. Units of Red Cross men in their gray uniforms and white helmets waited together, smoking and looking tired and occasionally shrugging their shoulders at each other and at the entire panorama. There were quite a few American and British tourists with cameras, taking pictures. Platoons of the *Gendarmes Mobiles,* different in their black jackets and blue pants from the CRS, stood around holding their unloaded carbines like quarterstaffs, waiting for orders.

For some reason I did not know, a platoon of these filed out and replaced the group of CRS who had captured the two-car barricade.

Public-service workers were already at work struggling to clear the streets.

A block away the students jeered.

The platoon of *Gendarmes Mobiles* got ready to advance another block.

I had noticed that the nearer you got to Maubert and the action the less talking and laughing there was among the crowd. By the same token, I had noticed immediately that the nearer you got to the real action, the less nervous the crowd became, and therefore the less prone to turn and flee a few yards at the first cry or wave of movement up front.

Harry was quite right when he said there was a curious ritualistic quality about it. It was as if there were a tacit but definite set of rules both sides abided by. The police did not really try to capture the students, and the students did not really try to stay and fight hand-to-hand on their barricades. The volleys of paving stones by the students seemed to reach a definite peak and subside, after which the police would prepare to make their charge. It was like a ritual dance almost. There was always a 20 to 40 yard no-man's-land between the two, with the students on the defensive and retreating slowly, while the police took the offensive by charging, but slowly enough to let the defenders retreat. Their strategy obviously was to take over more and more blocks of streets, while herding the students back away from the Sorbonne until they dispersed. The tactic of the police was to keep close enough and charging, so as not to give the students time to pull up paving stones and erect new serious barricades.

I followed them for maybe an hour. The students backed up rue Monge to rue des Écoles, then backed around to the left on Écoles. The police followed them street by street, charging but never quite reaching them. At the rue Cardinal Lemoine the students turned to the right back uphill, backing toward the Place de la Contrescarpe, another hotbed of student activity like Maubert.

Twice, following Harry's advice, I circled around on another street to change sides from one side to the other. On these unfought-over streets everything went on normally, and people shopped, though there was a saturation of excitement in the air. On the student side, there were many more students than were out in the street fighting, sort of following along and watching. There were tourists, taking the eternal pictures. Everybody was weeping copiously, and grinning, laughing. On the police side, I was belly-shoved once in the chest by a *Gendarme Mobile,* and told to get back, stay back, when I peered around a corner too quickly after a platoon that was just passing. The original unit of *Gendarmes Mobiles* had been joined by two others, so that they moved up the street after the students in a leapfrogging way, from both sidewalks and in the center.

I saw one student taken in. I did not see him actually captured, so I did not know how they got him. But I saw two *Gendarmes Mobiles* carrying their carbines at the balance in one hand, turn him over to three CRS who were lurking around. There were pairs and trios of CRS all around. It apparently was their job to take care of the captures. These three CRS carried the rubber *matraques* with the iron rod in the center, which while they probably shocked and hurt as much or more than the hickory sticks, did less physical damage. They clubbed the student to the ground with their *matraques*, while he tried to protect his head with his arms, and then got him by the armpits and rushed him wobbling away, his feet half dragging. His eyes were glazed and his mouth hung open, and there were various little streams of blood running down his head out of his long, somewhat greasy hair.

The clubbing was absolutely unnecessary, since he was half out and already bleeding somewhat, when the *Gendarmes Mobiles* turned him over.

And behind me out in the street the other fighting students were shouting and laughing, went on roaring and throwing, having the time of their lives, with a kind of marvelous self-righteousness I had not seen since my own college days and our 'raids'.

Soon after this I left them. They were still backing up the rue

Cardinal Lemoine toward Contrescarpe. The excitement was intense, and it never let up. It was so emotionally exhausting that in time it exhausted you physically as well. I walked back down the hill on Cardinal Lemoine, to pick up a carton of cigarettes at my local *tabac* at the corner of St.-Germain, cross the Pont de la Tournelle and go on home. On my way, I saw a CRS man who evidently had just come off duty, and was on his way home to supper. He had taken off his helmet, and was wearing his cloth overseas cap. He carried his helmet close to his leg, his hand wrapped in the straps, as if trying to make it unobtrusive; or as if signaling with it in a quiet way that he was not working now. He did not have a riot stick, and he did not look guilty. He looked like a working man going home to supper. I got my cigarettes, crossed the bridge past the two camions of CRS still sitting on it there, walked on home to shower and leave my cigarettes, and then went on down to the Gallaghers' where the American group should be meeting.

7

It is not difficult to describe Samantha Everton. The difficult thing is that once you have described her, you have not described her. The difficult thing was she seemed to be and act exactly what she was and thought. My grandfather taught me long ago nobody is ever that.

I was standing at the bar with Harry and some of the men when Weintraub brought her in. Louisa, instantly hovering over the black girl like a protective mother hen, escorted them slowly down the room, introducing her. The girl moved beside Louisa casually, but tensely.

Even from the bar Weintraub's stentorian voice, made falsely deep, was easily heard. The girl stood quietly behind him, almost submissively, with a thin-lipped ironic smile on her small face.

"That's Dave's new girl," Harry whispered. "He picked her up Tuesday night at Castel's. She's staying with him at his *pension*. He called Louisa about her."

"What do you mean, new?" someone said. "I didn't know he ever had any girl."

Weintraub went on introducing her loudly.

So there she was. She was a black, but so were a lot of the others who showed up at the Gallaghers'. She was 19. She was not unusually beautiful in the face. She was sleek-looking, but she did not have a special figure.

She was Rosalie Everton's daughter. Rosalie Everton was the great Haitian singer. All of us knew her by reputation, and some of us had seen her perform. But we all were used to stars and celebrities—and, in the last few years, to the celebrated children of stars and celebrities. Anyway Samantha was not at all celebrated.

Weintraub was making it blatantly obvious that she was at least for the moment functioning as his mistress. She accepted this, smiling her ironic smile. Louisa hovered around them both, looking distressed. Whether Samantha knew as we did that Weintraub had almost never had a girl of his own, I still don't know. Finally, they got to us.

"Gentlemen, this is Weintraub's new love," Weintraub told us in his deepest voice, with an arm flourish. "Take a good look. Samantha-Marie Everton. Yes sir, she's bunking up with me in my little one-bed *pension*. The old joint has never seen the like."

She smiled directly at Harry behind the bar. "Because I'm broke and have no place else to go," she said sweetly.

"That's true, that's true," Weintraub added quickly. There had been genuine pride and pleasure on his face when he looked at her, as well as a look of surprise at his luck. It made me feel sad for him.

There was a reliant compactness about her, as if she were holding herself all in solidly together. As she had moved further away from the door, and therefore further into someone else's territory, it seemed that this compactness got visibly more compact. She slipped up onto a bar stool.

She was clearly wearing no underwear at all. Her eyes were a striking green, and she had dressed to them. Above was a green knit pullover with no sleeves at all, which showed off her lean, exquisitely shaved armpits; and on the front of this the nipples of her small unrestrained breasts made two visible bumps. Below, she was wearing those lowcut, skintight summer stretch pants, of a lighter green, with a wide belt and big buckle. The tight crotch of these was up so tight against her that the pants outlined quite clearly for you the two lips of her little crack. This was not unusual, though, was par for the course, in the spring of 1968.

She was quite dark. But her features were not very Negroid. She had some white and some Indian in her. And she had a 19-year-old's body which, in my day, was a valuable asset one never appreciated until one had lost it. But that could not be said of Samantha. She was small. Her hips were narrow and boyish. But she still had that high, hard, large-buttocked Negro derrière that a great many find so attractive. Her hair was cut short, boy-like, around her ears.

We had been talking about our adventures of the day watching the riots. There were five of us at the bar. There was the famous TV commentator, there was the young UPI man, there was Ferenc Hofmann-Beck. He was the young part German, part Jewish, part Hungarian-American who was the French publisher's assistant. There were Harry and myself.

I would have thought that those tight pants would have been most uncomfortable, for a girl, but if they were, Samantha gave no sign of it either standing or sitting.

Samantha, it turned out, liked to be called Sam. She had an annoying, and arrogant social habit. When she shook hands, she would hold onto your hand and search your face, slowly, and quite openly, for something. Then, not finding it, whatever it was, she would drop the hand and turn away to the next, indifferent. I thought it had to be a ploy. Nobody could do something like that unwittingly. She lingered over some hands longer than others. She spent no time at all over mine. Somebody told me later that she had lingered over Louisa's longest of all. I looked around for her, but Louisa had left us.

I like to remember that moment, though now it is always with a touch of sadness. Nothing that I know of anywhere exists, now, as did that apartment at the moment before Weintraub hove into view through the entry doorway with Samantha-Marie in tow, for all the world like some tiny burly tug hauling, not some great ocean liner, but a sleek black-hulled racing yacht. His formidable voice, always too loud anyway, continued the metaphor and served as the tug's deep, belching steam horn, announcing to the rest of the harbor the acquisition of a new major prize, as he introduced her, hovered over by Louisa, to first one group and then to another.

"And this is your host Harry Gallagher," Weintraub's steam horn brawled.

"Hello, Mr. Gallagher. I know your films," Samantha said, and thrust her hand at him across the bar. She turned from me to Harry a smile that was much too ancient, much too ironic for any 19-year-old.

"This is some pad you got yourself here." She looked back down the room.

Down its length, polished Louis Treize refectory tables covered with art books and statuettes glistened in the fading sunlight. Around them Louis Treize fauteuils or smaller armchairs clustered, where people sat and talked or stood. Against the inner wall sat a rare hexagonal Louis Treize chess table, with the pieces laid out in some opening. On every bit of available wall space were paintings. The French windows were open on the summery May twilight, and the breeze riffled the white under-curtains, which had been drawn back against the drapes, to let the windows open and let in the night air.

Harry looked at it, too. "What can I get you to drink?" he smiled.

"I never drink," the dark girl said. "I might smoke a little if you've got some. A little pot? Otherwise, just give me a Coke. I love Coke. I like you," she smiled.

Harry went at once onto the defensive. "Well, I like you, too. Or I'm sure I will, when we get to know each other a little better." He looked flustered, and confused. He busied himself fixing her Coke.

"Oh, you will," Samantha said. She accepted the Coke gravely. Then suddenly she laughed, a rich, high, girlish tinkle, vastly amused.

I thought—we all thought—that she was darling. But I thought I just ought to cough a little here. Ferenc Hofmann-Beck had been entertaining us at the bar with one of his famous French-namedropping routines, when Samantha and Weintraub came up. Ferenc, thoughtfully, took my cough as his cue to continue.

Ferenc Hofmann-Beck had been coming to the Gallaghers for about three months at this time. He had met Harry and Louisa at a party somewhere and had fallen madly in love with both of them, but particularly with Louisa, and had sent her a huge mass of flowers the next day with a card asking if he might telephone. When he telephoned, he begged that he might come by on one of her Sunday evenings Louisa often had, was invited, and had been coming ever since.

Ferenc resembled nothing quite so much as a huge, cuddly, reddish-colored, American brown bear. Strong as an ox, and shaped exactly like an upright pear, he affected, or truly believed that he had, a condition of permanent ill health brought on by his liver. He had once had hepatitis years ago. His dull, carefully tailored English suits complete with matching waistcoats made him look like one of those roundbottomed dolls from your childhood which you could not knock over. He wore a Baron's coronet on his monogrammed shirts and handkerchieves, but suavely never mentioned whether he was a Baron or not. In fact, his grandfather Hofmann-Beck had been a Baron, in the long-evaporated Austro-Hungarian Empire of Franz Josef; and Ferenc knew by heart the right name and title, if there was one, of just about every family in Europe. He was a walking Debrett's. He had a serious eating problem of which he made much fun, hated all forms of violence including the bloodless, cocktail-party variety, and could easily have been mistaken for some kind of a fag if you did not have a good eye. Lately he had taken to wearing a monocle: a scallop-edged one: the latest, chicest type: which he would fix in his eye or fiddle with to punctuate his poking fun at French society engaged in a spelling-match, namedropping contest. Now he fixed his monocle and peered at all of us, but especially at Samantha, putting on his thickest Hungarian accent.

"As I wass sayink about the O'Donnells." Someone at the bar had mentioned the name O'Donnell. "O'Donnell? O'Donnell? Mit two Ns and two Ls? I knew such an O'Donnell in Boston. Two Ns and two Ls. Peasants. Bums. Family had to leaf Ireland durink the second famine. Made money. But American money doesn't make peasants not peasants. My grandmother used to say the silk purse iss not from the ear of the sow made. But now, O'Donel! Mit one Ns and one Ls. I know such an O'Donel. In London. Big estates in Ireland. Two big estates. I vissited there. Very fine family. Grows horses.

"Ziss is rather like Gramont in French. Gramont mit one Ms is more chic than Grammont mit two Ms, though both are good. Gramont one Ms old and a duke. Grammont two Ms less old and only a baron. But hass wines.

"Ah, Miss Everton! Ve have not met! I am Hofmann-Beck."

He seized her hand and bowed over it without carrying it quite to his lips, clicked his heels and stepped back.

"Everton? Mit one Rs and one Ts? I knew some Everrettons outside London mit two Rs and two Ts. Very large house. Excellent gardens. Could be of you some relations?"

Samantha smiled at him. "Are any of them niggers?"

At the bar there was a sort of helpless, full-stop pause, of utter silence, a sort of consternation of silent helplessness.

"Actually, no," Ferenc said. "None are niggers."

He said it in his sweetest, politest voice, with no accent, and he smiled.

"Then I doubt if they're relations," Samantha smiled back.

A short while later Ferenc drifted away, down the room, and I don't blame him.

It certainly put a pall over the bar. Of course, Samantha probably could not really be expected to get the joke. She had never heard Ferenc's name-spelling routine before. But she ought to have heard the laughter at the bar as she came down the room. The joke of course was that in a suave, handsome way Ferenc was totally ignoring her color. Maybe she didn't want that. Perhaps it was just that she was diffident. That was what Louisa thought later.

A long time afterward, weeks afterward, Samantha herself, during one of several long talks we had, told me in all seeming honesty that she had thought it was a funny line, thought that it would get a big laugh at the bar. I find that hard to believe. It certainly got no big laugh. At the time I thought it was one of the most wantonly cruel things I had seen in a long time.

And yet, there was about her that gamin-like quality, so coltish and innocently young when it cropped out in her grin, that delighted. You were continually being suddenly brought up short by the realization that this child after all was really only 19 years old.

From behind us Louisa, sensing potential upset or dissension, had come back up.

"Isn't there something else I can get you? I mean, since you don't drink? Isn't there something else you'd like to have, my dear?"

Samantha smiled at her, warmly. "Well, I don't suppose you'd have any—" She stopped. She looked at Louisa a long moment, smiling. "No, you wouldn't," she said. Then she smiled again, warmly, almost lovingly. "I think you're beautiful."

Louisa blushed right up to the roots of her hair. "Oh, now!" she said, in a sort of confused breathless way.

"I really think you're one of the most beautiful women I've ever seen. I love you," Samantha smiled. "I'll tell you. What I'd really like, is a Hershey chocolate bar. With almonds? I don't suppose you'd have any of those, would you."

"I do!" Louisa cried. "I do!" She was suddenly all eager eyes and bony smile. She positively glowed at the idea of doing something for this girl. "I do have some! I've got stacks of them, loads of them." She turned on her heel toward the kitchen door in the corner. "Our daughter happens to be an addict of Hershey chocolate bars with almonds."

I looked down the room to where my Godchild lay stretched out in front of the empty fireplace. McKenna was all curled up like some half-grown kitten, oblivious of the party all around her, her gold hair hanging over her face as she read one of her perpetual Tin-Tin books. Tin-Tin was a young French comic strip character, who had all sorts of adventures with a bearded sea captain as his sidekick. Not even quite eight yet, she could already read like a ten-year-old. I remember, now, how completely secure she looked there. Her hair caught glints from the various lamp fixtures in the room, and their overlapping lights and shadow lit up softly the small-nosed, wide-eyed, serious little-girl face.

"Can I have three or four?" Sam Everton asked, when Louisa came back with the box.

"Take all you want!" Louisa pulled out a stack of them like letter envelopes.

"Thank you. Thank you. I really do love you," Samantha said, and leaned forward on her stool and kissed the taller woman lightly on the cheek.

"Oh, now!" Louisa said, and blushed again. "Come on, now! It's only candy."

Samantha drifted away from the bar herself shortly after that, holding her stack of Hershey bars. Later, I was talking to Fred Singer the TV commentator by the chess table, and happened to glance down the room and saw that Samantha was lying on the floor with Mc-Kenna. The two of them were lying on their bellies side by side, propped up on their elbows, contentedly munching Hershey bars, and reading the stack of childish Tin-Tin books with equally complete absorption. I knew McKenna did not make friends easily. Soon after that, Samantha and Weintraub left. "She's taking me to some orgy," Weintraub whispered, grinning.

"Orgy!" Sam said, looking at him contemptuously. "Orgy! Orgy!"

"It's the truth!" Weintraub whispered to me, grinning.

I went back up the room to Harry, and the bar.

Ah, that bar.

Was there ever such a bar existed anywhere, in such an apartment?

I guess Harry's bar needs a whole paragraph to itself. It got to be famous in Paris. It was a wooden Renaissance pulpit, made over. What the French call a *chaire,* one of those pulpits which hang up on a column in the church, with a circular staircase mounting to it. In Harry's apartment it stood on the floor. He had hunted two years for it, to find it. It cost him a lot; and it cost him almost as much to have his *ébéniste* fix it up for him. The *ébéniste* repaired it, gave it a new, raised floor of ancient wood, and fitted it with two bar shelves of the same, for bottles. It was a five-sided object, with one side open at the back for the drink server (or priest) to enter. The other four sides were of wood panels, with peaked arches carved across their tops, below which dim worn figures carved in very low relief and vague with age could be presumed to be doing something religious. It jutted out from the far end wall of the room like the nose of a PT boat cresting a wave.

Harry had once seen one in an antique shop in St.-Germain, thought it would make a great bar, only to find it had been sold the day before, and then had waited two years to find another. It was the showpiece of the entire collection of things. It was also one of Harry's most prized possessions.

"After all," he liked to say, and said it often, especially when in his cups, "what are the *real* fucking churches of today, in mid twentieth century? Where is the one fucking place where a modern city man can go if he wants a dim, quiet place to commune with himself?

"Where nobody will fucking bother him. Or make him feel guilty. Or tell him what he ought to do or believe. Or try to change his philosophy or ideology or faith. Where in short he can be by himself in quiet contemplation and suck spiritual nourishment from the liquid Communion in his hand and clarify his head. Where! BARS! That's where! And that's the only where!"

Ah, that bar.

Behind it Harry had had the entire end wall covered with a pleated, silver-beige velvet curtain, to accentuate it. No paintings hung there. And against this drapery, on the one side leaned a beautifully made sixteenth-century German executioner's sword; and on the other, head down, leaned a horribly crudely made, brutally hammered, steel thirteenth-century executioner's axe with a brass studded, unlathed and unturned pole handle.

"The three greatest things mankind has given to the world!" Harry liked to say, waving at the three of them.

He meant, I gathered from questions I asked him after the first time I heard him say it, by the third "thing" not so much the exquisite sword itself as its clear evidence when compared to the axe, of man's vast and divine increase in mechanical dexterity, within which Harry hastened to include both the Industrial Revolution and our own Technological Revolution as well.

As if all this were not sacrilegious enough to suit him, or perhaps one could even say funny enough, humorous enough, Harry had completed the whole tableau with a clutch of five bar stools which were not bar stools at all but in reality those hardest to find and most expensive for their size Louis Treize items of all: the prie-Dieu prayer stools. There is a story that the first time Buñuel ever came to the place, he peered at Harry's bar and its accouterments and then seized the two-handed German sword and tried to cleave Harry from shoulder to waist as he carried a tray of glasses in from the kitchen, crying, "You son of a bitch! You son of a bitch! My mother used to pray on a prayer stool just like that!" And rushed from the house. Later, of course, he sent an apology.

In fact, "Harry's Bar" (everyone made the obvious pun on Harry MacElhone's New York Bar on the rue Daunou) had picked up quite a singular history all its own in its seven years of existence. Certain dedicated Catholics, though known to be hard drinkers themselves, had walked out of the house after seeing it. Several times there had been drunken near-fistfights over it right there in the living room. It had been dedicated by James Baldwin the first night Harry unveiled it, with a hellfire sermon on the evils of drink.

Ah, that bar.

Harry instituted a set of ground rules regarding it. The drunken political, social, racial, philosophical and artistic discussions got so hot and heavy around that bar that finally no one could get a word in edgeways, and if he did, could not hear himself, let alone the others. So one night Harry drew up rules. We had a lovely pulpit, why not use it? Therefore, in any future discussions, anyone who wished could *"Invoke the Pulpit"* by simply saying so. The invoker would then be allowed to mount behind the bar and for a measured five minutes could have his say, all alone, while the room remained silent. This would be followed by an optional five-minute question period, at the discretion of speaker and audience. There were cries of applause and of "I invoke the pulpit!" from all over the room, and the ground rules remained. Harry had them printed and framed and hung them up behind the bar on the silver-beige drape.

As I have said, it is with more than just a touch of sadness that I remember it. That apartment, and that bar. I imagine it closed and darkened, with the shining tables and rich fauteuils, antiques and statuettes all gathering dust in the gloom. I imagine it like that, even though I know that Harry has kept on a Portuguese maid to come in and take care of it twice a week. I am a romantic fool.

Ah, that bar.

I suppose that we are a generation of drunks, as Hill's younger generation are all the time so loudly proclaiming. I have talked with them about it, and about the cowardice, wastage, and lack of responsibility in it. But I fail to see much difference between that and the pot-smoking and LSD-taking of their generation: and the slush-brained pot-heads, acid-heads, dropouts and even junkies that they produce.

If we have failed to much change the world we inherited from *our* parents, and have not given *them,* our offspring, any real moral precepts to go by, they do not understand that the generation of our parents failed even more to change the world *they* inherited, and gave *us* even less by way of any honest moral outlook. And I can't help but wonder what *their* children will be like, if and when they have them, whether we are drunks or not.

And I suppose we are. I suppose we might go down in history (in this new cataloging of the generations that has become so popular) as "The Drunk Generation", were it not that we have before us as example the generation of Faulkner and Fitzgerald and Hemingway— The "Lost" Generation—all nervously itching to take the credit, and jealously yelling "We did it first!", while monitoring us, guiding us, leading us by the hand toward the concept that alcohol is the panacea for all pain and despair, while at the same time claiming the heavy consumption of it to be the quintessence of manliness.

Ah, that bar. I suppose most of all I miss those hot and heavy drunken discussions we used to have around it.

That was the Thursday night. The next night was the night of the Friday of May 10th, and the Great Battle of the rue Gay-Lussac.

I suppose it is silly, even dumb, to talk about that battle now at this late date. But at the time it was very important. It was really the first major turning point of the May Revolution, and from it the whole Revolution proceeded, probably.

Yet, I think the real May Revolution began at some point during the day on that Thursday of May the 9th. Some time during that Thursday the people of Paris went over to the side of the students. And I think they did it, and it began, in gaiety and a sort of hedonistic social irresponsibility, which passed by osmosis from the students to the populace of Paris. People just suddenly did not want to work for the Patronat, the Establishment any more, at least not for a while.

I know many believe it began the next night, the "Black Friday" of May 10th, when the night battle on the rue Gay-Lussac so outraged the French with its police brutality. But I believe they were already on the side of the students, and that there would have been no great night battle if the students had now known this. Certainly it was the students who set the battle up, and forced the police into it.

When more than three hundred people are hospitalized after a night of barricades (and there were many, many more than that, who preferred not to give themselves up to a hospital and be arrested for it) —when that happens, it is bound to be an important event with big impact. We followed it on our transistor radios at the Gallaghers, on both the Europe Number One and Radio Luxembourg stations. As usual, the French Government-owned television and radio said almost nothing about the fact that there was a student uprising.

It began late, after two A.M., and everybody had left the Gallaghers long before that. I had gone out to dinner and come back later because we were all wondering about Hill. Student leaders had been negotiating with M. Roche at the Sorbonne all through the evening, still about their same three demands, and the students themselves used the time to prepare themselves well; they built barricades in depth all over the upper half of the Quartier: rue Gay-Lussac; rue St. Jácques; rue d'Ulm; rue Lhomond; Place Contrescarpe; rue de l'Estrapade. The police, under orders to wait, could only stand at the ends of the streets and watch. Finally, shortly after two A.M., the negotiations broke down and the police were ordered to charge, to clear the streets, and the battle was on. Finally it coalesced itself in two spots, Contrescarpe, and Gay-Lussac.

Gay-Lussac was apparently far the worse. Fred Singer the TV man finished his nightly reportage and came back from there on his way home, and seeing the lights on in the apartment, came up. He was red-eyed and weeping and his nose was running copiously. "The damned CRS are beating up everybody. Strangers, foreigners, newsmen, photographers. I almost got beat up myself. And for a minute I thought we were going to get our equipment smashed."

The students had piled up cars parked in the street and set them afire. They were dropping Molotov cocktails down off the roofs of the buildings. The police kept on throwing in more and more tear gas. "I don't see how they stand it," Fred said, sniffling. "I didn't get anywhere near the heart of it, and I couldn't stand it." Harry made him a stiff drink.

It was too far away for us to see or hear anything from the windows. But an eerie glow lit up the night sky over Montparnasse, above the Left Bank houses.

We had the two American painters, one of them a woman, with us now. They were afraid to try to get home. There were no barricades near their area yet, but a lot of people were out and there was much activity in the street.

At one point Harry and I decided to go out. We would sally forth up to Montparnasse to watch the battle still raging up and down Gay-Lussac. But then Louisa said that if we went, she was going too.

Louisa's bright eyes were feverishly bright now, and her long-jawed face was grim with a kind of frenetic righteousness. If we were going out to look and take a chance on getting ourselves hurt, she was absolutely going, too. And if we were going out to get involved, she was going to get involved, also. She had a son out there. She had a son out there, too, she said. Harry took one look at her, and said she absolutely could not go, and that if it meant all that much to her, he would not go either. She subsided. But her face fell and she seemed depressed, and she began to brood, quietly.

As a sort of placating compromise, I offered to telephone a literary friend, an American writer who lived on a small street that crossed rue Gay-Lussac, the rue de l'Abbé de l'Épée, to see how things were. When I got him on the line, he advised us not to come out at all. "Things are really bad up here, Jack," he said, "I wouldn't try it." The agitation and excitement in his voice were apparent on the phone. "I'm not even going out myself. The police are really cracking down tonight. We've got half a dozen hurt students in here now my wife and I are trying to give first aid to, and every half hour there are three or four more taking refuge in our court. I don't see how these kids can stand it out there. Even the police, with masks, can't go into that tear gas they've laid down on Gay-Lussac. And yet these kids stick right in there and won't leave or retreat."

"All right, Clem," I said. "Thanks a lot. I guess we won't go." This was obviously something quite different than what I had seen the afternoon before.

We did not hear from Hill that night, nor did we hear from him the next day, Saturday.

In the morning we walked up to Montparnasse and rue Gay-Lussac to view the devastation. Lots of other people were out to look, too. It looked like a war had passed by. Turned-over and burnt-out cars littered the entire street in a series of fought-over barricades. Store windows were broken out, and some storefronts were burned black. The usual glass and debris, twisted metal signs, paving stones, and blackened fire filth were everywhere. Cordons of tough-looking police now held the street, and gave you a rough looking-over before allowing you through. You had to have business there or you could not get through. I gave my writer friend's name and address, in my best American accent. After a drink with him and his wife, who were high and excited, but exhausted, from their night of Red Cross work, we went back to the Gallaghers' to find that no word at all had come from Hill while we were gone.

That was the Saturday, you will remember, that M. Pompidou returned posthaste from Afghanistan. Only four hours later, and after more than 36 hours without sleep, the Prime Minister went on TV with a tight but remarkably well-delivered speech giving in to all the student demands. From it he emerged with a considerably enhanced, if slightly ragged-looking, dignity. Certainly it enhanced his popularity. "The great Zorro arrives in the nick of time to save the day," one Government official was quoted in the paper as saying. It was certainly something Monsieur le Général de Gaulle would never have accepted to do.

Hill did not call Saturday night, either. Saturday seemed to be a sort of night off for everybody, while police and students both patched up their ranks and their wounds.

8

Sunday was always a day off for everybody, student Revolutionaries and police alike. I suppose a lot of them went to church, and then had a big Sunday dinner.

Actually, student groups were meeting with workers' committees and union committees all that day.

I had news that afternoon late, when I walked down the quiet treelined quai to the Gallaghers for what had now become a recognized daily ritual. Hill had telephoned me just before I left to go to his parents.

"Where in the hell have you been!" I cried.

There was a kind of strange, frustrated pause at the other end. Then he said, "I've been busy. Haven't you heard about the great battle?"

I was outraged. "Do you have any idea at all how worried we have been about you! Never mind me, but your mother and dad! Why in the name of God didn't you telephone?"

"I don't think you understand, Uncle Jack," Hill said tersely. "We've got a lot of sick people on our hands here, and we've got to take care of them. Somebody's got to."

This slowed me down a little. I could imagine him in some loft, like the one he had roughly described to me, surrounded by wounded and moaning students covered with blood. "Well, is everything all right?"

"I'm okay," Hill said, "if that's what you mean. That's why I telephoned."

"I gathered that. And I will tell your folks. But what I meant was, well, all the rest of it."

"We're making out. We're making out. As well as can be expected."

"Can I help? Do you want me to come over there?"

There was a pause. "What could *you* do?"

"Well, I'm still pretty expert at first aid."

"We're past the first aid stage, we're into the medical. Now, we need oxygen, and anesthetics, and bandages, and medications. Do you know any doctors?"

"I know so-and-so and so-and-so," I mentioned two doctors that I went to, and who were friends of mine.

"They've both been here, volunteering their help already. There's really nothing you can do, Uncle Jack, really."

"Well, don't hang up for a minute. Tell me, were you out in the middle of all that?"

"Sure. And I think I got some pretty good shots. Tell Dad that. I won't know till we get them developed, and there's no place in Paris we can trust to send them to. The Government apparently has put a tag on all the photo-developing places with the idea of confiscating student film, if it is brought in. So we'll have to wait. The light was very bad, and we did not have any artificial lighting. And you know how it is with a hand-held camera, especially when you're breathing hard and standing unbalanced."

"Well," I said, "at least you have won, anyway, all of you. Pompidou has given in on all three of the student demands. The Sorbonne will be open on Monday."

His voice was almost a snarl. "Are you kidding? Pompidou's offer is only a token acceptance, to slow us down and cool us off a little. They will 'discuss reforms' with us, they say. Well, we're not quitting now. If the Sorbonne opens on Monday, we will occupy it." His voice suddenly got cautious. "And we may occupy something else, as well!"

What on earth could they occupy besides the Sorbonne? I wondered. The Assemblée Nationale? that would be real war. The huge Government TV and radio building; on the Avenue du Président Kennedy: the O.R.T.F.?

"Then you're not satisfied?" I said.

"Satisfied? You should be where I've been for the past thirty-six hours, and then talk about satisfied. No, we're not satisfied."

"Where are you now, Hill?"

"I'm calling from a pay phone in a café in the Place Contrescarpe."

I knew that area. There were ancient old lofts all over, all around that area, and on the rue Mouffetard. That was "Hemingway country", as George Plimpton might say.

"Well, where is it that you are staying?"

"I don't think I better tell you, Uncle Jack. The police are still out after us, you know. They'd love to find a loft full of us, wounded, and take us in to some hospital to show their humanitarian intentions. And then arrest us."

"I wish you'd call your folks yourself," I said.

"I can't. You tell them for me. That's why I called you. You're going down there now, aren't you? Jesus!" he said. "Can't you imagine it? Mother would be insisting to know whether I had my raincoat and my rubbers. Dad would be giving me revolutionary advice: 'Now, son, this is the way we did it in 1936.' No, thanks. They've never let me do anything on my own in my life. They've protected me."

"I don't think you're being fair to them, Hill," I said.

"Listen, Uncle Jack, I've got to hang up."

Some gleeful devil rose up in me. "And how is Anne-Marie taking all this?"

"Anne-Marie? Oh, she's having the time of her life. You never saw such energy, and bravery. People like her are in their glory in something like this."

"—" I could imagine.

"You've got a thing against her, haven't you?" Hill said. "You just don't understand. You don't understand that we don't believe in one-woman, one-man monogamy. We believe in love for all, love given to all, and accepted by all."

"I know, I know," I said.

"Listen, Uncle Jack, I've got to hang up."

"Well, I'll tell your folks," I said.

"I'm still your old buddy," he said.

That really made me feel bad. "I know."

"So long. I'll keep in touch."

He hung up, and the phone went dead.

I called Harry and Louisa immediately after, so they would not be kept in suspense about Hill longer than necessary.

"I'll fill you in on all the details when I get down there," I said.

Harry met me at the door. The apartment was already half full of people, the regular gang that was coming regularly every day now. "Come into the bedroom," Harry said. "Louisa's waiting. We can talk in there." I followed him, down the long hallway, away from the living room and the entrée.

"I guess it's my ego," Harry said. "But I just don't want those people to know Hill called you, instead of me."

Louisa was up on the bed, a mass of the satin throw-pillows against her back. She did not look depressed, or moody. She had on one of her at-home robes, and her hair was tied back. She had been cooking her curry in the kitchen apparently. The smell of it was delicious in the hall and in the entrée, when I came in. Instead of the normal daily gathering, this was to be one of her old-fashioned, pre-Revolutionary Sunday evenings. And she seemed in fine form, which sort of surprised me.

I told them everything Hill and I had said. They were interested, were not upset, and did not even ask any questions, except when I told them Hill had called from a café. "Where?" they said together. I told them Place Contrescarpe. They knew that area of old buildings and lofts as well as I did. It was actually only a very short walk from where we were sitting. We had all walked there many times.

"He just does not want any help from any of us," I kept saying over and over. "He insists this is something he has to do, and wants to do, on his own."

They seemed to take this easily enough.

"I think Hill doesn't understand that we are on his side," Harry said.

"I think he does," I disagreed. "And I think that that is exactly what he does not want. I think he would much rather have you be against the students, like the other parents."

"I don't think the parents are against the students," Harry said. "Not the French."

"Well, some of them must be," I said. "From what I've heard."

"Maybe not," Harry said, "maybe not."

Louisa suddenly got up off the bed in a bustling way. "Well, I'm going back to the kitchen. I have got to look after my curry. I'll be out in a few minutes."

She gave a distinct impression she did not want to be followed, and neither Harry or I followed her.

"I hope you won't say anything about Hill to the gathered assembly," Harry said, with a strange sort of gallant laugh, as we walked back down the hall.

"Sure," I said. "Of course, not. Of course, I won't."

But somehow it irritated me that he should ask it a second time.

The long salon was filling up with people when we came out into it. All of the old bunch who had been coming by every day were there, plus a number of others. There must have been 12 or 14 people, already in the room.

Louisa Gallagher's Sunday evenings had become quite a famous thing in Paris over the past six years. They were more known, though, in the Artist's Quarter than in the American business community. They had begun more by accident than by deliberate intent. Because all three of her Portuguese domestics had the full day off on Sunday, Louisa had started making curry on Sunday evenings, since they had to stay home to look after McKenna. Louisa could make a delicious, real Indian curry. A few people started dropping by, by accident, and then came back. The word got around, and more people tried to get invited. Louisa did not try to make a thing out of it, it was very informal. But she and Harry refused to let it become an open house where the people could come without being asked. Mainly we were artists, painters, writers, a few gallery owners; almost all from the Quarter; and of all nationalities. Hill sometimes brought groups of his French and American student friends. There was a smattering of movie people Harry knew. There was a smattering of people from the American business community, the established bankers, lawyers, engineers, and corporation people. The business community people came once, or twice, and then somehow did not come again.

I do not think it was because of any especial temperamental difference. I think we just made them uneasy. We were a pretty fiery bunch. We discussed everything. Nothing was sacred. There was a lot of drinking. There were a lot of four-letter words spoken, though Louisa never used them and neither did I. It was bound to make them uneasy. And I think the business community wives took a quiet but determined dislike to Louisa. It was as if, even though Louisa never spoke them herself, they felt she should not have tolerated the bad language or allowed it in her house—especially in front of her child daughter.

I gradually came to suspect that some of the men of the American business community, though not all, would have liked to come again, and again. But their wives were not about to let them.

Louisa, of course, could not have cared less.

That Sunday there did not appear to be any of the American business community present.

Harry and I walked up toward the pulpit bar.

McKenna was at one of the refectory tables, absorbed in some tiny homework she had to do for her school, and she came running over to me with her arms out, to be picked up, tossed and kissed by her Godfather. She was getting harder to toss. She was growing, a lot.

At the bar a group was talking over the events of the weekend: the surprising return of Pompidou, his even more surprising speech and acceptance of the students' demands.

The latest news was that a nationwide one-day general strike was being called for Tuesday the 14th, to protest "Police Repression". Electricity, gas, water, transportation, telephone, telegraph, mail and taxi service would all be affected. Everybody was coming out on the side of the students. There would be no Monday afternoon or Tuesday morning newspapers. Banks, schools and many businesses would close. Students, teachers and workers would be on the march all across France to protest "repression".

The feeling at the bar was that it was all over but the shouting. Someone said the phrase "The Students' One-Week War", and others picked it up. There was elation at the bar over the students' win, but there was a nostalgia for the now-finished Revolution. They were all so certain that it was finished. But I could not forget my picture of Hill, and the things he had said on the phone.

Down at the end of the room Weintraub came in with Samantha-Marie. Louisa apparently had invited them. They made their way toward us slowly, shaking hands and saying hello.

Several others more had come in before them and there were now 18 or 20 people in the room and two of them were black people. One was a slender, beautifully muscled dancer from the Folies Bergère, a friend of Louisa's, and of Harry's too, but more of Louisa's. The other was an old, aged painter, poor but famous in New York and Paris for ten or 15 years, who had the courtly manners of an old-time Virginia gentleman. He was a good painter. Weintraub introduced her to them. If Samantha felt any surprise or chagrin or anything else at seeing two other American blacks here, she gave no indication. And yet somehow I had a suspicion that she did.

From her table McKenna ran out to meet her and clasp her around the knees. Samantha patted her head and kissed her. McKenna rarely ran to kiss anybody, and I found myself feeling jealous.

Our discussion at the bar had centered itself on the question of whether the students would try to take over and occupy the Sorbonne tomorrow as they had threatened. Someone had asked if they would. Now that Pompidou had declared it would open.

"They'd be crazy to," Harry said. I stared at him. He went right on blandly. "Pompidou's given in to them on their demands. What's the point? Now's the time for them to sit down with the Government and negotiate. Get the reforms they want for the University. Not keep the Sorbonne closed down."

"Don't you believe it! They aint about to do it!" Weintraub boomed, coming up. He had his arm around Samantha.

At the bar Ferenc Hofmann-Beck, who up to now had been one of the most talkative, slipped off his stool and moved away. He gave Samantha a low bow as he passed her, and a sweet smile, his monocle in his fingers. He did not come back.

"But why?" Fred Singer the TV commentator said. "I have to agree with Harry. What's the point? After Pompidou's agreed to all their demands."

"Because they don't trust the Government," Weintraub bellowed in his deepest basso. "That's why. Every time the Government has given its word on something, and things have started to calm down, the

Government reneges on its word again and forces the students a step further. And then they turn loose their jackals, the police, and claim it was all the students' fault." I thought it sounded almost like Hill.

"That's true," Fred Singer said. "The Government *has* been playing a both-ends-against-the-middle game."

"All governments always do," I put in sourly. "Look at our own." Almost all of us were against the Vietnam war, if not for moral and political reasons, then for strategic and tactical ones. The Paris talks about it would be opening here tomorrow, in the midst of all this. This whole discussion was boring me suddenly.

"That's true enough," Harry said to me. Then to Weintraub, "If those kids want to play with grown-ups, they better learn how dirty it's going to be, when they finally get out there."

"They're learning," Weintraub said. "They're learning damn fast. The students want a firm, solid bargaining position," Weintraub said in his deepest voice. "And they believe the only way they can have that is to keep the Sorbonne closed and occupied." He sounded as if he was quoting some student leader.

"Then maybe they should occupy it," Harry said. Suddenly he scratched irritably at the close-clipped hair alongside his bald, sharp-ridged skull. "But hell, you know the police could throw them out of there any minute they choose."

"The police wouldn't dare right now," Weintraub said. "And the Government wouldn't dare let them. What do you think this big strike is all about? Everybody's on the side of the students. Even the shop-keepers on rue Gay-Lussac who had their shops burned, are on their side.

"And those kids are mad," he said. "Do you know nobody knows how many people were hurt Friday night? Literally hundreds haven't turned themselves in to the hospitals."

"Where do you get all your information, Dave?" I said thinly, and looked at Harry.

Weintraub's arm around Samantha had slipped down until his hand was on her hip, and now he threw out his burly little chest. He made one of his dramatic pauses. "From the kids," he intoned deeply. "From the kids themselves. That's where." He turned to Harry. "And your kid Hill is one of them. Incidentally, he's all right."

"Yes. Yes, we know he's all right," Harry said. "He's been calling us."

"Well, he told me to tell you that," Weintraub said, a little more defensively.

"Probably showing off to his buddies," Harry said, easily. "I guess it's not popular to be in with your parents right now."

I wanted to take some of the weight off. "Where did you see them, Dave?"

Weintraub was delighted to tell. He took his arm from around Samantha to give himself oratory room. He had met a group of them, at a little café-tabac in the Carrefour Odéon, a place called the Monaco, where a lot of American beatniks used to hang out years ago, and where he himself still went sometimes because it was cheap. I knew the Monaco, and it was a pretty low dive. Anyway, Dave had seen this group of kids, students obviously, all huddled up over a table in the back every day, and finally one day he noticed Hill was with them and started talking to them. They were all students of Cinema at the Sorbonne and most of them were studying Sociology too, like Hill, and they were planning what they were going to do when the Sorbonne was occupied, as all of the student groups had voted for. They were the leaders of a special *Comité du Cinéma des Étudiants* which was assigned the job of photographing the Revolution, the occupation of the Sorbonne, and everything that happened after that until the end of the Revolution, whenever that might be. They all expected a lot more fighting. From their footage they intended to make a film which would show the world the real Students' Revolution of France. When he described some of them, like Anne-Marie, and Terri of the long hair, and Bernard the bearded one, I recognized Hill and his group who had been to see me. Weintraub had offered them his help in any way he could be of help, and they had accepted it. They had a sort of perpetual rendezvous to meet at the Monaco every afternoon at three or three-thirty, if any of them could at all possibly make it; and they had invited Weintraub to come, too. He had seen them there this afternoon. None of them had been hurt Friday night.

"This afternoon?" Harry said, and gave me a look. "At the Monaco? You saw them?" Hill had told me he was calling from the Place Contrescarpe. But there was no discrepancy in that.

"Yes," Weintraub said. "Why? You know, the great thing is that they've brought the workers into it, now. They tell me delegations of the students have been working like hell all week to do that, going out to the factories, and the auto assembly plants. That's the important thing."

"That's abso*lute*ly true," Fred Singer put in, "that's going to make all the difference come Tuesday."

We were suddenly off into another discussion, about the workers now, and their plans, their demands, and their hopes for wage increases. Above this, Harry gave me a knowing, sort of conspiratorial look. But I did not know what he meant to do, or convey. It was perfectly possible that Hill could have been at both Contrescarpe and Odéon during the afternoon, and it didn't make any difference if he had, or even if he had not. I couldn't read what Harry was trying to signal.

Then suddenly Samantha Everton, Weintraub's little "mistress", who had said practically nothing at all up to now, burst into the discussion with both her pretty feet.

"I think it's all a lot of bullcrap," she said to us all with a covering grin, but there was an edge to her voice.

I think it was then that I first began to think of her as "Sam". She had said before she liked to be called that. Instead of Samantha, or Samantha-Marie. I think it was the grin that did it.

9

HARRY GRINNED AT HER. "Say shit," he said. "Bullshit. You can say bullshit here."

"Then, bull*shit*. I say, it's all a lot of bullshit."

"What is?" Harry said.

"The Students' Revolution. They're not going to change anything." She grinned up at Harry from the stool she had slipped onto. "Incidentally, I met your son, too. This afternoon. He's a nice boy."

"Yes. Well," Harry said. Then after a minute, "I'm glad he's all right. He is a nice boy."

"He's a lovely boy," Sam said. "But he's much too young, and much too idealistic, for me."

"He has your age."

"I know. Yes. But he hasn't my experience. I like them older, when they've been around a little."

"And you don't think the students are going to change anything?" Harry said.

"Men like you," Sam grinned at him. "What? Change anything?" She raised her voice, and the rest at the bar stopped talking to hear. "Certainly not. No, they won't change anything. Oh, they'll make the old folks give them a few little concessions and reforms. But they won't change anything. Revolutions can't happen in the kind of highly organized societies we live in today. And I'm not so sure they should happen. Look at what their Revolution cost the Russians. Anyway, today everybody's got to have his electricity and his water and his gas and his automobile. But Revolution? That's all horseshit. The TV wouldn't work."

Weintraub had put his arm around her, after finishing his oratory, and his hand now rested on the curve of her hip, just at the bone. Beside me, Sam twitched her hip irritably, and Weintraub's hand disappeared from it as if shot away. "These kids are out there in the streets having the time of their lives. They're having *their* 'war'. They're playing games. They're getting their kicks. All getting their rocks off. That's the truth about it all!" She grinned her street Arab grin at us all.

"I take it you don't think the Students' Revolt of Paris is very important," Harry grinned at her.

"No, not very."

"She just got in from America, you know," Weintraub said.

"Sure, I just got in from America. But I've lived in France. Quite a lot. I went to school here two years." Her voice got sing-song, "And I've been in CORE. And I've been a SNICK worker. And I've been SDS. Students are all assholes and jerks. If I could ever find one person who didn't have personal ambition mixed in with his altruism. If I could find one. Students give me a royal pain in the ass."

"What about Mickey Schwerner, and those other two boys?" Harry said. "Chaney and Goodman."

"James Chaney and Andy Goodman. What about them? They're dead," Samantha said. "That was a long time ago. So what about them? They knew what they were getting into. Or should have. They knew the chance they were taking. They went down there. Those two white Jewish boys were white Northern assholes. They were fools. They didn't believe those crazy rednecks would ever kill them. And the nigger, James Chaney, knew the chance he was taking in his home country. They all wanted to be there."

She shifted her little, high Negro behind on the old seventeenth-century prayer stool. "Oh, it's all sexual, all of that, down there, don't you know? At least for the white men. And probly for the niggers. Did you ever read that book? That Huie book? Did that man Huie ever speculate on how much the crazy redneck sexuality might have played in the murder of those three boys? No."

"He alluded to it," Harry said.

"But did he ever speculate on the real meanings of his allusions? All those white women making those crazy obscene phone calls about orgies at the Center? Down there, every crazy redneck believes black girls wiggle their ass better, and know how to clamp down inside better. And every white woman believes every black man's got a big enormous schlong, and can go on screwing all night long. They hate their white men for screwing nigger gals. And the rednecks are terrified of being cuckolded by big black bucks. And rightly so. Because if their white women don't do it, they sure as hell think about it. No, down there it's all sexual, sick redneck sex. They're not very swinging cats, those New York sociology cats. Not if they think they can answer *that* with some sociology textbook about the Rights of Man. The textbook hasn't been written yet about down there."

"You sound like you know the South pretty well," Harry said.

"Well, I've been down there," Sam said. "Students. Students make me laugh. You all make me laugh." She slid down off her bar stool. She had no drink. "Your students'll get their reforms. Or watered down half-assed versions of them. And so what? Meanwhile they're all out there running and yelling and having themselves a vacation, playing cops and robbers. They're enjoying it, you're enjoying it, the police're enjoying it, and the French're enjoying it. It's a bore. I'd rather talk about dancing."

I came in, here. "Do you feel that same way about the race riots in the States?" I simply could not not ask it.

She gave me a smile. "Sure, pretty much. But when I was there we had some guns, and we killed a few people, and we burned down some warehouses. There, at least old nigger ladies are smart enough to steal themselves a free new TV set out of it. But as for changing society, changing the world—" She shook her head. "The world," she said, and paused as if searching for an unaccustomed word, "the world *absorbs* *everything.* Finally. I wonder if anybody's talking about anything interesting down at the other end." And she walked away.

"Hey, that's pretty pro*found!*" Weintraub bawled from the bar. He made as if to go with her, but she gave him such a look of contemptuous dislike that he stopped. He turned back to the bar. She went off alone. Down the room, I saw Louisa come over to her.

Her talk effectively put a damper over the discussion at the bar. But in a minute it got going again. This time it was still about the workers, and about how far they might go on the side of the students. But it tapered off. People left the bar to walk down the room. Finally only Harry, Weintraub and I were left. We huddled together at one end. Harry wanted to know more about Samantha.

She had come on from New York, Weintraub told us, to Paris on her way to Israel, and had run out of money. In fact, that was incorrect, he said. She had come on from New York knowing she did not have enough money to get to Israel, but figuring something or other would turn up here to get her to Israel.

"What about her mother? What about Rosalie?" Harry said.

"Well, her mother doesn't give her any money apparently," Weintraub said. "She claims her mother doesn't have much money." She was going to Israel to live for a while with a friend.

"A boyfriend?" Harry said.

"Well, no," Weintraub said. "A *girl*friend. A Sabra girl." There was something about the way he said it.

"My God!" Harry said. "A *Sabra* lesbian?"

"Why not?"

"She's a lesbian?"

"I suppose. I mean, that is what she seems to like." Weintraub tried a bluff grin. "But from personal experience I can say it would be hard to contend that she wasn't double-gaited."

"Well, come on. Tell us all, Weintraub," I said.

He puffed out his really quite deep chest like a pigeon. He did not need much urging. She had been sitting in Castel's in one of her little yé-yé outfits with a French girl whom Dave knew vaguely but only vaguely, nursing a Scotch and soda she didn't want. Castel, whom she knew from two years before, had bought her a bottle as a welcoming-back gesture. Dave had picked her up. She had been hoping someone would pick her up she told him, because she did not have anyplace to stay. She had gotten off the plane from New York that morning with ten dollars in her pocket. Her bags were locked up in a tin locker at the Invalides Aérogare. Weintraub had taken her home to his one-room, one-bed pad in his *pension*. He had been feeling vague and strange and not very much with it that night because it was last Tuesday and he had been out in the streets with the students for a while. His clothes and his hair stank of tear gas. So did his room in the rue Condé, when they got there. There had been a fight in the Carrefour Odéon. He had taken a shower and put some stuff in his eyes. When he came back down the hall in his robe, Sam was sitting nude on the bed edge. She had looked at him quizzically and asked if he wouldn't like for her to call the other girl, the French girl. He'd said what the hell, sure, why not; and she had. While they waited (she insisted that they wait) he had asked her why she hadn't let the other girl pick her up if that was her action, and she said she had tried but the other girl hadn't made a play. And she herself hadn't felt she had the right to pick the French girl up, since she did not have a room to take her to or enough money to rent one. Also, she thought the other girl maybe liked having a fellow around, too. What about you? he had asked her. She had smiled and shrugged. I'm here, aint I, baby? was all she had said. Then the knock came on the door and they let in the other girl. Dave had seen her around with boyfriends a hundred times at least. And there they were. He had never suspected the other girl of making it with chicks.

"Man," Weintraub grinned, "I tell you, when you get together with two girls who really like it that way, there's nothing like it in the world."

I stole a glance at Harry. There was a kind of deep glow in the back of his eyes.

So they had gone at it for three days, Weintraub said, whenever the other girl didn't have to turn up at home and check in with her folks. Harry was squinting at him from behind the bar, leaning on his elbows on the back of it, but he had no comment to make.

"Hell, I've only known her five days," Weintraub grinned at us, "and she's already taught me a lot."

"Come on, Dave," Harry said. "Don't tell me there's anything left anybody can teach you at this late date. Not after this past winter."

It was a rare thing to see Weintraub reticent about anything. But he only grinned, and a special word about him seems necessary here. Weintraub for the past several months before the Revolution had been making it in the orgy circuit in Paris. It was common international knowledge that there were two or three paying places in Paris where you could go and take your wife, or some other girl, and check your clothes at the door, drink nude at the bar and dance, and if you were so inclined adjourn to one of the cushion-floored rooms upstairs where others before you had already adjourned, to play games. You might even be invited up by someone who was not your date, but it was perfectly proper to decline, as you would a dance. But these places were only the paying places. In addition, there was a whole set of orgiasts who held their meetings in private homes, and where it was not proper to decline an invitation. Somehow, after living nearly 20 years in Paris without them, Weintraub had gotten himself involved with this set, perhaps by having gone to one of the paying places first. I remember he was telling Louisa all about it one Sunday evening two months before, standing in the kitchen while she was cooking the curry, as I happened to walk in. Soon, in his inimitable way, he had told everybody else all he knew about it, and so everybody knew all about Weintraub's orgy experience. Louisa had been blushing when he told it to her that time in the kitchen, but she had been interested to hear it just the same. As who wouldn't be? Dear Louisa.

"Hell, Harry," Weintraub said. "You know I gave all that orgy stuff up, after a couple of months. I told you that. It gets to be a bore. I only did it just to see once what it was like." He paused. "At least I did until that Sam appeared on the scene. She seems to know more people, and more houses, in that set in five days than I ever knew existed." He paused again. "She likes to, *loves* to dance naked for a crowd of them, you see."

"She must have known them when she was here two years ago," Harry said.

"I suppose so."

"But what I don't see," Harry said in an intellectual way, "is what new she could have taught you that you didn't learn on the orgy circuit."

"Well, that's it," Weintraub said. "She didn't. I mean, not anything physical. It's something else. That girl is totally without any morality. She has no guilts. I mean, she isn't *im*moral; she's *a*moral. She's like a healthy, beautiful young animal." A kind of shadow crossed his face. "She has absolutely no guilts about anything, or anybody."

He turned back to Harry. "*That's* what is different. I have never seen anything like *that*. It adds a whole different dimension, different *kind* of dimension to sex, Harry."

"Yes. Yes, I can see that," Harry said. "But I find it hard to imagine."

"Well, me, too," Weintraub said, and the shadow crossed his face again.

Soon after that Louisa called us to eat, and brought in the huge pot of curry from the kitchen. Some of the other girls brought in the rice and plates and spoons and forks. Harry got out, and opened, the cold wine. McKenna was not allowed to eat the Sunday night curry, and had been given her supper earlier and had by now gone to bed. But the rest of us spent over an hour forking down the rice and curry and the chutney and Indian condiments Louisa bought at Fauchon, pouring the cold Beaujolais down our scorching throats at intervals to cool them. We were all disgustingly full, sweating, and a little bit drunk, when volunteers finally cleared the dirty dishes away.

Only Sam drank no wine. And she ate very little curry. After a token helping, she turned in her plate and sort of disappeared off by herself. I remember sitting on the floor and looking up from my plate, and seeing her lying by herself on her stomach in front of the empty fireplace. She was munching on a Hershey bar Louisa must have got for her and reading one of the Tin-Tin comic books McKenna had left behind—just exactly as, and in just the same position as, she had done four nights before when she was with McKenna.

It was she who suggested putting on some records. There was plenty of yé-yé stuff on the record shelves, because of Hill. With Harry to help her and manipulate the complicated hi-fi system, she selected a stack of them and put them on with the volume up high. Then she went off by herself and began dancing to it those strange, disjointed, jerky new dances my generation always looks so unnatural and silly doing. She stayed all by herself, totally oblivious to everyone, audience and non-audience alike. Some of us, some others, danced a little while and then stopped, gave it up. Sam went right on, all by herself, staring without seeing, jerking her body and snapping her crotch, all by herself in an out-of-the-way corner, until the stack was finished. I could imagine what she looked like doing it nude. And I could imagine Harry could imagine it. Everybody applauded when she finished and she gave us a sweet smile, but looked somehow startled, as if she had not been aware there was anybody else there.

Later, she came over to us where Harry and I were standing alone at the bar. We had switched to Scotch.

"What are you two 'older-generations' talking about over here so mopey?"

Harry grinned at her. He seemed in better control than he had the other time he had met her. "Nothing that you should worry your pretty head about. Have you a subject you'd like to introduce?"

"Yes. As a matter of fact, I do. I'd like to make it with you, Mr. Gallagher." She smiled a smile at him which warmed up her eyes so much that they suddenly looked furry and actively overheated. "I'm propositioning you."

"Well. Well, that's flattering," Harry said. He grinned at her, and his eyes squinted until they were only thin lines. Then his eyebrows went up, making a washboard of wrinkles of his forehead. "We'd certainly make an interesting couple in bed."

"There's something about tall bald men that really turns me on. Tanned heads. Tanned heads between my legs."

"Great!" Harry said. "But I'm afraid it's not possible, Sam girl." His voice lay down heavily on the hippie phrase.

"Why?"

"Because, unfortunately, I'm a monogamist. I'm afraid Louisa would take a very dim view of it."

"Well, bring her along. Bring her along, and we'll all go to bed together," Samantha said. "It's really her that I like. I like her better than you, anyway. In fact, I think I'm falling in love with *her*."

Harry was still smiling. "Well, that's an idea," he said. "That's certainly one idea. But I don't have that kind of control over Louisa. You'll have to ask Louisa herself."

"Okay, I will." She slid lithely off her bar stool, and went swaying down the room.

I was still dumbstruck. And I think Harry, at least now, was a little startled too. He stepped down and came around from behind the bar. I leaned out from my own stool, saw I could not see from where I was, and came and stood beside him.

Louisa was sitting on one of the couches at the far end with some of the others, talking about something or other. Samantha came up and knelt beside her and leaned on her arms on the low cocktail table.

"Will you make love with me, Louisa?" she asked.

Louisa stared at her. Then her face blushed red right up into her hair. "Why! Why! Why, what would your mother say, if she heard you say that?"

"Are you kidding?" Sam said.

Louisa was laughing now, in a flustered way. So were most of the others. "Why! Why, I'm going to tell your mother on you, you bad girl!"

Sam was laughing too, now. "Are you kidding? My mother was a lesbian before I was born. Whenever I think about it, I'm surprised she ever went with a man long enough to have me!"

"Well," Louisa said. "Even so. Whatever possessed you to say something like that to me?" She was still blushing, and she was still flustered.

"Because I think I'm falling in love with you," Sam said, still leaning on her elbows, still smiling softly up at her. "I think you're the most beautiful woman I've ever seen. Didn't you notice it the other night?"

"No," Louisa said, looking around in dismayed embarrassment. She was still half laughing. "No. No, I certainly did not."

"I just propositioned Harry at the bar," Sam said. "But I only did it because I thought he might bring you along, too. It was really you that I wanted."

Louisa looked around again. Her hand had fluttered up to her breast. "Now you just stop that," she said. "Get up from there. Me go out with girls? I never heard of such a thing. Ugh."

Sam got to her feet. "My luck. Always my luck." She walked away from the couch, dropping her shoulders in a very cute, charming caricature of despair. "That always is my luck."

It was one of the most outrageous performances I had ever seen. And yet she had cleverly, charmingly, turned it off into a half-joke so that nobody was really shocked and no one was insulted. Nobody, in fact, could even be sure she had meant it.

Grinning, Weintraub came up to us where we were near the bar. "Aint she something? Did you ever see anything like her?"

Sam, smiling her street Arab grin, came right after him. "Come on, Weintraub," she said sharply. "We got a party to go to." She turned to Harry. "I didn't have any luck, Harry. Maybe the next time I come. Come on, Weintraub! There's nothing to keep me here now. Let's go to our party."

"Party!" Weintraub grinned. "Party! She's taking me to another orgy."

"Orgy!" Samantha said, glaring at him contemptuously. "Orgy! Orgy, Weintraub! Bark! Bark!"

"Aaaaooo," Weintraub said, grinning. "Arf. Arf."

When they left, she shook hands with Louisa and kissed her tenderly on the cheek. Louisa blushed.

Almost everybody else was gone by now.

"Do you think we'll ever see her again?" I asked.

"I don't see why not," Harry said and laughed.

"If I were she I wouldn't be able to show my face here again," Louisa said, and blushed.

"But you're not her," I said. "I suppose if Weintraub brings her again, she'll come. But would you invite her?"

"Well, of course," Louisa said, looking alarmed. "I couldn't not."

I made my own goodbys and left to walk home along the quiet quai, for once not drunk.

The next day was Monday, and the students occupied the reopened Sorbonne as they had threatened and promised. I went over there with a friend from *Life* to look at it. It was like a five-ring circus. The next day was the big strike and march all around Paris and I stood in my darkened, electricity-, water-, and gas-less apartment and watched the workers and students crossing the Pont de la Tournelle with their furled banners, on their way to the Place de la République to begin their march. I had completely given up trying to work.

Then on Wednesday night an "unruly mob" of students sallied forth from their bastion at the Sorbonne and down the rue Racine and rue de Vaugirard and occupied the Théâtre de l'Odéon, after the performance of the Paul Taylor American dance troupe finished. And I understood what Hill had meant on the phone when he hinted they might occupy something else. The Odéon was occupied in the name of the students' new "Cultural Revolution".

"Our typical luck," a member of the Paul Taylor troupe was quoted as saying in the paper. Now they would not get to finish their engagement. "Most places they don't want us because we're too avant-garde. Here we're out because we're too bourgeois."

In all those days none of us saw Sam Everton, or Weintraub.

10

ON WEDNESDAY THE 2000 workers of the Sud-Aviation aircraft construction plant at Nantes seized and occupied their factory. They held the plant manager and his chief assistants prisoner in their offices. This was a spontaneous unorganized wildcat strike, and not a permitted legal one. In France the law is that strikers must give five days notice, and get the permission of the Government and police before they strike.

And on Thursday, although we did not know it until the evening papers came out, a number of the nationalized Renault plants were seized and occupied. Renault was the biggest automobile-maker in France. And since being nationalized, it had had one of the best records in labor relations in the country. In spite of that, a spare-parts plant of 4500 workers at Cléon in Normandy was occupied in the late night hours. Then later Thursday morning the 11,000-worker assembly plant at Flins, near Paris, was taken over. Later in the day plants at Le Mans, at Sandouville near Le Havre, and at Boulogne-Billancourt in the Paris suburbs were struck and seized.

It was on Thursday that Harry Gallagher called me and invited me to lunch with him at Lipp and afterward walk over and take a look at the Sorbonne. I had already been once, on the very first day, when the Press Card of my friend from *Life* was required to get us in. But now the kids had thrown it wide open, to any citizen who wanted to come and see. I did not mind going again. Especially with Harry, knowing how ambivalent he felt about Hill.

We walked to Lipp from his apartment, taking the footbridge to the other island, crossing the Cité behind Notre-Dame, and heading right on up the rue des Bernardins to Place Maubert: the exact same route I had taken a week ago the Thursday before.

Place Maubert when we came out into it was still a mess. But it was being cleaned up, the burnt-out cars had disappeared, and a crew of Italian specialists were re-laying the paving stones ripped up by the student rioters. This was still back before somebody in the Government decided to replace the ripped-up paving stones with asphalt. We stopped a minute to watch them work.

They were beautiful to watch. The men who laid the stones worked on their knees or else worked bent way over, swinging, at the waist. Each master stone-layer had two apprentice workers, one who kept him supplied with two creeping piles of the stones on his right and left which moved slowly forward with him as he worked. The other prepared and smoothed continually with a shovel the bed of sand on which the stones were laid, afterward throwing and sweeping in the sand that filled the minute spaces between the stones. Every so often the stone-supplier, usually a youth, would reject and throw out to the side a stone that was either too large, too small or too unevenly hewn. He would throw out about one stone in seven. But the stones he passed were not at all all that evenly matched, and that was where the miracle came in. The master stone-layer, without ever bothering to look at it, would reach behind him for a stone, heft it, heft it maybe several times, toss it so that another face of the roughly squared stone came down in his palm, perhaps toss it again, looking quickly all the while at the six or seven available places in front of him for laying the next stone. Then he would place it, smoothing and adjusting with his other hand the already smooth sand under it—and it would fit. Occasionally he would heft a stone and then toss it aside and pick up another. They worked amazingly fast, 15 to 20 seconds to lay a stone. Inches away right beside them just beyond the tapes which protected them the reinstituted traffic whirred down the one-way Boulevard toward the river on the surface of paving stones that had already been replaced.

Beside me, Harry gave me a look of appreciation and admiration, and I nodded. We walked on up the Boulevard under the shade trees. I was thinking.

The *pavés* of Paris were really something special. Made of some grayish speckledly stone that looked like granite, and maybe was, they were roughly squared off into cubes of somewhere between four and five inches and they weighed roughly five to six pounds each. The identical scene to what we had just witnessed must have been viewed by Villon in his wanderings around Paris. They were laid in concentric arcs which never got any smaller, and which blended in with the other rows of arcs beside them in a way that it was difficult for the eye to follow. None of that had changed since the Middle Ages. When it was wet and raining, they gave back an oily, iridescent, rainbow look with all the colors of the spectrum. The skill, and simple endurance, required to lay them like that were phenomenal. One of the *almost* lost arts. I was thinking it would be a shame to see them all replaced someday in Paris with the sticky-in-the-heat, evil-smelling modernity of asphalt. But during and after the May Revolution that was just exactly what they did in the *Quartier Latin.*

Along the shady, dust-smelling Boulevard the sites of other fights and barricades were plainly evident. Where it junctioned with the Boul' Mich' at the Carrefour was of course always one of the big fights, and it looked truly beat up there. Six big camions of the CRS were parked there along the Boulevard just in front of the park-like trees and grass of the Musée de Cluny. But there had been another at the carrefour of the rue Danton in front of the École de Médecine, and just beyond it still another at the Carrefour Odéon. It was like that all the way up to the Place St.-Germain.

There were other camions of CRS placed strategically around, the men in them playing cards, smoking, reading newspapers, or laughing and talking. But the streets were literally alive with kids, most of them with long hair, all of them laughing and strolling, and happy warmth and excitement on their faces. None of them were belligerent; rather the reverse. About two-thirds of them seemed to be wearing red shirts. Lots of others wore red bandannas. And in all the little yé-yé clothes shops around the rue de Seine and rue du Four (Street of the Oven, in English) the red motif had been picked up and showed conspicuously in the display windows: red shirts, red slacks, red socks, red scarves. *Les commerçants,* it appeared, were already riding the bandwagon of the Revolution.

We crossed the dusty, litter-blown *Place* with the light. Then we worked our way through the usual press of people, mostly youngsters, outside the popular Drugstore St.-Germain. Brasserie Lipp was just next door.

Across the street on the sunny side the famous Deux Magots and Café Flore squatted dusty under the trees in sunshine, their sidewalk tables spilling out almost to the curb. There were more American tourists this summer than anyone had expected. Maybe they had come to see and to photograph the Revolution.

Lipp was crowded with lunchers. At the revolving-door entrance, which had been opened back in the warm summer weather, "young" Monsieur Cazes, the owner, met us, told us we would have to wait. But he gave me a look that said though there were others in front of us he would slip us in ahead. We sat down at an outside table and ordered the big schooners of beer which are called *un sérieux* at Lipp. Here on this side out of the sun it was almost cool.

"It will be interesting to see what it is like over there," Harry said after his first long pull, and wiped the foam off his lip. "The Sorbonne."

"Yes," I said. "And I'll be interested to make a comparison to what it was like the first day."

So we sat and watched the faces and stances of the people passing in the street for a while, always one of the best of the fringe benefits of Paris outdoor café sitting.

"Young" Monsieur Cazes came and got us before our beers were even half finished and I told the outdoor waiter to put them on the bill inside. There were a number of dirty looks thrown at us by the other people waiting. But Monsieur Cazes, "young" Monsieur Cazes, who was aged about 56, only eyed them blandly with a cold smile.

As a matter of fact, he was not the "young" Monsieur Cazes any more. Although we all still thought of him as that. He was now the "old" Monsieur Cazes, ever since his father the original "old" Monsieur Cazes, a tough white-haired very bourgeois old gent, had died in the spring of that year. There was no "young" Monsieur Cazes now, because the new "old" Monsieur Cazes had no son.

We followed him inside and through the crowded tables, nodding or waving at various literati or movie people we knew. They never took reservations at Lipp. But if Monsieur Cazes knew you, and considered you adequate, there was always a place.

I cannot say that it was I who introduced Harry Gallagher to Lipp. He had been there before. But it was I who introduced him into its inner sanctum by introducing him to "old" Monsieur Cazes, and to the then "young" Monsieur Cazes. I had been coming there the ten years I had been in Paris, and had been introduced myself by Romain Gary. Once they knew who I was and what I did, and that Romain Gary thought highly enough of me to introduce me, I became one of the special clients, of which there could not have been more than one or two thousand.

I do not think any of them ever read much, though I may be wrong about that, or ever had time much to go to the movies; but they took very seriously, and with about equal importance, their literary and their film-world clienteles.

It was an old tradition, going back to Fitzgerald and Hemingway and Edith Wharton and Cocteau in the Twenties, and even before that. It went back even to before the turn of the century. And its decor had not been changed since then, either.

Since I introduced him, Harry had taken to coming there more than I had ever come and now was better known there than I ever was. Harry had really taken the place up.

The waiters always dressed in black tuxedo-like suits and aprons and black bow ties from an earlier day. They all wore numbered metal checks on their lapels which signified strictly their proper place in the waiter hierarchy, and their seniority was a very jealously guarded thing.

The most recent Number One had died about two years ago and the new Number One, who had been wearing the Number Two check since I had first come to Paris, was a tiny roly-poly man about as wide as tall, with white hair which stood out from his head and the flushed, veined nose and cheeks of a dedicated red wine drinker. He wheezed when he moved and seemed almost too feeble to work at all, but the others all seemed to help him out almost religiously.

"Numéro Uno!" Harry called out, when the head waiter Monsieur

Cazes had passed us to usher us into the back room. And Number One came trotting over to shake hands, his eyes almost disappearing behind his red cheeks. It was a big act Harry and I always did when either one of us came to Lipp. It helped preserve our much-liked Americanism.

"M'sieu 'Artley, M'sieu Gallag-her," Number One grinned. "Ease good toe zee hyou." It was about all the English he knew. He put my name first because he had known me the longest and respected seniority everywhere, even though Harry was now more of an habitué than I was.

"Comment ça va, Numéro Uno?" Harry cried.

"Very finne, very finne," the old man beamed.

When we were seated against the wall it was waiter Number Fifteen who waited on us.

The rest of the place was like its waiters. By stepping through the door you might have stepped back into the year 1900. There were no tables in the center of the floor in the back, only a big serving cabinet, which held the napkins and the bread and condiments and silverware: *les couverts*. The waiters continually clustered around it to get their serving stuff. The electric light fixtures looked like they should be gaslights. Each wall was decorated with a three-foot mirror above the seatbacks, and if you craned your neck you could see the lights and the mirror and the people reflected and re-reflected almost to an infinity. Between the lengths of mirror were murals made of tiny highly colored tiles which represented plants. The front was almost exactly like the back except that it was wider and a waist-high wood partition ran down the center making it two rooms. One side was for coffee and drinking only. The other side was for eating. Along its top was a slightly raised plate of glass, so that people could talk under it to each other and see who all was there. Upstairs on the first floor was still another *salle,* but nobody went there except the unknowns.

The *plat du jour* for Thursdays was always *fricandeau de veau rôti,* and *cassoulet maison.* On Fridays there was *brandade de morue* and *raie au beurre noir.* On Saturdays and Sundays there was *boeuf gros sel* and *gigot d'agneau. Sole meunière* and *choucroute garnie* were standard daily items.

Harry ordered Baltic herring which was served with sliced onions and whole peppercorns in a *vinaigrette,* and the *cassoulet.* I did not feel my stomach was up to a cassoulet, which was a delicious dish of various meats and sausages cooked with white beans in a red tomato sauce and served in an earthenware casserole but a little hard to assimilate. I loved it, but I ordered a *boeuf museau vinaigrette* and afterward a steak and *pommes frites.* We had another schooner of beer with the first course, and a bottle of Bordeaux with the entrée. But in the end we drank two bottles of the Bordeaux. We must have known at least half of the people sitting in the crowded back room.

"No Revolution here," Harry said and grinned, as we were served the herring and the *museau.*

"No," I said, "but they've had their hard times just the same. They've been through the troubles of '36, when M. Pompidou himself was on the student barricades. They've had two World Wars, and an Occupation. As well as the time of the Existentialists right after, which must never be discounted."

"Well, may this bastion never fall!" Harry said, and raised his big beer glass.

I answered with mine and we toasted that.

"Did I ever tell you about the time I was having lunch here and Louisa came in?" Harry said.

I lied. "No."

"Well," Harry said, "I was having lunch here with Zanuck and Ed Leggewie. About some screenplay job or other. And Louisa came in with this Canadian playwright friend of ours who happened to be in town. Well, we were sitting at that end table up front, right by the *caisse.* The head waiter—him—that little one, yeah, with the straight white hair—he got hold of Louisa and whispered to her, 'Madame, Madame, Monsieur est là!' She didn't know what he meant, of course. But he said it again. 'Madame, Madame, Monsieur est là!' He was warning her. He thought she was out to lunch with a lover, and that she had stumbled onto me by mistake. Now, how's that for French politesse?"

I had heard it before, at least three times, but it was a funny story. It was very French, I suppose. But it was funny. I laughed, and then Harry laughed too, but there was a sort of anxious look on his face also. When Harry was anxious his forehead got wrinkled like a washboard. I thought he had remembered in mid-story that he had told it to me before.

"That little girl's been calling me," he said suddenly.

"What little girl?"

"That Sam. Samantha. Samantha-Marie."

"What?" I said. "No. Come on. You're kidding me."

"No," he said, "I'm serious. Quite serious. She's called me five times since she and Weintraub were at the house Sunday."

"What does she want?" I said. "Outside of your money?"

"Me," Harry said. "Apparently, she wants me."

I think then I suddenly realized what was the purpose of our luncheon. And it had nothing at all to do with the Sorbonne.

"Well, Harry, what do you want me to tell you?" I said.

Probably I said it too sharply. In my middle-age I have become very short-tempered with people asking me for personal advice. I do not know where they get off thinking I know enough to give them any. I have found that the truth is personal advice is not at all what they want. What they really want is reassurance. And if you give them that, they are as often as not likely to come back and throw it in your face later, and tell you that whatever it was that they did was all your fault.

"I don't want you to tell me anything, Jack," he said. "I want you to be a witness, that's all."

"Witness?" I said. "Witness to what? I do not intend to be any-body's witness to any God damned personal junk."

"Witness to the fact that I'm not having any," Harry said. "Not any at all. I know what I am, I know where I stand, I know what is good for me, and furthermore I know what I really want. I think I know where I've been. And I'm making you my witness."

That was pretty hard to refuse. In fact, it was not possible to refuse it, under the circumstances. I had been impressed, like a sailor. Once he stated it, like that, I was already committed, simply because my ears had heard it. And anyway, under those circumstances, I did not want to refuse.

"Okay," I said. "I'm your witness. I fail to see how I can not be. Under the circumstances. Now what?"

"Now nothing," he said. "Let's go see the fucking Sorbonne."

We had about finished the herring and *museau* by this time. Our waiter Number Fifteen was hovering around waiting to serve the entrées.

"If you are going to visit the Sorbonne, gentlemen," he said in French, "I would like to offer very much the suggestion that you also pass by and view the Odéon. It is not possible that you could not find it amusing."

I thanked him. When he served Harry his *cassoulet,* I regretted my decision not to order it. But I stuck with my steak. We ate the rest of the meal without talking much, mostly nodding or saying hello to people we knew who came in or got up to leave.

"Do not forget to pass by and view the Odéon," Number Fifteen called, after we paid and were leaving.

That was what we did. The easiest way to get to it was to walk back down the Boulevard we had come up, to the Carrefour Odéon, and turn up there, away from the river. It was pleasant strolling along under the shade trees, with the excited kids all around.

"I thought it was Louisa she was after," I said.

"So did I," Harry said beside me. "But maybe that was just a ploy. Anyway, that's a joke!"

When we turned up, the whole crazy place was visible way off, straight up the rue de l'Odéon, in the Place de l'Odéon, where the famous fish restaurant La Méditerranée nestled on a warped corner of the *Place.*

The theater itself was called the Théâtre de France but everybody spoke of it as "the Odéon". It had been built by Louis Quinze in the eighteenth century, 1781 or somewhere around there, then was burned in the Revolution and later restored. It had a huge colonnaded façade with the columns running four or five low stories up to the pediment, very Greek copy, with low, thick, arched arcades you could walk under running around the other three sides. It was a big building with lots of storage rooms and dressing rooms backstage around in the back which butted on the rue de Vaugirard, and just across the street were the Luxembourg Gardens.

Now two huge red and two huge black flags were streaming in the breeze from the very top of the pediment, the tricolor had been hauled down, and the entire roof appeared to be alive with unkempt kids swarming around, or just standing, or sitting on the cornice eating their lunch of bread and meat or bread and cheese.

Huge banners had been fastened to the big columns just under the architrave. "Imagination takes power at the Théâtre de l'Odéon." Another said "Barrault is dead," referring to the theater director's own quote about himself on Wednesday night when he joined the invading students.

Another said "FREE ENTRY". The students intended to throw the stage and pit open to a perpetual dialogue that would go on 24 hours a day every day, everybody invited. Apparently this had already started, and lots of workers, waiters and *petits commerçants* appeared to be taking advantage of the invitation.

Up closer, we saw somebody had painted a smaller banner: "When the Assemblée Nationale becomes bourgeois theater, the Bourgeois Theater must become the Assemblée Nationale!" This referred to Prime Minister Pompidou's performances in front of the Assemblée at the beginning of the week.

The whole *Place* was alive with people, not all of them students by any means, and discussions, dialogues and arguments were going on all around. No auto traffic could have gotten through it. *Commerçants* argued with waiters, waiters argued with students, students argued with *commerçants, commerçants* argued with *commerçants.* A TV group was filming it all from the top of their truck. Coming up, the sidewalks and the street itself were jammed with students and other people grinning or laughing and going to or coming from the *Place,* but there had been no jostling.

The whole place was wild, laughing, scratching crazy.

"Do you want to try to get in?" I shouted at Harry.

The entire huge porch beneath the great columns was jammed with a mob of people, all evidently trying to get inside to hear the dialogue in the pit.

"No," he shouted back. "We'd never make it."

We worked our way across the *Place,* heading for the rue Racine, which would take us to the Sorbonne. It had the same look as the rue de l'Odéon had had.

The Boulevard St.-Michel when we came out into it had a soberer, saner look. We walked up it toward the Place de la Sorbonne. This of course was crowded with knots of kids. So were all the cafés along it.

"Well, Number Fifteen was certainly right," I said. "About Odéon."

Harry nodded. "He sure was. Great sport. But there's going to be a big bill. I just wonder if anybody is thinking about who's going to pay that big bill when it is presented."

This sobered me down a little. "Well, I guess they will all have to pay a part."

"*They* will," Harry said, "yes. Because the Government and the *Patronat* sure as hell aint going to."

The word patronat translated means "body of employers". *The Patronat,* with a capital P, means just about the same as our word Establishment, except that it is probably a little more precise in *who* it means. Everybody knew, at least every American did, just how antiquated the French *Patronat* was in comparison to our equally unloved American Establishment. It was about a hundred times worse, in just about every sense. It had hardly changed at all since Karl Marx started taking the Industrial Revolution to task. Their capitalism was still of the circa 1870 variety. Their Stock Exchange even, the Bourse, still worked by secrecy and hidden buying, without open declaration. Comparatively speaking, they were taxed almost not at all. And as a result the comparative richness between them and the French worker was enormously greater. Whoever lost in this "Revolution", it would almost certainly not be the *Patronat.*

"Well, it's the people's vacation," I said, a little lamely, but Harry did not answer.

The Sorbonne, when we got to it, looked about the same as it had on the first day of the occupation except that now everything looked a little dirtier. The streets and sidewalks outside were covered with litter: mimeographed pamphlets, tracts, mimeographed single-sheet announcements, candy bar wrappers, old cigarette packs. But the students were apparently trying to organize a clean-up group, because we saw a number of them wearing some kind of unreadable armband and carrying brooms. A few of them were sweeping away at the mess, but most were talking. We went in from the rue Victor Cousin side.

Inside, the famous court looked like some kind of Persian market. Booths made of card tables or old refrigerator boxes had been set up all over the place. Here the outside theme of increasing litter and dirtiness was continued, in trumps, but here nobody was trying to do anything about it. Each booth it turned out was the station of some particular political persuasion. There were Maoists, Ché Guevaraists, Stalinists, Leninists, Trotskyists, and I don't know what all. Huge portraits of Lenin, Mao and Guevara had been plastered on the columns. Slogans had been painted in red paint just about everywhere.

"Society is a carnivorous flower," said one. "I take my desires for reality, because I believe in the reality of my desire," another said.

They were all over the place.

"One pleasure has the bourgeoisie, that of degrading all pleasures."

"Be a realist, demand the impossible."

"Those who make a revolution by halves, dig their own graves."

"A Philistine's tears are the nectar of the Gods."

"Acid is yellow!"

"Imagination power!"

"Sex power!"

"Cunt power!"

"Commodities are the opium of the people."

There were hundreds of others. A steady stream of youthful comers and goers filed through the courtyard gate and milled about in the yard. Everybody had a happy, laughing, vacationing look. I went over to one booth and asked to buy a copy of *L'Enragé,* a paper with fairly funny cartoons the Anarchist group had begun putting out. The long-haired boy at the booth stared at me coldly, decided I was not ridiculing him but was simply not one of the well-informed, sneered at me, and said, "They're over there. Here we are Trotskyites. We don't mess with their garbage." I apologized, and sauntered away. I did not have the courage to try another booth. Anyway, I could buy the paper on the street in St.-Germain.

"Come on," Harry shouted at me across some heads. "Let's go see the amphitheaters."

The amphitheaters did not appear to have changed any since Monday. They were jammed right up literally to the rafters, with students sitting on the statues and in the niches in the walls. The "NO SMOKING" signs had been mutilated and made to read "SMOKE!", as if it were a general's command. They could have been exactly the same students that I saw on Monday, and as far as I knew they were, so that I had the strange feeling they had all been sitting there without sleep, bowel movements or any other normal function for the three full days that I had been away. We did not go in but stood in the doorway. Some boy had the gavel up on the stage and while we stood there he recognized some girl with long stringy hair and extremely tight gray corduroy pants, who had some indistinguishable amendment to make to something. The morning papers had said that the students had already voted to boycott year-end exams, but this group apparently did not know this, had not voted yet and was still discussing the wording of the proclamation. Bottles of red wine, long loaves of bread and hunks of cheese and sausage passed back and forth from hand to hand. The more or less laughing uproar made such a din it was hard to hear anything that was said.

Harry motioned to me and we started away down the crowded, ringing corridor and ran head-on into Hill and some of his friends.

I must say they looked pretty grubby. Hill appeared to be starting a beard, but it may simply have been that he had not had time to shave for some days.

Anne-Marie was with them, as was Terri of the long hair, and bearded Bernard, but Hill had his arm well around another girl and it was pretty clear they were lovers, at least for the time being. Anne-Marie did not appear to mind, in her militant way. Thin and small as she was, she nevertheless moved along like a sturdy little tank, whose turret gun never stops turning and looking. Even the militantly clean Anne-Marie looked a little grubby. But I understood—whether Harry did or not—that none of them had had a chance at an honest-to-God bath since the Monday of the occupation, if not since the Friday night battle in the rue Gay-Lussac.

I guess Harry did understand it; about the no-bath beatnik, hippie look. At least, he played it all very cool. So did Hill. I thought then that Hill was desperately wanting to avoid any big argument with his father in front of his friends. I think Harry wanted to avoid the same thing. You might never have known that they had ever argued about anything in their lives, looking at them shake hands and say hello.

"We just came over to look the Sorbonne over," Harry smiled. "But

I didn't have any idea we might find you here, run right into you in the corridors."

"We've been sleeping here since Monday night," Hill smiled back, and he squeezed the little girl he had his arm around and smiled down at her, so that it was pretty obvious with whom he, anyway, had been sleeping since Monday night. "A lot of the kids brought their sleeping bags. It's not bad at all.

"Actually, you probably wouldn't have found me," he said, "a day later. We're moving our Cinema Committee over to the Odéon. It is felt that since we in Cinema are basically cultural it is better for us to be in the headquarters of the Cultural Revolution. Anyway, there's a lot more room up in the backstage areas there than there is here in this jammed madhouse."

"We understood the place had been thrown open to the public," I said apologetically. "So we thought we'd look in."

We were speaking English and Hill's new girl suddenly answered, in unaccented American-English. "It has, it has, it has been thrown open. Wide open. To everybody in Paris. Workers, artists, everybody. We want everybody to come. We want to get acquainted with everybody, in a whole new way of life, of living."

"This is Florence," Hill introduced her. "She's a new member of our Cinema Committee."

It seemed pretty clear to me why she was a new member of the Committee, and I would have bet 50 dollars with anybody that Hill had certainly been her sponsor.

"She's half-American," Hill said. "But she was born and raised in France. She only returned from the States a few days ago, by accident. Without knowing anything at all about the Revolution."

"Well, I guess she's finding out now, though," Harry smiled.

"She sure is," Hill said, and squeezed her again smiling down.

"I'm loving it," Florence said.

"I'm about to be elected Chairman of the Students' Cinema Committee of the Sorbonne and Odéon," Hill said. "We're having the meeting this afternoon, if we can find an empty room. Otherwise, we'll wait and do it after the move to Odéon."

"Well, I think that's great, Hill," Harry said.

"So do I," I said.

The others stood silently smiling at us that peculiar innocent smile, Terri of the innocent face, and bearded warm-eyed Bernard, all of them except Anne-Marie. It is not true that Anne-Marie did not smile. But her smile, while equally innocent and pleasant, was so superior and openly contemptuous of us "Older Generations" that for me at least it did not seem a smile. It was more like a smirk. Probably she did not even know it.

"But the best news," Hill said, "the best news, is about the Renault plant at Boulogne-Billancourt. Don't you think? We've had our boys out there talking to them since Saturday, almost a week. And now they've finally closed up shop and seized the plant. At Flins, too. We are all going to march out to Boulogne-Billancourt late this afternoon and hold a solidarity meeting with the Renault workers in front of the gates."

"Do you think that's wise?" Harry said, pleasantly enough. "What about the police?"

"Strike while the iron is hot," Hill said. "We've got the whole bunch of them on the run, now. I don't think the police will bother us. But if they do, so much the better for us and worse for them."

Harry was still smiling. "Come on, Jack," he said suddenly. "We've got things to do and things to see. We didn't mean to bother you, or upset any of your timing or plans."

"Oh, you didn't bother us," Hill smiled. "It was good to see you."

He did not offer to shake hands now, and neither did Harry. Hill turned away and with his arm still around his little half-American girl led his group off down the hollering, reverberating corridor.

"Dumbass kids," Harry said, as we started off the other way. "They're monkeying around with dynamite. It's one thing to close down a couple of universities. Nobody really gives much of a damn, and nothing much is really hurt. But it's an entirely different thing to close down all the major industries of France. That's something else again. They do that and they're going to find their heads in a noose."

We were almost at the great front door now, that opened onto the rue des Écoles and the back view of the old Musée de Cluny across the street. A sandwich, coffee and soup kitchen had been opened up by the students in the big main hall near the front door. You didn't pay. You could contribute if you wanted.

"I think I'm going to leave you here," Harry said suddenly as we went between the columns and down the steps. "I just remembered I've got a producer-director's meeting with some guys. Over on the Right Bank." His face suddenly looked all pinched up. "Anyway, I don't want to see any more right now."

"Dynamite," he said again as he left. "Absolute dynamite."

I walked home alone through the buzzing, swarming Quarter.

Harry certainly appeared to be right. That night M. Pompidou went on television for the second time. General de Gaulle of course was already in Rumania on his six-day state visit which he refused to cancel, had left in fact on Tuesday. He would address the nation in a few days, the Prime Minister said in his speech. We all of us watched it, the same gang of Americans, at the Gallaghers' apartment.

There was no placating of the students this time, and in fact the speech was announced only 90 minutes before the Prime Minister spoke. It appeared the whole Government had become first terrified, then furious at the prospect of the workers closing down their factories and following the students. M. Pompidou declared that he was prepared to use force if necessary to stem the student rebellion, to keep it from spreading to French industry. "This Government will do its duty," he said. "Its duty is to defend the Republic. It will defend it."

And this time the Government tried a new wrinkle, one which appeared to be caused by desperation, and which also appeared to have backfired. The Government permitted the student leaders on TV for the first time. For maybe 15 minutes before M. Pompidou spoke the three boys, Sauvageot, Dany Cohn-Bendit and Alain Geismar held a dialogue with a group of Government-selected correspondents, and made absolute fools of them with their charm, good humor and good sense. Cohn-Bendit was especially good. He had a particular charisma. You could not help but like him. "We just do not like the society which we are forced to live in," he said over and over, smiling. "We just do not want to live like that any more." That was the first time that that particular student theme was ever given public voice, as I remember.

And after them the Prime Minister seemed very anticlimactic.

I looked over at Harry over the heads of the others, and he nodded.

"This could mean anything," he told me later privately at the pulpit bar. "Those kids beat him hands down. It could mean a generalized nation-wide illegal strike by everybody—and a continuing one, without any time-limit for stopping. The Unions have completely lost control over their younger element. But for God's sake, don't tell Louisa."

I walked home alone that night very thoughtfully.

Neither Weintraub nor young little Samantha had shown up that night, either.

11

My mistress called me and came by that Thursday evening of the 16th. I was relieved that she did. I did not have a dinner date that night. And I did not feel like going out and dining alone in some restaurant. The French are excessively rude about staring at lone diners. Somehow it seems to menace them, and they aren't careful about hiding their disapproval. Normally I am quite capable of handling this and am good at staring coldly back, but tonight I was pensive and I didn't feel up to it. Neither did I feel like slapping something together and wolfing it down at home alone. I was feeling low and depressed. It was one of those lag periods, one of those spells that come, when a bachelor's life doesn't seem all that good after all and you are inclined to start asking yourself what the hell it all means, and what the hell is it really worth? That was no kind of mood to have living alongside the dark, flowing river Seine twinkling oily under the tall quai streetlights. And yet I knew I would be drawn helplessly to my windows, to stare at it, and its dark, masked, massive indifference to my death. It was going to be that kind of night.

So I was glad she called.

Besides, I had been wanting to ask her what she thought about what was going on. Martine was sort of my barometer about everything French: economic; social; political. I had never known her to be wrong.

She had for example predicted to me several weeks in advance le Général de Gaulle's vicious attack on the dollar. Through this I was able to make myself a small piece of change on the Bourse through my illegal money man Monsieur Jardin. Naturally I was anxious to know what she thought about the Revolution. But our ground rules were that I was never to call her; never, under any circumstances. She was always to call me.

I could hear the phone ringing as I came up the one flight of stairs and I hurried with my key, and ran to get it.

A few minutes, and I might very easily have missed her.

"Yes?"

"Cheri?"

"Martine! I've been wondering—"

"I can not talk now," she said guardedly. "But you will be home tonight? Yes? You do not have one other date? No?"

"No. I don't have. But if I had, I'd cancel it. I—"

"I can not talk now," she said again. "I will come at nine-fifteen. I will cook tonight. I bring everything. He has to be out for Ministerial affairs. By-by, Cheri."

I started to say goodby but the phone had already clicked dead in my ear.

I sat and stared at it a while. I certainly did want to see her about the Revolution. And my *cafard,* my fear and hate of the river were quite suddenly gone. The river could be very romantic, even gay, at times.

As I've said before I'm apparently a low-keyed man sexually. That is to say, I can take it or I can leave it alone. It does not really bother me when I don't have it, as it does some people. I was that way even when I was young. But I hadn't seen Martine in over two weeks. And Martine had a private special habit of always cooking in her underwear. I contemplated the empty telephone and thought about this with considerable pleasure.

The reason she did it was purely practical. She did it to protect her wardrobe. She spent almost every dime she had on her clothes, and she took a great deal of thought and care with her outfits. She was not about to get grease spots on some thing, not even on a *robe de chambre.* She was not about to have her things permeated with cooking smells. So she cooked, at my place anyway, in her underwear.

I didn't care what the reason was. I enjoyed watching the result. By underwear I mean her bra and her panties. She had a fine behind, and lovely breasts. She also wore her high-heeled shoes, on her bare feet, after carefully taking off her stockings. Apparently she seemed to feel grease spots would not seriously hurt her Mancini shoes. And kitchen floors are sticky.

Somehow the shoes added quite a flair to the whole thing. Don't ask me why, but they did. And I was the observer. I would pull a chair around, and sit in my living room, and watch her, down the short hallway, concocting whatever dish it was she was making. Once in a while, rarely, she would turn her head from where she bent over the oven and peer at me with an amused smile and say, *"Et toi! Et voilà, toi!"* She preferred to keep her cooking and her sex separate. She was truly a fabulous cook.

Why she originally took up with me I have never figured out. I once asked her this and she grinned that funny, tough-as-nails grin the Southerners have, and said, "That is why, Jean." She always called me Jean, French-style. I sort of got the point, which was not flattering, but it never really answered my question.

She was a blonde Southerner, Martine. There is a race of them. God knows where they came from, maybe their origin is Tuscan, but they have the aquiline nose and same high cheekbones as the dark ones, only their skin is fair and their hair blonde. Even their body hair is blonde. It makes a striking contrast—I mean, that Roman nose and cheekbone with all that blonde skin and hair. And they were just as tough-headed as the dark Southerners, when it came to bargaining or buying. Maybe even tougher, if that's possible.

I had met her at a literary cocktail at Magdalen McCaw's, a type of function she absolutely never went to. But Maggie's husband George, who was with O.E.C.D., had had to pay off some social debts to minor Government people, and had invited Martine's, ah,—well, friend. God only knows why he brought Martine instead of his wife. Maybe he thought Maggie and George, Maggie being such a famous American lady writer, were Bohemians—which only shows how little he knew Maggie.

I must say, Martine stood out at that literary cocktail. She was tall, statuesque, broad shouldered, big breasted, wore lots of eye make-up, and she was blonde, long-haired blonde—all that blondeness on one whose features openly proclaimed that she ought to be dark like a Mediterranean type. She looked immensely sexy there. There just wasn't anybody at that literary cocktail like her. Or at any other Paris literary cocktail I have ever been to. Within five minutes after I started talking to her she had written down secretly my phone number. All around her were people like Maggie, with her hair skinned back, and her toothy smile, which I have always found innocent and charming, though many others have called it sharklike. The males were at about the same level, as was I myself: tweedy, hirsute, pipe-sucking. Why she picked me I have never found out. It could just as well have been one of the others.

"Do not call me," she warned. "I will call you."

Three days later she called me to make our first sexual assignation.

Her lover, the man whose mistress she was, was a banker, a wealthy banker. But he also had some kind of hush-hush function or other, that I never clearly understood, with the Government. Her lover: I guess I *must* call him that: he paid her bills and apartment: *I* certainly didn't: *I* was more or less *her* "mister", since it was she who spent money on me—at least when she cooked for me:—Anyway, her lover would pass on to her bits of sometimes important Government information for her to use to aid herself, and she would in turn pass these on to me. Like that thing about de Gaulle's attack on the dollar. She knew a lot of what went on.

But it was more than that. There was something about her, something hard and cold-blooded and sharply French, in that hard-hearted, no-nonsense, tough-minded French way, that seemed to make her know beforehand what France and the French were going to do at any given period or moment. And she could predict them.

I've always felt that maybe her life she had lived accounted for this strange predictive quality she had about the French. She had had an oddly comic if, for her, not very happy life and set of experiences in her 32 years.

I think I would have called it laughable, if it were someone else than Martine, somebody I didn't know. She had come from a small town in the South. It's hard to believe how primitive and backward and set in their ways most of those towns can be. Her people were *petits commerçants,* and at 16 her parents had farmed her out as mistress to one of the local richies. This was natural enough, as she was their only beautiful child. But this young man, a spoiled brat apparently, had treated her badly. So she had secretly saved everything he gave her, trading presents in for cash at another town nearby, and swiped a bit more from her folks until she had enough to cut and run for Paris. This had taken her three years. In Paris she had modeled a little, drifted into the boutique world, first as receptionist, then as head saleswoman, then into the managerial side, and there she met the man who became her first official Paris lover and took her officially as his mistress. He too had been a rich banker, and in fact was a good friend of her present banker. With him, the first banker, she had done very well. Unfortunately, five years ago he had died of a heart attack quite suddenly.

He had never put her apartment in her own name. Hardly any of them ever did, she told me. It made it too expensive to change mistresses. The result was that the man's family, with their lawyers, but led by the wife, had moved in immediately and locked her out of her apartment. Everything she owned in the world except the clothes on her back was in it: all her expensive outfits: her jewelry he had given her: her shoes: make-up: everything. His wife, the widow, through her lawyers, claimed it all, and the courts awarded it all to her.

Martine did not seem to feel that there was anything personally vindictive in the widow's action, but rather that it was a normal piece of hard-headed French business. In the wife's place, she would have done the same.

She had had a rough time of it for some weeks, but several girl-friends had helped out with small loans. After that there had been a series of men, a lot of them Americans in Paris for a few weeks or months on business, but none of these had seen fit to invest more in her than a few presents, dates with her and dinners. For a while she sort of moved from hotel to hotel, depending on where they stayed. Finally she went back to a job as a receptionist and assistant manager of an haute couture boutique. She couldn't really expect to model any more. And it was here that she was found by her other rich banker, the close friend of her first rich banker, who used to have dinner with them with his own former mistress. He took her up at once. He had always coveted her, it turned out. She had been with him since.

Now however she was taking better care of herself. She now kept a good deal of her clothes outfits in a storage place, to which only she had the key. She kept only about one-third of her clothes at her apartment, and exchanged these with others at the storage place twice a week. She allowed herself to keep only one-fourth of her jewelry at home, but exchanged it frequently with the rest which was kept in a safety-deposit box in her name in a bank. She still of course did not have her apartment in her own name. But she now had her own bank account, to which she kept adding small sums whenever she could.

You had to admit it was sort of a comic story, in a kind of sorrowful, sad way. She would accept absolutely no presents from me, let alone gifts of cash. And usually when she came to my place she bought all the food on the way and brought it with her to cook and had paid for it herself in the market.

And that was the way she arrived that night of the Thursday of the 16th. When the bell rang and I opened the door, she was hardly visible at all behind two huge sacks of groceries, plus two large net panniers, one dangling from each hand, plus her little overnight bag.

"Here," she said. "For the God's sake, take these."

I helped her get them all down somewhere, then helped her get it all into the kitchen.

"I have worried much over you," she said as she started to undress in the other of the bedroom cubicles, where she preferred to hang her clothes than among my closely packed hangers in my closet. "For more than one week. But his wife went to the country. To visit relatives, you understand. Because of the troubles. So he comes to me every night. He can not go, of course. He has much to do for the minister of his. But you, you have the much to do too, tu sais, darrling." There is no way to write the lilting way she said darling with the French "r".

She unfastened her lacy garterbelt and sat down on the bed to carefully remove her stockings, and then put back on her shoes. "I will tell you about the all of it when we are eating."

I do not remember in great detail what she made that night. She started with mushrooms, the *champignons de Paris,* cooked and browned in their own brown sauce, and served in little pastry shells which she bought already made at the *pâtisserie,* then heated in my oven with their filling in them. It was a simple enough dish, but God how good she could make it taste.

As a main course she made something out of thin strips of beef all cooked up with strips of pimentos and green peppers, a dish she said she had learned from a Brazilian cook she had once had. With it she served mashed potatoes, but puréed in the French way, not dry American-style mashed potatoes.

When she had all that ready, and could safely leave it in the oven hot to serve, she went into the second bedroom cubicle and got from her overnight bag her striped floor-length housecoat, which was slit on both sides all the way to her waist, and for this she took off the panties and put on red and gold Moroccan slippers. It must have been some kind of Moroccan or Arab material, and a long sleeveless vest of the same stuff cunningly half-hid the waist-high slits. She served us in that. I don't remember what other vegetable we had. I don't remember if we had a salad. I don't know what we had for desert.

"You must understand the most carefully what I will now tell you, Cheri," she said conversationally after we had begun to eat. "I have worried for you ten days more than this. But what happened to now is not even something. Now it will begin really. We have had the word. Most serious word. Very dependable. Tomorrow or Saturday, Sunday and Monday everybody, all of France will be making the strikes. You will not have much time, so you must do exactly what I tell to you. The railroads, all the transportations, the gasoline, the oil, all the industrials and manufactures, the Métro, even the garbage men. They will all make the strikes soon."

She forked up a bite of the Brazilian meat dish and chewed it daintily, if lustily. "It is good, this dish, no?" She waved her fork at me. "You see, the French of France are all with the students now. They are angry. How long this will be, I do not know. But it will be for some time, believe me. These will not be strikes of protestations that will stop in two, three days. They are really angry, the French people. They are angry with the police for beating the children in the street as last Friday. And they are angry with the General de Gaulle for letting it happen, when by lifting one finger he could have stopped it before the beginning.

"Also they are tired, the people. They love de Gaulle, he is their great hero, but they are tired of him now. They are bored with him. You must remember they get bored easy, the French people. They are bored with his kind of sacrifice *pour la Patrie* which asks the people and workers to sacrifice while the Patronat sacrifices by buying more old chateaux and changing their grounds into beautiful private parks for themselves and relatives.

"France seems to be a rich country. And it is a rich country, in the ground, in the agriculture. And especially now it seems to be a rich country. But it is not a rich country. It could be such a one: more things are coming in, more things are being made, more money is floating in the air. But the price of living is going up swiftly and the workers' wages are not going up in the same speed. The difference, a not inconsiderable sum, is going in the pockets of the nouveaux riches of the new and the old Patronat.

"Too, you must remember we are a race of anarchists. Maybe the last left. Periodically for no reason we want to change. It is some kind of mass hysterical. Do not forget that we still keep the *louis d'or* in the mattress. And we do not complain of the bruises caused by this, or the lack of good sleep.

"And now the people are tired, of all this, and they are what you say? pissed off, and they are going to just sit down. They will refuse to work or do anything, just like the students are.

"Now what you must do, Cheri . . ."

And she began to tell me. With great precision and in the greatest detail she laid out for me exactly what I must do to ride out the coming siege. It was going to be the worst time in France since the Second World War. It would not become civil war, she thought. But it would be bad enough. First, I must get in plenty of staples. I must buy flour, sugar and salt. A stock of honey was good to have. I must absolutely get to my bank and lay by as large a stock of cash francs as I could withdraw. I must buy plenty of soap, both for the bath and for the kitchen. And candles. Lots of candles were going to be a necessity during the electricity strikes. Lay in plenty of cigarettes and whisky. Any mail I wanted to get out I should send off right away. Canned goods of all varieties would always be useful in such a situation. Since I was a member of the American Commissary, I could get all these cheaper than in the large French stores like Samaritaine or Inno's. She had figured it all out perfectly, down to the slightest detail of my life.

I should not to try to buy all these things at once in the same store.

Go to different shops. Buy in small amounts. Go first to stores where I was known. Then go to stores where I was less known, or not known at all, which naturally would be less friendly to me, and therefore more suspicious.

While she lectured me on all of this, we had finished eating. Still lecturing me, she cleared the dishes away, then made us each an espresso on the little one-cup, one-handle *Comocafé* espresso machine like all the big five- and six-handle ones used by all the better cafés, and which she had advised me to buy. After she served the coffee, she went into the second bedroom cubicle and changed from her split-length housecoat into her green *robe de boudoir* while I poured us brandies. When she came back down the little hallway with the light from the kitchen behind her, you could see entirely through the robe, even to the spiky shadows between her legs of her body hair. After the brandies, we adjourned to my bedroom.

I suppose that we did just about everything that two people do together when making love to each other. Martine was very experienced.

When she left, carrying the little nightcase, she did not wake me. But I came awake enough myself to see by my watch dial that it was one forty-five A.M. I snuggled down, and fell back into sleep, peacefully and happily.

12

In the next two days I did everything exactly as Martine had told me. I felt like some kind of spy or undercover agent, but I followed her orders with as much precision as any Marine sergeant ever followed the orders of his commander.

The result of all this was that I was not only better prepared for what followed than all my French and American neighbors along the quai. I was even better prepared than the concierges along the block; which in Paris is really something to be able to say. I even went out and bought up some five-gallon plastic jerrycans, as she had told me, and had them filled with gasoline for my little car. Martine had said this would not become necessary for nearly a week. But since I had the time I went on out and did it. I stored the jerrycans in my portion of the deep *cave*, which I could lock up securely. This of course was strictly against the law, but so were a lot of things going to be against the law soon, and, in fact, already were.

While I was doing all this, I called Harry and told them about my inside information. They did not share Martine's Gallic pessimism the way I did. Of course, they didn't know her like I did. In fact, they did not know her or about her at all. Because I had never told them about her. But I was able to help them out later.

Martine was absolutely right about the gasoline troubles not coming on right away. But, as she also predicted, a lot of other things did, and they came fast.

On Friday, while I was doing all my necessary shopping and laying in, French workers all across the country occupied scores of factories. About half of these were in the Communist Party strongholds of the Paris suburbs. The other half were in the provinces. That same day General de Gaulle, with his usual caution and good sense, said, in effect, that he'd be damned if he would cut short his state visit to Romania for such silly tomfooleries. And on Saturday May 18th the major railroads, the post offices, and the airports began to go. Already by Saturday communications, transportation and production were throttled in a display of strikes that threatened to completely disrupt the entire French enonomic and political structure. Even the radio and television workers, technicians, producers and directors at the huge round O.R.T.F. building out on the Quai Kennedy had voted to strike, against the Government's muzzling of the news. As Martine had correctly predicted, the French people were just "pissed off". All these strikes were wildcat strikes, and even the Communist Party, grown fat and complacently nonmilitant over the years of its decent cooperation with the Government, was alarmed. It was like a huge snowball rolling downhill gathering momentum, speed and extra weight, and already threatening to turn itself into a real avalanche. And meanwhile, the students continued their strike and occupation of the universities in Paris and the provinces, as well as the Théâtre de l'Odéon. They were still marching and fighting in the streets every night, and cordons of police were everywhere.

Our by-now quite cohesive American group continued to meet every evening at the Gallaghers, and on Sunday the 19th, when we all met again to slurp up (that's the only honest word I can use) another of Louisa's curries, Weintraub and Samantha Everton were there. We huddled around the now nearly worthless TV, and listened to radio stations Europe Number One and Radio Luxembourg. In the last few days everybody seemed to have bought himself a pocket transistor radio, complete with earplug for use in the restaurants.

I think the thing that shocked us all most was the complete stoppage of trans-Atlantic air traffic at Orly. The great lumbering 707s, landing and taking off with such precision at two-minute intervals in front of that great new glittering chrome-and-glass terminal, heading out for and coming in from destinations all over the world, were as dependable a part of life, now, as the air they flew through. It was like the old blue-and-white Greyhound bus of your youth, which, in their interiors, I've got to say they resembled. The railroads were stopped, which we more or less expected. The docks were struck, and no shipping was sailing. But when Orly and the airlines went, and went totally and completely, I think we realized for the first time seriously that we were cut off. The only way out of France now was if you had a car, and that only as long as the gas held out.

And yet, there was a merry, excited quality about our gathering that Sunday night. As I've said, it was like those first exciting days of a major war.

As for Weintraub and Samantha, they were as merry as the rest. I was interested in observing both of them. I was interested especially because of what Harry'd told me about her repeated phone calls to him. But she and Weintraub seemed completely with each other, with Sam still holding her old position of master, naturally. In fact, it was as if they had not missed a day with us since the last time we had seen them a week before; and Sam made absolutely no reference or allusion to the passes she had made at the two Gallaghers the time before.

I found Harry's reaction to this last fact ambiguous. He seemed nonplussed. At the bar, alone, he told me he was relieved she hadn't, hadn't acted up. And yet I thought he was a little piqued.

Later, not without a little deliberate maneuvering, I found myself alone at the pulpit bar with Weintraub. There was never any need to urge Weintraub to talk, about anything.

"Yeah," he said, "we were out of town from Sunday night till Friday morning," without my having asked him. "That's why we never showed up. And all Friday and Saturday and today I was with the kids at the Odéon."

"What kids?"

"Hill's Cinema Committee. By the way, he didn't get elected Chairman. Did you know that? Some other kid did."

"But if—" I started, but stopped. But I don't think Weintraub even noticed.

He took a big slug from his drink and sucked at his cigarette. "Oh, boy. You talk about an orgy," he said. "I never saw no orgy like this, man. And, as you probably know, I made that circuit for a while, in Paris."

I kept my mouth shut.

"It was some chateau just out beyond Fontainebleau. Some little town. I don't remember. Anyway the chateau wasn't in the town, it was way off by itself in some big forest. And talk about chateaus. They could move this one to the Loire Valley and it would not be out of place, believe me, Hartley. I never did find out who owned it. I never even found out who the host was. Maybe there was not any host even. Where that girl gets her contacts I got no idea. But she's sure got them. You never saw so many—there was nothing but socialites and big-name film people and bankers and, and God knows what.

"Why that kid chooses to stay with me in my little one room pad—

"Anyway, we stayed there from Sunday night through Thursday night and did not leave for town till Friday morning."

I simply couldn't resist. "But if you were out there all that time, how could she make all those phone calls to—" I stopped myself.

He peered at me narrowly. "To who? Not to you. To old Harry? Hell, all she had to do was to step into some temporarily vacant room and pick up the phone, man. Life's freebeesville out there, man."

"How did you know they were to Harry?"

"She told me," Weintraub said.

"Did she tell you what they were about?"

"No. She didn't. I didn't ask her." There was a slight pause. "How did you know about them?"

"Well, Harry told me. Naturally. What else?"

Weintraub shrugged and slugged back more booze. "She sure is some strange kid." Another pause. "I asked her about why she chose to stay in my grubby little pad and she said, Weintraub you are naïve if you think knowing a few rich orgiasts is going to get me to Israel. She had no desire to become some cat's property, she said. And nobody was going to put her up in a place when they knew that as soon as she got enough loot together she was going to cut for Israel."

"She could hustle for it," I said sourly.

"Sure she could. And knowing her, I certainly aint believing *that* would ever make her feel bad, or guilty. Like I said, *I* think she's just having too good a time to want to move on."

I thought it was time I made myself another drink. I certainly had no answer, no riposte, for that.

"But let me tell you about the kids," Weintraub said proudly.

I will spare you his dialogue. On the Friday morning after returning he had gone around to the Sorbonne to look up Hill and his group. He was becoming seriously attached to them, and to their ideal. He found they had moved the day before to somewhere in the vast backstage interior of the Odéon. Sam was at his place, sleeping it all off, so he had gone over there to try and find them.

Well, you had no idea what it was like until you had been in there. In the first place it was so crowded around the entrance by people trying to get into the 24-hour-a-day marathon dialogue in the amphitheater itself that you could hardly get in the place at all. Once you did get in, and up through the marble staircases and columns to the first floor where the red-plush entrances to the old amphitheater itself were, you were completely blocked off from any entrance to the backstage area by gangs of young toughs, *blousons noirs* kids, with thick chains hanging around their necks. The chains apparently served as both their badge of office, and as weapons if necessary. They were guards, hired, or at least acquired, by the students. Certainly none of them could pass for University students. In fact, most of them appeared never to have finished primary school, let alone *lycée*. They were everywhere, and they were adamant about not letting anybody pass who did not have a *Laissez-Passer* card. Finally Weintraub had got one of them, a huge, broad, fat muscle-boy with an evil grin but an apparently ready sense of humor, to go up into the dim labyrinthine backstage interior and bring down Hill Gallagher, who got him through. And that was how Weintraub finally became a bona-fide member of the *Comité du Cinéma des Étudiants de la Sorbonne*. He took out of his pants pocket his permanent *Laissez-Passer* card and showed it to me.

What he finally found when Hill led him up through five or six crowded grubby floors was a tiny room under the eaves crowded with one table-desk, one large refrigerator box containing cans of film, and

13 or 14 rather smelly and not well-washed students, all talking at the same time. One of the floors they passed had been set up as a provisory hospital, where young boys and girls in dirty white coats often with bloodstains on them ran in and out saying "Shh!" to everybody. You could hear the moans and groans of the wounded, presumably students, as you passed it.

What the 13 or 14 students were arguing about Weintraub never did find out. Despite his excellent French the student patois coupled with a lot of argot made it difficult for him to understand, and besides as soon as he entered he immediately began to sweat profusely which distracted him further. The entire little room, which had only one small skylight, felt like a hot-house for orchid growers. The Chairman who had been elected over Hill, sitting behind the table-desk, was, or claimed to be, a Swiss student and had never been registered at the Sorbonne. He wore round steel-rimmed glasses, and looked and acted like a genuine Commissar. Two doors led off from the small room, in addition to the entrance door. Behind one was apparently a temporary kitchen which had been set up as a place for them to get something to eat occasionally, and beyond the other was a place a few of them at a time at least could snatch some sleep. Weintraub had spent all of Friday, Friday night, most of Saturday and all day today with them.

It was on Saturday that the great *crise* came, when they thought they were going to be raided by a flying squad of riot police and had transferred all their cans of shot film out of a rear door and spirited them all to Weintraub's one-room pad in his *pension*, where they remained hidden even now. Though, it developed, the police raid did not materialize after all.

"I'm pretty proud of that," Weintraub grinned at me across Harry's bar. "They really do trust me, those kids. You ought to come along with me and see it. It's something to have seen."

"I guess so," I said.

"As a matter of fact," Weintraub smiled, "I am commissioned by the Committee to *request* you to come."

"Me? Really? But why?"

"Well, I'm trying to introduce them to certain different stars and directors I know who might help them. Burton. Harrison. And when I mentioned you, the idea was brought up immediately that you might be the right one to write the commentary for their film for them. A lot of them read your Review, you know," he added as an obvious flattery.

I thought about it for a moment. "All right. I'll come with you one day. I'd certainly like to see it. When can we go?"

"Why not go tonight?" Weintraub grinned. He looked around Harry's crowded living room. "We can go as soon as we leave here."

"Tonight?"

"Sure. Why not? They'll all be there."

"What about Sam?"

"She'll go with us. She's been going ever since Saturday morning. She's got her own card. She loves it up there." He paused to suck at his cigarette, and grinned. "You're liable to see some pretty strange sights up there. So be prepared."

I looked around Harry's quiet living room myself. At the moment everybody was drinking and waiting for the curry, whose delicious odor drifted in to us from Louisa's kitchen. "Okay. Why not? What have I got to lose?"

"Not a thing in the world," said Weintraub cheerfully. "Oh, by the way, I think I better tell you that Hill voted against having the Committee to ask you to come."

That took me back a little. "But, why?"

Weintraub shrugged. "I don't know. I guess because you're such a close 'relative', so to speak. I guess he felt it would be like them asking his dad to come help them."

"That irritates me," I said.

"Don't let it. He was way outvoted. So we'll go? After?"

"Yes."

We took a back way route that mounted the rue Cardinal Lemoine and passed up and around the Panthéon. Apparently there was fighting again tonight at the Carrefour St.-Michel. As we climbed the hill toward Contrescarpe I could still taste Louisa's curry, and sucked at my teeth and gums appreciatively. We turned at the rue Clovis. Lots of people were out tonight, and a heady excitement floated on the air. But the Panthéon itself was deserted, and nearly dark. At least seven or eight big camions of CRS were parked square in front of the Panthéon, in the *Place* there, loaded with men and ready to move. There was a Commissariat on the opposite corner, and uniformed policemen moved in and out the door continually. Every few seconds a helmeted motorcycle cop roared up, or roared away. We took the rue Cujas down the far side. When we crossed the Boulevard St.-Michel to rue Monsieur-le-Prince, we could hear the roar of the fighting, way down at the Carrefour. The street was jammed with people craning their necks and looking. There were no cars.

I had seen the Odéon once with Harry on Thursday, but I was totally unprepared for the crowding and hysteria we encountered as soon as we turned into Monsieur-le-Prince off the Place Edmond Rostand. We cut left on Vaugirard, and before we turned back right on the rue Corneille beside the Odéon building we could see a huge cordon of CRS or *Gendarmes Mobiles* blocking off the entirety of Vaugirard in front of the building that houses the Senate. The low little walkway under the low thick arches that surrounds the Odéon building was so jammed with exultant students that we kept to the street, but the street was almost as crowded. The great majority of the crowd did not seem to be students.

When we got to the great front doors under the colonnade, it was hard to get close enough to the door guard to get admitted. The porch was mobbed by people trying to get into the talkathon in the amphitheater, and a lot of them were socialites. I recognized the Countess Something-or-other, and saw the Baroness de Whatcha-ma-call-it, whom I had met a few times, both of them with fairly large groups, the ladies all in their furs and escorted by tall handsome men in dinner jackets. Preferential treatment was obviously being given to celebrities of this type.

Once we were in and up the not-crowded marble staircase to the first floor I recognized Dave's great fat muscle-boy, who wore a bight of bicycle chain three feet long with both ends open and dangling near his waist. The armpits of his half-open jersey shirt gave off an odor that spoke of years of insufficiently washed-away sweat still lingering in them. He grinned and let us through when Weintraub explained who I was. "But be sure you get your pal a card for hisself, hunh?" he called after us in French.

On the back stairs and in the corridors, through half-open doors, every cubbyhole and room seemed filled with a committee of students violently discussing something or other and the cigarette smoke was thicker than fog. The corridor floors were filthy with ash marks and rubbed-out butts on the once-red carpet. But then the whole place looked like it hadn't been washed in over a 100 years anyway. We were properly "Shh!"-ed by the dedicated white-coated workers of the hospital, then after two more flights we were in the little room under the eaves already described to me by Weintraub earlier.

Terri of the beautiful hair was there, so was bearded Bernard, so was Anne-Marie of course, and so was the half-American girl Florence, who for some reason now seemed to have attached herself to Weintraub. Hill was there, too, but after an embarrassed perfunctory handshake he backed off into a corner and said little.

The first thing we took care of was my card. With crisp dispatch the Chairman, who was called Daniel, seized a white card and on it wrote: ODÉON—COMMISSION CINÉMA LAISSEZ-PASSER PERMANENT—and then looked up at me through his steel-rimmed glasses. I had already been introduced as Monsieur Hartley.

"What is your name?" he asked.

"Why, Hartley," I said.

"No. Your first name."

"Jack."

He wrote it JACQUES on the card, in red ink this time, explaining as he did it, "We never use last names here, on anything we write. It is a precaution. It is a safety measure, for you, as well as for the Committee. Should this card by any accident fall into the hands of the police, you know." His French had a slightly strange accent to the ear. He signed it with an illegible flourish and handed it to me and I put it in my left front pants pocket. Like Weintraub. I somehow appeared not to want it in my wallet, with my passport and my credit cards.

Then we launched into a hot and heavy and long-winded discussion about my writing the Commentary for the film they wanted to make. Weintraub was certainly right when he said it was hot in there. Would I be interested in writing such a Commentary? Yes, I certainly would. But I couldn't very well write it until I had seen at least rushes, and preferably a finished copy, of the film they would make. Here someone else broke in. Well, of course, that was the trouble at the moment. They had no way of getting developed the film they had already shot.

Whoever the boy was, he indicated the refrigerator box and the cans of film in it. The police were watching every shop and company that developed film in Paris, both still photos and *ciné*, and any student film that was turned in would certainly be confiscated. Well, I was willing to wait, I let them know. But I certainly couldn't write or even begin to write a Commentary for them until I could see some film. And anyway, I pointed out, the Revolution wasn't finished yet. Would I be willing to write and print some articles about them and their aims and the aims of the Revolution in my English-language Review? I was asked. I certainly would, and gladly. They would be willing to give me a boy, or a girl, to work closely with me on them. When did I expect the next issue of my Review to appear? I was asked sharply by Daniel. I explained that that depended on a number of things. I had an issue about ready to go, but my Review was printed in Holland, because it was so much cheaper there, and that presented a problem about getting the material up there, since the transportation and mail strikes. I needn't worry about that, I was informed by Daniel.

He grinned at me. "We—that is, the students, not the Cinema Committee alone—have cars going to Holland all the time. We could deliver the material for you. And by boys without long hair." His own hair was cut short, I noted. "We feel," he looked around, "at least, *I* feel that the sooner the articles on us are on the stands in Paris and in America the better it is for us, and for the Revolution. Does anyone have any discussion on that?"

Instantly there was a babble of voices that made my head really ache. They certainly did have a thing about discussion. I had noticed from the moment I entered that this thing of democratic discussion was as much a sacred ritual with them as some other ritual might be with a church, and it was beginning to give me a pain in the ass. Also, I found I was taking an active dislike to Daniel the Chairman for some reason I could not isolate or name. It was hot as hell in there, I was sweating, and the whole thing had been in French, which, though I speak it well enough, tires me when it is done in a climate of emotional excitement. And now Weintraub and that little girl Florence appeared to have disappeared somewhere.

Just as if he had actively read my thoughts, Daniel smiled at me and said, "Let one of us show you around the rest of our establishment up here, why don't you?" He then plunged right back into the discussion, which by this time had turned from the delivery of my Review through to Holland to something having to do with various shooting assignments the various teams were competing for for tomorrow.

The boy who took me around had long hair, and his long hair could have stood a good washing. He was called Raymond. The first place he took me was to the right, into the "cooking" area, which was in fact slightly larger than the "office". It was nearly empty, the floor was dotted with rather ripe-looking blankets, and over a tiny butane cooking apparatus one boy was heating himself some canned soup. And over in one corner Weintraub was fucking that half-American girl Florence.

The boy Raymond, he was quite short, did not turn one greasy hair. "Would you like to take a look down at the theater? We have our own special balcony," he told me quietly in French.

"Why, yes," I said. Neither Weintraub nor Florence looked up from their locked embrace, and as far as I could tell, without actually peering, did not even break their rhythm.

So Raymond led me past the boy, still concentratedly heating his soup, down the narrow room to another door at the far end. When we opened it and stepped through, shutting it behind us, we were on a tiny darkened balcony right up under the roof of the theater itself. Seven floors below us the nonstop dialogue which had been going ever since the students occupied the Odéon four days ago was in full cry. A tall blond boy on the stage who was chairing the debate with a large gavel, and doing it well, had recognized a citizen, obviously not a student, and certainly no executive, in other words a worker, who was asking to large numbers of angry boos whether the developing general strikes might not be doing more harm to the French people than good. Amidst lots of derisive shouts the man stuck to his point and developed his argument, which was essentially that what France really needed was more inflow of American capital investment, which according to him would automatically change the antiquated French capitalistic structure and bring it along to the more modern American corporate system and in so doing would both quietly and peacefully do away with the old entrenched French Patronat which was the root of all the trouble anyway. He sat down red-faced to a smattering of applause and a great number of derisive boos. The blond boy beat his gavel and recognized someone else, who rose to refute the first man. We went back in. I could hardly help seeing that Weintraub and Florence were still at it.

"Would you like to take a look at the sleeping quarters?" Raymond said politely.

"Why, yes. I would," I said. I hoped it sounded cool enough.

We went back through the "office", still vibrating with some democratic discussion or other, and through the other door. This room was narrower but considerably longer than the "cooking quarters", darker, its floor covered with sleeping bags, greasy mattresses and the same sleazy-looking blankets, and on one of these Hill Gallagher was humping Samantha Everton. The blanket didn't cover much of them, and Samantha, who was not a tall girl at all, appeared to have very long and lovely legs—as pretty as Louisa's in fact, which were the handsomest I'd ever seen.

"Very nice," I said, and ducked back into the reverberating office immediately, "but what do you do about baths?"

"Oh, we go to the public baths around the area," Raymond smiled. "When we have the time to."

The kids were still discussing. I could not quite make out what the new discussion was about, but Weintraub had reappeared, sweating and red-faced.

"She's quite a little chick, old Florence," he grinned when he came over. "Would you like to try her? She likes you, she said. Likes you a lot."

"She said that?"

"Sure. I wouldn't kid you."

"I wonder if she washed?" I said.

"Washed?" Weintraub said. "Washed? Oh, washed. Well, I guess so. There's a john right outside in the hall. She went there."

At that moment Florence, looking pleased and happy, came in from the outside door; and suddenly something took hold of me and I thought why not? After all, if this was the way it was going to be, why not see what it was like? I might be an "Older Generation", but I still ought to know what the new world was going to be like. So when Florence came over to us, I took her hand.

Actually, she needed no urging. We went immediately into the "cooking quarters", where the preoccupied boy was now eating the can of soup he had so laboriously and meticulously heated. We used the same blanket in the same corner she and Weintraub had used, and I was pleased to see that we did not upset the young man's meal.

I must say that she was not much of a lay. She certainly did not have any of Martine's experience or finesse. She just sort of laid there. But, of course, as Weintraub said later, she was very young, she was only a kid.

13

"YOU CAN'T EXPECT HER to have the ability of someone older who's had years of practice and education in bed behind them," Weintraub said reasonably.

"Perhaps not," I said. "But look at Sam. She's the same age. Nineteen, too." I was feeling bad now about the whole thing.

"Ah, but Sam is a different kettle of fish!" He grinned. "To coin an apt phrase. She's sophisticated. She's been around plenty."

"I suppose." I felt gloomy. "But what about her and Hill, now? I saw them in the—, you know." I coughed. "I thought Florence was Hill's—well, you know."

"But none of them believe in sleeping with just one person. Monogamistic love," Weintraub said agitatedly. "You know that. Unless, of course, both parties decide that that is what they want. Then it's their business. You know all that. So Sam's making it with Hill a little bit now. And Florence is making it with me. And you. And a bunch of others, I expect."

We were sitting in a bar. In fact, it was the old Monaco Bar, that bum's hangout, the same place where Dave had told me about first meeting the Cinema Group kids earlier in the month. We had left the Odéon around one-thirty, with the understanding I would do what I could about writing a Commentary for them when and if that were possible, and in the meantime would try to get two articles written for the Review, all of the material for which, the entire issue, the kids would guarantee to get out to my printers in Holland for me. They had offered me an assistant, and I had chosen the angelic-faced Terri of the beautiful hair when Hill, after his tête-à-tête with Samantha, had declined my request for him. Sam had not left with us.

I must say, the old Monaco did not look like such a low dive anymore, after the happenings of the past few weeks. We had walked straight down to it from the front steps of the Odéon along the rue de l'Odéon. Ahead of us all that way was a huge cordon of police and police camions at the Carrefour, blocking off rue de l'Odéon where it met Boulevard St.-Germain. The CRS boys were lined up across the entire street, at least three lines deep, and wearing their helmets, gasmasks and fighting raincoats, and carrying shields and the long *matraques*. They hardly looked human. The smell of tear gas was everywhere, but we all were used to that by now.

"Don't worry about it. You and me can walk right through them to the Boulevard," Weintraub said cheerily as he led me into his old Monaco stamping-ground. "Of course, if we were twenty years younger and had long hair we probably couldn't," he added.

We had picked an empty table at the back.

"I think Hill is falling for her," I said now, after the exchange on sex. "For Sam. I mean in a really serious way."

"Oh, come on! Of course he is! Just like he fell for Florence, and then turned her over to me and that other kid. What's his name? Raymond. The one that took you around."

He was probably right. In any case I didn't think it was that important anyway. "Listen, Dave," I said. "I've just had an idea. A really brilliant idea. It was playing around sort of in the back of my mind all the time we were up there, and now suddenly it has crystallized."

"So what is it?"

"I'm not the man to do their Commentary on their film for them. Oh, I could do one. And I'll certainly go ahead and write those articles for them for the Review, though I doubt if they will help them as much as they are hoping. But as for doing a film Commentary, I'm not really the man they want. I've never done any film work. Harry Gallagher is the man they want!"

Weintraub did not answer for a full minute, and then grabbed up his Pernod and drained its milky contents suddenly and almost savagely. "Well, Jesus! Why didn't I think of that?" Then he paused another very long moment. "But it's going to cause all sorts of hell's orchards with Hill, you know. He was furious enough when I suggested bringing you over. I told you, he voted against, remember? What'll happen if they ask his dad to come?"

"Are we doing all this for the Cinema Committee, or are we all doing it all for the sake of Hill Gallagher?" I said.

"That's true," Weintraub said thoughtfully. He signaled for another Pernod. "But somehow it bothers me. I don't know what could happen."

"Listen," I said. "If it's for the good of the 'Revolution'—and you know what *I* think this 'Revolution' is going to come out to in the end—I don't see how Hill can fight it. Is he for the *Révolution?* or is he for Hill Gallagher?"

"Well," Weintraub said. "*I* am for the *Révolution*. We could go back up there and present them with the idea, certainly."

"Harry would be *perfect* for what they want," I said. "And I'm not chickening out or anything."

He drained off his new Pernod savagely, after adding a little water, and I suddenly had the distinct impression, quite clearly, that he was not at all that happy or that much at ease about having had to give up his beautiful Samantha to Hill, or to any of the others for that matter. "Okay, let's go," he said toughly, and pushed the little cash register tabs for our drinks over to me suggestively. I picked them up.

"But will they be there still, now?"

"Are you kidding? They'll be there all night, most of them."

So that was what we did. We turned our backs on the massive cordon of CRS at the foot of the street and walked straight back up to the massive front steps of the Odéon where our *Laissez-Passer* cards got us admitted immediately through the crowds.

"You understand I hate to do this to Hill," Weintraub said to me as we went up the marble stairs to the first floor, "but I do think it is good for the entirety of the *Révolution*." I had not anywhere questioned his motives.

It turned out that Hill was not there when we arrived back up at the tiny moisture-laden little room up under the eaves backstage.

Neither was Sam. They had gone somewhere. And after my presentation of the case for Harry's nomination to do the Commentary, led on by Daniel the Chairman who harangued forcefully for Harry during the inevitable democratic discussion which followed, there was, with the absence of Hill and a few others, a unanimous vote in favor of asking Harry to do it. Anne-Marie voted for it, so did my now co-associate Terri, so did the bearded Bernard. And certainly Daniel the Chairman voted for it. It turned out that not one of the Cinema Committee knew or realized that Harry Gallagher, the famous avant-garde and radical screenwriter, was the father of their *Comité* member Hill Gallagher of the same last name.

"I'll talk to him about it tomorrow," I said to Weintraub as we made our dim way back downstairs and left through the crowd.

I called Harry the next morning.

"What? A Commentary? A Commentary on the film *they* are going to make? On the Revolution?" There was a pause. "Hell, yes! *Christ,* yes! I'd love to do it!" Then another pause. "But I'll have to see shot film. And I'll have to have cutting permission. I'll have to be able to work with whoever they have for cutters."

"I think they will give you all that, and more if you want. Look, I'll take you over there tonight. Around midnight. That is, Weintraub and I will take you," I added. "It was really his idea from the beginning."

"Okay. But wait," Harry said. "Wait. Wait a minute. I'm not sure I can go tonight. I've got a meeting. I guess you know what happened at Cannes yesterday?"

In fact, I did not. I had not yet seen the morning papers. Harry proceeded to tell me about it.

Apparently on Sunday night the Cannes Film Festival, which had been going on for some days, had been closed down five days early by a group of agitators composed largely of the younger French directors and actors like Godard, Louis Malle, François Truffaut, Jean-Pierre Leaud and Carlos Saura. There was some confusion as to why, but mainly it was supposed to be a sympathy strike with the students and workers of France. Geraldine Chaplin, the pretty young star of the Spanish film *Peppermint Frappé* had rushed up onto the stage and attempted to close the curtains on the showing of her own film. M. Favre Le Bret had proceeded to close down the entire proceedings after these demonstrations, to avoid the possibility of violence during film showings and "since circumstances did not permit projections under normal conditions." So the whole thing was definitely finished, for the year.

"So I've got to get down there," Harry said over the phone.

I didn't understand. "But why? If it's all over and finished, what's the point? Why do you have to go?"

"I'm going down to strike my own film," Harry said. "It's the only film still shooting in France, for Christ's sake." I could hear the clarion call of the old warrior in his voice.

"You're what?" I roared. "You're out of your mind. It's an American film, not a French one."

"Doesn't matter," Harry said. "They're using French crews. I'm going to strike it." It was a French-murder-Western-love-story which was being shot in the semi-desert Camargue country by Harry's old friend Allen Steinerwein. Harry had not only written it, but had worked on it all along with Steinerwein.

"You really must be out of your mind," I said into the phone.

"No," Harry said. "We had a meeting of the Directors and Actors Union, yesterday night, after the news came in, late, and voted to strike that film, too. I was selected to go down because I know personally just about every grip and cameraman-technician working on it."

"But what about poor Allen Steinerwein?"

"Tough luck. But he'll have to take his chances like everybody else. So we're having a strategy meeting this afternoon, to decide on the best approach. That's why I'm afraid I might not be able to make it to the Odéon with you tonight."

"Well, I suppose it will wait till you get back," I said. "But these kids are getting nervous and if anybody ever needed help, I think they do. How long will you be gone?"

"I don't really know. It depends on how much trouble I have when I get there. Five days. Maybe a week."

"Well then I think you really ought to try to make it to Odéon tonight. Before you leave."

"Actually I probably won't leave until Wednesday," Harry said.

"Look. I'll call you tonight. After dinner. Sometime around ten-thirty. I'll know more about what the situation is like by then. Okay?"

"All right. But I think you really are off your rocker."

There was a pause, as if he not only did not care about my comment, but actually had not heard it, something else totally occupying his mind. Then he said, "What is Hill going to think, or say, about all this?" he asked suddenly. "He's on that Committee, aint he?"

"I'm sure he'll be against it," I said. "He was already against Weintraub bringing even me over there. But he's already been outvoted by a massive majority."

Harry didn't answer for a moment. "Well, if he was outvoted that much, I think it's my duty to go anyway. Don't you?"

"I suppose I did," I said. "It was my idea in the first place. —But I do think you've gone off your nut to go to Cannes. Let somebody else go."

"Go fuck yourself," he said.

"Good-bye," I answered. "Don't forget to call tonight."

But the phone had already gone dead somewhere in the middle.

I dined alone that night. I went across the bridge, past the two little camions of cops who were there now 24 hours a day, to Chez René on the corner of Cardinal Lemoine and Boulevard St.-Germain, a favorite place of mine for years where I was well known by all the waiters and the boss himself, who had been a wheel in the *Résistance*. I had had a bellyful of students, film Documentaries and Commentaries, and film people in general. Who in hell gave a real damn about the Cannes Film Festival anyway? Whether they struck them God damned selves or not? It was some kind of macabre joke. And I was sick of Harry, driving all that way down to Cannes, to strike his own film. He must really be out of his head.

I was back home by ten-thirty, passing the ominous, yet gentle and preoccupied little blue camions. Several of the cops inside, who knew my face by now, waved and grinned at me. The phone rang soon after I was back in the apartment.

"I'm ready to go," Harry said. "Can you get Weintraub?"

"We're to pick him up at the Monaco Bar," I said. "I'll meet you at the footbridge, okay?"

I do not think I ever saw anyone take over a roomful of people the

way Harry took over that sweaty, steamy, overladen little room under
the eaves of the Odéon and its gang of democratic-discussion–oriented
students. Not one of them talked back, or offered to argue, or mentioned discussion. This included Hill. And anyway, Harry went right
to the prime point.

"You say you want to make a film about the Revolution. But what
kind of film is it you want to make? Something to be shown at Rotary
Clubs and Ladies' Clubs luncheons across America? Just what have
you got shot? Have you listed it down, for each can, like you should
have done? No. Of course not. Nobody thought of that. So what you've
got here is this. And nobody really knows what it is, really." He looked
at the refrigerator box. "Is this all the shot film you've acquired during
the past month?"

"No," said Chairman Daniel, who was looking less and less like a
steel-rimmed Commissar. "We have at least that much more stored in
the private quarters of Mister Weintraub here."

"Ha!" said Harry. "All right. That's not so bad. Except for one
thing—repetition. I'll bet you got about two miles of film, most of it
over- or under-exposed, showing groups of students marching toward a
stationary camera; and about two miles of film, over- or under-
exposed, of masked cops charging a stationary camera, which is probably hand-held and wavery anyway. And what kind of a film are you
going to make out of that? They probably won't even want to show it
in the high schools in the States, let alone the colleges.

"So. Questions:

"Have you even got remotely in mind any sort of a continuity, a
story? If you have, you've got to have characters. Have you got
characters, to whom things happen, and whom the audience can follow
the development of through-out?

"No. Of course, you haven't. You never thought of that, did you?"
Harry looked sardonically, and very professionally around the room.
"Take him," he said, indicating Terri of the beautiful hair. "He'd
make the perfect boy for your film." He looked again. "And take her."
He indicated Anne-Marie. "You give me those two, plus three camera
crews, with or without hand-held cameras, and I can make you a film
that will be begged for in every theater in America. And I can do it all
in ten days. I think the Revolution is going to last that long. And I'm

sure there's some footage in what you've already shot that we can use for fill-in, timewise.

"Now. Do you want to do that? Or something like that? If so, I'm your man. And gladly. And all for free. I don't want a dime of the take. But I'll get your story seen, and loved, in every moviehouse in Europe and America." He paused, and grinned. "Except perhaps in France."

"Well, we asked you over here for that kind of professional advice, Mister Gallagher," Chairman Daniel said, in an exceedingly unbrassy voice, for him. "I think we ought to discuss it, though, first. Since that is the method we hold to in a democratic Revolution of this sort."

"Well, you discuss it, gentlemen," Harry said. "I'm prepared to sit and wait half an hour. But I will not discuss. And if I take it on for you, there will be no more discussion once you designate me as the 'Man'. From that time on I'll have to be the absolute boss. Please understand that."

"I'm not sure we can decide in half an hour," Daniel said placatingly.

"Well, that's okay," Harry grinned. "I've got to go to Cannes to do a little job tomorrow or next day. You can have until I return, which may be anywhere from five days to a week. There'll still be plenty of Revolution left to shoot from, I expect. Especially with all this footage that you've got shot already, to splice in when we need it. I'll need to get to know your cutters, of course. Need to get to know them intimately. Because once the shooting is all done we'll be working together very closely."

"We haven't even decided on cutters yet," Daniel said.

"Well, like I said, you've got roughly five days or a week." And he stood up from the chair where he had been sitting uncomfortably in front of the "office" table-desk.

Young Hill had been standing far at the back, in a darkened corner, all of this time while Harry was making his big-time lecture. I guess I had sidled slowly over toward him unconsciously. He and Harry had said a brief "Hello" and passed a perfunctory handshake when we first came in. But after that, Hill had offered not a word.

Somewhere in the middle of Harry's statement, a statement which I must say I thought took too tough a line with these unprofessional kids and was also a bit egocentrically long-winded, Samantha Everton had slipped in through the outside door and quietly slipped over to us.

"I don't think you understand one thing, Mister Gallagher," Daniel the Chairman said now, looking up at the standing Harry. "We don't want to make a love-story movie, or something on that order. We want only to show the truth to the world of what has happened, is happening and will happen in this Revolution of ours."

"I am totally in accord with that," Harry said sharply. "But I must add one point. Do not forget that the audiences of the world don't give a damn about the truth, unless it is presented to them in a way in which they can personally associate. They do not, for example, give one good goddamn about seeing seas of anonymous student faces, or even thousands of fighting, attacking cops' faces—especially if they're covered with gasmasks. They want to participate in the agony of a few students, whom they can pick out, recognize, and as I said, associate with over and over through the film. That seems to me to be, gentlemen, your basic problem here.

"Anyway, you gentlemen discuss it. I've got to go. And as soon as I'm back from setting up this strike in Cannes, I'll be in touch. Ça va? Okay?" They had been speaking in French all the way, but he added the word "okay" in English, at the end.

"Okay," Daniel grinned back.

Harry had made quite an impression, I must say that. And I noted that he had held back his purpose of striking the film in Cannes until the very last, like a good professional. Now he turned away and, grinning, came over to where Hill and I stood in our darkened corner. He was a tall man, and he had his arms out, to put one of them around each of us. "Let's us go and have a drink, what do you say?" he said. He pretended not to see Samantha.

I have always been sure, by the look that passed swiftly across his face and was as swiftly swallowed, hidden, put away, that he at that moment knew what had happened and was in process of happening with Hill and Sam.

"You can come with us, too, if you want," he said to her.

"I thought you were magnificent," Sam said in a near whisper. "Although I only heard the last half of it."

Harry continued with his gesture, and put one friendly arm around me and the other around Hill. He somehow carefully excluded Sam from this embrace. "You can come too, if you want, Dave," he called across several heads to where Weintraub sat on a wood bench with Florence.

"No thanks," Weintraub said with a fine grin. "I guess I'll stay here and listen in on the discussion. I'll be your spy." Everybody laughed, and a fine feeling was in the room as the four of us went out the door.

I don't remember what bar it was we went to. It was not the old Monaco. We took to the rue Racine again, as Harry and I had done once before, which was not blocked off by any cordon of CRS. We came out onto the Boulevard St.-Michel which was still jammed with people craning to watch the fighting still going on down at the Carrefour with St.-Germain. We walked south, uphill, away from the river, and it was one of those bars along there that Harry stopped at, and went in, and sat down inside.

Almost at once I felt like, as my old grandfather might have said, the proverbial one-armed paper-hanger with an itch. Whatever it was was happening, or was going to happen, they none of them wanted me around.

So I left them there, and walked home up the rue Soufflot and past the darkened Panthéon, with its CRS-loaded camions all in a line, and then down Cardinal Lemoine. It was almost the same way we had come.

14

I MUST SAY I REALLY did not think anything had happened. I mean what, after all, could have happened? And Harry called the next day to tell me he was leaving for Cannes that evening, the Tuesday, instead of on the Wednesday. Then late on the Wednesday afternoon Hill called me.

I had spent most of the Wednesday at his parents' place watching TV. They were showing the second (and last) day of the debate in the Assemblée Nationale on the motion of censure against Premier Pompidou's Government and M. Pompidou was speaking himself. It was the first time the Government had allowed such a broadcast since the troubles started. But after Pompidou's own speech, a tough and fairly reasonable effort I thought, I got bored with the rest of it and went home hoping to work. Anyway, Pompidou's Government survived the attempt to topple it, though only by 11 votes.

It wasn't long after I got home that Hill called. I do not know where he called from. In any case, what he wanted to tell me was that Samantha had suddenly disappeared. Hill was in great personal distress. Naturally, I asked him to come right over to my pad, as we "Older Generations" all call our apartments nowadays.

"Don't say anything to Mother or Dad," he asked.

"Your dad's already gone."

"Oh. I forgot. Well, don't say anything to Mother."

"Of course not," I said. "Are you out of your mind?"

"Maybe," Hill said. "Anyway I just got to talk to somebody."

I was flattered by that. I also of course realized immediately that he was in love. Madly in love, probably. For the first time in his miserable young life. And, with all of the possible choices in that good young life, in love with Samantha-Marie Everton.

And, suddenly, not only that, I was reasonably sure I could give him the telephone number where she could be reached in Cannes. I knew the hotel where Harry always stayed in Cannes. It was the Carlton.

Hill certainly looked haggard when he arrived. He was gaunt almost to the point of emaciation. There were deep-blue circles under his eyes, and the eyes themselves I could hardly look at because of the depth of anguish in them.

What in the *name* of *God* could Harry have been thinking of? I thought secretly. Christ. Christ almighty. Christ, Christ.

I've got to say he did not mess around, Hill. "I'm in deep trouble, Jack—Uncle Jack," he said.

"Jack is okay," I said.

"I'm in deep trouble," he said, staring wildly at the floor, as if it were responsible for whatever it was that had happened to him. For a second I almost expected him to kick it viciously, in revenge.

"Well, it happens to lots of people around your age," I said. "It even happens to people my age."

"I'm in love," he said, dully, and flopped down in my best chair.

I was a little put off, startled. I had thought that that was already understood, between us. So I tried to be light. "Oh," I said, "I thought it was something serious."

"Don't joke around." He glared at me almost viciously.

Seriously, I said, "I did not mean to joke. I was only trying to get you to loosen up, maybe laugh."

"Well, don't. And don't joke," Hill said. "Do you know what this is doing to me? What it's already done?"

"I guess I have some idea. Don't forget I was married for nine years, before I was divorced. Anyway: So she's gone."

"Absolutely. I checked with Weintraub. And with the other guys I know who she made it with. And with the two girls that I know of that she slept with. Not one soul has seen her since Monday night. Not since she was with dad and me."

I went over to the bar. Hill leaped up from the easy chair and followed me two paces behind as if afraid to let me get anywhere beyond arm's reach.

I seriously did not know what to say to him. Whether to tell him the truth—or what I was reasonably sure was the truth; or to just tell him nothing. Which would be the worse for him? So many people believe in telling the absolute, unadulterated truth to everyone nowadays. It's come back into fashion again in this decade. But I didn't give a damn about the fashion. I wanted to tell him, or not tell him, the thing that would damage him the least. But I mean, or I think I meant, the thing that would damage him the least in the long run. *In the long run.* Not the short run.

"Here," I said, reaching for a bottle of Scotch. "Have a good stiff belt of this. Maybe it'll slow you down a little."

But before I could get him a glass, he seized the bottle out of my hand and downed a good inch of the straight liquor straight from the bottle's neck. Slowly, he screwed back on the cap.

"I didn't mean like that," I said.

"It felt good," he said. "It *feels* good." He seemed to be relishing the relieving, releasing burn in his throat and stomach.

"You've really got it bad," I said.

"I sure have."

I felt a little sick, myself. Certainly I did not want a drink myself.

"You don't know what it's like!" he began, in a kind of strangled shout. "You—"

"Hill, I think just about everybody knows what it's like," I broke in. "At least, almost everybody. Just about everybody I've ever met, anyway."

"But it can kill you!" he said. "I mean, literally. *Kill* you!"

"It certainly can. Even if you're not a particularly sensitive soul."

He went back to the one big chair and flopped down again. "It's jealousy, I suppose," he said, rather thoughtfully. "Some kind of jealousy. I don't want her going out with anybody else." He paused a moment. "I imagine so much. All sorts of things. All the details. With the boys. *And* the girls. Jealousy. Of some kind."

I guess it was then that I decided to tell him. The kill that cures, or something like that. Anyway, my main thought was that he would certainly find out about it eventually anyway. Would the preparation not be better coming from me?

"I think I can tell you where you can reach her, Hill, if you want to. By phone, that is. My suspicion is that she is in Cannes. At the Carlton."

Very slowly, he looked up at me. "With *Dad?*"

"I rather suspect so," I said. "Of course, I could be wrong."

He did not answer for a little while. Then he said, "Jesus. Jesus Christ." He seemed to collapse in the big chair.

"But what I don't see is why you'd want to fall in love with *her,*" I said. Now I found myself desperately talking for time. Was I wrong? Had I made the wrong decision? "Is it because she's a black girl? And you feel that's part of your Revolution? You were going to save her? From something? From herself? Why her?" I drew a deep breath; and I objectively, coldly noted that it quivered. "And incidentally, or not incidentally at all perhaps, where is all this philosophy you've been preaching me the past year about monogamistic love being for the birds? Remember Anne-Marie taking care of the entire sub-committee? You don't believe in monogamistic love, remember? That's crap. Hypocrisy. Crap for us 'Older Generations'. Your generation has changed all that. No more monogamy. Marriage and all that crap is out. —Unless of course two people, two young people, decide on it together. Remember the preachments you've given me? God, you must have given me a hundred lectures." My breath had run out.

"It's not the same thing," he said dully into the empty space. "I want her."

"Well, let me tell you something," I said, getting another breath. "I'm afraid you've run into one girl, who for whatever reasons of her own, really believes like you once not long ago thought you believed. I can't understand why you picked on her."

He did not answer. "But with *Dad,*" he said, finally. It was curious how he capitalized the name when he italicized it.

"But is that so shocking?" I said. "It ought not to be, according to your philosophy."

His voice was low and so dull, depressed, that it was almost inaudible. "I guess my philosophy's changed."

Then quite suddenly he looked at his watch, jumped up from the chair, reached for his jacket. It was almost as if he were being chased, running from the dark shadows of his own thoughts he could not control. "I've got to get over to the Odéon. There's going to be a surprise demonstration at Maubert this evening, students *plus* workers. I'm assigned a crew to shoot it. Look, I'll see you later, Jack. I'll call you."

And before I could agree, or say more, or do anything helpful—or even harmful—he was gone out the door and down the stairs.

From my windows I watched him legging it along the quai, fast. As if those shadows were still after him. I noted that he chose to go left, by way of the Pont de la Tournelle, rather than right toward the footbridge that would lead to Place Maubert itself. That meant he would use the old back road we were all so used to by now.

I sat around my apartment a long time after Hill left. I was trying to decide whether I should try and call Harry in Cannes. Maybe it was my duty. The very possibility of getting a call through to Cannes was highly unlikely. But even if I could, should I? Was it any of my business?

I was flopped down in my one easy chair, looking, I guess, as Hill had when he had been flopped down in it. Certainly I felt as bad. Finally I jumped up myself, much I suppose in the same way Hill had done. Only, I had no place to go.

I wound up at my windows, looking out on the new Paris scene— which hadn't changed any since I watched Hill legging it off toward Odéon.

Since Friday things had not changed so much on the Île St.-Louis perhaps, but by looking across the river you could see it very plainly. France, or anyway Paris at least, was fast approaching total paralysis. Almost nothing moved over there. Most of the shops were shuttered and closed. And almost no vehicles moved along the Left Bank quais, which together with the Right Bank quais really form the main East-West traffic arteries of the city. Police camions, singly or in large groups, roared along the almost empty avenues. Every now and then Army trucks passed along, stopping at bus stops loading and unloading not soldiers but citizens trying to get someplace. And in all that empty space the traffic lights blinked merrily from red to green to red again, serving only the Army trucks, and the police camions who totally ignored them. It was an eerie sight, like some shot from a science-fiction horror film when for some reason or other the world has ended, and humanity no longer exists. But the traffic lights go on.

Only once in a great while did a normal civilian car move along.

On the Monday, the 20th, with the Métros, autobuses, railroads, etc. all already on strike,—the same Monday on whose evening I had carted old Harry over to the Odéon—there had been immense traffic jams of private vehicles all over the city. They were so immense that hardly any cars could move, literally for hours. Gas stations were beginning to run low on gas by noon, and long lines of cars were stalled blocks long in front of them.

The next day, Tuesday the 21st, even the numbers of private cars had noticeably diminished and it was possible to at least see a taxi now and then, though next to impossible to get one.

And now, on Wednesday, with gasoline supplies exhausted in the city and the taxi companies themselves on strike, nearly everything was at a standstill. Most business offices were closed, because their people could not get in to work. The schools were closed or closing for the same reason. About the only thing that was running near to normal was the truckers bringing food into the city. The big truckers were obviously being urged by their unions not to strike, but to continue food delivery, so that the emergency situation in the city did not turn into real general disaster. Even so, long lines of would-be hoarders—coming along much later than myself, who had been forewarned—stripped shops clean of everything on the shelves; butter, milk, sugar and flour simply disappeared, were not to be had. Most banks had closed on Monday, after a general panic run on their cash supplies, or else were limiting withdrawals to 1,000 francs: 200 dollars.

Everything Martine had predicted for me had been absolutely accurate.

The other most noticeable thing from my windows, besides the emptiness of the avenues and boulevards, was the accumulation of garbage everywhere. The gray or yellow plastic garbage cans, jammed to overflowing, stood outside every building on the sidewalks, and now they had been joined by huge piles of crates and boxes, and by just plain piles of gunk composed of old lettuce leaves, rotting tomatoes, used fruit rinds, rotting meat rejects. The garbage collectors had gone on strike on Saturday the 18th. One had only to look at it and imagine the field day the big gray-black rats from Les Halles and from along the river banks were having. This applied on our Island as well as everywhere else, and when you walked along the quais or streets it was already beginning to stink. Across the river the piles of overflowing crates were so huge, so high that you could see them all the way from here.

Martine had been absolutely right about everything.

I turned from my window feeling a little shiver in my spine, and went to the telephone, to try and get Cannes.

It took me over three hours. The automatic system, never too good in this country anyway, where you dial 15, then 93 and your number, was jammed, so overloaded that after an hour I gave up on it and went directly to the operators. They still maintained a skeleton crew, though they were on strike too of course. It took me half an hour to convince the girl that it was an absolute life-and-death emergency to get her to take the person-to-person call, and even then it took her more than an hour and a half to get such an "emergency" call through. I certainly didn't feel guilty about lying to her. And now, when I think back on it, I'm not so sure I was all that far off, all that wrong, after all.

By the time I got through it was late enough in the day I was sure that I would catch him at the hotel, and sure enough, he was in his room there.

Harry was immediately guilty, defensive on the phone. I could hear it in his voice. And well he should be, God damn him, I thought grimly.

"Jesus, it must have taken you all day to get a call through to down here," he said, making it an exclamation.

"It did," I said. "Or nearly."

"What is the emergency that would make you go through all that?" he said.

"Well," I began, but was interrupted.

He began to talk about his film, and the striking of it. It was going very well. All the French groups but one had agreed to go out, and the one was visibly coming around. Of course, Steinerwein was pissed-off at him, was furious. But that couldn't be helped. That was to be expected. Until Harry had come down, Steinerwein had talked the French crews into staying on because it was an American production, not a French one. Finally Harry ran down. Finally he stopped.

"Harry," I said.

"Yes?"

"Is Samantha Everton with you there?"

He did not answer at once. "How would you ever, how did you ever, figure out a thing like that?"

"I just had a hunch," I said.

"Well, yes, she is with me," he said.

"Hill came over to see me," I said. "He is pretty distraught, to put it mildly. He is in love with Sam, and she has disappeared from the Odéon, and nobody who knows her, including Weintraub, knows where she is. What did you expect, Harry?" I tried to make it crisp.

"Now, listen," he said.

I interrupted. "Hill knows where she is. That she is with you. I told him my suspicion. I remembered that night three years ago, when you told me about your Fantasy." I deliberately capitalized the word "fantasy" with my voice.

"Christ. Did you tell him that, too?" I could hear some kind of irritable, irritated squawking somewhere in the room behind him.

"No, no. Of course not. Did you even think I would? I only mentioned it to point out to you that that was what led me to my conclusion."

"Well, what are you sticking your nose into this for anyway?" Harry said in a near snarl.

"Well, I guess you know how I feel about you, and your family, Harry," I said. "I helped to raise Hill. A little bit. And you know I love Louisa, too. And after all, I *am* McKenna's Godfather."

He smothered the mouthpiece with his hand, but dimly I heard him say, "Shut up! Just shut *up!* I'll handle this in my own God damn way."

Apparently he was not successful or forceful enough, because the next thing I heard was Sam Everton's voice, and it was as full of venom as any voice I've ever had directed at me—except possibly my ex-wife's on a few occasions.

"Listen, you old fag! Is that all you got to do for a hobby? What are you going around sticking your nose in other people's business for that doesn't concern you? Why can't you just fade?"

I am old enough by now and looked into myself enough, and have been a bachelor long enough (all bachelors are always suspect), that being called a fag, even to my face, neither surprised nor bothered me. "Samantha, I don't know if you know that Hill is in love with you, really in love with you."

She laughed, harshly. "That kid. Well, if he is, it is certainly not any fault of mine, nor is it any part of any contract or deal we made together." She could really speak excellent English, when she wanted to drop that Harlem jargon of hers. But of course, she had been educated almost half her life in ritzy Swiss schools.

"Well, I'd like to talk to you about it, if you would allow me. When you get back to Paris."

"I'll be glad to talk to you, honey. But it'll cost you. How much you willin' to pay?"

"I would even pay," I said.

"Maybe I'll let you take it out in trade, honey!" she cried. Then she laughed, harshly.

There was a sort of strangled struggle on the other end of the phone, and then Harry's voice came back on. He was breathing a little heavily, and over his breathing I distinctly heard another, third voice somewhere back in the room, feminine.

"Listen. Christ, Jack," Harry snarled at me. "You know how much I think of you, too. But what did you have to go and get into this for? It all would have been all right. Nobody would have known about it. Now you've told Hill. Have you told Louisa, too?"

"Of course not. Are you goofy?"

There was a pause, and he sighed. "Sometimes I don't know." He seemed, down there at the other end of the phone, to be shaking himself all over, as if trying to collect himself, his person together, and his thoughts. "But Hill might just as well tell her."

"Hill most certainly will not tell her. Nor will he tell anybody else. He's too ashamed of it all. That I'm sure of. But if Weintraub figures it out for himself, and he's perfectly smart enough to . . . Or if Samantha tells him . . . You're putting yourself into a pretty dangerous position, Harry.

"You've got that other little girl with you, too," I said, "haven't you?"

"Yes. The one from Castel's Weintraub told us about that first night. She's on strike like all the rest of the kids, was living at the Sorbonne. In a sleeping bag. So she had nothing to do, and her parents wouldn't know," he said, and suddenly his voice hardened. "And let me tell you, it's great! Just great!" Then his voice changed back to normal. "It was to be just for these few days. I made a deal with Sam to give her the money to go on to Israel to her Sabra friend as soon as we get back to Paris." Again there was the sensation of him shaking himself all over, not shuddering, but shaking himself to get himself back together. "But now I'm afraid I'm getting hooked." It ended on a hollow note, and he stopped.

"Well, it's your affair, Harry," I said, lamely. It was the best I could come up with. "I just wanted to tell you about Hill."

"Hill," he said as if he didn't even know the name. "Hill! God damn Hill. What the hell did he ever care for me in his God damned life. I'll talk to you when I get back to Paris." He hung up abruptly.

It seemed people were always hanging up on me abruptly, while I never hung up on anybody abruptly.

I looked at the black phone in my hand, and then put it back in its cradle. I had lots of work to do: get ready those two issues which the Odéon kids had promised to drive out to Brussels for me; and I had those two articles to write about the Revolution, one for each issue, which I had promised to do for them with the aid of Terri. But I simply could not work. I couldn't bring myself to do anything.

I wound up again at my windows, in the gathering dusk, looking out at the dead-appearing city. At least they were keeping half the streetlights on at night; electricity, gas and water, though nominally on strike, were still running. But across the way upriver at the Pont de la Tournelle the usually beautifully lit penthouse restaurant of the Tour d'Argent was closed down and dark. And down at our end of the bridge the two evil little black bugs of police camions were dutifully, resolutely, conscientiously keeping their 24-hour guard, their vigil.

In spite of Harry's absence the rest of us kept up our regular evening meetings at the Gallaghers' apartment. Most of us lived close enough by that we could get there on foot in the traffic-less city. The two correspondents, Fred Singer and that UPI kid Willy Something had now been joined by three other correspondents who had heard of the nightly meetings. All of them had been allotted enough gasoline allowance to get around the city. So it wasn't difficult for them to appear at the appointed hour. The "Witching Hour", somebody started calling it.

The French TV, after a great uproar in the press, had begun giving at least some coverage to the strikes and the rioting.

Of us all only poor Ferenc Hofmann-Beck had no way of getting home after our eight o'clock sessions. And if he did, he had no way of getting back to work the next morning to his office in St.-Germain from his apartment in Auteuil, except to hoof it. As a result he began to wind up, during the rest of that week, sleeping on the couch in the Gallaghers' living room.

In the morning he would stagger off to his office on the Boulevard St.-Germain through the thinning tear gas, to take up his "post". Though the workers' unions had long ago struck his French publisher boss, the offices, and everything else about the business, the executive branch had decided to keep to a business-as-usual policy.

Every now and then Ferenc was able to bum a ride to Auteuil with someone who had gas and was going there, for a change of clothes. But with Harry gone I had taken to staying to dinner with Louisa every night, and most nights of that week the last sight I saw as I left the apartment was the two unbelievably large bare feet of Hofmann-Beck sticking straight up in the air from under the edge of the coverlet Louisa had given him to cover himself with on the couch. He had brought back from Auteuil some shirts, socks and ties to leave at the apartment, so he would not look "totally disreputable", as he said, when he tottered off to his office with his bowler hat and umbrella in the mornings. It was rather nice to have him around, Louisa said with a smile. And I guess it was. Certainly he had become a great favorite with McKenna, with whom he played all sorts of idiot games which he made up on the spur of the moment.

He would eat his dinner with us, and almost immediately go off to sleep on "his" couch in his underdrawers, hanging his clothes meticulously over the back of a fauteuil. He certainly kept us all entertained, with his wild crazy stories of what went on at the office among the stiff-upper-lip, business-as-usual executives, and of the things he saw in the street coming and going.

He was, with his "eating thing", as he called it, and as we all called it now, a pretty heavy drain on Louisa's icebox, but I was able to help her out from my preaccumulated stocks. And food was never really scarce.

He had always loved Louisa and Harry. But now with the Revolution, possibly because of it, he had become almost pathetically attached to them. He seemed very distressed by Harry's absence. Much more than Louisa, I must say I noted. So Louisa and I would sit and talk while he snored, those enormous bare feet sticking straight up in the air like tiny skyscrapers.

We talked quite a lot those evenings, Louisa and I. As far as I could ascertain, there was never any suspicion in her mind that Harry was doing anything more down in Cannes than his stated purpose in going: to strike his and Steinerwein's film. And as far as Hill was concerned, she was unperturbed and adamant about it.

"He's only doing his thing," she said, and smiled, "as the young like to phrase it nowadays. I would never stop him from that. No more than I would have stopped Harry going to the war as a Marine private when he did not have to."

"You weren't married to him then," I said gently.

"But were I, I would not have stopped him."

There was a rough, hard, inflexible, Puritan morality about her that could not be touched. Or pushed. Or breached. Or even breathed upon, from outside. She was an impenetrable fortress of it.

"I would have stayed home, and remained faithful, and done my war-work like the rest, and held myself together while I waited and hoped."

"I'm sure you would, Louisa," I said softly.

As I tiptoed out that night, Ferenc was not snoring; but the soles of those immense feet stared at me, somehow cynically. He was a cynical man, Ferenc. But after all, he was a Hungarian, at least by culture. He would never understand a New Englander like Louisa.

15

WE HAD PLENTY to keep us occupied during that long weekend Harry was away.

On the Wednesday, the 22nd, the day Hill had come to see me so distraught, the French Government officially banned the re-entry into France of *Dany le Rouge*. Cohn-Bendit had gone off into Germany, hoping to begin an international students' revolt which would carry the French students' *Révolution* over the whole of Europe. Cohn-Bendit, aged 23, had been born in France, of German-Jewish refugee parents from World War II, and so nominally could claim French citizenship. But he carried a German passport, I have no idea why, and so the French could nominally be legitimately legal in barring his re-entry.

In Berlin on Monday the 21st, Dany claimed that from five to 11 people had already been killed in the Paris riots, but that he could not prove it because the information was being kept secret; also that there were many students blinded, presumably by tear gas, although he did not elaborate on that.

None of us had heard even the slightest rumor of anyone having been killed. I think some of us, especially the correspondents, would have if there had been deaths. It was pretty amazing there hadn't been any, actually. Anyway, Dany's allegations certainly were not going to endear him to the French Government.

When this news about barring him was released, it set off a whole series of student riots which ran on through the entire weekend, and which, finally, developed into the worst fighting since the beginning of the Revolution.

It was these demonstrations, beginning Wednesday night, that Hill was rushing off to help film—though in his state of distraction he neglected to tell me any part of this new development.

On Wednesday night the demonstrations were not so bad. There was a lot of marching and singing, and shouted slogans against le Général de Gaulle, who had finally interrupted his Romanian state visit to return on the Saturday night of the 18th. Since he had expressly stated that he would not do this for any such amateurish "childrens' revolt", it must have hurt considerably his nineteenth-century pride to do it. But the massive strikes were beginning to cut close to the bone on everybody, including him apparently.

A few fires were started in the piles of uncollected crates, rubbish and garbage on Wednesday night, none of them serious. But that was about all, because, strangely enough, apparently on the Government's orders, the police stayed completely out of it.

They had retreated from the Latin Quarter almost a whole week before. But the police were keeping the students from crossing to the Right Bank. The *Quartier Latin* had become a sort of student-owned-and-operated city in itself, though under a tacit siege.

This excepted, of course, all the bars, cafés, restaurants and *tabacs,* which were doing a land-office business from the "tourists" (which included Parisian Frenchmen) who came "inside the lines" to look.

Almost obviously, the Government, and the *Patronat,* with whom the Gaullist Government worked so closely, were just sitting back and hoping the Revolution would "rot" itself out as food funds for the students and the workers' unions dwindled, and as the people themselves, the whole French people, got discontented with discomfort.

Never have I seen such a clear-cut example of the fact that a modern Government must by definition be the paternalistic enemy of its citizens. At least, any kind of Government mankind has been able to discover or invent up to now. It made you scared, and it was scary.

On the Thursday it got worse. And as usual, it all ended up around the Place Maubert, which now looked like a real battleground in a real war. Apparently, the Government had told the police to go in and break it up. When the police advanced, barricades of paving stones immediately began to go up in the streets again everywhere, topped now by the iron grilles, which had been placed around all the beautiful trees along the boulevards. On top of these went all the crates and rubbish the garbage collectors had not collected, which were then set afire and left, forcing the police to charge into them.

Now it was not only the organized students and workers who were involved but also just plain bums and riffraff, the "lower depths" of Paris who had crept out from wherever it was they normally hid themselves and apparently were in all the fighting just for the hell of it, the fun of it. It was getting out of the hands of the police, and now was beginning to get out of the hands of the students themselves, and was turning into just a plain old destructive anarchy of human hate and rage, without any point to it at all except just to fight and commit mayhem and see blood flow.

When le Général had returned from Romania, one of his most-quoted remarks was the now-famous line, "Réforme oui, chienlit non." According to the papers *chienlit* was a French Army barracksroom term, a quite old word, almost impossible to translate. Translated literally, one source said, at least on the French Army level, it meant "Shit in the bed", or bed-messing. But the word was also used to mean "masquerading", as in the sense of children dressing up in grown-ups' clothes. So that, in another sense, the word did exist on a polite level as well. In modern *polite* usage it meant a just plain "bloody mess". But le Général almost certainly must have known this, and used the word deliberately, a sort of triple or quadruple entendre. Anyway, it *could* be considered a considerably gross term. I suppose, on that level, the most nearly equivalent in English would be, "Reform yes, bullshit no." In any case the students certainly took it on that level, and as they did with so many other things, they made a chant out of it: "*Chienlit, c'est lui!*", meaning: "The bullshit, it's de Gaulle!" except that in French it rhymed. You could hear this being shouted by hundreds, by thousands, all over the Quarter all day and all night, that Thursday.

The next day was Friday, Friday May the 24th, and le Général had announced some time back that he would speak to the nation on TV on that Friday. Why he chose to wait so long, in the midst of such a crisis, nobody knew exactly. Perhaps it was just his way. He was not about to be pushed, ever. There had been much talk and rumor that le Général was going to ask for a national Referendum on his continuing in power, and in his speech he did declare such a Referendum vote, for sometime in June, though he did not name the date.

We, of course, our gang of Americans, watched his speech on TV at the Gallaghers'. There was much speculation about it among us afterwards. He did not seem to be his old vital self, to say the least. Despite his usual vigorous, self-controlled, theatrical delivery, his old self-assurance seemed to be missing. For the first time since I had watched his talks, he gave the impression that he was not really sure his latest call would be heard by the people.

After it was over, and I had had dinner with Louisa and Ferenc, I decided to go out into the streets again.

I had been going out every night since Monday. I had become quite occupied with the Students' Film Committee of the Odéon. It was quite easy to get to the Odéon, if you took the back way up rue Cardinal Lemoine and around the side of the Panthéon. Once you got to the crowded, jammed-up Odéon, where the marathon discussion was still going full tilt in the theater amphitheater, you were perfectly safe from the police.

Of course, on the Friday of the 24th I did not really know what to expect.

It had already been a pretty rough day, according to my transistor radio. The day had been full of demonstrations in cities all over France. Even the farmers out in the countryside were coming into the towns to demonstrate for more Government protection of the small farmer and higher prices for French products. In Nantes, in Brittany, a mob of 3,000 farmers and students had attacked a police headquarters, first with stones and bottles, and then had cut down trees around it and tried to burn it down.

And in Paris people were out all over the place, and demonstrations were going on everywhere. After le Général's speech which was heralded with great boos and jeering, mobs had collected at the Place de la Bourse and set fire to the Bourse itself, France's sacred Money Mart and Stock Exchange.

It all looked pretty grim. But I felt I had to go, and I wanted to see what the kids thought about it all now.

As I was leaving the Gallaghers' apartment, Ferenc asked me to take him with me. He wanted to see it too, he said.

I was a little taken aback. I already felt that it was dangerous enough for me myself to go out. I didn't relish having the added responsibility of Ferenc. Besides that, it had finally begun to rain somewhere along in there, making everything slipperier and more evil-seeming. The May rains which the police officials had waited for so hopefully in the beginning of the month had finally come—much too late to do anything about the Revolution, now, except to make everything worse.

So I hesitated. But the crestfallen look on Ferenc's face was too much for me. "Okay," I said. "Come on, if you want to. But you have to follow me and follow my lead without any arguments. If we get separated, you're on your own." The big grin that came over his large face was almost worth the decision.

"I suppose I better take off my monocle? And put on my glasses?" he said thoughtfully.

"If I were you, I'd leave the monocle here," I said.

He nodded. "I'll do just that." And took it off with its black cord and laid it carefully on top of Louisa's fireplace mantel.

"One mustn't go around looking like a bloody executive or aristocrat on a night like this," he said.

"What about me?" Louisa said.

"You're staying here," I said positively. "There's no question about that."

"I think he's absolutely right, dear Louisa," Ferenc said gently.

"I suppose so," she said gloomily.

"For God's sake, think about McKenna," I said as we went to the door.

I had been worrying about my marvelous little Goddaughter ever since I had learned for sure what had happened to Harry in Cannes. In the fact McKenna, who after all was only in the third grade, had, after the Sorbonne revolt, organized and created her own tiny Revolution in her class at school (a bilingual school which taught both English and French) Louisa had told me. At this school, in a staggered sort of fashion, each class spent one day a week out at Meudon, a woodsy sort of suburb just up the hill from Sèvres, for some kind of vague outdoor health reasons, I suppose. Somehow they had got the use, cheaply, of some old quonset huts out there. Well, McKenna had canvassed her class, collected more than 50 per cent of them behind her, and had got up in class and made I gather a rather lengthy speech about the inadequate facilities of the Meudon installation. There was not enough heat, the children were always freezing cold, and the food served them at lunch was so bad that none of the children could eat it. When the teacher canvassed the class herself, face to face, only about 40 per cent stood up to back up McKenna. Although over 50 per cent had promised that they would. In any case it was still enough of a revolution for the teacher (a rather dislikeable sort I gathered) to take it to the Headmistress of the school, one of those exceedingly formidable woman educators, whom McKenna staunchly confronted in her office, and who then called up Louisa. Louisa and Harry naturally backed McKenna up all the way. But though promises of rectification had been made by the Headmistress with a harassed laugh (she was having a hard time, they said, just keeping the school running) so far nothing had been done, but it was supposed to be.

Also, on the day of the failed vote of censure against M. Pompidou's Government, the Wednesday of May 22nd, McKenna had organized her own little demonstration. I've often thought she would have made a hell of a General. Getting three little French kids that she played with on the block to help her, she had got hold of a set of red towels Louisa had and tied them to mop and broom handles. With the adults engrossed in the debate on the TV, the four children under McKenna's direction had rushed across the living room and begun waving their improvised red flags back and forth out on the little balcony above the quai crying *"À bas le Gouvernement! À bas le Gouvernement!"* The island was crawling with cops at the time, and those of us nearest them grabbed them back in as quickly as we could, afraid the police below would think it was an adult-organized thing. But when I stepped out onto the little balcony and looked down, smiling what I hoped was a confidently amused smile, all the flics below were roaring with laughter.

She was really such a precious, brilliant little thing. I would have given anything to have had one like her of my own, and sometimes when I thought of her I positively hated my ex-wife. And now, with Harry off on his irresponsible junket in Cannes, I dreaded the thought of something bad happening to the family that might injure Mc-Kenna.

Of course by now McKenna had long since been put to bed. But Louisa had not answered my last remark. However when I looked back at her from the door, with Hofmann-Beck close on my heels like an eager mastiff, she looked up from the mantelpiece, where she appeared to be studying Ferenc's monocle, and smiled and nodded at me.

"Well, come on, Ferenc," I said. "Let's go. Let's get with it."

"I'm right with you, buddy," Ferenc said, a term he would never have used to anyone before meeting the Gallaghers and us.

I nodded. "Don't forget your raincoat, now."

"I think I had better leave my bowler here, and take one of Harry's caps in the entry," he said.

We went out of the apartment and down out onto the quai in the drizzle. It looked as though it might be letting up.

Well, I sure need not have worried about Ferenc. Underneath his layers of fat and hypochondria he had a pair of legs at least four times as strong as mine. And when he raised up and showed forth that chest of his, instead of letting it droop on his belly as he usually did, it had a girth half again as large as mine, which was not small. He was as strong as a lion, that young man, and as brave as a fighting bull at least.

We crossed by the Pont de la Tournelle and started up rue Cardinal Lemoine. When we reached Boulevard St.-Germain, I turned up it toward the Place Maubert. We made our way up toward the *Place,* past shops and restaurants which were all carefully shuttered and closed. The French knew how to take care of their trade goods and property. Things like this had been happening to them since the beginning of the Middle Ages. It appeared the drizzle was stopping.

But the goddamned French had something else about them, too. As we sauntered up the half-dark Boulevard toward the *Place,* the inhabitants of the apartments of the four- and five-story buildings above the ground-floor shops were out burning their uncollected garbage and trash in the center of the street. By a sort of common consent, not led by generals or even by civic leaders, they had got together with their brooms and mops and rakes and squeegees or whatever, and had swept all the mountain of uncollected trash out into a row in the middle of the Boulevard and were methodically and carefully burning it up. Somebody had figured out that the center of the Boulevard would be the best place to do it in order to do the least damage to the leafage of the flowering trees that lined the boulevards on both sides and helped to make Paris the Paris they loved and liked to live in. A 100 yards up the way you could hear the fighting and shouting, but back here here they were, all out helping to preserve themselves and their health and at the same time not destroy the beauty of their city, Paris. Old Paris. God, the things it had not seen were few. There was not any possibility of traffic now on the boulevards anyway. And all the way up to the Place Maubert there was a long line of burning crates, cartons, old wet lettuce leaves, rotten tomatoes and fruit rinds and garbage, all of it being tended with old pushbrooms or sweepbrooms by the little bourgeois who inhabited the area. It was enough to almost make me weep. For them. For all of us.

When we got to the *Place,* it did not take long to see that the police had invested it. Beyond the Place Maubert the police were lined up three or four deep in their black fighting raincoats, helmets, goggles and shields. They had worked down from the Carrefour St.-Michel, and established a cutoff line here all across the Boulevard. They were not doing anything at all, just standing there.

Some distance away there was a mob of citizens, on our downhill side of the street. They kept a respectful distance, 50 yards say, and hurled insults at the cops.

There were no students, now. Mainly, they were all dark Algerians. There was not one student involved that I could see. Of course the area between Maubert and the river was all an Algerian quarter—which had been hurt hard during the time of the Algerian War. We sifted our way through them until we were out in the no-man's-land between rue Monge where the mob was and the police lines beyond the end of the *Place.* We were alone out there in the middle of the *Place.*

"Aren't we rather vulnerable out here?" Ferenc said from behind me.

"I don't think so," I said. "Really. I mean, look at them. They're not trying to hurt anybody."

"But we *are* very presentable targets," Ferenc said in his best King's English accent.

"Cut the shit," I growled, and then something strange happened to me. I discovered I had made up my mind to cross the *Place,* the no-man's-land, and pass peacefully through the police lines. Was I showing off for Ferenc? Was I proving that I was an old hand at the Revolution? Was I testing my own rather doubtful courage in some crazy way? In any case I absolutely knew suddenly that those police over there would not do us any damage if we walked toward them calmly and sanely, clearly unarmed with bottles or stones, and said to them "Excuse me, but I live up there." I knew they would not touch us. I just knew it. And I kind of wanted to walk up the rest of the poor old torn-up busted Boulevard. Just to see what had happened to it in the last 24 hours.

I really do not know what it was came over me. Anyway I forged ahead, out into the middle of the deserted *Place* and past the high stone pedestal from which the Germans had removed the metal statue of some unknown notable during the War to melt it down, and on toward the police line across the Boulevard. Ferenc was right behind me. I could hear his footsteps and there was not one sign of falter in them.

Then, suddenly, at the sharp corner of the rue Lagrange after the *Place,* just at the little café-*tabac* there, two young Algerians in dark clothes leaped out of the dark straight in front of me, shouting some insult, and one of them heaved a paving stone at the police line. Then they leaped back, and ran around the sharp corner onto rue Lagrange.

I did not see where the *pavé* landed. It either fell short or was blocked by a shield. A couple of the policemen shouted something back which I did not understand but the voices had a plaintive note to them, as if they might have been saying in English, "Come on! What are you doing, dumbass! We're not bothering you, are we?" They threw no tear gas, or anything else, in retaliation.

But suddenly my whole feeling changed. I could not be sure the police did not think we were friends of the Algerians, and were coming on to attack them. Probably they didn't. In any case, I did an abrupt aboutface, with Ferenc right alongside me, and started away, walking slowly.

"That was rather bad luck," Ferenc said in an even voice at my side, matching his stride to my slow one. He was indeed following my lead as I had asked.

"Yeah," I said. "It was. Come on, we'll go up here." And when we reached the pedestal, I took off across the empty *Place* toward the rue de la Montagne Ste.-Geneviève. Nobody contested us, or bothered us.

Rue de la Montagne Ste.-Geneviève is probably one of the most picturesque streets in all of Paris. It is full of tiny but very good restaurants, and mounts steeply and twisting from Place Maubert up to the Panthéon on top the hill. It is the street where Hemingway placed his *bal-musette* in the opening part of *The Sun Also Rises,* where Brett Ashley is introduced. I loved to walk it, and used to eat there a lot. But now the street was so absolutely full of crates and cartons and garbage from the restaurants and the apartments above that you could hardly see any of the groundfloor windows or the painted names of the restaurants above them. It looked as though if anyone carelessly dropped one match along it the whole street would go up in one great whoosh of flames.

We came out on the rue des Écoles halfway up. Now the rue des Écoles runs along the front of the Sorbonne itself. When I looked up that way, I could see that the place had been cordoned off by police units, and that the air was full of tear gas and smoke. I had a sudden fatigue reaction. "Let's go the other way," I said.

But at rue Monge we had the good fortune to witness how a Paris barricade is constructed, from its very beginning.

At the corner of rue Monge and rue des Écoles is a lovely little park called the Square Monge with big trees behind which are visible the handsome old buildings of the École Polytechnique. It is surrounded by a handsome fence of wrought iron, and has concrete benches both inside on the grass and outside on the sidewalk. When we arrived, a mob of people were just beginning to tear up the concrete benches and the handsome wrought-iron fence. Ferenc and I stood back against a building cattycorner across the street, and watched.

There was not one student involved in this barricade. These people were all Parisian workers of the lowest class. There were no Algerians among them. About one-sixth of them were women. And almost without exception they all had such badly rotting, mangled teeth that I felt sorry for them all and wondered how they could ever manage to eat their own fabled Parisian cooking.

They had crowbars with them and sledgehammers, and later we saw shovels. They shouted encouragement to each other in shrill voices as they tore up the lovely little park. The women were particularly good at the shouting part. But the women worked hard too. Whenever someone grinned at me, I grinned back. I advised Ferenc to do the same.

Directly in front of us, two men of about 24 began attacking the pavement with a crowbar. They were trying to force an initial opening between two paving stones. They kept at it with an intense concentration. Then a slender, gray-haired, partially bald man in a light-beige raincoat walked up to them.

Now, I do not know the mechanics of how the eyeball, all unwitting to the conscious mind, trains itself in an intelligent man to recognize a plainclothes cop. I have said elsewhere in these papers that my eyeball, all on its own, can recognize an Algerian man or a Chinese man a block away by the back of his head. And my eyeball, again all on its own, can recognize an American in the city of Paris as far away as I can see him, or her. It's something about the stance, the way they walk, as if they felt guilty, and when they come closer some look on their faces that my eyeball knows but which I do not, confirms me. They are just American, that's all. And I've never been wrong, to my knowledge. And, by the same token of eyeball judgement, I knew immediately that the man in the light-beige raincoat was a plainclothes cop.

Immediately I looked at Ferenc, and he nodded. I nodded back. This was interesting, and we strolled slowly over to where the two young men, now joined by a couple of others, were still trying intently to prise a paving stone from the tightly laid pavement. The man in the light raincoat had begun to remonstrate with them about why they wanted to do it. He talked calmly and objectively: There were no police around to fight; if they prised up the street, it would only bring the police; what was it they were after?

I do not think a soul there except us two knew he was a plainclothesman. But a crowd began to collect. He was certainly a gutsy cop. Slowly the voices got louder. They were talking French so fast, all of them, that I couldn't make out what forms the discussion was taking. But several citizens were taking the side of the man in the light raincoat. They did not prevail however, crowbars and youthful adrenalin prevailed, and when this became apparent the man in the light raincoat backed off, shrugged a typical Frenchman's shrug, and sauntered away, probably to telephone headquarters about what was happening at rue Monge and rue des Écoles. Ferenc and I backed away and stood again back against the building.

It was a fascinating thing to watch. It took them quite a long time to get the first paving stone out. But after that it became easier. And got easier and easier the more of them they removed.

Once they had a foot or two of the square stones up off their bed of sand, there was a great cheer all across the place, and the shovels were brought in. And then it went fast. The men, and the women, formed human chains to pass the stones which the shovelers were now loosening almost faster than they could be passed along. They wanted to make a V-shaped double barricade, that would cut off rue Monge from Place Maubert downhill toward the river, and would also cut off rue des Écoles from the west toward the Sorbonne. God knows who they were, or why they were there, or what they expected to cause or gain from it all. They were just there, and they were just doing it. To have stopped them would have taken machineguns.

It was amazing how swiftly the barricades rose. The concrete benches from the lovely little park were stuck in amongst them, while the beautiful wrought-iron fence around the park was set in in sections along the face so that they stuck forth like spears in the direction—the two directions—from which the police were expected to come.

"I think it's about time we moved on," I said. I had not forgotten that gray-haired man in the light raincoat.

Neither had Ferenc. "I expect so," he said calmly. Then suddenly he grinned. "Thank you," he said. "It's been a great evening."

We sauntered on down rue des Écoles to where it crossed rue Cardinal Lemoine, not far, and turned back down Cardinal Lemoine toward our sanctuary of the Île St.-Louis.

At rue le Regrattier we shook hands.

"It's amazing really, isn't it?" Ferenc said in an odd voice. "Really, it is amazing."

I let myself into my door with my key, and he went on down the quai to "his" now proprietary couch at the Gallaghers' apartment.

16

SATURDAY MORNING FERENC AND I walked Louisa and McKenna up to Boulevard St.-Michel to view the devastation. It was unbelievable. All the way up St.-Germain the streets were torn up, the tall gooseneck metal streetlamps were down, and turned-over burnt-out cars had been dragged to the gutters, sometimes encroaching up onto the sidewalk itself.

At Place Maubert the innocent little newspaper-magazine kiosk had been torn completely apart and dismembered—for no apparently good reason, because it clearly had not been strewn on the barricades that had gone up there later in the night after we left it. At rue St.-Jacques more tipped-over cars had been dragged to the sidelines.

Everywhere, work crews were at work trying to clean up. They were using bulldozers and those small one-man mobile cup-shovels and other pieces of roadbuilding equipment. But this time there would be no replacing of paving stones. Asphalt trucks and mobile road-rollers were already pouring and tamping their hot smelly asphalt into the places where the torn-up street had been cleared. People and students sat at the outdoor tables of the cafés having a coffee or an apéritif while the fumes from the asphalt rolled over them.

But the worst place of all was the Carrefour, and Boulevard St.-Michel itself where it ran from there up to the Place Edmond Rostand at the corner of the Luxembourg. At the Carrefour itself nothing had been left standing. Nothing. And up the Boulevard at least one-third of the lovely old flowering trees, such a beautiful and distinctive part of Paris and of the *Quartier,* had been downed during the night and lay out in the street or up onto the sidewalk almost to the storefronts. They could asphalt the boulevards, all right. But it would take a long time to replace those.

Hundreds of people were out strolling to view the destruction. They climbed over the tree butts when they had to, or passed around them out in the street when it was possible. We joined the parade.

It was hard to believe where last night there had been such violence and wild emotion and potential danger there was now such quiet and order and amiable calm.

At the rue Racine there was a phenomenon I knew about and I took the others to see it. Rue Racine was a short street which ran on an angle from Boul' St.-Michel to the Odéon and on it was a barricade which the students had come to call the *barricade pure,* the "pure barricade". It had been there for at least two weeks and had never been removed. It was made of nothing except paving stones. That was what made it "pure". It had become a joke at both the Sorbonne and the Odéon. Nobody was allowed to put any streetlamps, trees, tree grilles, or traffic signs on it. I took McKenna's picture standing up on top of it, from a squatting position in the street.

Then as an afterthought I took one of the *pavés* from it to save for her. I thought someday she might like to have it. I thought I could have one of the sides ground down smooth and polished and then engraved with the place and date of the Paris Revolution for her.

But then, after I had taken it, I felt peculiar walking along with it in my hand, as if some flic I met might think I meant to heave it at him. So I stuffed it into the pocket of my trenchcoat, where it hung down so heavily that it made me look like some kind of deformed semihunchback. So, in this odd fashion we made our way on up St.-Michel to Edmond Rostand and had a coffee there at the big café on the corner across from the Luxembourg. Everyone in the café certainly seemed happy and cheerful enough.

After that we walked over to rue Bonaparte and took it down to the Place St.-Germain and had lunch at Lipp, where everything was business-as-usual. It was funny to note that at every table there was a silent transistor radio, and that somebody at each table had the tiny plastic earplug in his ear for the news.

On the way home we took them past our own barricade at the rue des Écoles and rue Monge.

The lady painter from our American group who lived near Maubert was with us too, and we dropped her off at her place and went on home to the Île. She and Ferenc had been having a mild flirtation for the last week, and he had called her up, and she had met us at Maubert on our way up to St.-Michel. She, though I think not Louisa, was shocked as much as I was about the old trees. Louisa seemed to think it was all part of the Revolutionary game. Like the old saw: *If you want to make an omelet, you have to break some eggs.*

Actually, I had seen some of the first of those beautiful big trees come down myself the night before, along the Boulevard St.-Michel.

After saying goodby to Ferenc and letting myself in, I found I wasn't able to sleep. After standing at my windows with a drink for half an hour watching the heated glow in the sky over the Quarter, I had gotten dressed and gone out again.

This time I went straight up Cardinal Lemoine and around the Panthéon and down through the Place Edmond Rostand and straight over to the Odéon. It was still the same jammed-up crowding screeching place it had been on my other visits. But now tonight with the renewed fighting the excitement was more intense. There were noticeably fewer Countesses and Baronesses with their tall black-tied escorts "touristing". When I got back upstairs with my *Laissez-Passer* card, I found both Weintraub and Hill Gallagher there in the crowded steaming little offices of the *Comité du Cinéma des Étudiants de la Sorbonne.*

Hill looked awful. He stood around like some kind of stork with his shoulders all hunched up and when I went over to him particularly to say hello he mumbled something and turned away from me. He looked like he had more misery in him than there was in all the rest of the world. But not Weintraub.

"Hey!" he said cheerily, and came over to me. "I was wondering if you'd show up tonight."

"I almost didn't," I said. "But I couldn't stay away."

"That's the old Revolutionary spirit," Weintraub grinned, and slapped me on the back. But for the first time I thought I could detect a haunted look underneath the grin.

The usual groups of kids, all familiar faces by now, were all standing around the office. Daniel the Chairman with the steel-rimmed glasses was behind his desk. The usual democratic discussion and voting was going on just the same, at full tilt. It had become an almost unconscious ritual for them by now.

"What do the Cinema Committee kids think about all the renewed fighting?" I asked Weintraub.

"Naturally, they think it's all a deliberate ploy on the part of the Government," he said cheerfully. "The Government has been holding back hoping the Revolution would 'rot' itself out, as they say. When it didn't, they decided to send the police in again against the students, to make it so unpleasant for the people that they will turn against the students, stop all the strikes and settle down and go back to work. In other words, the new fighting is to try and alienate the working people from the students and destroy the solidarity."

"Um," I said. I did not know if I could subscribe to that.

"Well, that's what they believe," Weintraub said. "Especially now that talks are starting between the Government and the unions tomorrow." He added, "We've got three crews out shooting the St.-Michel fight tonight."

"They don't really think they've got any possible chance of winning, do they?" I said.

"We never talk about that." He moved. "Let's go in and have a coffee. I've got something I want to talk to you about."

We moved through the democratic discussion of something or other chaired by Daniel and went to the door into the "kitchen" part of the Cinema Committee's "offices", which also, by its other door, led onto the tiny balcony high above the main amphitheater. The by now almost goofy 24-hour marathon discussion was still going on down there. But it had lost a lot of its energy, and most of its sense. There was a pot of stew simmering on one burner of the tiny butane hotplate and a pot of coffee on the other. There was one young couple necking on the mat in the corner but not as far as I could see, while trying not to look, doing more than that. Otherwise it was empty. "Did you see the 'hospital' on your way up?" Weintraub asked as we shut the door against the discussion.

"I heard it," I said. "As I came up the back stairs."

"They've got over a hundred more in there now than they had on Wednesday," Weintraub said. He got two grimy looking cups. "They just won't turn themselves in to the regular hospitals because the police keep a check on them all and arrest everybody." He poured the hot black coffee for us both and then sat down against the wall on a mat at the other end from the necking couple. I sat down beside him, nursing the hot cup of horrible coffee.

"Hill Gallagher is flipping his lid," Weintraub began.

"Oh?" I said. "How so? Why?"

"You mean you don't know about Harry taking Samantha off to Cannes with him?"

"Do you know that?" I asked. "Or is it a supposition?"

"Well, I don't have any signed letters from either of them, if that's what you mean," Weintraub said. "And I haven't tried to call down there. But it's pretty damned obvious. Where else would she have disappeared to?"

"Lots of places. Well, if he did," I said, "I think it was a damned silly thing for a man in his position to do."

"I'll concede that," Weintraub said and again I saw that odd pained, battered look come onto his face that I was to see so many more times. "I guess I knew I could never keep her. Of course, she was shtumping Hill, and a lot of the other guys up here I suppose, but at least she was bunking up with me." He drank from his steaming cup. "She's still looking for that loot to get her down to Israel. Though I don't know how she would get out of Paris now if she had it. Shit, only a damned diplomat can get out now, from those military fields that are still operating, or a big big-business man."

"But what about Hill?"

"Well, I guess he's flipped over her," Weintraub said sadly. "I don't know how *he* found out. I certainly didn't tell him." I felt a twinge. "But then he was bound to find it out sooner or later."

"And you're absolutely sure about this, Weintraub," I said.

"As sure as I am about anything I've ever seen or done."

"Listen, Weintraub. If you ever intimate so much as one word about this, ever, to Louisa, I'll—I'll do something terrible to you," I said.

"Not to worry!" He raised his hand. "Poor Louisa is no concern of mine."

"Well, just remember that. I swear I'll hound you out of Paris."

He shook his head. "Of course, that is not to say that Hill might not tell her."

"No he wouldn't," I said. "Never."

Weintraub shrugged. "Who's to say? In any case, he's been flipping his lid around here."

"How do you mean?"

"Well, you know they voted in the Committee about Harry's proposal he made before he left. Well, Hill came out against it. Everybody was clearly in favor of it, but Hill makes this long wild gnashing speech against it in the discussion about how his father was a commercial, revisionist bourgeois, who wanted to use commercial, revisionist bourgeois methods to make the Committee's film, and that it would destroy the honor, the very precepts of the Committee, its film, and the Revolution itself, if they let his father make it his way, or even work on it at all. His father was a commercial hack, a paid pawn of the Establishment. He went wild. I mean, really wild. Waving his arms, and hollering, and grinding his teeth. I was there at the time."

"That's all due to Samantha," I said judiciously.

"I don't know if it all is," Weintraub said. "But certainly some of it is, I'm sure."

"He's fallen madly in love with her."

"Well, he ought to know better than to fall for a chick like that," Weintraub said, sadly. "She's not about to tie herself up with some guy. And certainly not some guy like Hill." Or you, I thought. He had implied it. "Anyway, she certainly knows her business in the bed," he said, "and maybe that got to him. He's so young." He sat musing for a moment, his back against the wall.

"Well anyway, they finally got the floor away from him, and some other kids made short speeches about why they were in favor of the idea, Harry's idea. It was plain they were all against him. But Hill couldn't leave it alone. He kept breaking in out of order, and trying to make more speeches, and Daniel kept having to gavel him down. Man

I mean but he really lost his cool, man," the 45-year-old Weintraub said. (I suspect him of being much closer to 50 than 45, if not already 50.) My sadness for him over Samantha increased. He was taking it really well.

"Anyway finally, they voted, and voted him down almost unanimously. The only two who voted with him were Terri and Bernard. And they clearly did it out of friendship, knowing they would lose beforehand." He grinned suddenly. "After all, Terri is going to be the star of it if they do it Harry's way.

"And since then he hasn't been the same boy. He just mopes around. The kids who crew with him say he isn't doing half the job he used to do on his assignments. That's why they didn't send him out tonight. I think he's in a pretty bad way."

We both sat in silence for a while, nursing our hot cups. I simply could not get that vile coffee down, though it did not seem to bother Weintraub. There just was not anything I could say about Hill that would do any good or help.

"Is there anything you can do to help him?"

"I never have been able to talk to him about Harry," I said finally. "And not now either, about Samantha."

Weintraub appeared not even to have heard me. "Then there's been another development. You know they stored all those cans of shot film at my place during that scare about a police raid. Well, they came and took them back, and all of them were kept out in the office there in those two big refrigerator boxes. There's no way to get them developed here in France without the police and the Government confiscating them.

"Well, about ten days ago one of the kids on the Committee came in here and took almost all of them, more than fifty, maybe sixty cans—that's a lot of film—saying he had a ride to Italy that night in a private car and he would take the film to Italy with him and have it developed and bring it back. There was only one girl in the office, alone, at the time. She had no authority to say yes or no and she let him take them. They've had no word from him at all since then, and they've been beginning to get worried about the film. Do you know about all that?"

"No, I don't," I said. I had not heard anything about it at all.

"Well, now they've got some garbled message back from Italy saying that he lost them all, in Rome. They were 'stolen' from the back seat of his car during a riot, or after a demonstration that he went to, or something. It's a pretty garbled message. The kid who brought it back doesn't even know him. And the kid himself who took them hasn't come back. He's still in Rome, trying to get a fix on where they went." Weintraub smiled a bitter smile. "There seems to be some suspicion among the kids on the Committee that he just swiped them and sold them in Rome."

"Jesus!" I said. "But that's irreparable."

"One bad apple in the barrel," Weintraub said. "That kind of a story. It sure is irreparable. Almost all the stuff they've shot from the beginning up to then. All the stuff that Hill shot on the barricades of the Friday night of Gay-Lussac. All the demonstrations. All the stuff shot inside the Sorbonne. It's more than irreparable. It's a catastrophe."

"The idealistic students," I said. "The idealistic students of the *Comité du Cinéma de la Sorbonne et Odéon.*"

"Yeah," Weintraub sighed. "The idealistic students, and one bad apple. They don't really know yet what really happened. They're just waiting to hear." He shoved himself up from against the wall. He had emptied his cup. I got up myself.

"That must not make Hill too happy either," I said.

"I very much doubt if he's even aware of it," Weintraub said. "What with his misery over Samantha."

"Where can I throw this?" I said, holding up my cup.

"There's a little sink there in the corner," he said. It was so dark and dingy in the corner that I had not seen the tiny sink before.

"I wonder what's happened to his live-and-let-live, screw-and-let-screw, anti-monogamy philosophy?" I said coming back.

"I suppose, after the first time in your life you fall in love big, you're more prepared for it," Weintraub said thoughtfully. "You're more prepared for the loss and the big knock."

"But you've got to survive that first time, though."

Weintraub sighed. "Yeah. That's true. And you really don't think there's anything you can do to help him, hunh? Look. Do you want to go down and take a look at the old Boul' St.-Michel? Have you been down there yet tonight? We can get that boy Raymond to steer us all around. He's well known just about everywhere in the Quartier now."

"No, I haven't yet," I said. "I've been around other places but not there. Okay, sure. Why not?"

The boy Raymond was out in the office, where some other heated democratic discussion was going on chaired by the tireless Daniel.

Raymond had sort of become my official conductor everywhere since he had first shown me the Committee's offices and the balcony over the theater. He said he would be glad to take us down to St.-Michel.

"You'll probably need a handkerchief if we get anywhere near to the Carrefour," he smiled.

I nodded and said I had one, and then he took us down past the moaning hospital and out through the kids with the chains around their necks, who were certainly not students. Grammar school dropouts or not, they were having the time of their lives guarding the Revolution with their chains.

As we went down I saw Jean-Luc Godard, Truffaut, and William Klein all wandering around separately in the crowded corridors. Only one of them, Godard, had a camera with him. There was still the same tension and sense of happy elation all over.

Out in the street we made our way across the crowded *Place* toward rue Racine and down it past the *barricade pure* to the Boulevard. There was room to get past it on the sidewalk. At the Odéon there had been gangs of students up on the high Odéon roof, armed with garbagecan lids for shields and wearing weird-looking Roman or Gothic or Frankish helmets. They had found stores of these among the theater's costuming department. They shouted down from the high roof unintelligible comments while brandishing their shields. It was a real bedlam.

Along Racine and on St.-Michel we found more gangs of similarly uniformed students moving along toward the fight or else away from it. There seemed to be little order to their movement. They all wore handkerchiefs around their necks ready to be pulled up over their noses in the tear gas.

Raymond really was quite small. He spoke no English at all and we spoke to him all the time in French. He was considerably older than the others, 25 or 26. He seemed to be more reflective. He was sweeter-looking and more nonviolent-looking than anyone I had seen around. He had been doing graduate studies in Cinema at the Sorbonne before the Revolution. He wanted to be a film director. As we moved along, he was hailed by students from all the groups we passed.

"Tell me," I said. "Do you think Daniel the Chairman could perhaps be a foreign agent?"

We were standing on the corner of the Boulevard now, by the little bookshop there. The wide street was jammed with people. Small civilian cars with red crosses painted on their sides and hoods, driven by shouting students, were honking and trying to get through the press. Some were going toward the fighting and some away from it.

"I have thought of that." Raymond looked at me with smart eyes and smiled his gentle smile. "No, I do not think he is. He has a strange accent. That is all. Well, he is Swiss."

"He also has the look of a dedicated Commissar," I said. "And those ancient style steel-rimmed glasses of his. Very Russian."

"That is true," Raymond smiled. "But no, I do not think he is. In any case we must use what we have at hand. Shall we go on? Or stop here?"

"No, let's go on."

We were able to get down to the Carrefour. It was only a short distance, and the actual fighting at the moment was further down toward the river. We could see the flashes, smoke and bursts of tear gas coming up down there nearer to the Place St.-Michel, and hear the shouts and the chanting.

Across St.-Germain gangs were ripping up what was left of the street, pulling down traffic signs and streetlamps to make a barricade. Up St.-Germain 200 yards, at the rue Danton, a police cordon blocked that boulevard, but they were not moving.

Suddenly, in front of us, at the Carrefour, four tough but vicious ratlike-looking individuals, in their early 20s I guessed, snaked out across the sidewalk and began dismantling with great efficiency the protective pedestrian railings that ran around the corner of the sidewalk. These consisted of eight or ten iron pipes set into the concrete and connected by chains. One individual opened the end links with a large switchblade as a lever, then carefully closed the links and draped the chains around his neck. Two others equipped with hacksaws began sawing off the pipes at the ground to use as clubs. The fourth collected the pipes as they came loose. They were dressed in what appeared to be Army fatigues and they wore the round-topped American-style forage caps pulled far down onto their ears with the brims turned flat up. They did not talk and their faces were absolutely cold, concentrated and expressionless.

When they had demolished the pedestrian railing, they snaked back across the sidewalk and disappeared as they had come, down toward the fighting.

"Did you see those types!" I said. I could not help exclaiming. They were like real rats, totally inhuman.

Raymond, beside me, made an embarrassed gesture. "It is no longer under our control, you know. It has not been since last night."

"But you have a lot of them working for you at the Odéon."

Again Raymond made an embarrassed smile. "That is true. And not only at Odéon."

"They gave me a chill up my back," I said.

"Me, too," Weintraub said simply.

"I would gladly knock those four young gentlemen off with a machine-pistol, and feel no qualms," I said. I was absolutely furious for some reason.

"And they would do the same for you," Weintraub said. Then he laughed, in his deepest voice.

"I am sure they would," I said.

"We no longer have control," Raymond said apologetically. "It has become completely out of hand."

I wasn't angry any longer. Certainly not at small gentle Raymond. "But when you did have control, you still were hiring types like those," I said. "Tell me, do you not find a philosophical discrepancy in what you students declare are the aims of your Revolution and in the fact that you hire gutter stormtroopers like that to fight for you?"

He smiled ruefully. "Of course it is there. But the police and the Government forced us to it. I could not get out on those barricades and fight like that. I wouldn't have a chance."

"You are small, but you are not smaller than those four boys," I said.

"I am not smaller than half the policemen in uniform, either,"

Raymond said. "It is not a question of the size. It is a question of the temperament. Of the mentality. I could not do it."

"But lots of the students have."

"Yes, but you do not know that in the fighting, the real fighting, they were fighting always side by side with boys like those four."

"No, I did not know that," I said.

"The only answer I can give you is that when we have won, when the Gaullist Government is toppled and replaced by a truly Socialist Government, we will try to rectify all the bad things we had to do to achieve it."

"Yes," I said. "And the Government says that, too."

"I know it," Raymond said. "I know they do. But it is the only honest answer I can give you."

"And you really think you can overturn de Gaulle?"

"That is why we are out here," Raymond said.

"You see?" Weintraub said to me.

We were still standing near the corner of St.-Germain. Behind us a spluttering, chattering noise started up, loud even in all that noise. We turned around to look. A crowd of people had gathered around one of the huge old flowering trees. It was impossible to see what was going on and we walked back up to look. Two young men had attacked the big old tree with gasoline-driven chain saws. They looked absolutely hysterical. As the saws cut through the tree, the crowd around moved fast suddenly, to get out of the way.

"We better get back," Weintraub shouted to us.

We backed off further up the Boulevard, watching. There was a warning shout, and the great tree came down into the Boulevard, where a group of students had cleared a space for it and were holding hands to hold back the crowd. I looked at Raymond and he shrugged sorrowfully.

"I guess I have seen enough," I said. "Let's go back to Odéon."

Further up the Boulevard on our way to rue Racine two other youths with big double-bitted woodsmen's axes were attacking another of the big trees.

"It will take a long time for your Government to rectify that," I said as we turned into Racine, "don't you think?"

"I hate to see it as much as you do," Raymond said. "Believe me, if I were giving the orders, I would not give such an order, or allow it. But now, now nobody is giving orders. It is completely out of hand."

"I do not think you can win," I said bluntly. "De Gaulle is tough. And the people will get tired of the discomfort and the misery. The workers will take what they can get from the Patronat and give up and go back to work. And they will be worse off than before, even with their pay raises. Because what your Revolution is doing to those trees along the Boulevard, it is also doing to the national economy of France."

"At least we will have made an impression," Raymond said. "Our existence will be proved."

At the corner of rue Monsieur-le-Prince I left them and cut back up toward the top of the Boulevard and rue Soufflot. I could not stand the thought of going back to the Odéon with them, or even without them. The narrow old street was filled with a visible thick mist of tear gas that made my eyes smart badly. I had to pick my way over the remains of barricades and debris, and around the weirdly dressed student fighters who moved along it. At the top of the Boulevard at Place Edmond Rostand where the crowds ceased I stopped just once and looked down the strife-torn Boul' Mich', then went on home by Cardinal Lemoine feeling very very down.

Saturday things were much quieter. The students were trying hard to get back control and all their unions issued orders against rioting in the Quartier. The next day Sunday things were even quieter, but they always were on the Sundays. The three-way negotiations between the Government, labor and management had begun and went on through the weekend. On Monday Harry Gallagher came home from Cannes.

17

THE REASON HARRY CAME BACK on Monday was because there was to be a huge joint parade of students and workers Monday evening, followed by a mass meeting at the Charléty Stadium in the south part of Paris.

This meeting had been announced on Friday and had received government permission. Harry was a big member of the main committee of the Film Directors and Writers Union, which would be taking part, and he felt he had to be present for the parade and meeting. Otherwise, he told me later, he might not ever have come back.

I did not see Harry on the Monday. He was not at the nightly gathering of Americans at his place because he was out all afternoon helping organize, and lead, the Directors and Writers Union part of the parade, which even as we met at the Gallaghers' apartment was already going on. Louisa told me he rushed in just long enough to shower, shave and change clothes before rushing off to his committee. Louisa did not appear to know anything about Cannes.

So Harry was not at our nightly meeting of Americans. Neither was Samantha, about whom and whose whereabouts I knew nothing at all.

But good old Weintraub was there. He had not missed an evening since Harry and Samantha had left for Cannes.

As soon as I got a chance I got him off in a corner.

"Harry's back," I said quietly. "Have you heard anything from Sam?"

"He is?" Weintraub seemed surprised.

"Louisa told me," I said impatiently. "He came back because of the parade and meeting tonight. That's why he's not here. But what about Sam?"

"I haven't heard a word from her," Weintraub said. "Maybe she's still in Cannes?"

"Could she have gone from there to Italy?"

"She could have," he said. "With Harry's money." He had that pained, battered look on his face again. "If she hired a car to take her to San Remo, she could catch a train there to take her to Rome and fly from Rome to Israel."

I felt a sudden great rush of relief. "Maybe that's what she did."

"Could be," Weintraub said. "Well," he said and suddenly turned away from me. "Well, well." Then he turned back. "Anyway, I was over at the Odéon most of the afternoon, and she didn't show up there. Nor has she tried to contact me at my pad."

The Odéon, I thought. "Did you see Hill while you were there?" I asked.

"Hill? Yeah. Yeah, he was there."

"How was he?"

"All right. Morose. Beat down, maybe. But he seemed okay." He sighed. "Maybe he'll pull out of it."

"Maybe he will," I said. "Tell me, how long did Hill know Sam?"

"Hill? About a week, I guess. I don't *really* know if she was screwing anybody else but him. And occasionally me. I suppose she was."

"That's an awfully short time to get rid of all those so firmly ingrained philosophies of his about free love," I said.

"Yeah," Weintraub said in a dulled voice. "Well, women can do that to you, I guess."

Before I could say anything else Louisa came toward us from across the room.

"What have you two got your heads together about?" she said.

"We were talking about Dave's girl," I said, truthfully enough.

"Oh. That beautiful little colored girl?" Louisa smiled. "I've been wondering what had happened to her."

"She seems to have disappeared," I said.

"Oh! That's bad luck for you, Dave," she said.

"Yeah," Weintraub said, equally truthfully. "It sure is."

"Let's all go and have another drink," I suggested. At the bar I patted Weintraub on the back, somehow unaccountably moved by his mood. Normally he was such a buffoon. But now even that shell had broken. And what was inside, a lonely man, shown through. I told him I would see him at the Odéon later.

Later, after the others had left, I had dinner with Louisa and Ferenc, who was going over to the lady painter's apartment near Maubert after dinner. It was a gay dinner. Ferenc was always an amusing and funny conversationalist. He had Louisa and me laughing much of the time.

Weintraub did not show up at the Odéon on that Monday night of the 27th. I stayed there until four A.M. waiting for him. Hill was there though, moping around, but he would hardly talk to me. He had it really bad.

Most of the kids were jubilant. The parade and the meeting at the Charléty Stadium had resulted in a resounding "No!" to de Gaulle and the Government's proposals of wage raises. They—the students; and lots of the younger workers—were out for a serious, complete Revolution. They wanted to bring down the de Gaulle Government and replace it with a "Socialist" one, though I don't think they knew what they meant by that. I could not honestly see, personally, how any of them could have run any God damned Government.

But then, when I finally left Odéon, I ran into Weintraub, entirely by accident. He was sitting all alone at an outdoor table of an all-night café across the square, looking bemused, and I happened to pass by.

"Hey, Weintraub!" I called and went over and sat down with him. "What the hell happened to *you?* You were supposed to meet me at the Committee office."

"I'm sorry about that," he said, a sort of dreamy look all over his face. Then, as he really became aware of me, I watched it change to that depressed, pained, battered expression I had begun to get used to.

"Sit down, Hartley," he said, though I already was sitting. "Samantha is back, all right."

"You saw her?"

"Did I ever," Weintraub said. "Did I ever. And her little French friend."

"You mean you—" I began. I did not know quite how to say it. "You mean you did them?"

"Did I not," he said. "Did I not. Did I ever."

I decided to shut up and just listen. After his frugal dinner on his hotplate in his room, he had gone around to Castel's, just to look in, and maybe have one drink if somebody offered, before coming to Odéon. And who should be sitting in the ground floor bar totally at home? Sam and her little friend. Castel had presented her with another bottle. Dave sat down with them and had a drink. He was full of questions. He wanted to know everything, and Sam told him. Yes, she had come back with Harry from Cannes. Yes, she was staying in a hotel. Yes, Harry was paying. Yes, he had given or would give her the money to get to Israel. Yes, she was looking into the possibility of flying out from Paris. It was possible, she thought. She knew some people who might help. No, her little friend was not going with her. What in the name of God would I do in Israel? the friend interjected in French. But why had she come back to Paris? Dave wanted to know, when she could have taken a car direct to San Remo from Cannes? Well, she hadn't thought of that really, that was the truth, and she did not quite feel like leaving Paris yet. She did not know why. Yes, Harry was very *sympathique, très sympathique,* one of her kind. She had known it from the moment she first shook hands with him. No, she didn't hate to leave him at all. They were not in love. They just understood each other, and what was fun. The hotel she was staying at was on the Île, on Île St.-Louis.

"Jesus Christ," I said in a low breath. That fact bothered me more than any of the rest of it.

It was one of those small hotels on the rue St.-Louis-en-l'Île, Dave said. I was sure I knew the one.

"Yeah," he said. Well anyway he had asked her why she wasn't with Harry tonight, and she had laughed. Harry was out doing his thing with the God damned Revolution. Well, if that was Harry's bag, let him climb into it. She was not about to go and sit in some smelly stadium with a bunch of students and workers who might flip out into a crazy mob at any moment. So she, and her little friend, had come here. No, there was no commitment between her and Harry. They were both free agents. Harry had paid, and paid elegantly, for the fun and she had delivered. That was it. Then she smiled at Dave. Why didn't they all three go over to Dave's place? she had asked. For old time's sake. Why not? Dave answered quickly. He was ready and willing, more than. Such a windfall. Did he have any booze in the joint? Well no, he was a little short, a little short on booze, at the moment. But he could sure as hell get some, somewhere. Never mind, was the answer, she had money. She would pay. She didn't like booze, but her little friend did and it turned her on. They would pick up a bottle on the way. So the three of them had gone to his place. That had been around eleven or eleven-thirty. The two girls had only just left about half an hour ago. Such a windfall. Weintraub peered at me with that dreamy look in the half light of the outdoor café.

"I really didn't feel much like coming up to the Odéon," he said huskily.

He was really so simpleminded about it. I could not somehow feel shocked at his going to bed with two girls who liked to have a man in the act when they went to bed together. It was just something I did not understand. I knew I ought to be shocked about it. But he was so simple and happy about it, like a child. Maybe Harry felt the same way? But Harry was not the same case as Dave. Weintraub didn't have a wife who loved him, and two kids. It was not the same at all.

"Oh," Weintraub said dreamily. "Incidentally. She asked me if I had ever been up to Harry's studio up under the roof. Said it was a lovely pad. I've never been up there. Have you?"

"She said what!" I exclaimed.

"Just that," he said. "Apparently she, they, were up there in the afternoon."

"Great God!" I said. "He must be out of his mind to do something like that!"

"Yeah," Weintraub sighed, "I guess he's hooked, all right." The battered look came back over his face. "Christ, I wish I had some of his money."

"You've simply got to keep quiet about this, Dave," I said. "You simply must."

"Oh, I'll keep quiet," he said. "Why should I not? Only, I've got to admit I'm hoping she don't leave Paris too soon, and that there are more parades and meetings to keep Harry occupied nights." He grinned at me. But it was a rueful battered grin.

I left him sitting there, one moment dreamy-looking, the next looking battered, and went home by my round-about way feeling very distressed.

I saw Harry the next day. There was no parade or big meeting of dissidents, and he was at home for the by now ritual meeting of Americans at his apartment. But so was Samantha there, also! And of course so was Weintraub.

Sam came in by herself. And she acted absolutely correctly. There were no sighs, or long flirtatious glances, or double-entendre statements, from that one. She spent most of her time with Weintraub, talking quietly, and the rest of it she spent with Louisa. There was certainly no indication that she was Harry's mistress. Perhaps mistress is the wrong word. Maybe paramour is better. I do not know what to call it, since there was no love involved at all between them. When she left Weintraub and went over to Louisa, she sat all curled up at Louisa's feet like an adoring kitten. They talked a long time. I had heard Louisa ask her earlier when she first came in if she had just returned from a trip, but I do not think Louisa made the connection between Harry's Cannes trip and Samantha's absence. Sam could not have been nicer to her.

Even so, it was all almost a little too much to stomach.

Finally I got Harry off in a corner alone, behind the bar.

"My God, Harry! What in the name of heaven do you mean bringing that girl in here like that?"

He grinned at me. He actually grinned at me. "She was lonesome," he said. "Said she wanted to be around some Americans. I didn't see why she couldn't come. She's not going to make any gaff."

"Maybe not," I said. "But even so, Harry, my God!"

"She likes Louisa," he grinned. "She told me so herself in Cannes."

"Harry, look," I said guardedly, after looking around to see there was no one near enough to hear us. "What are you now? Fifty? Almost. Do you know what in hell you're doing? Have you lost your marbles?"

He grinned at me narrowly, and those narrow eyes of his and his bald head suddenly looked eagle-ish. "Jack," he said, quite carefully, but in a conversational tone, "have you ever reached a point in your life where you just don't give a shit?"

"No, I don't think I ever have," I said.

"Well, I have," he said quite calmly. "And as for being fifty, which you are right I almost am, it seems to me it's time to move. Move. Move about what you want. Blink your eyes, Jack, and it'll be ten years from now and I'll be sixty. Blink again, and make it seventy. And where'll I be then, hunh? If I aint dead already."

"Well then, for God's sake, put her in an apartment somewhere. Set her up. You've got the money. But for God's sake don't bring her right here on the Island, and stash her in one of those little hotels. Everybody on the Island knows you, Harry. Get her an apartment in the Sixth."

"She wouldn't stay," he said, matter-of-factly. "She's going to go to Israel. And she'll go. I'm not at all sure, Jack, that I won't go down there too, after her. I think I may.

"You know about that, hey? The hotel," he added.

"Weintraub told me," I said. "He also told me she told him what a fine studio you had here in the building up under the roof."

"Yeah, I took them up there. As a matter of fact, we made love up there, yesterday afternoon. I told you, Jack. I've reached a point where I don't give a shit any more."

"You sure have," was all I could come back with.

"I have."

I was aghast. "You must be out of your mind," I said, feebly. "You've got to have some responsibilities. Do you remember that your own son is, or was, her lover and is crazy in love with her?"

"Yeah," Harry said. "For how long?"

"Well, a week. Or maybe ten days. But you know as well as I do that that is long enough. Time doesn't matter in a thing like that."

"Yeah," Harry said. "Him. Him, and those loudly spouted philosophies of his about free love." He grinned again, with that eagle-ish look. "It seems to be turning out that I'm more of a radical than he is.

"Incidentally, Jack. I know they spent most of last night with Weintraub. She told me. And I don't give a damn. What do you think about that?"

There was not anything that I could do. We had been there alone at the corner of the bar too long now already. Both of us had raised our voices at least once. I thought it was time to back off. I knew it was. "Make me another drink, Harry," I said, "and I'll circulate a little."

"With pleasure," he grinned.

I took my new drink and walked down the length of the long room, saying a word here and a hello there, and wound up where Louisa and Samantha were.

"Well, Mr. Hartley," Sam said immediately, from her seat on the carpeted floor. "Hello, Mr. Hartley. How are you, Mr. Hartley? You're looking good. It's nice to see that kind, decent face of yours again, Mr. Hartley."

"Yes," I said. "Thank you. I hear you've been on a trip."

"I have," she said. "But now I'm back."

I just nodded.

"And do you want to know who I've missed the most while I was away?" Sam said. "I've missed you, Mr. Hartley. But most of all I've missed Louisa here. She's the one I missed most of all."

Louisa was beginning to blush.

"Hey, Harry!" Samantha called down the length of the long room. "I'm still really crazy in love with your wife! Crazy!"

Everyone laughed. At the bar Harry merely grinned and nodded, with that eagle-like look I had never seen on him before. Louisa was now blushing completely.

"You're incorrigible," she said. But I had hardly ever seen her looking happier. "Really incorrigible. Your mother should have spanked you more."

"Oh, she did," Sam smiled up at her, "she did. She spanked just about everybody. Including my father, and most of her girlfriends."

Forcing myself to grin an appreciative acknowledgment, I went over to Weintraub and left them. He stared at me dreamily, with that dreamy look of last night. After a while, after a proper amount of time, I got my hat and umbrella and left. Since Harry was back, I had no obligation to keep Louisa company, and I did not want to think about them, any of them. I dined alone.

Later on that night Harry showed up over at the Odéon. Weintraub and I were both there. So was Hill. Samantha did not appear.

Harry had come to see what they had decided about his proposition. He had been given a *Laissez-Passer* card by the Chairman Daniel when there before. So he just appeared in the doorway, his always new, starched trenchcoat billowing with the collar up around his ears, a cigarette dangling from his jaw. He and Hill only nodded stiffly at each other. Then he asked Daniel what their decision was.

Daniel, always the Chairman, gave a long spiel about how they had discussed it and had voted, in the proper democratic way, which was the essence of the Revolution, and they had decided to accept Harry's offer. The two principals he had chosen would be ready any time he wanted them. They would put themselves at his disposal, for the good of the Revolution, but he would have to instruct them. Neither of them was a trained actor.

Harry accepted graciously. He would instruct them, all right. And he would bring his own camera, his own cameraman, a guy he had worked with, and he would buy his own film. What he wanted was the proper backgrounds for the scenes he would shoot. The whole thing would key in on a love affair between Terri and Anne-Marie, which would take place during the Revolution. He would shoot all that. Then they would mix it all up with the film the students had already shot to get the proper ambiance. But he wanted to get one thing clear. Once they had accepted, he was the boss—the dictator. There would be no democratic discussions and votings while he was the boss of the film. Otherwise, it would never get done. That was his only stipulation. Once they had accepted the idea, and he started shooting, they would have to accept that too: that he was the absolute boss. Was that all right?

Daniel fidgeted and turned a little red. Well, they should discuss that and vote on it before they finally decided. However, for himself, he was more than willing to go along with that. He understood and accepted that a director had to have full authority. Then he gravely told Harry about the 50 cans of missing film lost in Italy.

"I think you ought to know about that, before we begin," Daniel said.

Harry made a sour face. That was bad luck, he said. But they would have to do with what they had. It might mean his having to shoot more background stuff. But they could do that.

I was very tired. I had been working very hard the last two days with Terri, trying to frame and flesh out the two articles that I had promised them were to go into my Review. We had worked very hard at my place—in anticipation of this arrival of Harry's which would take Terri away from me for an unknown number of days; and I had got my framing all down. But I was beat. So I sat in a hot corner of the office yawning while the scene went on.

True to the old Revolutionary principle, Daniel called a meeting and got out his gavel, one of the girls took stenographic minutes for the record, and Daniel opened the floor for debate. Harry stood by the door listening, his cigarette still hanging. Nobody had any objections apparently. A couple of youngsters spoke shortly, saying the same thing practically, which was that as directorial students of Cinema themselves they understood the director had to have full authority. Then Hill stepped out front and asked for the floor.

Well, I had listened to Weintraub's description of his wild emotional speeches of a few days before, and Hill did exactly the same thing again. He did not wave his arms or gnash his teeth, this time, as Weintraub said he had done before. But the rest of it was the same: overwrought, far too high-keyed, much too lurid and with much too much hyperbole. He made a complete ass of himself. In the student jargon of Anarchism, which was not really all that different from the old-time Communist jargon, he accused Harry of just about everything except stealing the kitchen sink.

Harry simply stood by the door, his hands in his trenchcoat pockets, a little smile on his mouth, his eyes narrowed, occasionally puffing at the cigarette between his lips.

In his summation Hill used that ringing old French phrase of Zola from the Dreyfus Affair "*J'accuse*," and pointed a finger dramatically at his father. "I accuse this man of being a paid lackey of the very Establishment we are trying to bring down. I accuse him of having no moral precepts whatever with regard to our Revolution. I accuse him of just about every kind of revisionism and revisionist thinking that exist in our messed-up horrible world. True, he is a member of the Film Directors' Union. But what did any of those unions do, about anything, before we students started this Revolution? You all know that. Absolutely nothing. True, he went down to Cannes to strike his own film, but only after the Cannes Festival had been disrupted and abandoned and he could climb up on the bandwagon safely. I accuse him of using commercial, revisionist methods of the Establishment to impose on, and ruin, our own film of our own Revolution. A love story! He writes marvelous commercial love stories for the Film Industry Establishment, and makes a great deal of money at it, and all of them are full of commercial shit and untruths. I submit that he should not be allowed to touch or work on our Revolutionary film at all." Finally he dropped his arm and stepped back.

Daniel rapped his gavel. "Okay?" he said. "Okay. Now I suggest we vote. For myself, before we vote, I would like to add that I personally think that any methods that we use to get our film and our story out before the world are justified and therefore morally usable."

This time no one voted with Hill. Not even Terri and Bernard did. When the call came for the nay votes to the proposition, he stepped forward and gave his single nay staunchly and loudly and all alone.

"Okay," Daniel said. "That settles that." He rapped his gavel. "You have our vote and our support, M. Gallagher," he said from behind those cold steel-rimmed glasses. "And I, for one, think your idea an excellent one. We will give you everything we have within our limited resources."

"Well," Harry said from the door. "Fine. Okay." He stepped forward to the desk and turned to address the group. He really looked very romantic with his starched trenchcoat and a new cigarette in his mouth. "Tomorrow, Wednesday, there will be a big march by the Communist-led CGT Confederation. I want to photograph that march, with my principals in it. I realize that the Students' Unions are not taking part in that march. But my own, affiliated union is, and my two actors can march with that group. I'll have my own cameraman, and we will be moving in the parade in an open car. I have already set up this contingency, in case you people voted as you have. That's all set. But I also want two of your crews out there shooting the march from different angles. I want the two best crews you've got, but I don't know who they are or how good. Except for him there," he said, indicating Hill. "I want him to head one of the crews. You must pick the other one yourself. But it is important right now to get as much excellent footage as possible, especially with this apparent loss of shot film that you've had. I'll meet all of you here at around one o'clock tomorrow afternoon and we will set up the details here before we leave." He turned to Daniel. "Is that okay by you?"

"That is fine," Daniel said. "We will have your two crews and everything set up as best we can for you."

"My group are donating their services," Harry said. "Nobody wants to be paid. I will pay for my own film. But it's important that we all use the same film, you understand."

"We will fix all that," Daniel said. "We will have everything ready."

"Not quite everything," Hill Gallagher said from the back of the room, and moved forward again.

He had drifted back into the crowd of kids after the vote, and was standing almost against the wall into the "sleeping" quarters of the Committee, where I had seen him humping Samantha on that greasy mat that one night. I myself, in spite of all Hill's violent emotions floating over the place, was half asleep on the bench in the steaming crowded little room.

"I refuse the assignment," Hill said, moving forward to the desk.

Daniel tapped his gavel. "You can't refuse," he said.

"But I do," Hill said.

Daniel tapped again. "All right," he said from behind the steel-rimmed spectacles, "but I must then provisionally suspend you from this Committee. This is too serious a matter to vote on now, and we must wait until we have everybody here. But as Chairman I provisionally suspend you from the Committee until such time as a vote of approval or disapproval can be taken by all the members."

"Now, wait a minute," Harry said. "I didn't mean—"

"M. Gallagher," Daniel said crisply. "I do not know what kind of family matter is involved here between you and your son. But that is a personal matter, and has nothing at all to do with this Committee. We are concerned only about making the Revolution and we all took an oath of discipline when we became members of the Committee. Therefore, I have to rule that Hill is suspended, provisionally, until we can take a full vote on the matter." He banged his gavel.

"You won't have to take a vote!" Hill said. "I tender my resignation from this Committee as of right now!" And he was out the door, slamming it behind him. Harry, after fumbling with the door, was right after him.

I was groggy, and exhausted, and very nearly asleep. So I was slower. They were standing arguing about ten yards down the dingy, ill-lit corridor as I came through the door.

"You're an ass, Hill," Harry was saying as I came up.

"I may be an ass, but I am an idealistic ass," Hill said. "And these ideals are no longer quite up to my standards."

"When I selected you," Harry said patiently, "I only wanted to—"

"You've taken Samantha," Hill said. He glared at his father, his fists clenched against his thighs. "And now you've taken the film. And the Cinema Committee. And in the end, you'll take the Revolution itself, all of you. And turn it back into the same shit that we've always had."

"Look, Hill," Harry said. "Samantha would never have stayed with you. She'll never stay with me, either. Samantha's got no more morals than a snake, Hill. That's just the way she is. The way the world is. She'll never love anybody."

"She could have had," Hill said. "Don't touch me!" he said. "If you lay one finger on me I swear I'll swing on you."

"Come on, fellows," I said. I did not know what else to say.

"I won't touch you, boy," Harry said.

"Then go and fuck yourself," Hill said. "And the film. And the Committee. And the God damned Revolution. I'm through. And you better not try to stop me." He turned and stalked off down the dim, interminable corridor.

Harry stood looking after him a moment. Then slowly and elaborately he got out a cigarette and clamped it in the corner of his mouth. Then he put his hands in the flaring pockets of his starched trenchcoat with its collar up around his ears.

"Okay," he said to me. "Shall we go back in?"

At the door he stopped and said, "I think I can shoot this thing for them in three days, four at the most."

18

PARIS WAS SULLEN NOW. In the intermittent drizzle and frequent flurries of real rain that swept across the town all the flags on the ministry buildings hung wet and limp against their poles. The black flags and red flags of the student Revolutionaries over the Sorbonne and Odéon hung the same way.

The feeling in the air now was one of sullen patience, instead of enthusiasm. When is it going to stop? the faces seemed to say. You had the feeling that anything now, any act, might happen that would set off the final explosion of civil war.

Probably the increasing garbage in the streets, the crates, the cartons, the rotting food, contributed a lot to the feeling. The Army had sent out troops in trucks to try and do something about the garbage. At first the striking garbage workers had tried to fight with them and stop them. Now the soldiers went under armed guard. But they could only make a dent in the accumulating trash, the daily residue of the living of millions of lives.

There was no gasoline to be had anywhere now, and you realized how much the city truly depended upon a living flow of a continual supply of gas. The city really lived by its automobiles.

Only at the Sorbonne and the Odéon was there any enthusiasm. But both these places were becoming increasingly unkempt and grubby under the pressures and dirt of just simple daily living. This helped muffle the enthusiasm for us outsiders and even, I think, for the students.

The odd fight between Harry and Hill was on the night of Tuesday the 28th.

The next day, Wednesday May the 29th, was the day General de Gaulle disappeared from the Élysée Palace for seven hours. News of this was all over by the time our group of Americans met at the Gallaghers' that evening.

The word was le Général had abruptly canceled a Cabinet meeting called for ten A.M. that morning. Ministers arriving for the meeting were told there would not be any. Ninety minutes later le Général and his wife left by car for his retreat at Colombey-les-Deux-Églises. Normally that would be a three-hour drive. But le Général did not arrive at Colombey until six-fifteen P.M., and he arrived by helicopter.

Nobody knew where he had been in the intervening lost time, and he and the Government were not telling anybody anything. It was announced he would return the next day to preside over a Cabinet meeting at three P.M. to reveal his plans.

It was a very peculiar and erratic way for the old general, usually so precise and punctilious, to react. A great many people felt it was one of those secret signals of his that he was so fond of using, a signal that meant he was preparing to step down and quit without even waiting for his precious Referendum, to allow a new Government to be formed without him. And if that happened nobody knew what would come next.

The other development Wednesday was that during the day the Communist CGT unions, backed by the student unions, had for the first time publicly called for le Général to quit and lay on elections for a new Government. That seemed a pretty powerful thrust at the moment.

We discussed all of this excitedly at the Gallaghers' and watched the limp tepid Government–TV newscast. But nobody really knew anything at all. Everything seemed up in the air and I was beginning to think it was about time to get Louisa and McKenna, at least, out of the country to Brussels. I had the gasoline for it, all hidden away. I wouldn't stay out myself, of course. I would come back.

Besides, what with all this Samantha Everton business, it might be better to have Louisa away until it finished. I was positive one of her Portuguese maids or some *commerçant* on the street would make a remark to her about the Negro girl staying in the little hotel which was also now frequented by her husband.

About the only good thing I had to say for anything was that on the Wednesday the drizzle tapered off and stopped for a while and there was some sun.

I wanted to talk to Harry about my idea of driving Louisa and McKenna out to Brussels. It was getting that bad. But Harry was not at his place that evening. He was out filming the CGT march with his student actors. But Samantha was there. So was Weintraub. So was Ferenc Hofmann-Beck.

Feeling I had to trust somebody, I got Ferenc off alone and asked him if he knew anything about what was going on. I indicated with my head the supine Samantha stretched out on the carpeted floor reading one of McKenna's comic books.

Ferenc screwed his monocle in his eye and lighted one of his long black Russian cigarettes whose long cardboard tip he pinched carefully two different ways before lighting it, and grinned at me.

He put on his Hungarian accent. "I haf alvys said that one must expect some henky-penky everywhere." He dropped back into American. "Especially with that"—he sniffed—"that little girl there." Then his eyebrows went up, though he did not lose the monocle. "Not Harry?"

I nodded. "Yes. Harry is having an apparently serious affair with that little girl there."

"Is he now? Well, one must usually expect some sexual peccadilloes in any group relationship." He grinned. But he looked deeply hurt by what I had told him just the same. "Poor Louisa," he said after a moment. "But I don't really know them all that well, you know," he added. "I don't think I can offer any advice."

"But did you suspect?"

"Well, ah," he began. "To tell you the truth, I did have some small suspicion. But I am cynical. I have a dirty mind. I was hoping I was wrong. But I still can't offer you any advice, if that's what you're looking for."

"Well, keep shut about it anyway, will you?" I said.

"But of course," Ferenc said suavely.

"I mean seriously," I said.

He merely nodded. "I do feel sorry about it, though. Especially Louisa. It's always been she I liked the most.

"Poor, dear, darling Louisa."

I guess that was the first time the phrase ever stuck in my head. But it burned itself in. Poor, dear, darling Louisa.

"She is such a fine lady really," Ferenc said sadly.

"Yes, she is."

For a moment I debated with myself whether I could tell him the reason, or what I had decided was the real reason, for it and decided that I could. I was sure his discretion was impeccable.

"Harry apparently has this thing," I said. "He apparently likes to make it with two girls at the same time. And your young friend apparently digs the same action. I don't believe there's any love involved."

"Ah, my little colored friend," Ferenc said faintly in a thoughtful tone. He had not ever really forgiven her for their first meeting, I think. "Ah, well. I have a bit of a penchant for the same sort of thing, you know," he added. "And especially if one of them is a lady of color."

"You mean you too?" I said. "Tell me, what is it?"

"It's hard to explain," Ferenc said in a lofty way. "I don't know. I've never tried to analyze it. I don't like analyzing things. I'm not a writer. I'm a publisher. But I can sympathize."

"What are we going to do?" I said.

"I think the best thing is not to do anything at all. Let things take their natural course," he said. "And keep the fingers of the right hand perpetually crossed," he added.

"Maybe I shouldn't have brought the thing up at all."

"No. It's all right. Like I said, I suspected. You can trust my discretion." He took out his monocle and wiped it vigorously with his pocket handkerchief, an obviously emotional gesture. "It's just that I'm sad over it."

"You can say that again," I said.

Ferenc didn't answer. Then he said, "I simply love your American phraseology."

"Balls," I said. "Listen, I've been thinking that I might suggest to Harry that I drive Louisa and McKenna out to Brussels. I've got the gas. I don't like at all the way things are developing here in Paris. I have the feeling it might turn into a real blood bath any minute. Did you ever read *The Fall of Paris* by Alistair Horne? Unfortunately, I've been reading it lately. The bloody Parisians killed 25,000 of their own citizens in one week in Paris that time."

"I've read the book," Ferenc said.

"They could fly over to London from Brussels. They've got lots of friends there. Could stay a few weeks until we see what's finally going to happen."

"When do we leave?" Ferenc had broken into a big grin and was rubbing his hands together.

"What?"

"Marvelous. Marvelous. Great. I said, when do we leave?"

"You want to go too?"

"But of course!"

"To stay."

"No, no. No, not to stay. I will ride shotgun for you, as they say in the Westerns. And return. I wouldn't miss the dénouement for the world."

"Well, I'll have to talk to Harry about it first, you know," I said. "It's only an idea. But there's no school now."

"You just let me know," Ferenc said. "You just let me know."

"And with this Samantha business. I think it might be the best thing."

Ferenc made a pained face. "I think I'll take my drink, and wander down the room," he said gently. He put a large hamlike hand on my shoulder. "But you just let me know." He turned away.

"Hanky-panky, hanky-panky," I heard him mutter under his breath as he moved away. "Always the hanky-panky."

I was left alone at the bar with no more help than I had started out with. But I felt somehow relieved. And I trusted Ferenc completely. Suddenly, for no apparent reason, I liked him very much.

I took my own drink and went down the room from the bar. I noted that Ferenc had again avoided Samantha, after a polite hello, as he always did. No, I could trust the guy, all right. He would do what he could. Though, as he said, the only thing was to let things take their natural course. Actually, Sam had left Louisa and gone over and was talking to Weintraub. After the lousy Government–TV coverage of the situation we were all, or almost all, talking excitedly about the meaning of what de Gaulle had done.

I sat down beside Louisa on the big couch. She immediately turned to me with that curiously fierce and at the same time oddly vague-eyed smile of hers.

"I would like to do something for that little girl, Jack," she said, incredibly. "She needs some help."

Yes, she needed help like a rattlesnake needed help, I thought.

"Yes, I guess she does," I said. "I guess she's a nice girl. But I must confess I've never understood her."

"There's nothing to understand," Louisa said. "She's never had a mother, that's all. And she needs one."

"And you think you could fill the bill?" I said. Dear God, I thought.

"Not permanently. But for the time she is here, the little time she is here, maybe I might," Louisa said.

I had absolutely no answer to that at all. I simply could not think of anything to say to her. "So Harry is out shooting tonight, is he?" I asked.

"Yes. He was out absolutely all night last night. And he said he's likely to be out all night again tonight," she said.

I happened to know he had left the Odéon at two o'clock the night before, because I was with him. It was not hard to guess where he might have spent the rest of the night.

"I didn't know Harry ever harbored secret ambitions to be a film director," I said, hoping it sounded easy enough.

"I don't think he ever did. He's doing this for them, for the students. And for the Revolution." She paused and looked thoughtful. "But perhaps he may have such ambitions now, after this. After all this mess is over. And I for one would like to see him do it." She turned that smile on me. "He's really such a big man, Harry. But you know that."

"Yes," I said. "I know." I was getting decidedly uncomfortable. "What do you think is going to happen with de Gaulle?"

"I think he's going to quit," Louisa said positively. "Step down. I don't see how he can do anything else, now. And I'll be glad. His isolationist policies of the last five years show how old and blind he's gotten. He's like an ostrich. His pride has made him blind to what's been happening in the world."

"The old guy's tough," I said. "He may be able to pull it out."

Personally, I felt de Gaulle's chances were a whole lot better than that. I didn't believe le Général would ever give up and step down, as long as he got his proper Referendum vote. But I did not want to argue with Louisa, who could become quite distraught on the subject of de Gaulle.

"I don't think so," she said stubbornly. "Not this time."

"But who would replace him? Mitterrand? He's offered himself up as candidate for a united Left."

"Not enough power," she said immediately. "He could never make it."

"Mendès-France?"

"*Non plus,*" she said immediately. "He's got even less of a chance than Mitterrand."

"Well, that's what I'm saying! Then who? There just isn't anybody," I said.

"Probably it would be Pompidou," Louisa said.

"But he's simply de Gaulle's creature," I said. "Why throw out de Gaulle and then vote in Pompidou?"

"He is his creature now, I grant. But I have the feeling he is more flexible. If he were elected, I think he would slowly—and delicately—make the changes necessary toward a more flexible policy in keeping with the world of today. With the Technological Revolution." She turned those vague dreamer's eyes and ferocious smile on me. "I like this new young man Jean Lecanuet, the quote Centralist unquote. He seems to want to bring things along in keeping with Servan-Schreiber's ideas, in *The American Challenge*. That's the way things *have* to go if France is ever going to modernize itself."

"But he hasn't got a ghost of a chance, Louisa," I protested. "You know that."

"No," she said, staring at me. "No. Maybe not. Well, we'll just have to wait and see."

Just then Fred Singer, the TV commentator fellow, came over and sat down with us, and I excused myself and went away. I was glad. It was about all I could do not to run.

Later, when everybody left, I left too and did not stay to dinner. Ferenc was going over to the lady painter's place to eat, and apparently was going to spend the night there, instead of on "his" couch at the Gallaghers, and I could not bear the thought of having dinner with Louisa alone.

I noted that Weintraub left alone. Sam hung back. She continued to lie on the floor, reading alone as we all left.

Myself, I left alone too. I did not really feel like talking to anyone. I wandered up the car-less street by myself to my own place, thinking I would drift over into the *Quartier* and have my dinner by myself in some unknown, unsung little bistro. It would be an enormous relief.

I had not been in my apartment five minutes, not long enough to have gotten down my first Scotch-soda, when the phone rang. I somehow had a hunch who it was.

"Âllo, Chéri!" Martine's voice came over the apparatus. *"Tu es là tout seul ce soir? J'ai envie de te voir si c'est possible. Je peux venir préparer le dîner si tu veux. J'ai des nouvelles."*

"Good?" I said. "Or bad?"

"Good. Ver-ry, ver-ry good," she said. "But I do not wish to speak of it *sur* the phone. I will arrive *chez* you in one half the hour. Hokay?"

"Okay," I said and grinned. I hung up and went to stare out the windows at the river and the empty quais. What good news could she possibly have? What good news would change anything now? What possibly?

When she arrived she was carrying two netted-cord panniers containing the makings of an excellent dinner. While she stripped down to her bra, panties and shoes to begin the cooking, she talked to me from the bedroom.

"It is all over. You do not need to worry any more. It will begin to start stopping on the Friday coming. Day after tomorrow. Le Général is not quitting. He will announce tomorrow. Cabinet meeting three o'clock. Television and radio address by him at four-thirty." She came out of the little bedroom into the short hallway, looking magnificent.

"But more important, much more important: There will be gasoline. Much, much gasoline. For the Pentecost weekend. The Government made a deal with the gasoline companies, and the suppliers. The truckers. They will begin trucking the gasoline into Paris tomorrow night. They will use soldier drivers, too, wherever necessary. Unlimited gasoline for the Pentecost weekend. Everybody will vacation it.

"A great ploy, no? It will change the mood of everything. And it is predicted great weather for all of Pentecost. But it is a great secret. You must not tell one people."

I must say, she really did have a magnificent body. She turned into the kitchen and went on in a louder voice.

"So it is finished. After Pentecost the unions will agree. They will have to. And all because of the gasoline. They will be working on it all the night tonight. But the deal is already made. My friend and protector will be working furiously at his ministry all the night." That was the way she always described her banker-lover. She smiled sweetly at me from the kitchen.

"It is good news, no? So I can stay all night."

I went to stand in the little hallway. I never liked to bother her too much in the kitchen when she was cooking.

"And how do *you* know all this, Martine?"

"From my friend and protector. Who else? It has been many phone calls between Colombey. Everything is being prepared."

"Where did le Général go today, when he disappeared for seven hours?" I asked.

"To talk to the Army. To his generals. He visited the Generals Massu and Hublot at the home of his son-in-law General Boisseau in Mulhouse."

"In Alsace," I said.

"Oui. Massu commands the two Divisions in Germany. Hublot commands the three Divisions in France itself. They have promised to back any legally constituted Government, which of course his Government still is. And two regiments in Germany have been put on alert for return to France if it is necessary.

"Le Général will have to pay for this. In a short while he will declare an amnesty and release the Général Salan and other officers who are still in prison from the Générals' Revolt in Algeria. But it is a small price to pay. They are not longer dangerous.

"It is good news, no?"

"It is," I said. "It is also good to have a girlfriend who has the ear of the mighty."

"Ah, oui! It is what you Americans say an extra," Martine smiled. She was already in the midst of cooking. "But you must remember it is a secret, hah? The deliveries of gasoline will not begin until in the night tomorrow night. They will continue all through Friday, so that the citizens will have sufficient gasoline for the weekend of the Pentecost. Of course the vacation will include the Whitsuntide Monday of the June 3. Nobody will come back till Monday night or Tuesday morning."

She grinned. "It is anticipated it will break the back of everything. It will prove the Government is still the Government and is in control. But you must say nothing. Not even to your friends the Gallaghers. Not until Friday."

"Don't worry," I said. "I won't. But it is nice to know. I had begun wondering if I shouldn't drive Madame Gallagher and the baby out to Brussels."

"Two days ago I might have said yes. But is no longer necessary," Martine said crisply.

She had bought us what in French is called *petits poussins,* what we would call spring chickens, but smaller than we use in the States, young birds not even half grown. She baked them in the oven with a black sauce made out of the giblets, then she pan-cooked them again in a skillet with the sauce, and they were delicious. I ate two entire birds myself. And Martine ate two whole birds also. I enjoy women who like their own cooking. I also like women who have a real and honest healthy appetite.

As we sat down to table, after she had put on her loose-flowing robe split to the waist, I was thinking that I did not now need to talk to Harry about driving Louisa and McKenna out. In one way I was relieved. But in another way I was sorry it was not going to be forced on us, what with all the Samantha business. Also, there had been no word from young Hill as far as I knew.

"So you're going to be able to stay all night?" I smiled across the table.

"All the night, Chéri," she smiled. "The whole night."

19

I WENT AROUND all the next day and night with my private information locked up inside me like a ticking timebomb. Every time I opened my mouth I shut it again and thought twice. There were so many people to whom I could tell what I knew and relieve their anxieties.

But I kept my word.

Everything turned out exactly as Martine had told me that it would.

At three o'clock there was the Cabinet meeting, apparently. At four-thirty le Général went on radio and TV, pre-taped, with a remarkably strong address saying he would not resign but that he was dissolving the Assemblée Nationale and calling for new elections which would take place, as prescribed by law, in a certain number of weeks.

The theme of the address was "Participation"—of the citizenry in Government, and of the workers in industrial management; and the keynote was the "terrible threat" of a Communist conspiracy that wanted to destroy *la belle France*. Particularly when compared with his feeble speech of a week before it was a powerful address.

Nobody believed that stuff about the Communists, whom he did not actually name, but it was a convenient and dramatic handle with which to present his attitude to the French bourgeoisie, who had always feared the Communists, and were still the most powerful voting group in France.

An odd fact about this address was that on TV there was no visual image, only a blank screen with le Général's voice recorded over. I was told later by somebody that this was because the TV employees were on strike against the Government's policy of censorship of the Government-owned TV, but I do not know if this was true.

That night, of course, I could talk. But who in life ever wants to hear anybody say, after the fact, that he had known before but hadn't told? Anyway, that night the gasoline ploy was still a secret, since deliveries would not begin until some time around eleven-thirty or midnight. So I really could not tell my whole story anyway. In the end I kept shut.

That afternoon, the afternoon of the Thursday of May the 30th, there was a huge, a massive demonstration on the Place de la Concorde and the Champs-Élysées in favor of the Gaullists. It went on before, during, and after le Général's big speech, and it had people like Malraux, Debré, Roger Frey, Maurice Schumann, and François Mauriac leading it. The Government did everything it could to make it a success. They even provided Army trucks to haul people in from outside Paris for it. Not only that, for the first time since the last serious street fighting they allowed the independent stations Radio Luxembourg and Europe Number One to come back on the air to report it. The radio reporters were rather droll when they thanked the French Government for allowing them to recommence broadcasting and hoped that they would do the same for the student demonstrations in future.

In spite of all that it was a pretty impressive demonstration. The Champs-Élysées was one huge living sea of people for de Gaulle, from the Concorde to the Arc de Triomphe. An interesting note about it was that there were lots of American flags in the street, along with the Tricolor. In spite of le Général. Americans in the office buildings along the Champs waved their own little American flags from their windows and the French people in the streets cheered and waved their bigger flags in response. Certain sources, usually Government sources, claimed it was a bigger crowd than the student-worker march across town on May the 13th. Certainly it was a better-dressed crowd and a louder one. And surely it was a richer one. There was a much higher percentage of older people in it.

At least I heard that, on the radio. I did not go to it myself, any more than I went to any of the big student-worker demonstrations.

There weren't many of us at the Gallaghers' that night at seven. Harry was out filming the Gaullist march for the student film. The UPI boy and the TV commentator Fred Singer were both out reporting it. The American businessman with the string of Left Bank girls was either out demonstrating or stuck in his Champs-Élysées office. But Samantha Everton was there. And Weintraub. And old Ferenc. The lady painter was there, too. She was obviously rather infatuated with Ferenc now. I figured they had done the dirty deed. I hoped so.

When we all left this time, Samantha hung back again. She did not make it obvious, but I noticed it this time. Outside, Weintraub asked me to have dinner with him someplace in the *Quartier*.

I declined but said, "Haven't you got anything better to do than eat with me?"

He made a wry smile. "Sam told me to fuck off. She's busy, she said. And she intends to remain busy."

"But isn't Harry out shooting?"

"Yes," Weintraub said. "Yes, he is."

We walked along.

I looked at my watch. It was nine P.M. My ego got the better of me. After all, what harm could Weintraub do if he knew?

"Listen," I said. "Did you know that by morning this city will have sufficient gasoline for the entire Pentecost weekend?"

"What?" he said. "I don't believe it!"

"Or at least a lot of it," I said, wanting to be absolutely honest. "And by Friday night there'll be all the gas anybody could want."

"But that will be the end of everything!" Dave said in an odd panicked voice.

"Yes," I said. "Exactly."

"How do you know?"

"I can't tell," I said. "Can't tell who, I mean. But it's what I consider a reliable source."

"But that's the end of the Revolution and everything," he said.

"Yes," I said. "Probably."

"How the hell did they do that?"

"I'm not at liberty to say."

"But shouldn't we tell the kids at the Cinema Committee?"

"I'm not at liberty to," I said. "I only told you in a moment of ego weakness. Anyway, there's not a damn thing they can do about it."

"Yeah!" he said, drawing it out like a sigh. "So— He's won."

"I always said he would," I said. "He's an old fox."

"Whoever thought that one up for him deserves a medal," Weintraub said.

"And he'll probably get one," I added on.

"Do you think the newspaper stories about him going to see Massu and Hublot in Mulhouse are true?" Weintraub asked.

"That's what I hear," I said.

"Then it's all over," Weintraub said.

"Pretty nearly, I would imagine," I said.

"Now, how the hell did you find all that out?" he said, in a kind of wondering tone.

"Not at liberty to tell," I said.

I left him on the quai at my corner.

But I didn't much like myself. Damned ego. But what he had said about Samantha had set me to thinking. Was Samantha giving up her little friend and Weintraub? For *Harry?* Or was Louisa getting through to her and making a straight girl out of her or something? Louisa certainly had been mothering her. And I remembered what she had told me. This made the second—or was it the third?—night that Sam had stayed behind when the rest of us had left. And if so, my God what would that do to Harry?

I thought about this while I had my first, and then my second, Scotch-soda looking out my windows at the empty Left Bank quais. I didn't find any answer. I wasn't even looking for one.

Anyway, it looked like de Gaulle had won. And that Louisa was wrong.

Poor, dear, darling Louisa.

Harry showed up at the Odéon that night.

He was with his "principals" and his two student crews, and his own volunteer cameraman, a professional who was on strike like the rest of them and who was scouting the Odéon hoping to shoot for Harry some short scenes there in the Cinema Committee offices. He was a likeable guy, politically as uneducated as Harry or Hill, or me, or any of the rest of us.

De Gaulle was the one who was politically educated.

There was an awful cloud of gloom over the kids' offices. And I assumed the same was true of the Sorbonne. They had come up against a professional of long experience and been bested. And I think by then, that Thursday night, May 30th, they all sensed it.

When I could, I got Harry off by himself. "What do you make of it, Harry?"

He raised his eyebrows and pursed his lips. "I think he's got it made. If he doesn't use any more violence, if he gives the idea of being patient, I think they'll follow him."

"Do the kids know it?"

"I think so," Harry said. "Christ, can't you smell the misery around here?"

"I thought I could."

"He's really such an old fox," Harry said.

"That he is. That he is. He told them that, as a matter of fact. In effect. He said don't mess around with the pros until you're dry behind the ears and know your business."

"Are you pro-de Gaulle?" Harry said.

"I'm not pro-anything," I said. "I'm an observer. I write a Review. You know about the gas," I said.

"What? No."

I looked at my watch. "Right this minute trailer trucks are unloading gas in every filling station in Paris. By tomorrow noon there will be more than enough gas for the Pentecost weekend. By tomorrow night there will be unlimited gasoline."

Harry squinched up his narrow eyes, and suddenly looked excited. "By damn! Then it really is over." He was silent a moment. "By God, I've got to shoot that!"

"How will that affect your film?"

He stared at me. "It won't affect it at all. We'll have to hurry up a little, that's all. When I said it's all over, I did not anticipate that there wouldn't be a few more riots. We'll just have to catch them all, that's all.

"Oh, by the way. Saturday I'm taking what film these kids have got out to the Boulogne studios to get it developed. The guys on strike there all belong to my union, or a subsidiary. I'm arranging for the striking technicians to develop it for me. Would you like to go along?"

"Hell, yes. Sure. Why not?"

"I'm arranging the actual appointment tomorrow. I'll call you and let you know the actual hour. It will probably be early."

"That's okay," I said. "I always sleep late."

He grinned.

It was just then that Weintraub came in and came over to us.

"Hello, Dave," Harry grinned, in a gimlet-faced way. "What are you doing here?"

"Whadda you mean? I was the first one in this," Weintraub said.

"That is true," Harry said. "On the other hand, you better make your hay now, Dave. I told you, I'll likely be through shooting in a day."

This was a direct lie, because he had just told me he expected he would have to be shooting whatever riots were remaining. I said nothing.

Weintraub took a little while to answer. And before he did he gave me a long cautionary but unreadable look which I did not understand. "Well," he said finally, and grinned, "I'm just tired, if you want to know. I can't take it any more like I used to. I'm plumb wore out."

Harry threw back his head to laugh. "I can appreciate that. I get the shaky knees myself, now."

Weintraub's grin was courageous, probably one of the most courageous I'd ever seen. "We aint none of us getting no younger," he said.

I left soon after that. There weren't many cars at the filling stations I passed on the way home, but there was at least one trailer truck at each of them pumping away, and sometimes there was an extra one waiting.

20

ONE OF THE THINGS General de Gaulle announced to the nation in his extraordinarily tough address on Thursday was that "civic action" must be immediately and everywhere organized. He added that to achieve this the local *préfets* would, in fact must, return "to the functions of commissars of the Republic".

I do not know the derivation of that term, but this was the actual term le Général had used when he returned to France during the end of World War II, when all of France including the Resistance organizations was in the throes of local lynch law and civil strife. By backing the local, duly elected law enforcement agencies he had been able to head off civil war and at the same time head off a Communist takeover, which at that time was a serious threat.

Now he was evoking the same process. It was this that caused the Leftist leader Mitterrand to call his speech a "call to civil war".

Well, M. Mitterrand could not have been more wrong.

On Friday morning, while the massive gasoline deliveries were still going on, almost the whole of Paris headed happily for the country for the long weekend. It was a marvelous bright sunny day, as if even the weather were conspiring to aid de Gaulle. Hordes of people filled the highways and Autoroutes in their newly reactivated cars. It was an exodus almost as great as the great annual August vacation rush. Since practically nobody was working that day anyway they did not even have to wait till the end of the working day and by mid-afternoon Paris appeared as empty as it did in August. About the only people left were the students occupying the Latin Quarter, and the cadres of workers occupying their plants—and the politicians holding feverish strategy sessions about whom to run for the various Assembly seats in the elections scheduled for June 23rd.

It seemed all the big unions, including the Communists, wanted no direct political confrontation with the General. Without exception they issued statements withdrawing the political demands of two days before and seemed pleased to settle for purely economic ones. It seemed that, like children, they were all glad to have the heavy paternal hand of le Général there still in power.

It appeared it was all over but the shouting, as my old grandfather would have said.

A "Back To Work" movement was said to have started, although nobody seemed to know quite by whom. Probably it was a deliberate Government leak. That was what all we cynics thought.

M. Pompidou announced the line-up of a new Cabinet, most of whose members had merely changed places as in musical chairs. But a few of the old ones were dropped, and without exception they were replaced by men who were a clear conciliation gesture to the Left, to get more Leftist votes for the Gaullists. In general, old fox de Gaulle appeared to have won again.

There was a fire in the attic of the occupied Sorbonne on Friday, which burned away a fair portion of the roof on the rue des Écoles side before it was brought under control by firemen. This incident seemed to increase the feeling among the people that the students had about had it. I heard one man in the street saying, "How do they think they can run a Government when they can't even wipe their own asses?"

This seemed to be pretty much the general opinion.

All in all, it was a quiet weekend, the first in a while. There was some strike-breaking by the police, but usually in the Government post offices, and the sit-in strikers all left peacefully. There was a general change in ambiance everywhere.

There was still no news of Hill Gallagher.

While all this change and rearrangement went on in the May Revolution noisily, it seemed a lull had developed in the Gallagher family's story. Harry was out shooting all night almost every night and slept in the day. Sam was spending the evenings quietly with Louisa. Hill was gone. It was not likely Harry would be seen too much at the little hotel in the rue St.-Louis-en-l'Île. It gave me a feeling of hope that Samantha might leave, or be got out of, Paris in time. Maybe no Hiroshima explosion was necessary. No more, anyway, than had already happened between Harry and Hill.

It was on the strength of this hope, plus the hunch that I might catch her in if I went before one P.M., that I bestirred myself Friday morning and went down to the little hotel on the rue St.-Louis-en-l'Île to see her. I wanted to talk to her.

Well, I had known that hotel man to say hello to a good ten years. So had Harry Gallagher. I had had friends from America stay in his place. So had Harry. It was cheap, and clean, and quite presentable, if it was a little old-fashioned. But that only gave it charm. In other words, I was certainly not any stranger to the man—who, incidentally, did not own the place. It was owned by his great-aunt, whom I had never seen (she didn't live on the Island) and who allowed him to live there and run it for her. She gave him his board and keep, and some small salary I guess. The gossip along the street was that if he did not mess up and make her mad he stood a good chance to inherit the whole thing since there was no other living relative—always provided of course that the old lady did not outlive him. She apparently seemed intent upon doing so. And the poor man drank much too much, apparently out of frustration.

Well, when I looked him in the eye and asked for Samantha Everton, he gave me such a peculiar look as I have seldom had since my college prankster days.

"*Ah, oui! Ah, oui, M'sieu 'Artley,*" he said. "*Bonjour, M'sieu 'Artley! La petite, uh, Américaine! Allez! Montez! Allez monter.*"

Go right on up, he was saying.

"She is a friend of all of ours," I said in French.

"I understand!" he said. "I understand! M'sieu Gallagher was just here, last night. And his son the night before."

Was there a faint gleam deep in his eye? Or did I only think I saw it, because of some guilt in me? I hasten to add, some guilt in me for Harry.

"*C'est la chambre cinquante-trois,*" he said. "*Au cinquième étage.*"

The fifth floor was the top one, and up there under the eaves there were only three doors. Fifty-three was the third one, on the left. When I got to the landing I stopped to get my breath before I knocked. When I did knock, a voice which I recognized as Sam's said, immediately, "Come on in."

So I opened the door.

She was lying on the one bed on her back absolutely stark, bare-ass naked with her hands along her flanks palms down and her feet together like a springboard diver. Her head was turned toward me at the door. She grinned with flashing white teeth in her dark face in the half gloom of the little room.

"Why, hello there, Mr. Hartley," she said. She didn't move a muscle. She certainly didn't try to cover herself. I noted that the bed was a three-quarter one, and that it was already made, including the coverlet.

I was so taken aback that whatever I had meant to say to her completely fled my mind, the way an avalanche flees beneath your feet. I remember that I closed the door rather quickly.

I fumbled with my umbrella foolishly, looking for someplace to put it, in order to gain some time.

"I'm sorry I don't have an umbrella stand," Sam said, without moving. "Put it anywhere. Then sit down. Sit down, sit down. What brings you here, Mr. Hartley?"

I did not sit down, but seconds later I was sorry I hadn't. It would have been much more cool. So I tried to brazen it out standing, and gave her a long and detailed cool inspection.

She had medium large nipples, with definitive but not very protruding paps, and even lying down her breasts were so young and firm at 19 that they did not appear to slide down toward her armpits at all. Her navel was a shadowed indentation in the flat concavity of her belly that actually dropped below the level of her hipbones, the way she was lying. She took a couple of deep breaths that raised her chest and dropped it without even moving the concavity of her belly.

Ah, youth! Youth. One never knows how much it's worth until one's lost it; not, at least, in my set. But the most extraordinary thing was her crotch, her bush. It had an amazingly thick, lush growth so black it seemed almost blue, as the black night sky is blue. A hairy triangle of such thickness and depth that you felt you might never be able to find your way through that jungle. But the amazing thing was that it wasn't curly. It was, instead, sort of spiky. You felt it might put out your eyes, if you were not careful. I had never seen a female whose crotch hair, whose bush, was not curly.

"Who was it you were expecting?" I said coolly.

"I wasn't expecting anybody," she said, in what I thought a rather languorous way. "Harry's out working. Or sleeping at home."

"Hill, then?" I said.

"I haven't seen Hill since before the trip to Cannes," she smiled.

"He was here the night before last."

"Ah, yes. But I did not see him. Harry was here, too. Hill did not get in. He beat on the door a while and then left."

"Oh, God!" I said. I couldn't help it. Even though I knew it was losing my cool.

"Would you like to fuck me, Mr. Hartley?" she said. There was a distinct languor in her voice now, and she suddenly turned her hands over, palms up.

"No, thank you," I said. "I simply came to talk."

"Maybe you would like to go down on me, then."

"No."

"Would you like me to masturbate you?"

"Really, no. But thank you," I said.

"You're really pretty much of a bust, Mr. Hartley," she smiled, even more languorously.

"I don't think you understand that I have other things on my mind." I felt I was maintaining my cool, now.

She only stared at me. "Maybe you would like to watch me masturbate?"

"I, uh." I was confused, and I stumbled. "Really, no." It would not be honest to say that I was not somewhat excited by her.

"Different people have different bags," she said, still in that languorous way. Then suddenly her voice changed, and sharpened. It became a command voice. "Sit down! Sit down in that chair there! Right now! Sit down! Mama is going to punish you! Sit down, I said!"

For a moment I was almost carried away. I sat down.

"Mama's going to punish you," Samantha Everton said. Then her voice softened. "Mama is going to masturbate herself, and you must sit there and watch, as your punishment. And you're not allowed to do anything. You cannot touch yourself. You can only watch."

She had opened her legs, languorously, and was manipulating herself with her first two fingers. Her head was turned to the side, and her eyes were closed. She crooned to herself. I had never been with a Negro lady, a colored lady. Her inside flesh was not bright pink at all, it was dark brown. I was seriously afraid I was going to lose control of myself. Then, suddenly, or it seemed suddenly to me, though it may not have been so quickly as I thought at the time, she screamed.

It was not a loud scream, and it was very low in tone. It was certainly no soprano. It was more like a contralto scream, if one could say that. Then she snapped her legs back together in that pose of a springboard diver and looked over at me. She ran the fingertips of her two hands lightly over her nipples. "Now would you like to fuck me, baby boy?"

"I would love to," I said, trying to make it cool. But my voice was trembling, and she knew it as well as I. "I really would, and that's the God's truth. But I really did come to talk."

"You really are quite some cat," she said. "That one always knocks Harry dead. Okay, talk."

"Would you mind if I took off my trenchcoat?" I asked. "I really do feel quite warm."

"I wouldn't wonder," she said. "No, go ahead. Then talk. I'm perfectly comfortable, myself."

I have often thought that hypocrisy is really strictly the province of youth. I swear I am convinced it is all a question of sheer physical stamina. We older people simply do not have the energy to lead a life of true duplicity. It requires youth and its marvelous, unbelievable, boundless energy to do that. That is why we older ones get crotchety and go around telling people the truth. We are simply too tired, too worn out not to be honest.

But it is hard for youth, with its energy, to understand that. It takes time and the ageing process itself to get to know what that is like. It takes just plain years passing. And that is exactly what you cannot have when you are young, no matter how hard you holler.

I simply could not get one honest word out of that girl, no matter how hard I tried.

"Do you have any idea at all what you are doing to the Gallagher family?" I said.

"No," she said. That was already a lie. "And if I did, I wouldn't give a damn."

"I don't believe you," I said. "I believe you know, and what's more, I believe you give a damn. A very large damn. I think you know exactly what you are doing, and that you are doing it deliberately—for some personal reason which I do not fully understand."

She smiled, flashing white in sweet dark face. "If some guy wants to fuck me, is that my fault? If some guy likes to go to bed with me and my little French girlfriend, is that my fault?"

"It could be," I said. "And in your case, I think it is. You flirt. Who was it suggested that you go to bed with Harry and Louisa together? It was you. You put the idea in his head, about him and you and another girl."

"I disagree," she said simply. "The idea was already there."

"Perhaps. As a matter of fact, true. It was there. But it was buried. It was controlled. You deliberately stimulated it and brought it to the surface. Deliberately."

She smiled again. She really did have a lovely, black, spiky crotch. She said, "You can't make somebody feel something that they don't already have a hankering to feel."

"No. Maybe not. But you can help them to control it. That's what civilization is. Control. *Self*-control, finally. That's what the result of any really deep education is, finally. Education is not only getting knowledge, it's learning control. That is civilization."

"Fuck civilization," Sam said. "I don't give a shit for civilization."

"You wouldn't say that if you didn't have it all around you, protecting you," I said.

"Maybe I would. Yes, I *would*. I don't give a damn how long I live. Or how soon I die."

"Why?" It snapped, exploded out of me. But before she could even answer, I interrupted myself and went on. "Look. I've known this family a long time. I've followed their fortunes, as they say, for more than ten years. I'm practically Hill's Godfather. I *am* McKenna's Godfather. I used to take him fishing, for Christ's sake."

"Fishing!" Samantha jeered.

"Never mind. What I'm trying to say is that you've already, as far as I can see, successfully ruined that boy. And now you're about to do the same thing to his father. They're not even speaking to each other, because of you. God only knows where Hill is now."

"I didn't ruin him," Sam said in a clear voice. She had not moved her hands from along her flanks since she had had her little orgasm. "Life did. If he can't handle life when it comes around the corner and gibbers at him, that aint my responsibility."

"Where did you learn that word?" I said.

"Gibbers," she repeated, and smiled. "Oh, I've read a little, Mr. Hartley. My mama sent me to some pretty ritzy schools. I even read a couple copies of your Review. They aint much good. You did not answer me."

"What you say is true," I said. "In a way. In one way. But the whole process, the whole point of civilization is to help each other make life less cruel. Not *more* cruel."

"Horseshit, Mr. Hartley," Sam said. "You are full of it."

Actually, I felt I was myself. I felt she was absolutely right. I had somehow gotten way out of my depth with all this do-gooder talk. I hadn't meant to. But somehow she had led me right that way. "Probably you're right. In fact, I think you are right. Look, all I'm asking, all I came here to talk to you about, is to ask you to leave, get out of Paris now. You've got the money to get to Israel. From Harry. I can get you on a plane, if you can't do it yourself, which I'm sure you can. Just to leave. That's all. Before Louisa Gallagher finds out about you and Harry. Okay?"

"The answer is no, Mr. Hartley. N O, no."

"What if I killed you?" I said. I could hardly believe it was me talking. But I was furious. "I could, you know. Easily. Right now."

"So go ahead," she said, and smiled. "It wouldn't solve anything. And you know it. I told you, I don't give a shit how long I live, or how soon I die."

I moved my head. "I'm not the killing type, anyway," I said. I had to grin.

"I know," Samantha said. "And you are not the *solving* type, either. You just float."

"Well," I said. "Will you at least think about what I said?"

"I'll tell you something," Sam said, and smiled at me again. It is hard to describe the striking quality, the beauty if you will, of the flashing white of her teeth in the dark of her face in that gloom-covered room. "I'll tell you something, Mr. Hartley. All of you white motherfuckers are out after my little old black ass. Don't you think I know? You want to fuck it, fondle it, eat it, rub your noses in it. And then you'll go away, go home, and pretend you didn't do it, pretend you didn't even think it." She stopped, and the time seemed to run on—as if there should have been more for her to say.

"Do I appear like that to you?" I said, finally. "After what's already happened here?"

"Sure," she said. "You want it. You're just a coward, that's all. I had you misjudged. You're not a fag. You're just a coward."

I got up. My old trenchcoat was across the room. I got it, and my umbrella. "Well," I said. "I suppose I'll see you at the Gallaghers tonight."

"Probably," Sam said. Once again she turned her hands over, palms up, an offering. "Wouldn't you like to fuck me, Mr. Hartley? Or suck my cunt? Or let me jerk you off? Or masturbate me?"

I was at a loss. I did want to. Anything. Everything. "Maybe later," I said, trying to be cool. But she could tell. I was sure she could tell.

"See you later," I said.

As I went out, the hotel man saluted me with a wave of his hand to his forehead. Half a salute. I was sure he thought I had been up there having sex with *"la petite, uh, Américaine"*.

21

THE HARSH FIERCE SUMMERS and harsh fierce winters of New York and Ohio would make cloud-covered France a melancholy place for any American. They wrote about the rain all through World War I. At least two generations of Americans have used French weather as a large part of their literary capital. Especially Northern France. Every kilometer north and east that you get from Paris you find the French more and more like the Germans: melancholy, alcoholic, therefore intensely military, big eaters of pig sausages against the long, gloomy, dull and chilly winters, big eaters of fats, big eaters period. I remember coming out of a Berlin nightclub half-stoned one night at about one-thirty and finding it was daylight already. That would make a gloomy kook out of anybody. New York City is on just about the same latitude as Madrid, Spain.

As a matter of fact they didn't have central heating anywhere in Europe until we Americans introduced them to it. That's why the Scots make such great sweaters. And yet, after you've lived there long enough, you find those gray cloud-covered days no longer depress even that eternal and oppressive American optimism we have. The gray drizzly cloud-cover becomes a natural, and pleasurable, part of life.

But even so, anywhere above the Loire Valley a sunny day always comes as a bonus.

On Saturday it tried hard to be a bad day but couldn't make it. That was the Saturday of June the 1st. It was as if the old sorcerer mon Général had made up some witches' brew to make it go his way. Cloudy early in the morning, by nine the sun stood forth up there in all his glory, making his own personal contribution to the making of le Général's Pentecostal weekend. It did not rain.

On Saturday Harry took me with him out to the Boulogne studios to get the student film developed, as well as his own. He wanted to see some rushes of his stuff, and at the same time get some idea of what the student stuff was like.

He had told me it would be early. Well, it was. Friday night he told me to meet him outside his place at seven-thirty. When I got there at seven-thirty-one-and-a-half, he was pacing up and down the quai in front of his car, a cigarette dangling from his mouth. In that early morning light, which comes from the east and therefore makes shadows slanting to the west, a thing my eye is not at all used to (being used to afternoon shadows that slant the other way: to the east), I noticed Harry had a very cruel mouth. It was sort of like the mouth of an Arab pasha as the Victorians used to draw them: thick, sensual, curving with a sense of power not to be stopped. That might have pleased Harry, if I had told him (which I didn't). But it didn't please me. Maybe the son of a bitch *ought* to go to Israel or someplace.

We did not talk much on the way out. It was a long drive, through the Bois and further. Harry smoked, squinting as he drove. There was a big student march set up for Saturday, but we would not be able to get to it. But Harry had his two student crews shooting it just the same. He was worried about their work, he said.

"I'm really concerned about the way they shoot," he said. "They're terribly sloppy. They seem to feel that if they just get a picture of it, any old damn kind, it will be enough. That's why I want to get a look at rushes of the stuff they've done up to now."

At the studios in Boulogne it was weird. I had been out there before with Harry when he was working on some production or other. It had always been teeming with people and excitement and hollering. Now it was nearly empty. Only a skeleton force occupied the place. We were met at the gate and required to identify ourselves beyond doubt. Then we wandered through empty halls and corridors and sound stages where high ceilings flung back to us our own footsteps with a frightening hollowness. In the labs three guys from Harry's union who were going to do the work met us; and Harry gave them the cans of film.

"Now there's nothing to do but wait it out," he said to me. "It will take them till two to get it developed and ready to look at. There's a student meeting at four where I'm supposed to show the stuff. They'll work right on, all through lunch. But you and I might as well go for a long walk and have a couple of drinks and then have a bite of lunch."

That was what we did. We were back by two-fifteen. When we got through all those empty corridors and sound stages to where Harry's guy was working, the technician gave Harry a look and shook his head.

"What is it, Jerry?" Harry said at once. "Bad?"

"It's pretty thin shit," the man said. He was an American.

"Have you projected some of it?"

"I don't have to," the man said. "I strip-read the frames. It's enough."

"Shit," Harry said. "I was afraid of that." Then he smiled. "Well, let's have a look."

"Go on in," the man said, indicating the projection room. "It's dry enough. I'll run it for you myself. I'm sorry about it, you know. I like those kids."

"So do I. Why do you think I'm doing this?" Harry said. "But liking them and wishing is no excuse or help for amateurishness."

"You're so right," Jerry said. "Well, go on in."

In the projection room when we were seated and Harry had lit a cigar, the lights went out and the screen lit up.

Well, it was awful. It was worse than the technician Jerry had said. Most of the film that had been shot in daylight was very over-exposed. Of course, all the night film was under-exposed. But the over-exposed daylight film was also marred by marks, dust and pieces of lint that had gotten on the lens. But it was not only the technical part, it was also the approach. There were long, long minutes of a shot, all of it taken from the same angle, of an approaching march or parade, with students holding large banners out there in the distance, faceless, unreal, approaching the camera. In the one or two scenes where police figured, and could be seen running to attack the scurrying students, everything was too far away to have any reality for a viewer. I could see all that myself.

Even to me it was clear that it was hardly worth looking at the rest of the students' cans that they had fought so hard for, and had guarded so preciously.

By his chair Harry pushed a button. "That's enough, Jerry!" he called. "It's worthless," he said to me, bitterly. "I was afraid it would be. Even if we processed it, we'd only get about six good minutes out of the whole lot." He called again, "Now show us some of my stuff!"

By contrast, Harry's material was superb, much more professional and interesting. All of it was properly exposed, except for those night scenes when he had deliberately partially under-exposed, to create an effect. His two characters, his "principals", Terri and Anne-Marie, were good in their close-ups, sweet and beautiful in their love scenes against the backdrop of the violence. They came through as people, real people, with whom and with whose misery one could associate. And the few violence shots he had been able to get added to the poignancy of the young student lovers.

We did not see it all. After five minutes of his stuff Harry had seen enough of it to be satisfied. He pushed the button again and called out to the technician. Instantly, before he could even finish, the screen went dark and the lights in the projection room came on.

"Okay, Jerry. I've seen enough. It's okay. It's adequate. I wish theirs was! Can it all for me, will you? Mark my stuff with red tape and theirs with blue." Then he sat smoking his cigar pensively.

"What are you going to do?" I said.

"I don't know," he said, after a moment. "I don't know. If the caliber of the stuff they lost in Rome is the same as this shit it doesn't much matter whether they lost it or not. Most of it's absolutely unusable.

"You know, Hill shot a good deal of this stuff," he added, and paused. "I didn't know he was that bad."

"They were shooting under pretty difficult conditions most of the time," I said. "They had a lot of handicaps imposed on them."

"A cameraman takes care of his lenses, and keeps them clean," Harry said. "All you need is a brush and a sheaf of lens papers. And a lens cap. There's no excuse for daylight over-exposure if you got a light meter."

"Do you think you can squeeze enough out of it to squeak through?"

"No," he said bluntly.

"I suppose that their emotion kept carrying them away all the time," I said tentatively.

"The camera unfortunately is not subject to the emotion of the holder," Harry said. "That's the first rule. —I mean, that's the first rule after the elementary ones, like keeping your lens clean." He got up and he looked suddenly tired, beat. "I guess I got to hold some elementary gradeschool classes up there in that damned sweatbox. We might just be able to shoot enough riot stuff to fill it out. If there are enough riots between now and the end. Come on. Let's go. I've got to show this stuff to those kids. I wonder what they'll say about it."

We walked out through the bleak, empty studios.

The student showing had been arranged for at four o'clock at the Censier, an ugly collection of cheaply made modern-French buildings built as an adjunct to the overflowing Sorbonne. I guess nothing is quite so ugly as modern-French building because they don't understand concrete like we do and try to save money by not putting in enough cement for a rich mix, and a year later the whole thing begins to crack out. That was the Censier. But, it had a large amphitheater with a screen and projection equipment often used by the Cinema students to show things, back before the Revolution. Incongruously the Censier was set into a maze of skinny little medieval streets, beautiful streets, that ran below rue Monge down the hill. We drove there from the studios in Boulogne in about three-quarters of an hour and arrived a little early.

The previously arranged, police-permitted student march which I mentioned earlier—from Montparnasse to the Gare d'Austerlitz—passed not far from rue Censier and in fact was in full swing, indeed was nearly over, as we drove back in. We listened to the reporting of it on the car radio. Young Dany Cohn-Bendit, who had returned from Germany the Tuesday before with false papers and his red hair dyed black, had left his sanctuary of the occupied Sorbonne to lead it. The police had threatened, had *promised,* that if he ever left the Sorbonne they would get him and deport him. But today he was closely surrounded by a horde of student security forces, the commentator said, and the police though they stood all along the route of march did not try to go for him. There was apparently little or no confrontation between the police and marching students.

Almost as soon as we reached the Censier and went inside, gangs of students began to arrive back from the march all flushed and laughing and glowing with a sense of triumph and with their adrenalin up high. The showing had apparently been well advertised among them. I sat and watched them as they trooped into the amphitheater hooting and calling and waving bottles of red wine, baguettes of bread and long sausages. Harry was checking out the two student operators in the projection booth. When Harry came back, we sat and watched them together.

"I wonder what they'll think of this," Harry said to me in English.

"They probably won't even know," I said.

"I'm afraid the Cinema Committee won't know, either," he said. "That's what I'm afraid of."

It turned out we were both exactly right. The Cinema Committee kids began coming in from the march soon after, and most of them sat near us. Terri and Bernard and Daniel the Chairman and young Raymond my erstwhile guide all sat down near Harry and me, along with some of the others. Then a little while later Anne-Marie "the Commissar" came in. She was white-faced, and had her left arm in a plaster cast and a sling.

"What happened to *you?*" Harry said in French.

"The flics," she said contemptuously from between tight lips. "What else?"

"I thought there wasn't any violence today," he said. "According to the radio."

"There never is any violence according to the radio of the capitalistic imperialists," Anne-Marie said, true to form.

"But we were listening to Europe Number One and Radio Luxembourg," Harry said.

"It's still the same," she said.

"They beat you up?"

She waved her cast up and down contemptuously. "What else?"

"Is it broken?"

"Yes," she said. "The elbow. But not too badly, they said."

"They caught a bunch of us," Daniel the Chairman explained. "After we had cut off from the march and were starting back."

"Was anybody else hurt?" Harry said.

"Two boys had their heads cracked," Daniel said. "But they were not of the Committee."

"Were you there?"

"No, I was with another group." Suddenly he grinned wolfishly behind his steel-rims. "But you see what can happen to anybody. I have been caught, too."

"I'm sorry," I said to Anne-Marie.

"Thank you," she said, with great contempt. "But I care nothing for them. What can you expect? when the hireling killers of the—"

"—capitalistic imperialists are present," Harry finished for her.

"Exactly," she said.

"Come on, you guys. Shall I tell them to start?" Harry said. He went to the booth.

He showed them every bit of the student film that had been developed. He did not show them any of his, which in fact he had left locked up in the car. It took about an hour and a half. The students in the crowded amphitheater all loved it. They hooted and cheered themselves, groaned or booed at the few shots where policemen figured, passed red wine bottles and sausages back and forth along the aisles. But, as Harry had figured, the Cinema Committee kids seemed to like it, too. They chuckled, laughed, poked each other with elbows, reminisced in whispers about shots they had worked on. All of them seemed to love it. Even Anne-Marie apparently thought it was fine. It began with a long long shot, badly over-exposed, of a student march in some totally unrecognizable street, with students holding a huge unreadable banner and moving interminably toward the camera. Minute after minute. The screen was marred by crooked dark lines and dark spots which were the lint and dust Harry had referred to. There was very noticeable jiggling of the hand-held camera as the holder breathed or moved his hands or arms. And none of the rest of it was very much better than that first bad shot. The night shots were almost unrecognizable as anything at all, all black with occasional splashes of light that momentarily lit up an indistinct face or two. And yet the kids, including the Cinema Committee, seemed to love it all. Only little Raymond seemed to feel it might not be marvelous. He slipped over into the empty seat beside me and whispered in French, "It is pretty bad, no?"

I nodded.

"Is any of it usable?"

"He says six minutes, maybe."

"Damn. God. I was afraid of that," said Raymond disconsolately.

When the lights finally went up, and the bottle-wielding, sausage-wielding, ordinary students began to file out in happy groups, Harry turned to the members of the Committee who were still sitting all around us.

"Did you like it?" he said to all of them, then signaled out the girl. "Anne-Marie?"

"Yes. I thought much of it was very moving, very touching. It is perhaps a little too long."

"Daniel?"

"Very much. I think it shows our Revolution exactly as it is, was."

"Terri?" Harry said.

"Bernard?"

"François?"

"Georges?"

Without exception they all liked it.

"Well, you're all wrong," Harry said. "It is plain shit," he said. "Just plain shit."

There was no arguing with the bitterness in his voice, and nobody tried to.

"Nobody in the world," Harry said. "Nobody in the world would sit through an hour of this. Or even a half hour."

Nobody answered him.

"I'm shocked that you could think it was any good at all, any of you," Harry said. "You're letting yourselves be carried away by your own participation, by your own subjectivity, as opposed to objectivity.

"Now, look. Somebody pick up the film cans and bring them back to the Odéon. I'll meet you there. I guess I'm going to have to give you all a lecture. Can we get the use of that little movie theater at Odéon?"

"I have permission to use it whenever I want," Daniel the Chairman said, in a subdued voice. "Nobody else ever uses it."

"All right. I'll meet you all there," Harry said getting up. "Can we get a projectionist?"

"I can get one," Daniel said positively.

"Okay. I'll meet you there. We'll go over this stuff, or part of it. Some of it."

When we got into the car outside, he was cursing savagely.

Back at the Odéon he did indeed give them a lecture. He was as tough on them as a Marine first sergeant on a platoon of recruits. "There's no point in showing all of this over. I don't even know if I could stand to see it all through another time. You all ought to be ashamed of yourselves. And you ought to be doubly ashamed of yourselves for liking it."

In the beautiful little gray-and-black movie theater of the Odéon with its modern black swivel chairs for seats, which back before the Revolution had been used to show special films occasionally to very select avant-garde audiences, he ran several sections of their film over and over, reversing it and then running it again, pointing out to them all the mistakes they had made, which were manifold. At one point he blew up a little.

"Jesus Christ! I didn't think I'd ever be in the position where I'd have to tell advanced Cinema students of the University of the Sorbonne that they should keep their God damned lenses clean! Don't any of you know how to use a God damned light meter properly?"

But then he cooled down. After the actual demonstration was over he got up in front of them, for all the world like a harassed professor before a class.

"As I've said, almost all this stuff is worthless. Unusable. That leaves us with the following logical problem, and question. Are we going to go ahead and try to make a film, or are we not? Is it even possible to attempt to shoot enough riot stuff in the next two or three weeks to make up what we now lack? I am not sure we can, myself. But I'm willing to try. A lot depends upon how much more rioting there will be. I am sure there will be some. But will we be able to get there and photograph it? We all know that the General has won. It is only a matter of time now before the so-called Revolution," he grinned at them, "the *almost* Revolution, is a dead duck, finished. The point is, can we get the stuff we need to fill out the film you want to make in the amount of time left? This is a problem and a question you will have to decide."

Before anyone could answer, Harry held up his hand.

"I can tell you that I am reasonably certain that if I shoot again tonight, with my two 'principals' here," he grinned at Anne-Marie and Terri, "I can pretty well finish up the *personal* story I've been wanting to get. As a matter of fact, Anne-Marie's broken arm ought to be a big aid to us. I never would have thought of faking that. I just wouldn't have thought of it. In fact, if we had faked it it might have come out sentimental and have hurt us rather than helped us. But since it *did* happen, we can use it in all honesty.

"Now, I am not going to show you any of my film today. I'll show it to you when it's all finished. I'll want to edit it a little. I may let a few of you help a little with the editing, if you want to learn it. I'll bring a good cutter. A good cutter is vital to film editing. But for the moment I don't want to show it to you, largely because it is so noticeably better than what you people have shot that I'm afraid you might all go off and commit suicide. Even the little bit of what you've shot that I may be able to save is going to look so different, so noticeably amateurish, that I may not be able to use it anyway.

"However, none of this solves the problem and the question about all the earlier material we are lacking. Without it, we won't have any film. That's for sure. It is up to you people to decide whether we want to go ahead and try or not." He folded his arms across his chest.

At the back Daniel the Chairman rose to his feet. "Regarding that, I think I can speak for all of us to say that we want to go ahead. I don't think we even have to debate it and vote on it. If there are any disagreements, will they please say so and enter their dissensions?"

Daniel waited, but the small room was entirely still. Nobody moved or uttered a word.

"Then I think I can safely say we are in agreement with your suggestion, M. Gallagher," Daniel said. "Whether we can succeed in getting the material we need is another problem. But we want to try. We put ourselves at your disposal. If we don't succeed, we don't. But there is a chance we might. If we don't try we might as well dissolve this Cinema Committee of the Sorbonne and Odéon for the Cultural

Revolution, and forget it. I do not want to dissolve the Committee. So I guess we have to try." He sat down.

Harry unfolded his arms. He did not grin, or even smile. "Okay. If that's the way you want it. Now, I have something I have to do now, this afternoon. I will meet the two crews and the actors here about nine o'clock tonight. I'll be wanting to shoot a few outdoor shots, in which we may have to fake a little rioting, and I'll be wanting to shoot some indoor shots here at the Odéon—in the hallways, the hospital, and in the offices themselves upstairs. Okay? See you then. Come on, Jack."

He was outside the door almost before I could follow him. "Fucking dumb pricks," he said, as we went down the hall.

"What is it you have to do, Harry?" I said. "And where is it you are going?"

"Where do you think, dumbass?" he grinned.

When we were outside the Odéon and down the steps into the *Place,* he stopped and turned to me.

"Do you want a ride back to the Island? That's where I'm heading."

I hesitated. "No. I think I'll wander around a while, and then walk on back," I said.

"See you, then," he grinned. "Will you be here tonight?"

"I don't know. Probably."

"See you then, then." He marched off, his starched trenchcoat ballooning, the collar up around his ears. I thought briefly that he looked like Floyd Gibbons or Ernest Hemingway or some damned body. I started to turn away, and stopped.

"Harry!" I called after him sharply. "I guess you know I don't approve of all this business!"

He stopped and turned back, trenchcoat ballooning, collar up around the bald head, and grinned. "I rather gathered that."

That night Samantha Everton did not show up at the seven o'clock meeting of Americans at the Gallaghers' apartment. But about eight-thirty, just as everybody else was leaving, she appeared suddenly, her short hair looking curly and cute.

When the rest of us left, she stayed behind, quiet and somber and reading another comic book. As we went out, Louisa went over to her.

22

NOTHING HAPPENED ON SUNDAY.

Almost nothing happened on Monday, either. In Monday's Paris *Herald* a piece by some reporter, Koven I think it was, stated that le Général had proclaimed himself winner in a serious test of strength against the Communists.

In Monday's paper it also said that Helen Keller died in her sleep at 87. The item was datelined Westport, Conn., Sunday, June 2nd.

I thought that was kind of funny. Apparently, nobody else did. Or at least nobody mentioned it.

Also, in Monday's *Herald-Tribune* a piece told how *Pravda,* the Soviet Union's official organ (I like that phrase, official *organ*), had stepped up its criticism of le Général. I confess I found that nearly as important as the fact that Helen Keller had died.

Then, in Tuesday's Paris *Herald* there was an item datelined New York, June 3rd, stating that Andy Warhol, painter of the Campbell's Soup can and underground film-maker, the rage of the Jet Set, had been shot and seriously wounded by some woman named Valeria Solanis, leader, and apparently sole member, of an organization named S.C.U.M. (Society for Cutting Up Men), who had once acted in one of his dirty movies. I was almost glad that Helen Keller had not lived to hear about that.

It looked like it was going to be a good week all around.

Meantime, the Pentecostal weekend was going on, went on, had been going on. Frenchmen by the millions picnicked in the country, or visited relatives there.

On Monday Prime Minister Pompidou went on TV for a 12-minute address, his first since le Général had dissolved the *Congrès* for new elections. He warned the strikers of the injury to the National Economy, stated that the strike had cost the nation six billion dollars so far. I could not help remembering what Harry had said that day, when we first walked over to the newly occupied Odéon.

On Tuesday there was the biggest traffic jam in Paris history. People coming back from the Pentecost vacation tried en masse to drive their cars in to work in town. The railroads, Métros, autobuses, and taxis were all still striking. Almost no policemen were available for traffic duty. In addition there was a Young Gaullist demonstration marching from Trocadéro to the Champ-de-Mars which further disrupted circulation. Some people actually sat in their cars in the same spot for three or four hours. I, of course, did not go out into the town. Neither did Harry. It was very pleasant and quiet, on the Island.

But all in all things seemed to be tapering off. Another point was that tobacco was again being delivered to tobacco stores, and the smokers' crisis appeared to be easing.

It was on that Tuesday that Hill Gallagher called me. He called rather early, around noon, to make sure I would be there. I was. I was still in bed. As a matter of fact, I had waked up only about a minute before he called. When he ascertained that I was home, he said he wanted to come by and see me.

"Jack?" his voice said when I picked up the phone. "Jack?" His voice sounded peculiar, different.

"Yes?" I said. "Who is it?" I was still a little dopey.

"Hill," he said. "Hill." When I did not respond immediately he repeated it again. "Hill!"

"Yes, Hill, yes," I said. "What is it?"

"Did I wake you?"

"Well, yes. Just about."

"I wanted to make sure and catch you. I want to come by and see you, if I may. I was afraid you might go out. I'm leaving Paris. I wanted to say goodby, and talk a minute."

That *I'm leaving Paris* woke me up a good deal more. "Well, can you give me an hour?" I said. "I'm not really awake yet. And I haven't—"

"Oh, sure," his voice said. "I'll be over in an hour and a half, say, okay?"

"Fine. Do you want to have lunch?"

"No. I've eaten already."

"All right. See you then."

"Fine," he said.

I hung up.

I could not place what it was about his voice that sounded so different. But there was certainly something changed. I buzzed my Portuguese and addressed myself to my coffee and juice and the morning papers. I do hate to be disturbed in my morning ritual. I suppose that sounds old-fashioned, even ridiculous, to a younger generation. But this meant I would have to hurry through the papers, if I wanted to shave at leisure.

When he came in I was ready for him though. He appeared to have put on a little bit of tan, as though he had been in the country for the Pentecost weekend himself. But under the new bit of color he looked extremely haggard, as if he had not slept at all since the last time I had seen him a week before. Also, he was clutching some book. Wherever he moved around the apartment he did not let go of this book, which was quite thick. I could not see the title, and preferred not to peer too obviously, but it was a blue board cover and it had what looked to be Chinese characters in red on the front and on the spine.

Well, we got into it all soon enough. It was when I offered him a drink.

"Do you want a bash of something?" I said. He was moving around restlessly.

"No. I've stopped d—" Then he said, "Oh, sure. Why not? Give me a Scotch. A Scotch on the rocks. A good big one." There was a peculiar condescending tone in his voice.

"You don't have to have a drink," I said.

"No, no. No, no. I want one, I want one."

I made them. I took a cold beer for myself. It was a little too early for me for Scotch. But not for Hill. He gulped his down like a man just returned from the desert.

"You've picked up a little sun," I said. "Where've you been?"

"Sitting on the quai," he said. "You know, the one out in front of Notre-Dame there. Below that little park with the statue of Charlemagne. On the lower level."

"I see," I said.

Well, I did. I knew the place. It had become a hangout for all sorts of hippy kids, in sunny weather. Penniless or drifting or perhaps both they would stretch out there and take the sun with their shirts off. I had always thought it charming. But not for Hill.

And that was when he brought the book forward.

"Do you know this book?"

He held the spine toward me and above the red Chinese characters, which I could not read, I read the English letters. It said: *The I CHING, or Book of Changes.* It was published by some American firm.

"I got it at Galignani's," Hill said.

"I think I've heard of it," I said. But I was thinking to myself in dismay, Oh, no! I had been through that whole routine myself, in my youth. With us it was Annie Besant, and Madame Blavatski, and finally Paul Brunton.

"You just open it anywhere and get the answer to what you want to know," Hill said. "Of course, you have to concentrate first. Empty your mind.

"Shall I show you?"

With us it was a book called TRISMEGATUS. It was even bigger. And for a subtitle it had, *Trismegatus Revealed.*

"Well, sure," I said. "But what if you get the wrong answers?"

"You don't," he said. "That's what's so marvelous. Here, let me show you."

He held the book in his right hand, and placed his left hand flat on the cover, and frowned. After half a minute he opened it.

"Changes and movements are judged according to the furtherance that they bring," Hill read. "Good fortune and misfortune change according to the conditions. Therefore, love and hate combat each other, and good fortune and misfortune result therefrom. The far and the near injure each other, and remorse and humiliation result therefrom. The true and the false influence each other, and advantage and injury result therefrom. In all the situations of the Book of Changes it is thus: When closely related things do not harmonize, misfortune is the result: This gives rise to injury, remorse, and humiliation." He stopped and looked up. "Now, isn't that *profound?* Isn't that *great?*"

"Well, it's certainly profound," I said, cautiously. "I don't really see how anybody could quibble with a statement like that. But what was your question?"

"My question was: What shall I do? You see, that's what I mean. It answers everything," he said, and his eyes started to glow. "Guy I met turned me onto this. And now I wouldn't be without it." He wrapped his hands protectively around the book.

"Well," I said, "you know."

"You ever read Alan Watts?" Hill said. "Alan *W.* Watts? You know, *The Way of Zen,* for instance, and *Nature, Man and Woman?*"

"Yes. I know his work. I've read some of it."

"Well!" Hill said. "There! You see?"

"See what?" I said. "Watts is English, isn't he?"

"Is he?" Hill said. "I didn't know. What difference does that make?"

"I think he was English," I said. "Maybe he's American now. The English have a long history of association with, and immersion in, Eastern philosophies. That's largely because their warrior race conquered so much of the East, and thus were brought into intimate contact with the stuff."

"So?" Hill said.

"So nothing," I said. "Do you know the *Zen in the Art of Archery* book? By this German Herrigel?"

"I've got that, too!" Hill said excitedly. "I've got that, too!"

"Good," I said. "But have you got a bow?"

"I'm thinking of getting one. And some arrows. And a target. That's what I came to talk about."

"Archery?" I said.

"No, not archery. I mean, not just archery. I told you I was leaving Paris."

"I used to be quite an archer," I told him.

"Did you?" Hill said. "That doesn't seem like you. It's hard to believe."

"Well," I said. "It's true, all right. Matter of fact, I could send you to a damned good archery shop on Avenue Malakoff just off the Place Maillot. They've got everything there, and bows from a 50 pound pull up to 140 pound pull, if anybody can go that high. And double reflex bows; they've got the lot."

"Well, what do you know!" he said. "Did you get into that through Zen?"

"Well, no," I said. "Not originally. But then I did."

"How did that happen?" he asked eagerly.

I didn't know how to answer. I decided to tell the simple truth. "Well, I used to believe that men ought not to kill animals with rifles, especially deer. Forest deer, I mean. Whitetails. Like in Pennsylvania and New York State. That you meet at close range. I thought they ought to give the animals more of an even break, and do it in the style of the ancient days. With spears or bows. It was a moral point. I've killed four deer you know, with broadhead arrows. I've killed running rabbits with the straight-tip target arrows. —Not often," I added, "but I have."

"I don't want to kill anything," Hill said.

"Neither do I," I said, "anymore."

"You don't?"

"No. You want to know why?"

He nodded.

I did not know if I ought to go that far, really. But it was the truth. The truth of my youth. And he was so obviously going through a bad time. And I wanted to help him. I really so much wanted to help him. "Well, I was gutting out a deer I'd shot. It was the last one I ever shot. Now, deer contain an awful lot of guts. As do we. I might say that deer are about 65 per cent digestive system. Anyway, the day before, I had skinned my right hand badly, saddling a horse. That was out in Wyoming. And there was a big scab on it. I mean, a big thick scab. Well, after dipping my hand into that deer's belly for so long, I found that the contact with the deer's blood had completely dissolved my big scab. I happened to look at my hand, and the skinned spot was absolutely pink and clean. That shocked me. I don't know to this day why it shocked me so badly, but it sure shocked me. I might even say it horrified me. And that was when I went to target archery and then somebody told me about this Zen book and I got a copy of it."

"Jesus!" Hill said.

"Yes," I said. "Exactly what I felt."

"But then why did you give up the target archery after?"

"Well," I said, "to tell you the truth, it got so it bored me, finally. It just got so that I was bored with it. So I quit. I suppose I got older."

He didn't say anything for a moment. I was hoping it all would get through to him. "I don't believe in killing anything," he said, finally.

"But you got to eat," I said.

"Eat plants, vegetables," he said. "They don't feel."

"How do you know?"

That slowed him up a little. He clutched that crazy book. "Well," he said. "Well. At least they don't feel as much as sentient animals. They don't scream."

"Nobody can be sure of that. How do you know that they don't scream on a decibel level, or in a different medium, that we simply can't hear?" I had been through all this for years, when I was younger.

Hill came up out of the chair and started walking around, still clutching that *I CHING* book. "Well," he said. "Well. I don't know. I don't really know. That's why I'm going away from Paris. I want to think about all these things. I think I'll go by your shop there and get me some archery gear before I leave."

"Where are you going to go, Hill?" I said. "And what about money?"

"Cadaquęs. In Spain. It's just over the French border, on the sea. I've been there."

I knew he had. He had been there a couple of summers ago, with his father and his mother and McKenna.

"But a guy I know told me there are some great caves there," Hill said. He sat down. "It's a nice town, you know. Lots of younger people come there. And these caves, apparently they're great. They're outside of town about ten miles, and quite dry. Nobody owns them. Or if they do, they don't holler about people using them. I've got two buddies who've been there for quite a while. Sleeping bags. That's what I'm after. That's what I'm looking for."

"Why?"

"Meditate. Same way you have to meditate over your archery, if you want it to be good, perfect. I'll sit there and meditate. Think a lot. Try to figure it all out."

"I see," I said, again.

He did not say anything at that point, and sat clutching his *I CHING* book and staring at it.

"If you figure it all out, will you send me a wire?" I said.

"I sure will!" he said, looking up eagerly.

I found I had nothing to say to this. After a moment I said, "But what about money?"

"Oh I've got a little money you know. You know," he said. "From my maternal grandmother. I've even got my own bank account. The folks have never touched that."

"So you're going to become an Oriental philosopher?"

"No. No, no. Not at all," he said. "But there's a lot of things."

It seemed to me his entire language had changed, in the week since I had seen him last.

He looked up.

"Why is there so much hate?"

"Well," I said judiciously, and coughed. "I don't think there's as much hate as you seem to think. Actually I guess it's what one could call, in the parlance, a conflict of interests. But when you're raised up in a background, like you were, that keeps pounding into you that everybody should be full of love, and then you get out there and see that not everybody is, I guess it comes as a kind of shock."

"I suppose," he said. "I suppose."

I wasn't sure he'd heard a single word I'd said all during the afternoon. Suddenly he got up and turned half away from me, placed his left hand on the top cover of his *I CHING* book, frowned for half a minute. Then he turned around and opened it again.

"Heavenly bodies exemplify duration," he read. "They move in their fixed orbits, and because of this their light-giving power endures. The seasons of the year follow a fixed law of change and transformation, hence can produce effects that endure.

"So likewise the dedicated man embodies an enduring meaning in his way of life, and thereby the world is formed. In that which gives things their duration, we can come to understand the nature of all beings in heaven and on earth.

"The Image:

"Thunder and wind: the image of *duration*.

"Thus the superior man stands firm, and does not change his direction.

"Thunder rolls, and the wind blows; both are examples of extreme mobility and so are seemingly the very opposite of duration, but the laws governing their appearance and subsidence, their coming and going, endure. In the same way the independence of the superior man is not based on rigidity and immobility of character. He always keeps abreast of the time and changes with it. What endures is the unswerving directive, the inner law of his being, which determines all his actions." He looked up.

"True enough, I guess," I said. "But?"

He closed the book.

"That's what I've got to do!" he said.

"What?" I said.

"Just that! My God, can't you see?" He put the book under his arm and looked around vaguely. "Well, I got to go."

"Hill," I said. "Have you been on a lot of pot lately?"

"Oh, sure," he said. "Down there under the bridge there's nothing but pot. It's great."

I had no answer to that.

"I met a couple buddies there who have spent lots of time in them Cadaquęs caves. They know all about it down there the scene.

"The scene, and the cave scene."

I said nothing at this point, but I had my suspicions.

"Well," he said. "I better go. I just wanted to come by and say good-bye."

"What about your folks?" I said.

"Shit on them," he said. "Mom deserves everything she gets."

"I understand you were down there at the room at the hotel last Wednesday. The Wednesday of May the 29th."

"Yes, I was." He looked up eagerly. "I hung around for a while. Knocked on the door a few times. There wasn't anybody answering. But I knew they were there. You can sort of tell. You can tell an empty room from one with people in it." He half-shrugged, in a peculiarly French way. "Then, finally, I went away."

I had absolutely nothing to say to that. "Look," I said. "If there's anything you want, or anything you want done for you from down there, you'll let me know, won't you? Hunh?"

"Oh, sure," he said. His eyes were eager. "And if there's anything you want me to do for you, you'll let me know, too, won't you? You can always reach me General Delivery, Cadaquęs."

"What do you want me to tell your folks?" I said.

"I don't give a shit what you tell them. No, wait a minute. I guess I don't mean that. Don't tell them anything."

"You don't want them to know where you are?"

"I sure don't want them coming after me. Tell them nothing."

"All right," I said. "If you're sure that's what you want."

"I'm sure."

He went to the door, clutching his book.

I was standing by my little bar. "Look!" I called sharply. "I guess you know I think you're all fucked up and full of shit, don't you?"

He turned. "Oh, sure," he said, and grinned. It was the first time he had grinned since coming into the apartment, and it was singularly like Harry's grin I had seen so often. "Oh, sure," he said. "Who aint?"

He went out.

The next day was Wednesday. The Wednesday of June the 5th. That was the day that Bobby Kennedy was shot. Of course, in Paris, with the time lag, we did not know about it until later in the morning. In any case, the word was out that the French transportation and mail services would be going back to work sometime during Thursday. Some other industries, steel, automobile plants, weren't giving in yet. But the trend was clearly toward getting French society back into harness. De Gaulle clearly had won.

23

I HAVE OFTEN THOUGHT that if I had been smarter, or more prepared for what Hill was going to throw at me (or not throw at me, rather), I could have helped him more, instead of failing him. I feel I have to take responsibility for that. But that sudden mysticism routine of his threw me. It was so unexpected. And by the time I was able to muddle through it all, and try to come up with some sort of understanding statement that might pull him out of it, he already was gone. Long gone.

And that was the last I was to see of Hill. I have not seen him since. I assume he is still in Cadaquęs, sitting crosslegged and meditating in some cave, but I do not know. He was still there, and still meditating, when I received his second postcard in late June. I did not answer it, and that was the last word I have had.

I'm sorry he ever met those hippy flower-people types, who apparently from his postcards are living with him, on his money, of course. He told me that much. There apparently is a whole colony of them.

Anyhow, the assassination of Bobby Kennedy pushed the May Revolution completely off the front page of the Paris *Herald*. It did the same with almost every French paper. Of course, the word had been flashed, and everybody across the world had heard about it on the radio before any of the papers could come out with the news. But of course, everybody wanted to read the details.

I remember it was my Portuguese who brought me the news. She came into my bedroom at eight-thirty in the morning and woke me, an absolutely unprecedented thing for her to do. Actually, she was a young woman, much younger than she looked, and unmarried, a virgin apparently, perpetually saving something which no one any longer wanted to bargain for. She never came in my bedroom unless I called her. But now she was wringing her hands and tears were streaming down her trusty Portuguese face. She had apparently just heard it on her equally trusty transistor in my kitchen. "Oh, Monsieur," she kept saying. "Oh, Monsieur!"

I guess everybody felt the same sense of horror and chill. It was as if God had truly abandoned us all, by letting the lightning strike twice. At least, that was what everyone I talked to later in the day seemed to feel. It was certainly what I felt.

I remembered when John Kennedy was assassinated back in '63. This second time, there was not the totally struck-dumb desolation and total despair, the numbness we all felt when the older brother was shot in '63. Maybe we were more used to it now, coming so soon after Dr. King. But by the same token, in a way, this hurt worse. I remember that time, when Jack was shot, I wandered around Paris in a daze for two days—going to bars I knew that were frequented by Americans, searching out Americans, and finding them, in all the American-frequented bars, where we all sort of just stood together like wet birds buying each other drinks and nodding our heads and saying almost nothing.

There was not that, this time. But in another way there was an even greater desolation, a greater horror, because of its having happened twice to Kennedys. And of course this time there was hope. Robert Kennedy could be operated on. Everybody hoped, hoped against hope. Of course next day he was dead. I guess nobody really ever believed that he would make it. But there was always this thing of it having struck us twice.

I had met Bobby Kennedy a few times at parties in New York when I was back in the States on business for the Review. But I had never formed any real opinion of him. He certainly appeared to be quite an egotist. And he certainly took great and careful care to maintain and project his public image and role as the Young Defender. Also he had let his hair grow longer. I always had the feeling that, politically, he had seized a cake that he did not have a knife big enough to cut. But then who did have? Nobody.

But then in addition to all of that, which sounded carping to me now, there was something definitely tragic about him. Almost as if he definitely knew what to expect.

Sitting with the newspaper in my apartment, I remembered one night at a lawn party in Martha's Vineyard where I was visiting, when some of the Kennedy clan had whipped over in their boat from the Cape, and when after all the shouted hellos and laughter and drinks and the barbecue itself, I saw him sitting by himself on the old porch rail, a porch rail which came right out of another time. He had one foot in its expensive loafer up on the rail and was clasping his knee and looking out over the lawn and smiling, all alone, enjoying the moonlight and the party. There were lots of children squealing and playing on the dark lawn, and there was a local band of sorts playing a modified rock. Kennedy simply sat, smiling, enjoying, his blond shock of longer hair hanging down over his forehead.

In my Paris apartment, reading the June 6th issue of the Paris *Herald,* suddenly I turned away choked up, and tears spurted into my eyes making it impossible to read further. I put the paper down.

I always was an awful slob.

Still, others felt the same way.

We saw it all that night on TV at the Gallaghers.

Louisa was practically beside herself. Her eyes were stary and wide like a mad woman's and she hardly spoke to anyone. In a soft voice Harry told me it was McKenna who had informed them, apparently at about the time my Portuguese was informing me. She was up and having breakfast with their Portuguese, when they heard it, on *their* Portuguese's transistor radio, and she rushed into their bedroom and woke them up to tell them, sobbing and crying. McKenna had once met Bobby somewhere too, and he had played a minute with her, and tossed her up, and so for her he was a sort of special private possession.

Only Samantha Everton seemed completely unmoved. But I am convinced she was much more moved than she was willing to let on.

"Well, he was ambitious," she said with a shrug.

"We're all ambitious," I said, with deliberate ambiguity. "In one way or another."

"True," Sam said, and smiled at me. "But political ambition carries with it certain things. You takes your chances."

"Well, he was certainly a good and great thing for your people," Ferenc Hofmann-Beck said suddenly.

Samantha turned to smile at him. "I aint got any people, baby," she said. "Didn't you know?"

Louisa was staring at her with those wide, goofy eyes, but not even seeing her I think. A sort of contortion of revulsion writhed itself across her long horseface and thin-lipped mouth. "I think that is incredibly calloused."

"I suppose," Sam said, and smiled at her too. "But you've led such a protected life with all that money that you don't know what goes on out there in real life. You're safe."

At this point Harry stepped in. "You haven't led such an unprotected life yourself," he said with a smile. "Born in Europe, and going to all those ritzy Swiss and Parisian schools. Like Brillamont."

"I've been out there," Sam said, and smiled again. "And I'm here to state that it aint at all like you cats think." She laughed suddenly. "Now America can choose between two slobs. Two slobs so much alike you can hardly tell them apart. It's Tweedledum and Tweedledee. That's America for you. That's America, to me."

Louisa had already turned away and was standing looking out the window at the river, hardly listening, probably not listening at all. I thought it was high time I tried to break it up.

"Well," I said, "I suppose a lot of interpretations will be put on it. Yours is one. I have one of my own. I think it is a case of a nonman trying to assert himself. A silly little Arab immigrant boy, probably certifiably insane, but whom society hasn't even bothered to look at or test, whom society stares through like a plateglass window and doesn't even bother to see, tries to prove his existence

in the only idiot way he knows how. A boy who's never done anything—and hasn't the brains to, I hasten to add—except deliver
groceries on an old bicycle in that great sprawl of smog called Los
Angeles decides to force society to notice he is there. So he guns
down the richest, handsomest, most fortunate, most publicized
member of the world celebrity set that he can get access to. His
motives as stated by himself, all that Arab junk, don't mean a thing.
The real motive is that he wanted attention, wanted to make the
world admit he existed.

"I think that's the real problem, and I think that's the problem
somebody has to try to solve.

"You could do what Sirhan Sirhan did," I said, smiling at Sam. "I
think you could very well do that."

"No, I couldn't," Sam said at once. Then she smiled. "Or maybe,
by God, I could." She gave me a long look. "Yes, by God, I think I
could, Mr. Hartley."

"Anyway," Harry said in a soft sad voice, "that's an interesting
proposition, Jack. I'd like to discuss that with you."

He took me by the elbow and led me off toward the bar. "Maybe
he wanted to prove to *himself* he existed."

"No. Too romantic," I said.

At least, I had succeeded in changing the drift of the conversation.

When I look back on it, it seems to me now that the killing of
Bobby Kennedy, whom we all knew—or at least had met—was the
trigger point where everything began to go bad for us. By us I mean
the Gallaghers, and me. I can't call myself a Gallagher, really.
Though I was very close to them, and I *am* McKenna's godfather.

It is my well-thought-out certified opinion that if the rest of what
happened had not happened, there would have been no problem
with Hill. I can't prove that, but I believe it. He would have come
home eventually I think, and straightened himself out. But what
happened, did happen.

So I have to address myself to that. And I can not avoid this
obscure feeling that if the second Kennedy had not been killed like
that, so totally uselessly, by a stupid silly little Arab boy, what

happened to us mightn't have happened. I know this is a superstitious idea. Dumb, stupid, idiotic, animal. Like making up a God to account for why the lightning struck your hut. But then, I am a superstitious man. Damn it all, I am. But maybe Sam might have reacted differently, with less cynicism. And maybe Louisa would have been less distraught, and more capable of thinking her way through.

In any case, on June 6th, a Thursday, police cleared out the Government-owned Renault auto-assembly plant at Flins, out the Autoroute de l'Ouest near Mantes. The move came at dawn, and caused new street demonstrations that day in Paris which nearly turned into renewed street fighting. In a case of mistaken intention, a demonstration of students at the Arc de Triomphe thought that a group of several hundred middle-aged ex-paratroopers marching up the Champs-Élysées was a deliberate counter-demonstration to their own. In fact, the ex-paras were only holding a march to pay homage to the Eternal Flame of the Unknown Soldier that rests under the Arc. Students and workers started singing the "Internationale", and the middle-age veterans countered with the "Marseillaise". Fist fights broke out all over the Champs-Élysées, and were stopped only when a student leader and a para leader climbed up on the roof of a car together to explain to the battlers that neither group knew about the other's demonstration, or when or why or what for. By this device renewed street-fighting was averted.

On Friday of June 7th French workers and students fought day-long skirmishes with the police at Flins, while trying to reoccupy the assembly plant which the police had thrown them out of the day before. The students apparently drove out all the way from Paris for the fight. The Government claimed that at least 1,000 workers were trying to get back into the plant to clean it up in the hope of getting back to work.

That night, the Friday, le Général went back on TV in a widely publicized interview that went on for a whole hour. He was interviewed by a journalist named Michel Droit, the same man who had interviewed him back in 1965 during the last crisis of his Government, and it was ·a pretty intellectual discussion, with le Général doing most of the talking. He talked mostly about the "mechanical society" and its great accomplishments, but he added that on its debit side it tended to make objects out of the workers, and that he felt that both Capitalism and Communism tended to contribute to this soulless mechanization. He was hoping, he said, that his new plan for "participation" would be a third way which would give all workers a sense of identity by having a say-so in what their firms and their management decided to do. But, he added, the Unions had always been against him on this because it would take away some of their power. He talked some about University reforms, too. It was a real old-fashioned fireside chat, and he made himself look pretty good. It was an interesting soft-sell after the "hard" line he had taken on May 30th. And you certainly could not fault him on his intellectual ideas or his statements. In the end though it was the same pitch. All was lost, he warned, if the French did not follow him. The only alternative was a massive Communist take-over, which with its totalitarian system would cause the very dehumanization process he was seeking to avoid.

I found it difficult to care much, after the Bobby Kennedy California debacle. It was hard to be interested.

It was on Saturday morning, Saturday June the 8th, just as I was getting out of bed, that Harry Gallagher called me from his own apartment down the quai. It was just noon.

"I've got to see you, Jack. And I've got to see you right now."

"Well, can you give me an hour?" I said, perhaps a little plaintively. I do hate to be disturbed during my morning toilet. And Harry knew that. I was suddenly reminded of Hill his son, calling up the other day. I had not yet decided to tell the parents about Hill's departure. "Can it wait that long?"

"No, it can't," Harry said. "I've got to see you now. I've been hanging around cafés since dawn, not wanting to disturb your repose. But now you're up. It can't wait any longer."

"Well, you don't mind if I shave while we're talking, do you?" I said irritably.

"No, I don't mind if you shave," he said. "I don't mind what you do. I don't give a damn if you jerk off while we're talking."

"That's highly unlikely, I think," I said drily.

"I'll be right down," he said, as if he hadn't heard me.

I was in my bathroom when he arrived.

He perched himself on the side of my bed like some long tall nervous bird, an ostrich maybe.

"Well, what is it, Harry?" I said, "God damn it?" I peered out, my face still two-thirds lathered. I had a bath towel wrapped around my waist.

He did not answer immediately and I ducked back in and wiped my razor carefully with the hem of the towel and began to strop it. You must always be quite sure that no beard hairs are left on the razor when you strop it because they will mix in with the *pâte* and cause a dulling effect. "Do you want a drink or something?" I said.

"I already made myself one on the way in," he said, holding up a glass and coming to the door. He leaned against the jamb.

I went on shaving, skimming the first layer of beard and the lather from the right side. "Well, what the hell is it, Harry?"

"I don't quite know how to say it," he said. He took a deep breath and let it out in an explosive sigh. "Well, Louisa is having an affair with Samantha."

I flatter myself that I didn't nick myself badly. I pulled up the skin of my cheek, to see if I had gotten it all under the jawline. That is always one of the hardest places to get baby-pure clean. "What's the matter with you, Harry?" I said. "You're losing your mind or something like that?"

"Of course I'm losing my mind," he said in what I have to admit was an icy-cold, steely voice. "There's more. Sam left today."

"Left?"

"Left Paris. For Israel. At Louisa's suggestion. She's going via Rome."

"That's good news," I said.

"For whom?"

"For youm, that's whom."

"You may not find it such good news in a few minutes," Harry said.

"Now, look," I said. "You go out there and sit down. Let me

finish shaving without cutting my throat. Make yourself another drink or something. Then we'll talk about your suspicions and everything, when I don't have to concentrate on two things at once. Or do you want to lose one of your best friends?"

Without a word he turned and strode out away from the bathroom door and out of the bedroom, still holding his glass as if it were a cracked egg.

When I came out into the living room after applying my cologne water and having put on my kimono, he was standing with one foot up on the sill of the open double-doored window and staring out at the noontime river. A barge was passing, and we could hear as though through a megaphone the steady throb and beat of its diesel as it made its way up-current toward the Pont de la Tournelle. He had clearly made himself another drink because when he stalked out of the bedroom his glass was nearly empty and now it was a little more than half full.

"I think I'll have a drink myself," I said. "Now, what is all this tripe?"

Harry turned to face me, and at the same time took a long draught from his glass.

24

It appeared he had come home the night before somewhat early. He had been out shooting some more demonstration stuff, with his two "principals", in order to try and pick up some more backlog film to help the Cinema Committee kids fill out what they had lost and what they had done so badly. But the demonstration had fizzled out, and they had knocked off early. So he had come home early.

Well, he let himself in (it was about one-thirty) and shut the door carefully, and then took off his shoes just inside the door. He always did that when he got in after midnight, in order to avoid waking Louisa. This time, as he usually did, he went in through the entryway into the living room salon, to make himself a nightcap, but this time as he stepped through the doorway in his stocking-feet he became aware of two silent figures lying under the night light on the couch in the small-salon part, to his left. They had an ancient wrought-iron stand-up floorlamp there which they kept lit all night every night, and this stood at the head of the couch in the corner. It was easy enough to see the two silent figures lying there.

It was clear enough to him that they were Louisa and Sam. They were lying there together on the couch, fully clothed, necking. He himself had not made a sound. They weren't making any sounds either, not even an occasional rustle. It could not actually be said that one of them was on top of the other. They were lying side by side, though Samantha had one leg thrown across Louisa's thighs in a rather possessive way, thus hiking up her own skirt to expose her cute little bottom in its panties, which she clearly was still wearing. She was kissing Louisa deeply on the mouth, soul-kissing was the phrase he used, I believe. Louisa's eyes were closed. Her hands were not visible but it appeared from her position that they were lying along her sides. He had a number of seconds to take this all in, in a kind of frozen film shot. Then he turned and tiptoed out again, and silently left the apartment. He put his shoes on outside, in the hall.

He had been so startled, shocked, in a way, if you will, that he had not known what else to do. Mainly in his mind was the thought that he did not want to catch Louisa and thus embarrass her. He had gone up to his studio and double-locked the door with the key left in the lock, and then had lain on the bed a while. He was not sure whether he dreamt or not. If he hadn't dreamt, then he had thought about them, envisioning it, imagining it, seeing in his mind's eye them making it, taking as his jumpoff point the way he had seen them on the couch. The slow taking off of the clothes, the languorous disrobing, the kissing of each other's breasts, the further necking, soul-kissing, nude, the whole lot.

I interrupted him here. "How did you see them doing it, Harry? In your dream. —Or in your envisioning."

"Oh," he said, "sixty-nineing, of course. Or at least, Sam going down on Louisa. I'm not sure I even remember. But it was that."

It was his fantasy, his Super-Fantasy, of course, as he had told me a number of times, he pointed out. But he had never envisioned it with his wife as one of the participants. That was very upsetting. It was like that thing about not going to one of those undress places with your wife. You could take somebody you didn't love, take somebody you weren't in love with, but not somebody you were. He had certainly never meant for his wife to get involved in things like this. He had lain there in his studio, dreaming or imagining, he could not be sure which, for some time. A couple of hours? Three? Then he had gotten up and gone out, leaving whatever was happening up there in the living room salon to handle itself, take care of itself. He had looked up once at the lighted window, from the quai.

He had wandered around, sitting in one all-night café for a while, then in another. He had gone home around nine-thirty in the morning, his eyes feeling scorched and burning. He had waited there, in the curséd damned living room until he knew I would be up and then had called me. He had had four Scotches, not counting the two he had had at my joint, and he felt considerably better. He was preparing to leave for Rome today.

He stopped and a kind of awful silence, waiting for me to respond, hung over the apartment.

"Harry, you know, I just don't believe Louisa could be having, could have, an affair with any girl. Samantha or anybody else. I just can't believe it," I said. "I think you thought you saw something you didn't see. After all, it is your *fantasy*, you know."

"Fantasy, yes," Harry said, his eyes blazing suddenly. "But I don't hallucinate. I don't have waking hallucinations. I know what I saw."

"Well," I said. "I just can't believe it. I suppose, I don't want to believe it."

"Possibly," Harry said. "But you've got to take my word."

"I'll accept it," I said. "But I find it very hard to believe. Did you, uh, talk to her about it?"

"Of course not."

"I think you should," I said. "Maybe she'll have some reasonable explanation."

"What reasonable explanation is there?"

"Maybe she'll deny it."

"Of course she'll deny it. That changes nothing."

I thought, God damn. Men. They certainly were peculiar. They would go around screwing everything they could get their hands on. And then if their wives did something of the same sort of thing they would scream like wounded baboons.

"Well, I think you should talk to her," I said trying to keep my voice equable. "About both."

"What both?" he said.

"About what you saw," I said. "Maybe she'll have some explanation. And also about your decision to go to Rome."

Suddenly, I had a peculiar feeling of *déjà vu*. All this same damned scene had happened to me before. And, of course, I immediately realized it was with Louisa, the time she had come to see me in September of '59. About leaving Harry. My God, I thought, now they'll have another child, for which I shall have to be Godfather also.

Harry was looking out the window. As I stood grinning idiotically at his back under the stress of my sudden revelation, he turned back toward me.

I tried to compose my face, and succeeded. "At least you owe her that," I said reasonably.

"I don't owe anybody anything," Harry said evenly. "Particularly now, I don't owe anybody anything. I'm going to Rome. After Sam. And I'm going on to Israel with her."

"Well, at least go and talk to Louisa first," I said. Then something hit me. "Say, how did you know it was Louisa who suggested Sam's leaving, if you haven't talked to Louisa?"

"Sam told me. I saw her this morning at nine o'clock before I went on home. She had her bags already packed, and was just preparing to get a taxi out to Orly. She wasn't even going to say goodby. 'I figured you'd know where to find me,' she said, 'if you wanted me.' Want her? I've never had anything like her in my life."

It was useless to keep on saying to him that he was losing his mind. Even if it might be true, there was no point in keeping on repeating it. Then something else struck me. "Say. Tell me. Will you answer a personal question? Did you have sex with her at the hotel this morning?"

"Of course I had sex with her at the hotel this morning," Harry said.

"You really must be going out of your mind, Harry," I said, I suppose in a kind of wondering voice. I couldn't help it. "But what about the other girl?"

"We don't always have to have another girl," he said, and suddenly he grinned. "There are other things."

I was suddenly reminded of that "punishment" routine she had used with me, when she masturbated herself. I guessed there were other things. "I can't imagine it," I said, in a feeble way.

"Don't try," Harry said. "I don't think you've got the imagination for it." He set down his empty glass. His eyes were looking red and scratchy, and I remembered he had not been to bed last night at all. Then he said, with it exploding out of him, "But, God *damn* it, why would she leave like that and take off on me like that?"

"I don't know," I said. But I thought I did know, after all he had told me. She had said several times to all of us that it was really Louisa she was after. "I know I've been counseling her to leave but she always refused to."

"You? You!" Harry said. "You've been trying to get her to leave, too?"

"I've been hoping to get her on her way before some kind of horrible catastrophe occurred," I said. "But I guess it's too late for that now."

"It sure is," Harry said. "Only it's not such a catastrophe."

"Please do talk to Louisa before you cut out," I said. I grinned. "You do owe me that, for our many years of friendship. Anyway, you have to go home to pack, don't you?"

"All right, I'll do that," he said. "I do have to pack."

"You didn't see Louisa at all this morning?"

"No. She was still asleep. Or at least she was still in the bedroom. I didn't go in there and she didn't come out."

"Please do talk to Louisa."

"Damn it, I said I would, didn't I?" Suddenly he yanked the Scotch bottle off my bar with a kind of furious gesture and poured some in his glass. He did not even bother with ice or soda. "Damn it, I can't understand why she would cut out like that, and not even tell me good-bye."

I did not answer. He drained off the straight Scotch and straightened up and looked at me with his hard, haggard eyes, and turned on his heel and walked to the door. From the door he said, "I'll stop back by on my way out of town."

"Okay, Harry," I said, and kept my mouth shut for the rest.

Well, it didn't work. It didn't work at all this time. He was back in about two hours and when he rang and I opened my door, I heard him set down two heavy suitcases on the ancient hexagonal tile that covers the entry on the ground floor.

"This stuff'll be all right here, won't it?" he called up.

"Sure, Harry," I said.

I went back inside and waited for him. I had been having a rather rough time. I certainly did not feel like eating anything. Especially since if I went out, I might miss Harry if he called or came back. There was some sliced ham in the refrigerator, and a baguette of bread from yesterday that was not yet stale, and there was mustard. But though my stomach was a little bit hungry, the rest of me wasn't. So I just sort of paced back and forth across the apartment, or looked out the windows at the river, and tried hard not to drink too much. I am not used to early in the day drinking. In spite of that I had at least three Scotches while I waited. I was expecting him to call, and tell me everything was all right, not for him to come back, and certainly not to come back with two loaded suitcases.

Well, he came up the stairs and into the place, in a kind of flood of energy, and availed himself of the bar. This time he did it quite calmly, carefully pouring himself a normal Scotch, adding ice from the bucket, adding soda. He did not say anything at all. Neither did I. I was not about to question him at this point.

"Well," he said finally, sipping from his drink and looking at me. "It was quite an experience."

I chose not to answer.

After a minute he began to talk. I looked away, out the window at the river, as I listened. I thought that might help. Louisa had been sitting in the living room, the salon, having her normal breakfast of coffee, juice and buttered toast. Normally, she was an early riser. She was wearing one of those sheer nightgowns of hers, with an even flimsier robe thrown over her shoulders over it, and her rather heavy breasts were both visible and excitingly noticeable through the stuff. Her eyes had that wide, stary look they had had the night of the Bobby-Kennedy-killing TV program.

"I came home last night," Harry said he said to her. "But then I left."

"Oh?" she said. Her lips sort of writhed at him, like two whipping snakes, in the exact same way I remembered them moving that other night, with me. "Why was that?"

"Because I didn't want to disturb you," Harry said.

"Disturb me?" Louisa said.

"At whatever it was you were doing. Whatever it was you and Samantha were doing," Harry said.

"Oh? Yes?"

"On the couch there." He waved his hand at it. "In the corner. The night light was still on, even."

"Ah, yes. I was trying to comfort the poor girl. It's strange I didn't hear you. But you could have come on in. The poor thing. She's never had a mother, you know, really." And she had looked at him with that wide, stary look, her lips writhing as she spoke.

"Comfort!"

Harry said it exploded out of him, but then he tried to get hold of himself, and smiled. "It didn't look much like comfort to me."

"Well, that was what it was," Louisa said calmly. "Why didn't you come on in? Oh, incidentally, she told me you had been sleeping with her. Is that true?"

"Yes, it's true," Harry said. "Or at least I was. She left Paris this morning for Rome, on her way to Israel. So I'm not sleeping with her any more."

"She did? Oh, good," Louisa said. "I advised her to do that. And she agreed with me. I thought she might get into a sort of insoluble situation, if she stayed around here and around you."

"Well, she left. She took your advice," Harry said.

"I'm glad," Louisa said calmly.

That was when he wanted to hit her, Harry said. Of course, he didn't. "Well, it may interest you to know that I'm going to Rome after her. If I don't catch her there, I'll follow her on to Tel Aviv and catch her there."

"Well, of course, that's your decision to make, isn't it?" Louisa said calmly, looking at him with that wide, stary look. She turned to go back to her breakfast.

"It sure is," Harry said with some heat. "Now, listen! Do you mean to try and tell me that you were *comforting* that girl when you were lying on that couch necking with her? You mean to tell me you didn't have sex with her?"

"You must be going out of your mind, Harry," Louisa answered calmly, looking up at him. She picked up a piece of buttered toast.

"What's wrong with you? I always knew you had a dirty mind. Are you?"

"Am I what?"

"Going out of your mind?" She bit into the buttered toast daintily, then picked up her coffee cup. Over it she stared at him calmly, with that wide-eyed, stary look. Then, looking away from him, she calmly went on with her breakfast.

He had stalked out of the room then. In the bedroom he threw some clothes in the two valises, and then carted them out into the hall. Louisa had not moved from her breakfast. He left. And here he was.

It was a pretty dismal tale, all the way around. I stood looking out the window a moment longer. I simply couldn't imagine Louisa, poor, dear, darling Louisa, having sex with that little girl, or any girl, particularly in the way Harry had said.

And yet, I thought, and yet. I was suddenly reminded of all those old New England and San Francisco ladies, who had all come over to Paris in the early 1900s. It wasn't only Gertrude Stein and Sylvia Beach and the other famous ones. There had been a whole exodus of them. And, whether from San Francisco or Boston, they had all had the same sort of background Louisa had had: liberal thinking, political, politically liberal, with a strong sense of public service and duty, and sexually repressed. And what had happened to them? What had they come for, to Paris, in fact? Because they were lesbians, down to the last one on the list. Lately, in the past three years, I had kept meeting nephews of theirs at parties, usually law graduates at some very good school, all come over to settle up some maiden aunt's estate, after her recent death. Always they looked apologetic. The old gals always had lived with "companions". Always they had bought themselves, out of their family's wealth, a quite nice if now old-fashioned apartment on the Left Bank, usually between the river and Boulevard St.-Germain. Always they had excellent English-language libraries.

It was the libraries that interested me. That was how I got into the whole thing. These nephews, all law graduates, were about as interested in books as they were in rugby. Sometimes less. They were always just about to give them to the American Library, which would be a chore. They didn't want to take the time to try and sell them. They certainly didn't want to have to pay to have them all packed up and shipped back to the States for sale. But their New England consciences wouldn't let them just leave them, in the apartments, which were all always going to be sold. My response was always, "Well, let me have a look at them. If there's anything there I want, I'll take care of the whole thing for you." All of them were always more than eager that I should do that for them. As I said, none of these young lawyers gave a damn about books. I guessed that in the past three years I had taken care of at least six libraries of maiden ladies from New England or San Francisco or from both. I found a number of marvelous rare books. There were at least three first editions of Joyce's *Ulysses,* the 1922 edition published by Sylvia Beach's Shakespeare & Co., two of them autographed by the great man to the maiden lady in question. And once I found a complete set of first editions of Vachel Lindsay, a little musty and moldy perhaps, but four of them were autographed by the author to the maiden lady who had them, or to her "friend". The rest, the things I didn't want, as I had promised, I packed up in my small car and carted over to the American Library for a donation given in the name of the lady. The young lawyers were always pleased to get rid of that chore.

But all of that only flashed through my mind in a series of thought-memories impressions. The main point was that if these ageing ladies from an earlier time, with the same identical background as Louisa, could have this particular hangup, why mightn't Louisa from a later generation have the same damned thing, only in a latent way, like one of those butterflies fixed and preserved in plastic?

"Well, what do you want me to tell you, Harry?" I said, turning back from the window.

"I don't want you to tell me anything, sport," he said. "Not a thing."

"What about this film you're working on?" I said. "You can't just up and leave it like that, can you?"

"The Western? Sure I can. I got a contract says I can stop and leave the production any time I don't like the way things are going. I always get that kind of contract. So, I don't like the way things are going."

"What about all those Cinema Committee kids, who are counting on you so much?"

"That's a lost cause, anyway. They haven't got a chance. Not in God's world. There just isn't enough good backlog film. You saw the stuff with me. They all mean well, they're just damned amateurs. They don't know their trade." It was about the worst condemnation Harry could give, I suspect. "I only did it for Hill, you know that. And now that dumb asshole has flown the coop. But I'm leaving them all my film anyway. I've set it up. They already have it."

"Did you do it *for* Hill, Harry?" I said. "Or did you do it in competition with him?"

"*For* him," Harry said. "You know that as well as I do. I would never have bothered to get myself involved, otherwise."

"Well, what about little McKenna," I said, "my Goddaughter?"

"Her?" he said. "Hell, she's fixed up better, and better off, than all of us. That young lady is likely to become the first female President of the benighted Nunited States."

"Maybe I better tell you about Hill," I said.

"What about him?" he said sharply.

"Well, I promised him I wouldn't tell either you or Louisa. But under the extraordinary circumstances that exist now I think I have the right to tell. He's gone off to Cadaqués. You know, where you went that summer two years ago. Apparently he fell in with a bunch of American hippies, or beatniks, or whatever they're called now. He's become a hippy Zen Buddhist, and renounced the world. He's gone down there to live in one of those caves outside of town and meditate."

Harry laughed suddenly. "Oh, that's only likely to last for a year or so. We all go through our period of that. Didn't you? Sure you did. Hell, in a year I'm likely to be back here, back in the old harness," Harry said. And then he grinned. "Or off somewhere in India or Bali, living it up."

He had come over to where I was, with his glass, and we were both standing on the sill looking out at the deeply throbbing barge traffic on the river, making its way upstream with loads of sand, or oil, or gravel.

"Well, what about Louisa?" I said.

"That one can certainly take care of herself, I think," he said in a cold tone.

And so there you were. He had apparently arranged everything about his flight to Rome, and beyond, with some executive and PR man at TWA that he knew. This man had been able to get him on the Rome flight at such short notice, particularly since he was going first class. The PR man had arranged for him only to pay tourist, but to ride up front in first. As, in fact, he had done for Samantha the day before, through Harry's instigation. He looked at his watch.

He stepped down from the sill and back into the room. "Can I call a cab from here, Jack?"

I did not turn away from the river, and did not answer for a moment. But then I thought what was the use? "Sure," I said softly. "Use my Chèque-Taxi number."

"Five minutes," he said, when he hung up the phone.

"They always say five minutes," I said. "Usually it's three."

It was three. We both stood in the window till the taxi came. Then Harry slapped me on the back and shook hands.

Down in the street on the quai, after he and the driver had stowed away his bags, he looked up and grinned a kind of glittering, eyes-bright, teeth-bright grin, and waved.

Then he climbed in and disappeared, and the cab moved off, and became lost in the traffic on the bridge.

25

I DID NOT GO DOWN to the Gallaghers' apartment that night, for the usual daily meeting of Americans. I just was not up to it. I dined alone and turned in early. I assume Louisa presided over it, in spite of the absences of Harry and Samantha. But then, she had done that before. Unless she brought it up, there would be no curiosity or distress because neither of them was there. So I assume she did not bring it up. Anyway, nobody, including Weintraub and Ferenc Hofmann-Beck, told me that anything unusual had happened Saturday.

On Sunday morning Louisa called me at about eleven-thirty. Fortunately, I was already up and had completed my toilet and had shaved. I was having my light, meager breakfast, preparatory to going out for the Sunday papers. There is no Paris *Herald* on Sunday, and I would have to walk up to St.-Germain-des-Prés to get the English Sundays that I liked, the *Times* and the *Observer*. The French do not have much of a tradition of Sunday papers. They have them of course, but it is not like the tradition we English-speaking peoples have for Sunday papers.

"I have to see you, Jack," she said into the phone. "I have to see you right away." She spoke in that peculiar toneless voice she had taken up in the past few days, since Bobby Kennedy's death. Although her lips writhed a lot, and she stared hard at you, the voice had taken on a peculiar tonelessness.

"All right, darling Louisa," I said. "I'm having breakfast. Will you have coffee with me? Shall we go out to an outdoor café? It's sunny today. It's Sunday." I tried hard to make it light.

"No. I want to see you by yourself," she said. "In your pad."

"Okay. I'll be here."

"Thank you," she said, in the tone of a young miss getting her diploma from a young ladies' finishing school.

I suppose all that should have warned me. It did not. It only took her a few minutes to get up to my place from their place further down the quai. I had moved my coffee tray out into the living room, and was sitting there still in my kimono, when she rang.

Well, she still had that wide-eyed, stary look and her lips still writhed. Staring about an inch above my head, she did not take long in getting to the point. She got to the point right away. After accepting a cup of coffee, which she did not even sip from, she said, "Jack, I would like for you to have an affair with me."

You must note here, if only in my own defense, that she did not say: "I want to have an affair with you." She said, "I would like for you to have an affair with me."

I tried to laugh it off. "Why, darling Louisa! Nothing would give me greater pleasure!" I said, and tried to grin impishly. "But you must know that I was raised in a very stern school. I couldn't possibly have an affair with my best friend's wife. It just isn't in me."

"Your best friend," she said, still staring an inch over my head. "I suppose you know Harry's left for Rome. Chasing after that little girl, that I tried so hard to help."

"Why, yes. I do know," I said. "He stopped by here on his way out of town to say good-bye."

"I thought you might. You know, I could have saved that little girl. If it had not been for him. I think she has some kind of a buried, latent nymphomania problem. I was getting her straightened out. Or I thought I was. But all the time everything I did was already negated beforehand by the fact that he was already sleeping with her. So—I want you to have an affair with me. To clean everything up."

"But darling Louisa, darling," I said. "You must know I can't do something like that."

"But, why not?" she said. Then she said an extraordinary thing. "You've always been in love with me."

I was knocked back. I wondered if I had been? Had I been giving her that impression, over the years? Was it her ego? Reflecting on it, in the few seconds left me, I decided that perhaps I had been. But it had not been that kind of love. It had not been the kind of love where I would want to see and fondle those nicely heavy breasts, peer at and kiss those tightening nipples that she must have, grope and rowel with my hand in that dark triangle of mystery to find the opening into her, that path, that opening that most women are so damned overly eager to have explored. It was not that kind of love I had for her. I had that kind of love for Martine, perhaps. But I didn't have it for Louisa.

"Louisa, I can't," I said in a kind of panic. "You must realize that. For me, you must realize it. At least let me think about it. Surely you don't want us to just up and take off our clothes and mate, fuck, here on my Second Empire couch, or on the floor, do you?" I choked a little on that one word. I was hoping it would snap her back.

"Why not?" she said, peering at something, some vision, just an inch above my head. "Yes, that's exactly what I do want. Exactly that."

She stood up, suddenly, and began taking off the jacket of her suit.

I stood up, and stopped her. I grabbed the shoulders of the jacket and made her slip her arms back into the sleeves, then pulled the collar onto her neck. She didn't resist me. Instead she let her head droop back, her eyes closed, prepared for kissing, her mouth a little bit open, but I did not kiss her. "Louisa, we simply can't do that. Not like that. Louisa, you're distraught."

"I suppose I am distraught," she said vaguely. Then she straightened up, and shook her jacket back into place, still staring at some point on my forehead just above my eyes. "Yes, I suppose I am. Yes, you're right. I guess it wouldn't have worked anyway," she said, vaguely. "Well, Jack, so long, I guess," she said. "Good-bye. We must see each other soon, you know. You must come for dinner." She was heading for the door.

"Louisa!" I cried. I was terribly distressed. "You have to realize I'm just not built that way! You must understand that!"

"Oh, I understand," she said. "I understand. I understand everything. Or almost."

"Louisa! I'm not rejecting you!" I cried.

"Oh, sure," she said. "I understand that. I understand that much.

Please do call. We'll have dinner soon." She went out and shut the door. She slammed it, but she did not slam it with any sense of fury or frustration. It was just a normal slam.

I sat down on my Second Empire couch and put my head in my hands.

I just never had thought of her that way.

She called me again that evening, around about eight-fifteen, I think it was. I had not eaten anything. But I had put away a certain, if not a sufficient, amount of Scotch. Just the same, the peculiar misery in me, the feeling of having made an irreparable mistake, burned up like a Bunsen burner all the alcohol in my blood and left my mind as clear and sober as a child's—and about as knowledgeable.

In any case, I was in full possession of my faculties, if not very happy, when she called. So I was able to get the tone.

"Jack?" she said.

"Yes. Yes, Louisa."

"Jack?" she said again. "Dear Jack. I've always been in love with you, you know. You didn't know that, did you? But I have. You are all the things that Harry has always pretended to be, but never really has been. I had to hide it, you know. You know. That was my duty. But I've always been in love with you, Jack. Since the time you came to us to start your review. Did you know that it was me who made Harry put the money in it? No, I suppose you didn't. And maybe it wasn't me who made him. I'm sure he wanted to himself. He just didn't have the courage. Anyway, your review is beautiful, Jack. It's much better than the *Paris Review*. And I've always loved you, Jack, since then. I just wanted to tell you." There was a silence then. There was a peculiar sing-song to her voice, a flat quality.

"Louisa? Louisa? Louisa, are you all right?" I said.

"Oh, yes," she said. "Oh, yes. Oh, yes, I'm fine. I'm going to Switzerland."

"You're what?" I demanded. "Switzerland?"

"Oh, yes," she said. "Switzerland. You know. Switzerland. It's beautiful there. St. Moritz. And you can meet everybody. At least, everyone who is anybody. And you can ski. You can ski off the tops of the mountains there. You know. Right off the tops of them, and you can float forever. I'm going to float forever. I'm going skiing. But always remember I've loved you, Jack, since the very first day you came to us. Please don't forget that."

"Louisa," I said. "Louisa? You're going skiing?"

"Oh, yes," she said. "Oh, yes. I'm going skiing. I'm going skiing, Jack. Oh, it's so beautiful, skiing. Right off the tops of them. And down below there is nothing but the pure, white snow. Pure. And white. No evil, no dirt, no filth. A few cottages of faithful villagers, who love their cows and their land. Don't want to kill. And there you are up there, way up in the air, and it all belongs to you, and you love it. Oh, yes. I'm going skiing, Jack. Good-bye, my love, my darling love. My lovely Jack." She hung up and the phone went cold stone dead.

I was in a panic. I didn't know whether she had flipped her mind or what, but I knew instinctively something bad had happened somewhere. And I thought I ought to get down there. I hadn't eaten anything, and I hadn't dressed. That scene of the morning had really done me in. I threw off my kimono, and bare naked dragged on a pair of chino slacks, an old shirt and a jacket, loafers without socks. I ran all the way to their apartment, which was more than three blocks.

Well, it was a pretty awful scene. A bad scene. In the time it took me to get there after her phone call she had become unconscious and her maid had found her. The sweet, lumpish Portuguese lady, a friend of my own Portuguese, was on her knees beside the big daybed couch in the center of the living room, wringing her hands and wailing. When I knelt and tried to find a pulse in Louisa's delicate fine-boned wrist, the Portuguese mumbled something in a high piercing shriek, and ran out the door.

Fortunately, McKenna was in bed asleep of course. Louisa had calculated that. She had also left the front door unlocked, so that I was able to barge right in. Had she calculated that, also? So she could leave herself room for me to come and save her? At that moment I thought so. Later on, when I saw what she had taken, I changed my mind.

She had dressed herself for the occasion. She was wearing one of her sheerest, flimsiest robes, perhaps the same one Harry had described to me the day before. She would do that. Under it she had on a fine-textured white bra through which the two dark spots of her nipples showed like two dark eyes, and below a very brief, very low-waisted pair of panties through which the dark of her triangular bush made itself visibly felt.

I did not bother with any of that. I was unable to find any pulse in her wrist, but she was a fine-veined person, delicate, and probably had a light pulse. So I pushed my fingers into her neck above the collarbone, but I could not be sure I could feel a pulse there, either. Where was that damned Portuguese? I put my ear to her mouth and nose, but if there was any breathing at all it was very shallow and light. With my thumb I peeled back one eyelid, and an apparently insensate eyeball that seemed dilated stared back at me glassily.

I considered giving her mouth-to-mouth resuscitation, but I thought I ought to get an ambulance on the road first, right away, beforehand, so I got up to go to the phone. But then I thought that they might ask me about what she had taken, and give me advice about emergency treatment, so I ran into the bedroom to look. Sure enough, on the bedside table there was a large aspirin bottle, totally empty, and there was a large tinfoil plaque of sleeping suppositories, empty also, eight or nine of them. There was also a Nembutal bottle, empty too. I had already noticed that there was a glass and a half empty bottle of vodka on the floor beside her beside the couch. Apparently she had taken enough stuff to kill a whole army. That was when I changed my mind about the unlocked door.

I dialed the American Hospital in Neuilly for an ambulance. I thought it was better to call them, rather than the police, because of the question of public scandal. The French police take a dim view of suicide, and an unsuccessful one can be prosecuted as at least a misdemeanor, I believe, if not as a felony, if they wanted to push it. But as the phone was ringing, a French doctor with a small beard and wearing a dark suit darted into the apartment carrying his black bag. Apparently he lived around the corner, and the faithful Portuguese had gone to get him.

Then the phone was answered. "Will you please send an ambulance immediately to number 49 Quai de Bourbon?" I said into it. "Yes, the third floor."

The little doctor had knelt down to examine her. "Who are you calling?" he said, in French.

"The American Hospital," I said.

"It's too far," he said immediately. "They'll never get here in time. Call the police. We'll take her to the Hôtel-Dieu, on Île de la Cité."

"Really?" I said.

"Her heart has stopped," he said. "I don't know for how long. I'm giving her a shot of Neosynepheraine. That may start it again. But we must get her to a hospital very fast. And the police camions carry oxygen bottles."

"Yes, sir," I said. "Fine. I'm dialing them."

"If her heart has stopped for over four or five minutes, she could have serious brain damage. Even if we save her."

I dialed. The weeping Portuguese had retired to a corner, where she sat wringing her hands, and wailing. The police answered, took the message very efficiently, and hung up. I knelt, staring at the black phone I had replaced in its cradle. The doctor was working over Louisa. And suddenly, I became furious. Why are we trying to save her? I thought. If some stupid bitch wants to die, why not let her? Why are we so concerned with the saving of life? But we were. We all were. And suddenly, I was furious at the unconscious Louisa. I wanted to go to the big couch and turn her over and kick her in her unconscious ass. What was she doing to us, and how dare she?

The doctor was still working over her. "It's started again," he said suddenly, and leaned back. "And she is breathing." There was an enormous look of relief on his small bearded face. "I just hope it hasn't stopped for long enough to cause brain damage."

"I can't tell you," I said. "When I arrived I didn't find any pulse, but I don't know for how long that state existed. And the Portuguese didn't take her pulse. Doesn't know how."

He nodded. Then he rose, looking tired. I wanted to embrace him.

Outside there was a siren. Swiftly it grew louder, then much louder, then stopped. Seconds later four efficient French cops came marching up the last of the stairs in large boots and into the room, carrying a stretcher and an oxygen bottle with a nose-mouth mask.

They were an efficient team. One man turned on the oxygen, another held the mask over her face, the other two opened the stretcher and unceremoniously yanked her soft female's body off the couch onto the stretcher, tucked a blanket around her, and started for the door, the man holding the oxygen tank walking alongside.

"I better go with them," I said.

"Yes," the doctor said. "Do you know exactly what she took?"

"I don't know how much. But there is a large bottle of aspirin, empty. There is a sheaf of eight or nine sleeping suppositories, also empty. Also a bottle of Nembutal. A bottle of twenty, empty. And there was a half empty bottle of vodka beside the couch."

"My God!" the little doctor said. Again, I wanted to embrace him. Instead, I shook hands with him warmly.

"You had better take the evidence," he said. "To help the doctors."

I ran into the bedroom. We had already been heading for the door. Downstairs the policemen were all ready to go. I waved to the doctor. Then, siren beeping in that peculiar two-toned sound French sirens have, we wheeled around the end of the Island, and crossed the Pont Louis-Philippe to the Right Bank, heading for the Hôtel-Dieu on Île de la Cité. One of the policemen, the one who was holding the mask over Louisa's mouth and nose, looked over at me and winked, and made a face and shrugged.

In the little camion there was no sound except the sound of the oxygen pouring from the bottle, and the sound of Louisa's labored breathing.

I had never been inside the Hôtel-Dieu before. It faced on the square called Place du Parvis Notre-Dame just in front of Notre-Dame, which is where they used to pull people apart with horses for having committed some crime or other. The assassin of Henri Quatre was dismembered that way there. Hôtel-Dieu had a medieval look about it, at least from the outside, and I believe it had been started, a long way back, as a maternity hospital. There were two rows of trees out in front on the square, and a marvelous old pissoir. I must have walked by it a million times, mainly because I liked in warm weather to utilize the old pissoir, but as I said I had never had occasion to go inside.

Well, that police camion wheeled in there as though it had been doing it for scores of years, as it may well have done. Inside, behind the great oaken doors, there was a beautiful medieval courtyard, all paved with cobbles, with high slender lovely columns all around it. Almost before I could follow, those four policemen had the stretcher with Louisa on it out of the camion and inside to the all-night emergency room. A young Doctor Kildare complete with stethoscope and white jacket looked her over in the hall and whisked her into the emergency room, where I was not allowed to follow. The policemen shook hands with me and left. So I sat down on one of the benches there in the hall and waited.

They must have worked on her for about fifteen minutes. During that time I saw three other emergency cases brought in by other policemen. One was an old man who had been mugged somewhere in Montmartre, a poor man, I don't see why anyone would want to mug him, who had had his head cracked open by his attacker. Another was a young man who had had an automobile confrontation with a city bus. He had a large blue lump as big as two eggs on his forehead, and his eyes did not track, though he could sort of walk, if aided by two police. The third was a knifing victim of some fight in Pigalle, a pimp probably. He was carried in on a stretcher, and uttered not a sound from his pale face. All of them were whisked into the emergency room immediately. Finally, the young Doctor Kildare came out and looked for me.

"Do you know what she took?" he said in French.

I produced the bottles and the tinfoil suppository container. "Also a lot of vodka. The bottle was there by the couch. I don't know how much of these," I said. "But the maid told me she had just bought the aspirin that day."

The young doctor made up his mouth as if to whistle but actually made no sound. "Well, I think we can save her," he said. "But I'm not absolutely certain. She must badly have wanted to go. Anyway, you might as well go on home. There's nothing you can do more now. It will be several days before we will know."

They had just instituted a new intensive-care unit in the Hôtel-Dieu, and apparently they had taken her up there by another exit corridor. The young Doctor Kildare seemed very proud of the new unit. If anybody could save her, they could do it up there, he said.

"Are you her husband?"

"No. Just a friend," I said. "A friend of the family. I found her."

"She seems to think that you are her husband," he said.

I shrugged. "Well, I'm not."

We shook hands. I thanked him and walked out of there into the cool fresh night. In the medieval court with the columns the ambulance from the American Hospital was waiting. The maid had sent them to Hôtel-Dieu after us. Of course, now we didn't need them. I told them to go on back, and paid them. It wasn't so much.

Then I started home. The cool fresh air felt marvelous on my face. I walked along the side of Notre-Dame up river to the Pont St. Louis, crossed the ugly old Bailey bridge, then walked up the quai to my apartment.

I drank three Scotches looking out the window at the dark, flowing river.

Finally, I took a Mogadon and went to bed.

I knew there would be a big day tomorrow.

26

FOR THE NEXT FIVE DAYS I did not pay much attention to the Revolution. It took them that long, five days, to declare definitely that Louisa was out of the woods. Though she had babbled once something or other, to the young Doctor Kildare I met, she afterwards lapsed into a coma and did not come to until the fifth day. I was over there every day, damned near all day, although there wasn't really anything I could do and they must have gotten damned sick of seeing me.

Of course, I didn't entirely lose track. I would scan the papers in the morning, and later when I got back home, but I must admit I didn't take too much interest.

For instance, on the Monday of June 10th a young student of 18 was killed, drowned in the river, out at Flins, where workers and students were still demonstrating and fighting the police. Drowned in the Seine, in the good old Seine, in water that had flowed right past my windows, and that I had probably stared at in the dead of the night. The police claimed he, along with some others, had thrown himself in the river to escape an identity check, but could not swim. The students claimed that it was an "assassination", that the police had deliberately pushed him in. This was almost the first death to occur in the entire Revolution. At Lyons, earlier, a police commissioner had been crushed against a wall by a runaway truck full of stones which students had released and let run down an incline, but that could hardly be called deliberate. Then, a little later, a young man (apparently not a student) had been knifed outside a café-bar in the rue Soufflot in Paris in some altercation over a girl. Police were not involved in that at all. Now we had the Flins case, but it was impossible to tell who was lying to us in the press for propaganda reasons. That night, Monday, student demonstrations broke out all over the Latin Quarter and a number of fires were lit, before police drove the students off with tear gas and percussion grenades. The police, as the Government had warned and promised, were acting tougher now, and the students were no match for them.

But I was really not very interested. I did not go out to watch. I had Louisa to worry about.

On the Monday they told me at the hospital that her condition was very grave. She was surviving, in the new intensive care unit, but she was not showing any signs of recuperating. I was allowed to see her.

For some reason it seemed this case had been taken on by all the young nurses and doctors of the intensive care unit as a personal challenge. I sat by her bedside for more than two hours.

I must say, it was not a very pretty sight. If Louisa had been conscious, she certainly would have thought it undignified. They had her under this plastic tent, completely nude. A young nurse was constantly in attendance. Louisa's body (I hesitate to say Louisa) was constantly sweating profusely, and the nurse was constantly mopping her off. There were tubes up both her nostrils, and her arms were strapped down to the bed. Above her left arm hung a glucose bottle, its needle taped into a vein in the arm. If I had ever wondered about her nipples and her bush, I did not have to wonder any more. Her legs were sprawled, so that even the labia minora peeped through. But the attendants couldn't have cared less about that. And neither could I.

I sat by the bed and talked to her under the plastic tent. Of course, I didn't know if she could hear me, but I thought it was worth the try. The young nurses and the doctors said she wasn't trying, so I kept telling her that she had to try. I thought it might get through. If only she could hear me. If only she could hear me, even in her unconscious mind.

After two hours of it, I was exhausted. I left, walking out past the beds of all the halt and the injured. In one bed I recognized the poor old poor man who had been brought in mugged while I waited in the basement emergency room the night before. His eyes were not tracking, and he did not seem to see anything.

It was a nice walk home, alongside the sprawl of Notre-Dame. The day was sunny and I stayed on the sunny side. There are some nice little cafés there, tourist cafés, and I stopped in one of them for a drink. When I got back to the apartment, I put in a call to Harry in Rome.

I was pretty sure he would be staying at the Excelsior on Via Veneto, and sure enough he was. But he was out, the clerk said. He was out having lunch somewhere, I supposed. I said I would call back, and left my name, after carefully spelling it. Then I went out and had some lunch myself.

When I got back home and called back, he was in. Apparently he had waited for me.

"Did you try to call me?" I said.

"Yes. But there wasn't any answer." There was a pause. "What's up? Why are you calling me?"

I considered. "Louisa's in the hospital," I said.

"Oh? She is? What for?" Harry said.

I was beginning to feel irritated. "A suicide attempt," I said. "She apparently took enough stuff to knock off a whole damned army of guys."

Again there was a pause. "Well, how's she doing?" he said finally.

"Not so very good," I said. "She's in a coma. Her heart had stopped. I found her. I took her there in a police van, with oxygen. They're trying to save her. But they say she may die."

"Christ," he said. "Oh, shit." Again there was a pause. "Well, look. Keep me informed on what happens. You can always get me here at this time of the afternoon. I won't leave today."

"Leave for where?"

"Tel Aviv," he said.

"Samantha has gone?" I said.

"I missed her by about three hours."

I was really angry now. "Well, look, Harry," I said coldly. "I'm not going to arrange the God damned funeral for you. There is a limit to what a friendship can ask."

There was a pause on the line. "I suppose if she dies, I'll have to come back, won't I?"

"If you want to get her buried, you will," I said furiously. "I know I sure as hell aint going to do it."

"Oh, somebody would," he said. "Edith de Chambrolet. Have you called Edith?"

"No, not yet," I said. "I was trying to keep it quiet."

"Well, call her. Call Edith. She's a do-gooder. She loves to do good works."

I thought I had never heard anything so absolutely calloused in my life. Then he said, suddenly, "Look, you know, she's done this a couple of times before. And I've bailed her out of it. At great financial and spiritual cost to myself. I'm getting tired of it."

"Oh? I didn't know that," I said.

"Well, it's true. We've tried to keep it quiet. Once out on the Coast, at a lake. And once here in Europe ten years ago, when she was visiting in England. She almost didn't come back from a country weekend. I flew over. But I'm getting God damned tired of it."

"Well, I'm getting damned tired of it, too," I said. "Hell, Harry, I never even fucked the woman, you know." I was furious. "You did," I said.

"Maybe you should," he said.

"Thanks a lot," I said, and stopped talking. I was boiling.

"Look," he said finally after a short silence. "Call me back tomorrow and tell me how it goes. Will you? I'll cancel my reservation for Tel Aviv. So I'll be here at the hotel at this same time tomorrow. Okay?"

"Yes," I said caustically. "I'll call you back at the same time tomorrow, Harry. With whatever news." And I hung up.

I was so angry I went to my bar and had three Scotches in a row, staring out the window at the river.

He had told me to call Edith de Chambrolet. I did. I had met Edith at their place for the first time, and afterwards had had dinners with her frequently at her place. Large dinners, always very formal, eight to 12 people. Edith was a remarkable person. She was one of the richest women in America, and had married some impoverished French Count and had four sons by him, all of whom were now grown up and gone from the nest. To occupy herself she had taken up the study of Anthropology and was taking courses in it at the Sorbonne. She also believed in Oceanography, thought it was the only way to save the Earth from the population explosion, and had taken skindiving lessons as well as taking current courses in Marine Geology and Marine Biology. She had become an expert on shark identifications, for example. She spoke with just about the broadest, drawling A I have ever heard, and had stary eyes. There was something enormously sexually attractive about her, but she had never given me any signal, and I had never tried. But I liked her a lot.

"But dahhhling," she said, when I told her the whole story. "Of course I'll come." I can't begin to spell the way she talked.

"Can you be at my place tomorrow at ten, then?" I said.

"Of course I'll be there. We must straighten this thing out. You know, this isn't the first time. I know the whole story."

Apparently, in spite of Harry's attempt to keep it quiet, Edith knew all, though I had never heard of it anywhere before.

She arrived promptly at ten. I had had my Portuguese wake me early, and was up and dressed. Together we walked over across the bridge and down past Notre-Dame to the Hôtel-Dieu.

"You mustn't worry," Edith said as we went in through the court of slender columns. "This is a marvelous place. If anybody can save her, they can do it here. I've checked the place out."

She rapped on the uniformed guard's door brusquely.

"She's such a real idiot and moron, Louisa," she said as we climbed the old stone stairs. "She should get herself a young man. One of those faggot types that are always in attendance. An Italian hairdresser. They all look like fags, but we girls all know amongst ourselves that they're not really fags at all, darling."

As we walked in through the bed rows of beat-up, near-dead people, she said, "Isn't it marvelous, now? Extraordinarily efficient."

I was tongue-tied, and felt totally incapable, with her there.

"Now, Louisa," she said at the bed, lifting up one side of the plastic oxygen tent. "We must stop all this nonsense. We must pull ourselves together and I know that you will." She let the tent flap drop. "We'll talk to her again a little later. Let it sink in, first. I'm sure she heard us. In her unconscious."

We stayed about an hour, and Edith talked to Louisa once more, after checking the lapsed time on her watch. "Marvelous place," she said as we walked out. "Just look at the technology. It's a great innovation for France. I only wish they could do the same in business."

"What are we going to do about McKenna?" I said, as we came out of the great oaken doors under the two rows of trees. Up ahead, toward the Notre-Dame side, I saw my handsome old pissoir.

"Well, she can always stay with me, darling," Edith said.

"Maybe that's what we ought to do," I said.

"But of course. But I think we should wait a day or two, get a real prognosis on Louisa, before we decide that. What have you told her?"

"I haven't told her anything so far," I said. "I just told the Portuguese to keep her damned mouth shut. At least in front of McKenna. I tried to scare her badly. I think I did."

"Good," Edith said. "Fine. They will talk, domestics. It's what they have in life instead of drink."

We had come abreast of the old circular pissoir. "Do you mind?" I murmured.

"But, darling! Of course I don't mind!"

So while I went into the pissoir and had my leak, relieved myself, Edith stood outside and talked to me through the open top in the light summer breeze.

"Men always have to pee when they're nervous," she said in that drawly voice. "Women, on the other hand, find trouble holding their water when they're terrified, deeply in love, or about to drop a child."

"Yes," I said, coming back out. "I've noticed that."

"*Have* you?" Edith smiled, as we went on. "Now, about McKenna. I think the very best thing is just to tell her that mother was taken sick, and is in the hospital, and that she should come stay with me until momma is better."

"I would take her myself," I said. "But being a bachelor—"

"And sot in his ways," Edith said.

"Yes. Somewhat. Also, I only have this one rather neurotic Portuguese lady servant."

"Don't say servant," Edith said crisply. "They don't like to be called servants any more. They like to be called domestics."

"I don't really see how I can take her," I said. "But after all, I am her Godfather."

"Absolutely not," Edith said. "You couldn't possibly. Anyway, McKenna and I are great friends. We'll get along fine in my house out there."

"Could you possibly come to my place and wait out the afternoon?" I said. "Until McKenna gets back from school? It'll only be until four-thirty." Suddenly I wondered if I had designs on Edith without knowing it.

"Darling, I couldn't possibly!" Edith said. "I have a class. The Sorbonne is closed, but we meet privately, with the professor. At three-forty-five. In Marine Biology. But I'll tell you what. I'll meet you at the Gallaghers' at around seven, when all the Americans are congregating. I understand you've kept that up. After the news, we'll talk to McKenna alone, you and I, and explain our lie about what's happened, and then I'll take her home with me. It's much better than leaving her with their hysterical Portuguese, I think. Don't you?"

"Yes," I said. "I do."

"Could you possibly call me a cab from your place, darling?"

"Of course," I said.

We were just crossing the old Bailey bridge of Pont St. Louis. There was a fine breeze.

I called Harry back that night in Rome, a second time.

"How is she?" he said immediately.

"No change," I said. "No visible change."

"Well, all right," he said. "I'll stay here another night, and another, and another. And *another*. Until we find out the ultimate prognosis. But, well, if she doesn't die, I'm not coming back."

"Do you expect me to take care of her, Harry?"

"Well, no. Of course not. But there's Edith. We have lots of friends there, lady friends, in Paris. Edith can organize them. She'll love it."

"McKenna is going to stay with her," I said. "I saw Edith today."

"Good," Harry said.

"What if Louisa has brain damage?" I said.

"What brain damage?" Harry said.

"Well, the doctor who gave her the shot to start her heart going again, after a stoppage of we don't know how many minutes exactly, said if it was over four or five minutes, she might have permanent brain damage. That apparently means she'll be a vegetable, or half vegetable."

"That means we'll have to put her permanently in some kind of a sanatorium, won't it?" he said.

"Yes," I said. "Am I supposed to take care of that?"

"Of course not," he said. "I'll get somebody to take care of it. If it becomes a necessity."

"Okay, Harry," I said. "I think that's very kind of you."

"Fuck you!" he cried suddenly. "You don't know what I've been through."

"You don't know what I've been through, either," I said. "I've been through a lot of things. In my time."

"Well, I've been through a bunch myself," he said.

"Yes, but it's not my wife," I said.

"I know it's not your wife," he said. "I never claimed it was."

"Well, just lay off of me!" I said. "I'll go and visit your God damned wife! In that damned intensive care unit! But don't ask me to do any more than that!"

"I'm not asking you to do anything," he said.

"Go and fuck yourself!" I cried. "Of course you are! You're asking me to save your damned wife's life! And I'm not at all sure I want the God damned job! Listen, I guess you know I think you're a cheap fucker, and a totally irresponsible man, totally irresponsible husband and father! Don't you?" And I hung up, slammed down the phone.

Then I realized I had forgotten to tell him I would call him back tomorrow. I worried about that a little, but I didn't feel up to putting through another call to him. And I guessed he knew me well enough to know I would call.

The next day Louisa did not appear to be any better. Her condition had not deteriorated, the doctors at the Hôtel-Dieu told me. She had not sunk. But they had been hoping for a massive move back toward normalcy, after treatment. And this had not occurred. I sat by her bed for an hour or more in the late morning, trying to talk fight into her. Edith had said she would do the same thing later in the afternoon. Louisa's stentorious breathing was a very enervating thing to be around. I left and went down past Notre-Dame, feeling exhausted, and crossed the bridge to the Brasserie for some lunch. There was no point in my even thinking about working.

Apparently everybody on the damned Island knew the whole story. Madame Dupont left her cash box and came over to my table to ask about her.

"Et comment va la pauvre Madame Gallagher?"

I said not bad, and that I thought she'd be all right. Later, when she came in, the little daughter came and asked me the same thing. I gave her the same answer. After saucisses and choucroute I went home and lay down on my bed. My Portuguese came and stood by the door and asked me the same question.

I called Harry again that evening in Rome, and gave him my latest report. He had apparently been in touch with the hospital authorities in the Hôtel-Dieu, who had told him the same as what I told him.

"I was afraid you might not call back," he said over the phone. "But I should have known."

"Oh. You know me," I said feebly. "But I want you to know that I still think you're a prick. A prime prick."

"I suppose I am," he said slowly. "It's just that— It's just that, I thought of all people you might understand me when I told you I couldn't help it."

"Well, you ought to be able to help it," I said with some heat.

"I suppose I should," Harry said, "I suppose I should." This time it was he who hung up in my ear.

The day before a series of street battles had spread all through Paris. Students and workers were out all over the place, battling thousands of helmeted police and CRS. Another death had been reported in the morning, this time a worker in a town called Sochaux near the Swiss border, where a strikebound factory full of sit-ins was being cleared out by police. Union leaders claimed the bullet which killed the worker, a young man of 24 named Jean Beylot, was a 9 mm bullet. Many of the police were armed with 9 mm handguns. The police, of course, claimed—and proved—that workers and rioters had robbed police vans of guns and ammunition, and said that none of their men had fired any shots.

In any case, it set off in Paris another frantic day of rioting. In Toulouse, in southern France, a demonstration by 2,500 students turned into a melée with the police in which the students set up a large number of barricades and burned out the Gaullist election headquarters.

I had not gone out. I had the feeling that it was the last flurry before the end, and anyhow, I was too worried about Louisa. But the police and troops had gotten much tougher now, and a strict curfew was imposed on the Latin Quarter, and the students were really no longer any match for them. It was tapering off, or would soon. The consensus of public opinion was no longer with the students. Lots of workers wanted to get back to work. That night I had stood in my windows drinking Scotch, while across the river the Latin Quarter blazed with action and burning cars. Percussion grenades by the hundreds cracked their explosions across the water and into my ears, lighting the tops of the buildings with their flashes. I stood and watched it, and thought about Louisa.

I could not escape the feeling that if I had been more thoughtful and considerate, that if I had realized what was really bothering her when she came and asked me to have an affair with her, and had gone ahead and done it, then she would not be where she was now. So that, in a way, it was my fault, and I was guilty.

Still, I just don't see how I could have done it like that, on such short notice.

Late Wednesday the doctors said she had improved a little, slightly. At least, her blood pressure was more nearly back to normal.

27

FOR THE NEXT THREE DAYS I kept in constant touch with Harry in Rome. This was fairly easy since all the Government postal, telephone and telegraph people were now back at work. Harry remained adamant about not coming back unless Louisa actually died. And even then he was not absolutely sure.

He seemed to care nothing for her at all. Although, I have to admit, he said several times that he felt sorry for her. He seemed to actively detest her and have no patience with her at all since the night he saw her with Samantha.

Louisa, or I should say Louisa's body, was showing marked improvement on Thursday. At least, physically—in her blood pressure, pulse, temperature, breathing capacity, etc. But she remained in the coma.

Then on Friday she came to, throwing an enormous fit, and thrashing about. She managed to work one arm loose and tore the glucose needle out of her arm. Fortunately, they were able to get to her and hold her down before she could tear the tubes out of her nostrils, which might have done her really serious damage. And after that they strapped her down completely, legs and all.

After the Tuesday night rioting, there was a sort of cooling off, and nothing much happened during the next two days. There were a couple of interesting developments that appeared in the papers, however.

On Wednesday, after the two nights of renewed rioting in Paris, the French Government officially banned all street demonstrations throughout France. They would be banned indefinitely, and at least until after the National Election campaign. They also dissolved seven extreme-left student groups. The decisions were made and approved at a cabinet meeting presided over by de Gaulle himself.

The principal group banned was the 22nd of March Movement of young *Dany le Rouge* Cohn-Bendit, who was now in London, seeking political asylum, and posing for news photos in front of the gravestone of Karl Marx—whom, if I understood Hill Gallagher right, Dany had consistently repudiated in favor of Anarchism.

The ban on the seven groups meant that the Government could seize their offices, that they could not hold meetings, publish newspapers or have bank accounts. Although, none of this was likely to bother the 22nd of March Movement which had never had any official organization.

And on Thursday, Thursday the 13th, the Paris *Herald* carried a front-page piece on the fact that it appeared likely that le Général in the next few days would pardon the remaining Army Officers still in jail because of the celebrated "Generals' Putsch" in Algeria back in 1961. One of them was General Salan, one of the leaders, and another was some hot-shot Colonel named Jean Lacheroy. The rumor was all over that this was part of the deal le Général had had to make with the Army, in order to get their backing. Certainly, it was not going to alienate any Rightist votes for Gaullist candidates in the up-coming Assembly elections.

Right alongside, another article, continued on the second page, told how the student rebels of the Sorbonne were planning an evacuation in order to "clean house". They were afraid the police might try to take them over on the grounds of health and sanitation. So they were going to scrub the place down, get rid of all the garbage, and in the process throw out a group of young toughs who called themselves "les Katangais", who were inhabiting one corner of the huge Sorbonne cellars. I knew nothing of the "Katangais", but I could testify to the fact that they ought to get rid of the garbage. It would be a good thing.

On Friday, the day that Louisa came surging and fighting out of her coma, the police took back the Odéon from the students. There was not any fighting. Everybody left quietly. The lions were turning into lambs.

The newspapers gave conflicting and garbled accounts of it. But apparently the Government's reason, or excuse, for the move was that they wanted to oust a group of "mercenaries" who had taken refuge in the Odéon after being thrown out of the Sorbonne. Apparently, these were "les Katangais". In their "clean-up" campaign, as they had promised, the students had also cleaned out the "mercenaries" in the Sorbonne's basement. Apparently the name "Katangais" came from the fact that one of the leaders of the group claimed to have been a mercenary in the Congo fighting. Whether this was true, no one seemed to know. Several other armed and organized groups were ousted with them by the students, but the "Katangais" were the only ones who put up any fight. In any case, 80 students overwhelmed the 30 "Katangais" in less than half an hour, and no one was seriously hurt. So it could not have been much of a "battle".

This apparently was when the "Katangais" descended on the Odéon, and now late on Friday morning the police were knocking at the door, on the pretext of getting out the dangerous mad-dog "mercenaries", but incidentally clearing everybody else out at the same time. They sent in a young doctor who had been working there in the students' hospital with a message that anybody who left of his own accord would not be arrested. About 130 came out, several of them young student mothers with what appeared to be new-born babies, but of the 75 who stayed inside, a lot of them hospital patients and personnel, none offered any resistance when the police entered. The "Katangais", apparently, had quickly shaved and cut their hair and changed their clothes in order to walk out with the students, but several of them were recognized anyway and apprehended. The first thing the police did inside was to remove the big red and black flags that floated on the roof and replace them with the Tricolor. So, the month-long, 24-hours-a-day "cultural dialogue" was finally ended. And the Odéon had fallen, back into Government hands.

There were reports in the French afternoon papers that day about how filthy the students had left the place, but they said that nothing had been seriously damaged except for the costume department, where all helmets, shields and spears had disappeared.

I could not help feeling a little nostalgic. And I could not help wondering what had happened to our poor little Cinema Committee. But Weintraub, who stopped by the Gallaghers' apartment that night, told me that evening that they had moved to the Sorbonne, as had most of the other student committees housed there. But what about all their files, and their film? I wanted to know. Oh, they had gotten those out before, Weintraub told me, about two hours before the police arrived. The minute the "Katangais" had moved in they had begun getting their things out. I nodded, and then asked Weintraub over to Harry's pulpit bar to have a drink.

I had, as Edith said, kept up the evening meetings at the Gallaghers, even though now there were no Gallaghers there, including McKenna. I somehow felt Louisa would want me to do that. I suppose I am a sentimentalist. But I told their Portuguese to stock up on booze and to lay out the bread and plates of different sausages and hams as usual, all paid for by me of course. I told the other guests only that Louisa had been taken ill. If any of them knew the truth, they did not mention any suicide attempt. It was only on Sunday, the Sunday of June 16th, when I began these papers, that I stopped the evenings, and told the Portuguese to turn off the lights and lock the place up. That was the night Weintraub, I suppose with nowhere else to go, stopped by my place.

The maid, of course, had been retained by Harry to come in once a day and clean and take care of things.

They moved Louisa, in an ambulance, to the American Hospital in Neuilly on Saturday. The whole thing was handled by the American-trained French doctor we knew who worked there, and whom all of us, including Edith and Weintraub, used as our doctor. I had called him up on Friday evening. He was a remarkable man, and an excellent doctor, who worked himself into exhaustion just about every day. His name was Dax, like the colonel in Humphrey Cobb's novel, and he had the same humanitarian qualities as the colonel. I was not worried he would not handle it perfectly. I did not feel up to riding out with her myself, but Edith de Chambrolet went with her. It had already been established that she had a certain amount of brain damage, maybe a considerable amount. The thing now was to establish just how much.

I had visited her on Friday. I had called the Hôtel-Dieu that morning, and they had told me how she had come out of the coma fighting and tearing.

"Come," the nurse said, "but don't come until late in the afternoon."

When I arrived, walking in past all those sad, horrifying beds, the glucose bottle and the needle in her arm had disappeared, and the tubes in her nose were gone also. But she was still nude and under the oxygen tent and still strapped down, this time with straps across her legs and thighs and chest stretched all across the bed. Her eyes were glassy.

Her stomach seemed strangely swollen and bloated, and I commented on this.

"Well, she's had a lot of water, fluid in her lungs, you see," the nurse told me in French. "That was one of the worst problems."

She could move her head, and she rolled it over toward me and stared at me rather wildly. For a while she said nothing. "Do I know him?" she said finally, in a husky whisper.

"Yes, dear," the nurse said, and smiled and nodded sadly. "She's had some throat damage, too," she said to me. "From the tubes. We don't know yet just how much."

"I'm Jack," I said to Louisa in English.

"Jack," she said, as if tasting the name for the first time. She seemed to have more trouble with English than with French. Then she made a ghastly smile. "Well, hello, darling! How are you!" It was as if she was having trouble remembering the words.

"I'm all right, I'm fine," I said. "But you've given us a pretty scary time."

She simply stared at me as though this had no meaning for her at all. Then she rolled her head to the other side toward the nurse. "Is he one of them?" she said in her husky whisper in French.

"No, dear," the nurse smiled. "He's not one of them." She stood up. "I'll leave you alone," she said to me. "I have to get back." She spread her arm toward the other beds down the ward. "There's so much to do."

I thought, there certainly was.

"They're trying to get to me," Louisa said in French after she had gone. "They're trying to do things to me."

"They saved your life," I said in English.

"They're trying to do horrible things to me," Louisa said in French.

"No, they're not," I said in English. "They're trying to help you. Help you get well."

"They're trying to do terrible things to me," Louisa said in French. "I know."

There did not seem to be anything more for me to say on that. There was a chair beside the bed and I pulled it up and sat down.

"Will you loosen that strap on my arm a little? It's hurting me," Louisa said, in English now, but with that strange seeming to fumble over the words. "I know what they're doing. Believe I do. I see them. I see them coming and going. They move all around me. In and out. Really they do."

I did not say anything, but moved forward to the slip buckle of the strap across her arms and chest. It did look awfully tight.

Well, I was totally unprepared for what happened next. I slipped the buckle just the tiniest fraction. But before I could do anything more than that, as quick as a cat Louisa had her arm out, was slipping the buckle on her other arm, then bending to slip the buckle on the strap across her thighs, then the one across her ankles, and then was sitting up and swinging her legs over and pushing the oxygen tent aside. Her feet were already on the floor.

I was astounded. "Stop!" I cried. "Stop!" I had to dive in under the oxygen tent and throw my whole weight on her to stop her, and even then it was almost impossible to hold her. She fought like a tiger, and seemed possessed of an almost inhuman strength. "Nurse!" I yelled.

The nurse came running, consternation on her face, and from the other side of the bed got Louisa by the shoulders and threw all her small weight on her. From up the corridor a young doctor came running to help us. With him there, the three of us were able to contain her. We got her back under the straps and tightened them. We stood up, all three breathing hard and staring at each other.

"You must never do that!" the nurse wailed. "Never do that!"

"I'm sorry," I said, through my heavy breathing. "I didn't know."

"You must never do that!" the nurse wailed again. "We've all tried so hard to save her!" She wrung her hands suddenly, in a kind of despair.

"I know you have," I said. "And I'm grateful. And I'm sorry. I just didn't know."

In the bed Louisa rolled her head and glassy stare toward my side. She did not appear to be at all disturbed or upset and did not even seem to be breathing hard. "You see," she said in French in an insanely calm voice. "They want to do things to me."

I looked down at her and tried to give her a smile. Then I looked at the others. "Thank you, Doctor," I said in French.

"Oh, that was not anything," he said, and turned to walk back to whatever it was he had been doing.

"I think I'd better go," I said to the nurse.

"Yes, I think you should," she said. Her face was still full of consternation. "I don't mean as any punishment to you. But she's going to be upset now, and I'm afraid she's going to go into a catatonic state. I think I had better give her a shot. She'll sleep it off."

I nodded, and shook hands with her. Then, impulsively, I leaned down over her diminutive form and kissed her on the cheek. "I am sorry," I said.

"She's not herself yet, you see," the girl said.

I nodded again, shook hands again, then walked out of there down between the two long rows of beds filled with badly damaged people.

Outside, in the sunny air and under the leafy trees, I stood a minute breathing the air in front of the hospital, still shaken up. What was the point in saving her, really? If she was going to be like that? Better to let her die. But, of course, they didn't know she was going to be like that, when they were working on her. They could only work and hope.

Settling my jacket and tie and breathing the air, I thought of Edith and walked off toward my favorite pissoir.

I had told them at the Hôtel-Dieu about moving her to the American Hospital, and they had assured me that they would have her ready. After I got home, I called the American Hospital doctor, and then Edith. After I talked to Edith, I put in a call to Harry in Rome. I did not catch him the first time. It was a lot later in the evening this time and he was not in. But when I called back an hour later I got him. He had just come in.

"Well, what's the story?" he said. "Is she going to be all right?"

"Well, she's out of the coma."

"I know. I talked to the hospital."

"We're moving her to the American Hospital tomorrow."

"Good." There was again that curious pause he had developed since we began these telephone conversations. "So she's out of the woods."

"Well, physically, yes, I think. But she's got some throat damage from those tubes they had to shove down her throat. And there's this question of brain damage. They seem to think she has some. But just how much, they're not sure."

"Did you talk to her?"

"I tried to. But she didn't respond much. She didn't seem to know much of what she was saying. And she didn't recognize me, Harry."

"She didn't recognize you?"

"No."

"Well, they've probably got her all doped up on something right now, anyway," he said, after another pause.

I was suddenly enormously fatigued. "I suppose that's possible," I said.

There was another pause. "Well, I'm going on to Tel Aviv, then," Harry said crisply. "There's absolutely nothing I can do for her when she's in that state. So there's no point in me coming back there. I'll keep in touch from down there. You can let me know what happens."

"What if we have to put her in a sanatorium, Harry?" I said.

"If you do, let me know and I'll send the necessary authorization. If you need that. And then call Edith. She'll handle it all."

"But where will I find you?"

"The Hilton. Naturally. I always stay there."

"It certainly seems pretty damned calloused to me, Harry," I protested.

"I suppose it is," he said. "You said that before. But that's the way I'm going to play it. Anyway, I'll keep in touch. So long, Jack. And thanks."

He waited; there was a pause, as though he were expecting me to say something, maybe offer him good luck or congratulations or some damned thing. When I did not answer, he hung up the phone. I took mine away from my ear and stared at it.

Late Saturday I talked to the American Hospital doctor. But there was nothing much he could tell me. She had only just come in today. They had begun a series of tests on her, and would continue them on through Sunday, but it would take a while to complete the tests, let alone evaluate them. But at least her physical condition was continuing to improve.

"She was just about as dead as you can get," he said equably, "without actually dying."

"God," I said, "it would be awful if she came out of it a vegetable."

"Yes, it certainly would," he said. He did not say more. That left me with the burden of conversation.

"Well, thanks a lot," I said lamely, "anyway."

"What about her husband?" he said. "What about Harry?"

"He's in Tel Aviv."

"Chasing some girl," the doctor said.

"Well, I think he's working on some screenplay."

"Well, that's where all the girls are," he said, "isn't it?"

"I guess so," I said. "I guess there're always some around every film."

"Jesus!" he said. "Is he coming back?"

"Well, I think that depends a lot on what happens."

"Well! Well, fine! Just fine! Good! Okay, Jack. I'll keep you informed as to whatever comes up. Goodby, Jack."

"Goodby." I was just about to drop the phone into its cradle when I heard his voice say, "Jack?" from the instrument.

"Yes?" I said.

"I can't run peoples' lives for them. All I can do is try to patch them up after they've done whatever it is they've done. I'm just a glorified super-mechanic, that's all." He hung up.

"I understand," I started to say, but it was too late. I hung up myself. Then I got my worn, old man's body together and all girded up and ready to go down and, though I did not know it then, hold what would be the last of the American meetings at the Gallaghers'. I felt like an old man.

Well, they were all there. Just about everybody who had been there during those weeks of the "Revolution". Only, there were no Gallaghers. Not even McKenna was there, to add her small child's ambiance. I circulated, being a host. But I was already, even then, beginning to feel I would not be up to it another time.

It was somewhat later, as the first ones were beginning to leave, that Weintraub came in. He had just left the Sorbonne, where he had gone to watch the last of the students' "clean-in". With big buckets of sudsy water and brooms they had just finished cleaning out the garbage and mess that had accumulated during the occupation. There had been cheers when the students they had evacuated for the clean-up began to move back in.

But there seemed to be another problem, he said. Apparently late that evening the student patrols had picked up in the street a man who had been knifed in some altercation. They had taken him inside to their own infirmary for emergency treatment. Now rumors were floating around that the police intended to come inside the Sorbonne tomorrow, Sunday, to look for the man and make sure he got proper treatment. But the students claimed that, after giving him emergency treatment only, they had sent him to the Hôtel-Dieu. However, the police were claiming that the Hôtel-Dieu had no record of ever having received any such man. There was a big mystery about it all. And the students were afraid, were sure, that this was only a pretext of the Government to come in and throw them out, in spite of their massive clean-up.

My mind being full of the Hôtel-Dieu so much lately, I could see in my mind the intensive care unit as clearly as if it were a projected movie. Would those people, whom I had gotten to know so well in the last five days, actually deny they had received such a patient, when in fact they had? They might, I thought, if the Government and police put enough pressure on them. After all, Hôtel-Dieu was a Government hospital.

"Can I walk along home with you?" Weintraub said. "And come up for one drink?" He seemed pensive.

Most of the Americans at the Gallaghers' had left, and those who hadn't were in process of leaving.

"Why, sure, Dave," I said. "Why not? Come along."

I was pensive myself.

As we walked up the darkening quai, he told me it was not the same any more, with the Odéon cleaned out. He felt a little lost.

"It's just not the same. Oh, sure, I can go to the Sorbonne and hang around. But I don't really know anybody. And the Cinema Committee is moving way out there to Censier. That's out in left field. I must say, I miss them, the kids. I was quite a help to them, you know. I brought them you, and I brought them Harry."

"And a fine lot of good that did," I said. "Tell me how they are getting along out there."

"Well," he said. "Well, they're floundering. That's the truth. They don't know what to do with themselves, now that Harry's gone. He's in Rome, you say?"

"The last I heard," I said. "On a screenplay."

"They got used to depending on him," Dave said.

"Do you think they've got any chance of making it now?" I said. "The film, I mean? On their own?"

"I don't know," he said. "Maybe." Then he paused. "No. No, that's not the truth. The truth is, I don't think they've got a chance in God's world. Harry left them all the stuff he shot with his two principals. But they haven't got any good cutters. Harry was supposed to bring them in all that. Gee, I sure do miss them at the Odéon."

"Well, that's a shame," I said. "I don't suppose there's anything we can do about it?"

"I don't see what," Weintraub said gloomily.

We had reached my place. When we went inside I rummaged in the mailbox and came up with a telegram that had been delivered. It was hard to read in the light of the *minuterie*. I took it up the stairs and inside with me.

When I had the lights on, I saw that it was from Harry in Tel Aviv. Harry must have taken the very first plane out after my phone call, for it to get back to me so quick. I read, SAM NOT AT ADDRESS WHERE SHE TOLD ME I COULD FIND HER. AM CONTINUING TO LOOK. WILL KEEP INFORMED. HARRY. I did not see any reason why I should not show it to Weintraub.

He looked at it a long time. Then he handed it back slowly. "So he went," he said. "It could have been me down there, if I'd had the money to go. *And* the money for us to live on. She didn't give a damn who it was who came along."

"I suppose," I said.

He was looking out the window across the river at the lights on the Left Bank. "Well, it was an experience. A once in a lifetime. A great experience."

"I'm not so sure I can agree with that," I said. I had made us drinks.

"What do you say we go over to Boulevard St.-Germain and have a couple of Wimpy hamburgers at the Wimpy's and walk around the Quartier?" Weintraub said in a muffled voice. "It's quiet over there tonight."

"Fine," I said. "Okay. Why not?"

28

ON SUNDAY THE 16TH, as already explained, the Sorbonne fell. And that was the day Weintraub got himself knocked about by the police. Everything Weintraub had predicted to me Saturday night, about the man with the knife wound, and the Hôtel-Dieu, and the student infirmary, came absolutely true. It was the exact same story in the papers.

And on Sunday I began this—what shall I call it? This exploration? This research? This piece of crud.

As I have said, there were demonstrations and a lot of streetfighting on the Sunday. And all through Sunday night there were short, sharp fights between students and police, but not much tear gas, or the cracking percussion grenades. The police were using a new tactic of charging and disrupting the students before they had time to build new barricades; and anyway, most of the Latin Quarter was asphalted over now, so that paving stones were hard to come by. I liked to think of it as the "modernization" of Paris. All of this aided the police, and it was clear the students were holding the losing end of it.

On Monday there was more streetfighting in the Quartier, but by then it had taken on the appearance of the annual, traditional fights between students and police on Sorbonne graduation day. The "Revolution", the real "Revolution", the "almost" Revolution was clearly over.

But the most important piece of news on the Monday of June 17th was that the Renault auto-workers had voted to return to work. Over 70 per cent of them had voted for "Back-to-Work". That would just about end it. Now the students were alone again. In return for their vote the Renault workers would get pay increases of up to 14 per cent; payment of 50 per cent wages for the strike period; and, important new union rights and concessions inside the Renault plants.

The other important point was that the Paris taxi drivers suddenly appeared on the street again, startling their eager clients with the fact that their basic meter rates were up 66 per cent. Until the meters could be changed they were posting notices on their rear-door windows explaining in four languages the addition of 2 francs 25 centimes (45 cents) to each fare. Rates would also go up for the pieces of baggage carried and for trips from train stations and airports.

It was really all over, and Weintraub came by to see me that night, the Monday. He was not nearly so sanguine as he had been the night before. The students were quitting and going home in large bunches. They still held the Censier, but even there large numbers were cutting out, and leaving it to a few diehards. He had been out there during the day.

"What about the Cinema Committee?" I asked.

"Hardly any of the kids are showing up," he said. "They've quit all shooting. Daniel the Chairman has disappeared."

"Probably gone back to Russia," I said.

"Yeah," he said. "Maybe. You really think so?"

"Those steel-rimmed spectacles," I murmured.

"Yeah," Weintraub said. "Still. — I always thought he was too young to be an agent," he added.

"They train them young," I said.

"Maybe so," Weintraub said without conviction. He was visibly depressed.

"What about little Anne-Marie?" I asked. "The baby Commissar?"

"Gone," he said. "She's probably out organizing streetfights some-where."

"And Terri?"

"Hasn't shown up."

"And Bernard?"

"*Non plus.*"

"Looks like it's about the end," I said, sympathetically.

"Looks like it." He was standing at my open window leaning on his elbows on the little balcony rail and looking at the river. He turned back to me and grinned ruefully. He drained off what was left in his glass. "Well, it looks like it's back to the God damn fucking harp for me. God, how I hate that instrument."

"Well, anyway, as you said, you've had a great experience," I said.

He grinned. "Yeah. And especially with that Sam there in on it! — And at my age, at forty-four, you can't expect too many lucky breaks like that."

I noted that he had dropped a year off the accustomed 45 he was willing to own up to.

"What do you say we go over on St.-Germain and have a couple of burgers at the Wimpy's?"

"Not tonight, Dave," I said. "I'm feeling too depressed."

He looked at me and there was a sudden sympathy and sensitivity on his small tough ageing Jewish face.

"How's Louisa?"

"Not so good. Oh, her body seems to be recovering well enough. But it looks like the brain damage may be even more extensive than we imagined. It looks like she may come out of it a real vegetable."

"Jesus God," he said. He breathed it rather than said it, a sort of sigh.

"That's how I feel about it," I said.

"Well, I'll be going," he said. He paused. "But we'll see each other. We'll see each other soon. Won't we?"

"Sure, Dave," I said. "Would you like a last drink?"

"I guess not," he said.

He left.

From the window I watched him legging it up the quai and across the bridge where the little black police vans still guarded our end of the Pont de la Tournelle.

Then I just stood, looking at the dark river.

In the afternoon addition of *Le Monde* that day there had been a small article saying the Government was preparing to announce strong economic aid measures to help injured and embattled French businessmen in surviving the month-long strike. So, it looked like the price for the Great Vacation was already adding itself together, getting ready to demand payment.

I looked at the river.

I had been out to the American Hospital to see Louisa that afternoon. Afterwards, I talked with the American Hospital doctor and he was not at all encouraging. He was just the reverse. And after my visit with Louisa, I could not do anything but agree with him.

When the nurse brought me into the private room, it was plain Louisa did not recognize me. Her eyes were not glassy any more, but they were vague and wide, stary. Before, at the Hôtel-Dieu, she had been able to talk a little bit, however incoherently. Now she did not speak at all.

"She can talk a little French," the nurse said quietly to me. "But her English seems to be almost gone."

I nodded.

"You mustn't be surprised if she doesn't recognize you," the nurse said.

I could only nod again.

"Go ahead," the nurse said encouragingly, and smiled.

I nodded again and slipped over and sat in the chair beside the bed.

"Louisa? Louisa? How are you, Louisa? It's Jack," I said.

She turned her head and looked at me stary-eyed. They still had her all strapped down.

"Jack," I said.

"Ja—" she said. "Ja—"

"That's it. Jack. I just came by to see how you were, and to see if you got my roses."

She stared at me.

I looked around the green-painted room. It was airy and sunny. My two dozen red roses were in a vase on the bureau beside the bed. The nurse nodded at them and smiled at me. They were nice enough. They were quite fine in fact. Louisa had neither seen nor smelled them.

"Well, Louisa, I'll come back soon another time," I said. "You try to get better." I got up from the chair and left the room, trying not to run. Outside in the hall I stood leaning against the wall, my face in my hand. I was crying, and I could not help it.

The nurse followed me out. "I'm sorry, M. Hartley," she said. "But, you know, it may do her good to just see you. We can't tell just yet."

"I'm sorry," I said, and got out my handkerchief. It seemed to me suddenly that I had been saying that same sentence all my life. Then I bolted, down the corridor and out of there, to a taxi in the sunny afternoon.

When I called the doctor later at his Avenue Hoche office, after the sunny taxi ride back home, he was less than encouraging.

"It seems to be worsening," he said. "The tests all seem to be getting bleaker and bleaker. There isn't anything we can do."

"Some kind of operation?" I said, feebly.

"There isn't that kind of operation. Not today. The electrical currents in the brain are just about the most subtle electric currents that man knows about. In surgery we don't have that kind of electricians. We only have knives."

"Then I suppose we must start arranging for a sanatorium."

"Not just yet. I want to keep her here a few more days anyway. Maybe a little longer. We want to check her out as thoroughly as we can."

"You better get hold of Edith," I said.

"I will," he said. "I did."

After that, I called Edith. But she already knew about it all. She had talked to the doctor and had been out there herself.

After that I simply brooded until Weintraub rang the bell.

Now, after he had left, I simply stood, in the window, and stared at the river, the dark river.

Across the river there was still some fighting in the Quartier. Some tear-gas grenades popped, and some percussion grenades cracked. But not many.

And down on the corner of the bridge the two ugly little black bugs still waited patiently for whatever their destiny would be.

29

WHEN I GOT BACK HOME on Tuesday from the American Hospital, after another futile interview with Louisa, I found another telegram from Harry in my mailbox.

It said simply, FOUND HER.

My first impulse was to tear it up, savagely, and then to bite into the pieces. But I stopped myself, and took it upstairs. I figured it ought to go into the record. If you could call it that: a record.

Then, staring at the postmark date on the telegram, something thudded lightly in my head several times, like a light tap on a door. What day was today? Tuesday June 18th? Then McKenna's birthday was on Thursday. McKenna was born on June 20th.

How could I ever have forgotten that? I called Edith immediately. Luckily, she was home. She had just come in.

"Great God!" she said in a shocked voice. "I totally forgot it, too. How could I ever have forgotten that?"

"When will she be home?" I asked.

"In about half an hour," Edith said.

"I'll be right out," I said.

The taxi let me off in front of the old-fashioned porte-cochere and wrought-iron gate of Edith's house out near the Avenue de la Grande Armée. There was a leafy garden with some big trees and the garage in it alongside the house. The suave, silent butler let me in without saying a word. He bowed. McKenna, I found, was already there ahead of me. She ran to me, and I grabbed her up in my arms.

"Aunt Edith and I want to give you a birthday party," I said, and grinned. "Since Mommy is sick and Daddy has to be away." I looked at Edith. "I thought maybe it might be fun if we invited all your little school chums, like we did that time we had the party at my house, your first year in school."

McKenna stared up at me with her flat blue New England eyes. I had put her back down on her feet. "I'd rather not have them," she said.

"You wouldn't?" I said. "But we could have lots of fun. Like we did that time at my place."

"Yes, darling!" Edith said. "We can have funny paper hats and prizes and lots of balloons and games. It would be great fun."

"I'd rather not," McKenna said.

It was thundering through my head, with a great question-mark attached to it, Does she know? How much does she know? I smiled. "All right, dear. If you say so. We'll just have our own party. How's that? How would you like it if I invited some of your grown-up friends? Some of the people that used to come to the apartment all during the Revolution?"

"No," McKenna said.

"Oh, all right, then. We'll just have our own party. Just the three of us. How would that be? But I just couldn't let your birthday go by without giving you a party. I'd be unhappy forever."

"All right," she said. "I guess that would be best." Then suddenly, she flew to me and grabbed me around the legs and buried her face against my thigh. "Oh, Uncle Jack!" she said.

"What is it, lover?" I said. "What is it? What's the matter?"

She didn't answer. She gave my legs an enormous squeeze, and then stepped back and looked up at me. Her eyes were dry. "I think that would be the best," she said gravely.

"Okay. Then I'll arrange everything. I'll wear a funny hat, and Aunt Edith will. You don't have to, if you don't want to."

"I want to," McKenna said.

"You don't have to, if you think it's too childish. But you'll laugh like Woody Woodpecker when you see your old Uncle Jack in a silly funny paper hat."

Suddenly she grinned. I felt as though I had won a medal. Across from me Edith's face was still.

"Don't worry. And don't you worry, Aunt Edith," I said. "I'll take care of everything. This is my party. After all, I am your Godfather."

I kissed them both and took my leave, the butler bowing me out. I preferred to walk over to Grande Armée to find a cab. I felt I just could not wait there while they called me one.

I headed immediately for Paris' ritziest toy store, the Nain Bleu.

Next day, I headed over to the Bazar de l'Hôtel de Ville.

So, we had our birthday party on Thursday June the 20th. During the festivities the butler arrived solemnly bearing a large box which contained a doll that did all sorts of things. Gravely he presented it to the "young miss". Apparently he had bought it all on his own hook, without asking anyone. Apparently he thought a lot of her. Or did he know about the trouble?

Just as gravely, McKenna accepted it. "Thank you, Charles," she said. Then she insisted that he put on a paper hat and blow a horn. He did, seriously, gravely. He was also enjoined to eat some of the ice cream and the cake, which he did, seriously and methodically.

After it was over I gave her a bearhug, squeezed Edith's hand and left. I told the taxi to take me straight home. I was really hungry for a Scotch.

But as the taxi crossed the bridge of the Pont Louis-Philippe in the warm sunny summer air and went on in under the big trees I changed my mind. I leaned forward and told the driver to stop and let me off at the Brasserie. I paid him and went inside and had myself a big schooner of beer, the biggest they had, the "formidable". The sun was streaming in through the open windows and the two doors, making gold bars on the sawdusted floor. It was a great day. As I watched, moisture beaded on the big mug and began to run down in rivulets. Madame Dupont, Mlle. Dupont, Marcel the brother-in-law, and the master himself with his bulldog grin were all there. All of them asked me about Madame Gallagher. I told them she was fine. They would not let me pay.

When I had shaken hands all around and come outside, I heard the thin, piping sounds of penny whistles. I realized that I had been hearing it earlier, inside, through the open windows, but it had not registered.

It was coming from the vicinity of the old Bailey bridge of the Pont St. Louis and I walked over there. Two young men, neither over 20, with long hair, blue jeans and beards, students almost certainly, were sitting on the deck with their backs against the bridge wire playing in two-part harmony on cheap recorders a flock of old British and Scottish marching songs. The thin, brave, piping music spread itself up into the air and was carried to the Island and upriver in the breeze. On the deck between their outstretched legs was placed an old cap. Sometimes people crossing the bridge would drop a coin in it.

I stood and looked at them. It was over. It was really all over. Well, lots of things were over.

Yes, lots of things were over. Though those boys might not know it, I happened to know (because Madame Dupont had indignantly told me) that the old rusty green Bailey bridge was coming down and that the City of Paris was going to build a new modern four-lane, super-highway bridge there to take its place.

The Duponts had fought it hard apparently, as had other inhabitants of the Island, but they had lost and the bill to change the bridge had been voted in by the City Council.

So I stood and looked at them, the young recorder players. Then after a minute I climbed the steps and walked out onto the bridge to them. They were almost exactly in the middle. I dropped a ten franc note into the old cap, then changed my mind and added two more ten franc bills. The boys stopped playing and looked up at me in surprise.

"Are you boys students?" I asked.

"Yes, sir," they said in unison.

"I like your music," I said in explanation, and shrugged.

They grinned. "Well, thank you, sir," they said.

"Could I see some of the music?" I asked. They had a beat-up old portfolio with sheet music in it beside them, and were playing not from memory but from the sheets.

"Sure," one said. "Take a look."

They were songs I had vaguely heard somewhere but did not know the titles to. When I leafed through the frayed, faded, dog-eared sheets, I saw titles like *Lord Randal, Gude Wallace, The Bonnie House of Airlie, The Jolly Young Waterman, I Attempt from Love's Sickness to Fly.*

"Thank you," I said. I put the sheets back carefully into the old portfolio and laid it down.

"Sure," one of them said. They had already gone back to their playing.

I turned and walked off the bridge. The thin, incredibly brave, piping music followed me in the light breeze as I walked on home in the lengthening sunlight.

TEXT TYPE IS BASKERVILLE

AND THE DISPLAY IS GOUDY BOLD.

DESIGNED BY JOEL SCHICK